Stuart Donald's

*Complete New Tales of*

# PARA HANDY

Stuart Donald's
# Complete New Tales of
# PARA HANDY

The continued voyages of
the Vital Spark

Chronicled with affection,
acknowledgement and apology
to Neil Munro

www.vitalspark.co.uk

© Maureen Donald 2009

The Vital Spark is an imprint of
Neil Wilson Publishing Ltd
G/2 19 Netherton Avenue
GLASGOW
G13 1BQ
Tel: 0141-954-8007
Fax: 0560-150-8007
www.nwp.co.uk
email: info@nwp.co.uk

The moral right of the author has been asserted.
First published in 2001.

A catalogue record for this
book is available from the
British Library.

ISBN: 978-1-897784-62-4

All photographs courtesy of Argyll and Bute District Libraries, Dunoon,
with the exception of page 81, courtesy of Dan Macdonald Collection and
page 201, courtesy of Hulton Getty Picture Collection.

Typeset in 11/12pt Caslon 224 Book.

Printed and bound in Great Britain by Cpod, Trowbridge, Wiltshire .

To the memory of my parents

MY FATHER
who had the kindness and good sense
to introduce me to Para Handy at an early age

MY MOTHER
who worried about my childhood wanderings on the Firth
but still encouraged me to make them

and

For our next generation
ANDREW and SUSAN
with love

THE AGE OF THE VITAL SPARK — *This fine picture of passengers disembarking from Williamson's turbine Queen Alexandra captures perfectly the atmosphere and the ambience of the turn-of-the-century Clyde as Para Handy knew it. Here are the well-dressed daytrippers he longed to carry, the gentry en route to their estates, the curious crowds thronging the pierhead for the social event of the day, and the confident elegance of the new breed of ships, with the grace and the silhouette of liners in miniature. Sadly we shall never see their like again!*

# Contents

# Publisher's Note

I first met Stuart Donald in 1992 in that bastion of Cowal bookselling, Fiona and Gregor Roy's Bookpoint in Dunoon, and after we got talking he mentioned that he was working on some Para Handy stories, written in Munro's style and set in authentic West Coast locations. In that wonderful timbre which he exuded when taking someone into a confidence he lowered his head to my level and murmured conspiratorially, "I can't expect them to compare with Munro's originals, but I think they are fairly good!"

Some sample stories duly arrived and it did not take me long to agree with Stuart's belief. They were very good stories indeed. We agreed that there should be a trilogy of tales brought out a couple of years apart under the titles *Para Handy Sails Again*, *Para Handy All At Sea* and *Para Handy At The Helm*. The first two books sold quickly and reprinted, but sadly, the final volume never made it to press. In September 2000 Stuart lost a long and brave battle against cancer.

My quandary was what to do with Stuart's literary legacy and after taking advice from both Gregor and Stuart's wife, Maureen, I decided to reissue the first two books as a compendium volume in order to maintain the corpus. This is it and I am proud to publish it.

Stuart wrote of Munro's creation in *Para Handy Sails Again*, "Nobody could ever manage to recreate that world with the same matchless quality of craftsmanship, affection or accuracy. My hope is that my own efforts in that direction will entertain rather than irritate, and provide an acceptable extension to the Para Handy repertoire."

Well, Stuart's misgivings were unfounded as he did manage to recreate Para Handy's world and his stories have irritated no one. Long may they remain in print.

Neil Wilson, September 2001

# Introduction*

Anyone who is planning to tamper with a national institution approaches the task with some trepidation and, in my efforts to extend the repertoire of the much-loved tales about the Clyde puffer *Vital Spark* and her kenspeckle Captain and crew, I am no exception.

Neil Munro's characters are a national institution to many Scots, and the tales have a remarkable provenance. They were first created to feature in Munro's anonymous columns in the *Glasgow News*, on which paper he rose to become editor. Although they were dismissed as 'slight' by their creator (who saw them as an interruption to the writing of his serious, and nowadays sadly neglected, historical novels) they have rarely, if ever, been out of print for three-quarters of a century. Year on year new generations of readers are captivated by the gentle humour and kindly atmosphere of these chronicles of a long-lost world and a gentler society, on which we tend to look back with much affection, and nostalgic regret for what has gone for ever.

Trying to live up to the expectations of such enthusiasts while having the impertinence to try to recreate Para Handy and his people was always going to be a daunting task.

However, at the risk of offending the purists, I have to say at once that writing these stories has been great fun — which, in an ideal world, all writing should be; and that there were occasions when they wrote themselves, in the sense that I would embark on a particular tale with no clear idea of where or how it would come to its conclusion.

In retrospect, however, I am surprised that a volume of new Para Handy tales has not been attempted before this. There have been no less than three television reincarnations of the *Vital Spark* and only in the most recent of them was there any serious attempt to dramatise some of Neil Munro's

---

* This is the same introduction which appeared in *Para Handy Sails Again*.

original storylines: the others were, basically, 'new' creations. The most faithful of all the attempts to transfer Para Handy from the printed page was, in my view, the 1953 film *The Maggie* which, though never formally acknowledged as being based on Neil Munro's own characters, so obviously and so successfully in fact was.

Whether I have succeeded in creating an acceptable extension to the original tales will not be for me to judge, and I offer no attempt to defend my efforts in terms of their authenticity or readability. That is a matter for the personal judgement of those who may read them.

I would, however, defend the concept of writing new tales built round Neil Munro's creations, for I believe it has in fact been done before — and during his lifetime. In my documentary volume *In The Wake Of The Vital Spark* I put forward the proposition that the 18 'new' stories published for the first time in the recent Birlinn edition of the original tales were, in fact, the work of hands other than Neil Munro's. I won't reiterate the arguments here, but my conviction about that point was one of the factors which encouraged me to proceed with the present work.

I close the case for the defence by stressing that I believe Neil Munro to be one of the finest writers of humorous fiction which this, or any other, country has ever produced. I grew up with the Para Handy tales, and know them — literally — almost off by heart. I therefore approached the whole task with both affection and respect for their creator. I like to believe that Neil Munro would not be taken too aback by imitation, for it is, we are told, the sincerest form of flattery.

And I am certain that he would not look too unkindly on whoever was rash enough to attempt it — for that surely is the kind of sympathetic and forgiving man he was.

I certainly don't ask the readers to be either sympathetic or forgiving, however — but simply to read on, and come to their own conclusions and form their own judgements!

My one intention and my only wish is that these new tales might entertain and amuse, for if they fail in that, then they fail in everything.

Sandhaven, Argyll
September 1995

# 1

## The Encounter at Inveraray

As the *Vital Spark* chugged past the hamlet of Newtown, tacked almost as an afterthought onto the Lochgilphead road at the southern limits of the Burgh of Inveraray, the town's capacious pier came into view. Para Handy was astonished to see a huge crowd thronging both that structure and the stone quayside onto which it abutted, all of them staring across the water towards the approaching puffer.

"My Chove, Dougie," he said, "we've not always been such a centre of attention in the past! But I've always said, the time would come when the finer points of the shup would at last be recognised by the public at large. I'm glad we gave the lum a fresh coat of pent at Tarbert yesterday mornin', for she's neffer looked bonnier and plainly the news hass got around!"

"It's either that, or the Inveraray polis huv managed tae work oot jist whose punt wis up the mooth of the river Shira wi' a splash net efter the Duke's salmon the last nicht we wis by here," called a doom-laden voice from the engine-room at the Captain's feet. "Is there no sign of a Black Maria at the head of the quay?"

"I'll thank you to attend to your enchines, Mr Macphail," said Para Handy with some dignity. "And Jum! will you look lively and break out our best heaving-line ready for when we tak' our berth. There'll be no problem today findin' someone to catch it for us seein' ass we're the star attraction at the pier!"

The traditional place for the puffers at Inveraray is on the inner, west side of the pier and the *Vital Spark* was manoeuvred round the quay-head with just a little difficulty, for the tide was turning and the current threatened to push her back out. In the event, with some dexterous application of the helm and a touch of extra power to the propeller, Para Handy brought the boat safely into the slack water of the inshore berth.

"Right, Jum," he called, "stand by to heave the line!" And he turned triumphantly towards the pier preparing to wave a happy acknowledgement to the crowds who must have been watching his manoeuvres with interest and approbation, and who would now be surging forward to welcome the little vessel to her Inveraray berth — only to find that he was looking at some 200 disinterested backs, for the people on the quay had taken not the slightest notice of the approach and ultimate arrival of the puffer, but were still standing, as they had been when he had first caught sight of them, staring out towards the middle of Loch Fyne as if hypnotised.

"The Chook of Argyll himself must be expected aff a yat," said a somewhat chastened Para Handy to Dougie once they had finally secured the puffer to the quayside — Sunny Jim, as usual, having to leap for the jetty with the handline and haul the hawser in to the first bollard on his own. "And this iss his loyal lieges with their reception committee."

Squeezing their way through the crowd, the crew managed to gain a viewpoint, but found themselves staring across an empty loch with not so much as a fishing smack in sight.

Para Handy was just turning to seek some enlightenment from the nearest bystander, when there was a collective gasp from the assembled throng, followed immediately by a ragged cheer.

A squat, grey rectangular object was rising slowly out of the waters of the loch about 200 yards offshore.

～

The Captain had heard all about submarines but this was the first which he and the crew had ever encountered at such close hand. They watched in awed fascination as the conning-tower, then the gun, and finally the hull of the vessel emerged from the sea.

When the figures of the submarine captain and three seamen appeared on the bridge there was another spontaneous

3

cheer from the Inveraray crowd, and the vessel turned in towards the pier where eager lookers-on fought for the privilege of catching and securing the heaving-lines which two seamen now threw ashore from bow and stern of the grey hull.

Half-an-hour later the onlookers had dispersed homewards to discuss the excitement of the day over their teas.

On the pier, the submarine crew had deployed a spick-and-span gangway from her foredeck to the quay, a small pillar placed at the head of it carrying a coat-of-arms and the ship's name, *HMS Bulldog*. The white ropes which looped from posts at either side of the gangway were finished with turk's head knots and two seamen, immaculate in white jerseys and navy-blue bell-bottoms, stood guard at either hand with grounded rifles. On the ship's deck sailors in fatigues were polishing glass and brass on the bridge of the conning-tower, and from somewhere deep within the vessel came the constant deep throb of one of the new-fangled diesel engines.

The crew of the puffer, crammed into the wheelhouse, stared with undisguised and undiminished curiosity at their unexpected neighbour on the far side of the pier.

Eventually Para Handy squeezed his way out on deck without a word and vanished down the hatchway to the fo'c'sle.

Ten minutes later he reappeared in his best — indeed his only — pea-jacket, and wearing the cap with the white top and the splash of gold braid which he had picked up cheap at the Barras in Glasgow some years previously, but (thanks largely to the considerable amusement with which his crew had greeted its acquisition) had rarely had the courage to wear.

"Boys," he said, scrambling up the iron ladder let into one of the pier uprights, "it iss only right that I should present my complements to a fellow captain when we find oorselves neebours in a strange port."

And he straightened his shoulders, puffed out his chest, and marched across the quay towards the submarine's gangway.

~

Later that evening, in the bar of the George Hotel, the Captain and Dougie sat in a corner by a narrow window nursing two halves of beer. Sunny Jim they had left on the pier fishing, more in hope than expectation, for the makings of the next day's breakfast. Dan Macphail was in animated conversation at the far end of the bar with one of the engineers from the submarine and had been promised a guided tour of her diesels the following morning.

Para Handy's reception at the submarine's gangway had exceeded even his wildest imaginings.

"Whit way are they all keepin' at the Admirulity?" had been his opening sally to the sailors on guard duty. Before either could think of an appropriate reply, the submarine's Captain had appeared on the conning tower to take a breath of air, seen the puffer's skipper on the quayside, and invited him on board.

"A proper chentleman," Para Handy now enthused to the mate. "A proper chentleman, Dougie. But a hard life. They have no space at aal on the shup. Chust like livin' in wan of the caurs on the Gleska Subway, but wi' watter aal round ye.

"I would not wish to change places with them, for aal their chenerosity" — the Captain had enjoyed the hospitality of the wardroom, including the very first Pink Gin he had ever encountered — "for why would ye want to run a smert shup and then hide her under the watter where naebody can admire her?"

The immediate effect of his kindly reception aboard *HMS Bulldog* had been a change in the attitude of the burghers of Inveraray towards the puffer. From the moment that Para Handy was spotted leaving the submarine and shaking hands with her Captain at the foot of the gangway, the status of the *Vital Spark* was revised upwards.

As if to underline that fact, the landlord of the George Hotel now appeared with a cloth in his hand, wiped the top of the table at which the Captain and Dougie were seated, and placed two drams on it.

"Compliments of the house, gentlemen," he said, and whisked their empty beer glasses away.

"My Chove," said Para Handy. "What's got into Sandy McCallum tonight?"

"You were goin' to tell me why the submarine iss in Inveraray at all, Peter," prompted the mate.

"It's because the loch iss so deep," said Para Handy. "They iss going to use it for the diving trials of aal the new submarines built on the Clyde. *Bulldog* iss the first, but there will be plenty more.

"They are putting something aboot it aal in the papers, which iss where the Captain hass gone tonight. There iss an Inveraray man who iss quite namely ass a writer, and who does some work for the Gleska Evening News. Captain Morris from the submarine hass gone to have an interview with him, which iss why he wass not able to choin us for a dram."

~

Just at that moment the street door opened and the submarine Captain walked in, flashing more gold braid than Inveraray had seen in many months.

With him was a man of middle-height, aged about 40, with a high-domed forehead, a receding hairline, and a mild and kindly countenance.

The submariner looked round the crowded, smokey room and caught sight of Para Handy.

"Ah," he said to his companion. "There he is, that's the chap I was telling you about. I'm sure you'll be able to get a lot of interesting material from talking to him. He certainly kept me well entertained. He's a real character, and a bit of a teller of tall tales too, I would think!"

And, taking the other man by the arm, he pushed his way through the crowd and, reaching the corner table, clapped Para Handy on the shoulder.

"Captain, here's somebody I've been telling all about you, and he's very keen to meet you. I'm sure the pair of you will have a lot to talk about!

"May I introduce Captain Peter MacFarlane — Mr Neil Munro!"

*FACTNOTE*

Certain minor liberties with chronology must be admitted to in this story. Firstly it is unlikely that a submarine of the size hinted at would have been around the Clyde in the years before the First World War; secondly it was not until after that war that submarines were given names. Previously they were identified simply by their Class Letter followed by a numeral.

The Firth has, however, been closely associated with submarines for almost 100 years. Many were built in the Clyde yards such as Fairfield, Denny, Scott and Beardmore. The deep waters of the sheltered lochs — particularly the Gareloch, Loch Fyne and Loch Long — were ideal for diving trials and the testing of torpedos produced by the huge factory at Fort Matilda, Greenock, which Neil Munro referred to in the original Para Handy story 'Confidence'.

Much later, the Americans moved in to Holy Loch and for 30 years this was the European base for the US Nuclear Submarines which were such a crucial element of the NATO deterrent during the cold war. Now the Americans have gone, but Faslane on the Gareloch, and Coulport on Loch Long, serve the United Kingdom submarine fleet in a similar if lower-key capacity.

~

The real liberty taken in this tale, of course, is to place Neil Munro himself in it — but the temptation was absolutely irresistible! He must have revisited many times the community which meant so much to him and made such a lasting impression on him and influenced everything he did.

He was born and brought up in Inveraray and his first job was in the town, working in a lawyer's office. At the age of 18 he left for Glasgow, to lay the foundation of his future career as a working journalist and a talented novelist seen by many critics at the time as the natural inheritor of the mantle of Robert Louis Stevenson.

The chronicle of the gradual public indifference to his serious writing, and the rapid growth in their esteem and affection for works which he saw as slight and ephemeral, is well known. The tales of puffer skipper Para Handy, of waiter/beadle Erchie MacPherson and of commercial traveller Jimmy Swan, were all written for his regular columns in the Glasgow *Evening News*. And written anonymously for he did not wish to tarnish with trivia his reputation as a novelist of significance.

The real strength of his short stories, and the reason for their undiminished popularity, is that as well as being both highly amusing and beautifully crafted, they bring to life the people, places and pleasures of a long-lost world.

# 2

## *The Marriage at Canna*

I t was a Friday evening in July and the *Vital Spark*, on one of her rare sorties beyond the Firth, lay alongside the inner arm of a Skye pier which she was visiting for the first time.

An atmosphere of lethargy appropriate to the hottest day of the summer was evident not just in the village but particularly on board the puffer. Macphail thumbed the pages of a new romance with little enthusiasm, his eyelids heavy and his head nodding with the effort of staying awake. Sunny Jim sprawled across the tarpaulin covering the hatchway of the hold, sound asleep and spasmodically producing a staccato series of loud snorts to Para Handy's considerable annoyance.

The only cloud on the crew's horizon was that they had just returned from the local Inn and now faced a dry weekend, having spent their last coppers on a small canister of beer. With little prospect of more where that came from.

⁓

It had been a bad week for the puffer. More accurately, it had been a *very* bad week for her owner — but a splendid one for the crew — and all because of a partly-deaf clerk in the main Post Office in Glasgow.

The previous Monday, after shedding a cargo of coals at Crarae, Para Handy had gone ashore to telegraph the owner's Broomielaw office for instructions. Two hours later the postmaster's son appeared on the quayside with the reply. "My Chove," said Para Handy as he perused the familiar yellow form,. "it's foreign perts for us, boys."

What the telegram should have said was "Proceed Immediately To Ormidale To Load Pit Props".

What it actually said (thanks to the aforementioned clerk's hearing difficulties) was "Proceed Immediately To Armadale…"

Thus the *Vital Spark* lay at a Skye pier two days steaming from Loch Riddon on the Kyles where her cargo awaited. Her owner's language on receipt of Para Handy's telegram complaining that nobody at Armadale had ever heard of the puffer or her pit props is best left to the imagination.

However, as a man of some resource (or more accurately a man unwilling to see the costs incurred in getting the puffer to Skye becoming a total loss) he had told the skipper to wait for further instructions and was now hunting the Highlands and Islands for a cargo she could profitably bring back to the Clyde, while the crew enjoyed an unexpected holiday.

His most recent telegram had promised a decision about their next move on Monday morning, with money wired then too; but since that was a promise that neither the innkeeper nor the grocer at Armadale regarded as adequate collateral for 'tick', the crew faced a thirsty and hungry weekend.

"There's no food on board save yon barrel of salt herrin' from Campbeltown," Para Handy complained to the mate. "And nothin' to quench the thirst it gi'es ye except tea. Tea!" And he gave a shudder of distaste.

At that point came a discreet cough from the quayside and, turning, Para Handy was surprised to see a handful of men with the innkeeper at their head. "Captain," said this worthy, "we hae some business tae propose. May we come aboard?"

∽

"Man, Dougie," said Para Handy early next morning, "this iss the life, eh?" The *Vital Spark* was an hour out from Armadale heading west into the Cuillin Sound. The sun shone on a bright blue sea, the puffer's deck was crowded with a throng of smartly dressed men, women and children — all in holiday mood.

"This iss what she wass built for," he enthused, beaming with pride. "The *Vital Spark* wass never meant to cairry

coals an' stane an' sichlike ass if she wass a common gabbart. People iss oor merket — passengers! MacBrayne himsel' would be prood to have her in his fleet if he could see
her noo!"

He leaned from the wheelhouse to gaze fondly at the
colourful pageant below. A gaggle of children played a boisterous game of tag despite the protests of anxious mothers,
and young couples promenaded arm-in-arm. A huddle of
men in shiny blue and brown suits passed a bottle surreptitiously from hand-to-hand, with a wary eye on the hatch
where their prim womenfolk sat silently knitting. Perched
at the very point of the bows, Sunny Jim was obliging with
a virtuoso performance on the melodeon.

The innkeeper's 'business proposition' had been simple.
There was a wedding on Canna, one of the small islands to
the south of Skye, on Saturday: his own son was marrying
one of the island girls. The Armadale men had never seen
eye-to-eye with the men from Canna till now: here was a
fine chance to heal old wounds.

But the Mallaig fishing smack which had been booked to
ferry the wedding party to and from Canna was late getting
back from the herring-grounds thanks to the calm and
windless weather. If the *Vital Spark* didn't come to their aid
there would be no wedding. Of course, there would be a
generous whip-round for the crew and in the meantime
drinks would be 'on the house' at the Armadale Inn.

∽

"If she chust had another lum sure you would tak' her for
the *Grenadier*," enthused the captain. "I wish we'd room
for wan of they Cherman Bands. At least we've got Jum's
melodeon — but I'm vexed we cannae gi' e them a cup of
tea."

"It's no tea they're wantin'," cried a cheerless voice from
the engine-room below. "When did ye ever see a Skye man
wi' a *cup* in his haunds? Ah'm tellin' you Para Handy, ye'll
be gey sorry aboot this trup afore it's over, wait and see,
there's troubles tae come."

"Chust keep stokin', Macphail, and leave dealin' wi' passengers to them that ken what they're at," said the skipper
with some exasperation. "You're nothin' but a right misery!"

And indeed so it seemed. They tied up alongside Canna's

jetty just three hours out of Armadale after a crossing as calm as if they were sailing a millpond. The crew were invited to join the wedding party at the hall after the nuptials in the little church. There was an accordion band, and two pipers, pretty girls a-plenty, tables groaning with the weight of the food on them and a most astonishing quantity of whisky from the illicit stills for which the island was notorious.

"Man, Jum," said Para Handy as he reached out for another glass later that evening, "this Canna iss some place for high jinks!"

Even the morose Macphail had come out of his shell and was in animated argument with the bride's father — himself a retired engineer. Dougie had been coaxed onto the floor for a polka by the bolder of the two bridesmaids.

∽

The shattering of the idyll began a couple of hours before their planned departure for Armadale, when Para Handy stepped out for a breath of air. Behind him the jollification was ever more raucous and the first casualties of the bride's father's hospitality were to be seen, propped up in various stages of inebriation against the dyke which surrounded the hall.

The first warning of impending doom came when the skipper felt a fresh westerly wind on his face and saw, looming over the horizon, a growing mantle of ominously dark cloud. He returned to the wedding-party to give Dougie the bad news and see if the Armadale folk could be persuaded to leave sooner than planned.

It was too late.

Afterwards nobody could say what had happened, nobody was aware of hearing the first harsh word or seeing the first blow, but when Para Handy got back to the hall battle had been joined with a will and now the bride's and bridegroom's friends and relations were trading insults and punches. The women and children of Canna fled to the adjacent church, those from Armadale headed for the jetty.

Not even the puffer's crew could escape involvement in that general melee.

"You're to blame, bringin' godless Armadale men here at all!" cried the bride's father to Macphail, loosing a haymaker which that worthy luckily side-stepped. Two sidesmen frogmarched Para Handy to the doorway and threw him out with threats of horrible vengeance if he ever returned. Sunny Jim ran for the boat as if the hounds of hell were at his heels, but the slower mate was caught by the brothers of the girl he had been dancing with and given a very undeserved black eye.

From the comparative safety of the deck of the *Vital Spark* they eventually watched in disbelief as the Armadale men were forced to fight their way to the pier and back on board.

"My Cot," exclaimed the skipper, as the warps were loosed and the puffer moved out of the harbour. "Cross Canna off the charts boys. We never daur put in there again! Thank the Lord that's over."

Something almost as bad was still to come, however. The calm water of their outward journey was now a sea of white horses and with a rising wind dead astern the puffer, riding light, was tossed hither and thither uncontrollably as a cork. In the late evening light the deck began to look like a battlefield, strewn with moaning, whey-faced bodies as the relentless pitching and tossing took its toll.

"You and your bluidy passengers," protested Macphail from the engine-room. "D'ye see the state of this boat! She'll hae tae be hosed doon when we get tae port!"

～

Armadale was a ghost town on Sunday, a dead, deserted community on which the combined effects of over-indulgence and mal-de-mer wreaked dreadful havoc. The crew of the *Vital Spark* passed most of the day in the fo'c'sle, snapping at each other, reading old newspapers, or indulging in desultory games of cribbage or whist.

"I'm tellin' you it's me'll be glad to see the back of this place the morn," said the skipper. "Islands! I've had enough of them to last a lifetime. It's the Clyde for me from now on."

Following an early night — there was nothing else to do — the crew were up sharp on Monday and waited with anxiety to hear from the owner.

The telegram arrived just after nine and Para Handy eagerly tore open the flimsy envelope. His mouth dropped open in horror.

"Have we no' got a cargo, then?" asked Dougie anxiously.

12

"Oh, he's got us a cargo all right," said the captain. "A cargo of sand. From *Canna*!"

FACTNOTE

Armadale remains the terminal for the southernmost ferry crossing to Skye, from Mallaig at the terminus of the famed West Highland Railway Line. Run by CalMac, the route offers a vehicle ferry in summer, with a smaller vessel providing a passenger-only service over the winter months.

Of the four inhabited islands which lie between Skye and the Ardnamurchan peninsula, Canna is the most westerly. Rum, with its Victorian 'castle' of Kinloch, huge and mountainous and now run as nature reserve, is the best known. Smaller Eigg and tiny Muck lie south of Rum. Properly known collectively as 'The Small Isles' they are often (for obvious reasons!) irreverently referred to as 'The Cocktail Isles.'

Poetic licence has been taken in order to allow the wedding to be located on Canna. The island has the finest harbour of any of the Small Isles, and is a green and fertile spot, but even in Para Handy's day the population was too small to sustain the sort of spree which the story suggests. Things would have been different just 50 years previously, when the island peaked at a population of almost 400. However within two generations that figure had plummeted to less than 100.

Whether there were many illicit stills on Canna in years gone by, I do not know. But there were stills a-plenty throughout many parts of the Highlands well into the twentieth century and there may be a few in business yet! My first paid employment, in my student days in the late 1950s, was as a waiter in a (then) very well-reputed hotel in Wester Ross. The allocation of the weekly days-off for individual members of the dining-room staff hinged on the needs of the one permanent, year-round waiter — a local — to attend to the still which he 'ran' (if that's the word!) in the hills above the village. By custom and usage, he always had first choice for his day off, so that the still was properly cared for as and when the need arose.

Occasionally, too, puffers really did have the chance to carry large numbers of deck-passengers — though this was never in accordance with the rules or with the approval of the relevant authorities! At the time of the 'strike' against the resort of Millport on the island of Cumbrae by the Clyde steamer fleets in early July 1906, the puffers *Craigielea* and *Elizabeth* each carried about 100 residents and holiday-makers across to the island from Largs. The reasons for the boycott (reaction to demands for heftily-increased pier charges at Millport) are too complex to go into here, but the whole story is well chronicled in Alan Paterson's seminal *Golden Years of the Clyde Steamers* (David & Charles, 1979)

# 3

## The Race for the Pier

I was strolling along Princes Pier at Greenock, waiting for the arrival of the Dunoon steamer, when I noticed a familiar figure seated on a bollard, attempting to light a clay pipe with an expression of great concentration.

"*Home is the sailor, home from sea*, eh, Captain? But where is the *Vital Spark* berthed today?" I asked, for there was indeed no sign of the puffer anywhere on the long frontage of the pier.

"Well, she's no chust exactly berthed," said Para Handy. "She's on Ross & Marshall's slupway gettin' her shaft replaced. We kind of blew the main bearin' off Bute last week and had to get a tow home."

"Not by any chance from the *King Edward*?" I asked.

The captain's face reddened. "Aye, chust that," he said, and resumed his efforts to get his pipe to light.

"I should have guessed when I heard about it that it was likely to be the *Vital Spark* that was involved," I said. "You'd better tell me exactly what happened, Captain. There's some very strange stories going about Glasgow, and this could be your chance to put the record straight."

Para Handy sighed. "Aye, I heard it wass aal the talk o' the steamie, as ye might say. But none o' it wass by any streetch of the imagination the fault of the shup. If Dougie wass here he would tell ye himself.

~

"This wass the way o' it," he said, returning the stubborn pipe to the pocket of his pea-jacket. "I'll no' devagate wan single iota from the facts and maybe ye'll can pit it in the

15

papers and clear the good name o' the *Vital Spark*. I'm vexed that such a namely boat should be reduced to nothin' but a laughin' stock for the longshoremen. It wass no laughin' matter for us at the time, I can tell ye.

"We had been to Skipness wi' a cargo of whunstone, and wass headed back to Bowling in ballast when chust off Garroch Head, at the sooth corner o' Bute, there wass this most monstrous crunchin' sound in the enchine-room and then chust silence, and we started to druft.

"Macphail came burstin' out o' his cubby like a thing possessed and it iss chust typical o' the man that he tried to blame me for the breakdoon.

" 'Ah've telt ye for years,' he shouted, 'Years! And ye've never paid a blind bit o' heed tae me, naw, nor spent a penny on the engines and noo ye see the result! Ah've worked ma fingers tae the bone tae keep yon antiquated tangle o' scrap-iron turnin' ower, wi' nae thanks for it. But this time yer chickens is come hame tae roost for she's feenished, feenished. Yon's the shaft gone and since it cam' oot o' Noey's Erk in the first place ye'll no' find a machine shop tae fix it. It's the breakers' yerd for the shup, and the scrap heap for us!'

" 'My Chove, Macphail,' says I, quite dignified, 'that's quite a speech for you: but maybe you'll stert thinkin' about what we can do to stop her goin' ashore, and leave the highsterix till we've more time for them.'

"And sure enough, what wi' the southerly wind and the floodin' tide we wass setting quite fast onto the Head, her bein' light, and things wass lookin' pretty bleak.

"Macphail retired below to nurse his feelin's — there wassn't a lot he could do to nurse the enchines — and Dougie and Jum got the lashin's off the punt so that we would be ready for the worst if it came to it. I wass near greetin' mysel', I'll admit it. This looked like a terrible end for the smertest boat on the Firth, and her wi' a brand new gold bead on her paid for out o' my own pocket chust last week.

"Suddenly there was a roarin' noise astern like aal the steam whustles on the Clyde goin' off at the wan time, and when we aal recovered oor composure and turned to look, what wass it but the *King Edward*, inward-bound from Campbeltown, and closin' doon on us like a bat out o' hell.

" 'Puffer ahoy!' came a megaphone from a young officer on the brudge, a real toff by the sound o' him, 'are you in some sort o' trouble?'

"The upshot o' it all wass that in chust a matter of three or fower meenits the *Edward* had thrown us a line and sterted to pull us safely awa' from the Head.

" 'We'll give you a tow into Kilchattan Bay,' called the toff on the brudge, 'We're putting in there to pick up an excursion party but we can't take you any further up the Firth because we'll have to slow right down to tow you safely, and we can't afford that sort of delay in arriving at Gourock.'

"And off we went at a very douce eight knots or so which to the folk on the steamer must have seemed ass if they wass standing still.

"Well, it's me wass the mighty relieved man I can tell you, for though the owner wouldna be right pleased at havin' to pay for a tug to come doon and fetch us up the river, at least it wass better than the shup broken to bits on Garroch Head: and he'd have to do somethin' aboot the enchines at last.

"So I wass even beginnin' to think the break-doon might be a blessing in disguise, when we heard another great blatterin' o' whustle blasts astern. Comin' up on us very fast indeed wass the *King Edward*'s great rival, the *Duchess of Fife*, on her way hame from Brodick, the beat o' her paddles like chungle drums and the crowds linin' her rails to cheer as she swept past the turbine steamer ass if she had been lyin' at anchor.

"The paddler's Captain wass out on the wing o' the brudge and he doffed his kep and bowed very courteous-like to Captain Wulliamson in the wheelhouse of the *Edward* as he went by, but when he put it back on he waved very mockin', and blasted oot a sarcastic toot-toot-toot on the steam whustle.

"Even from the deck o' the *Vital Spark* two chains astern, you could hear the murmur of anger goin' up from the truppers on the *King Edward*, and I saw Captain Wulliamson come runnin' oot to the enchine-room telegraph on the starboard wing: it wass plain he wassna in good trum at aal. Next thing I could hear the shrill bell of it clanging furiously ass he rang loud and long down to the boys in the enchine-room.

"Ass you know the *Edward* hass three propellers aal druven by this new-fangled turbine enchine, and she hass aal the go of a greyhound. Wulliamson had called for emergency full speed ahead and she near enough lifted her bows out of the watter as she took off after the paddler.

"The trouble wass, of course, that she near pulled the bows of the puffer *under* the watter ass soon ass the tow rope tightened — which it did so fast I feared it wud snap: and I could wish it had, for I thocht every last wan o' the next fufteen minutes wud be my next. If Dougie wass here he would tell you himself."

I nodded: "The laws of physics, Captain," I said. "If I remember aright, any smaller vessel towed at speed by a significantly larger one is liable to be dragged under by the downward distortion of its normal centre of static gravity caused by the stress momentum associated with any uncompensated horizontal acceleration ..."

I am glad to say that the Captain looked unimpressed by this explanation.

"Whateffer you say yourself," he said at length. "But we were near sinking and the bows wass gettin' lower and lower in the watter as the *King Edward* went even faster. Things wass lookin' black for the shup! Wulliamson had completely forgot we wass there at aal, and we had nothin' which we could cut the steel hawser he wass towin' us wi' and no' way o' sluppin' it."

"So Captain Williamson just couldn't resist the challenge to the turbine's reputation?" I asked.

"It wassn't chust that," said Para Handy. "He knew fine that the *Duchess of Fife* was making for Kilchattan Bay chust like himself, and if she got there first she'd lift Wulliamson's excursion perty, and leave the *Edward* sadly oot o' pocket. So they were both hell bent on gettin' the first berth at the pier, and each had a man on the brudge keepin' a close lookout on the pierhead semaphore boards to see which o' the two the piermaster wass givin' the right o' way to — the *Duchess of Fife* in the offshore poseetion, or *King Edward* inshore of her.

"Wan o' these days there'll be a colleeshun, the way they boats iss aye racing to the piers. But aal I wass worried about wass what wass likely to happen to the *Vital Spark*, and I had chust wan way of remindin' Williamson that we wass there, so I hauled doon on the steam-whustle and held it wide open. But we wass chust like the banshee howlin' in the wilderness, as it says in the Scruptures, for Wulliamson neffer heard a thing but kept the steamer flat out for the pier, an' by now the sea wass running green over our bows.

"It wass the piermaster at Kilchattan Bay who saved us,

for ass the two steamers rounded the point and lined up for the pier he must have realised that there wass effery likelihood of a real smesh, and so he closed up both their semaphores and brought in the old *Texa* instead as she came limpin' in from Glasgow on her cargo run to Loch Fyne.

"Mercifully Wulliamson's eyes were better than hiss ears and he bided by the piermaster's instruction. It's us were the happy men when we saw the way come off her, and our own bow liftin' above the watter again ass the tow-line slacked off. But it wass a near thing.

"Ass it wass, both steamers were late on their run home for by the time the *Texa* had finished unloading they were sadly behind their schedules, and I'm told both Captains got a reprimand from the owners efter passengers had complained aboot the delay — and the piermaster had protested aboot the race.

"But — for all the pierhead gossip I hear aboot — it wass not the blame off the *Vital Spark*. How could it be?"

~

I shook my head sadly.

"You've obviously not heard the full version of the story as it reached Glasgow, Captain," I said. "The Kilchattan piermaster's report didn't blame just the two steamers.

"He said he had been confronted with *three* vessels racing for the pier."

I took a crumpled copy of the previous day's *Glasgow News* from my pocket, found the report I was looking for, and read aloud: "The Kilchattan piermaster reported to the Clyde Port Authority that he had denied access to the pier to the packet steamers *Duchess of Fife* and *King Edward*. Though they were racing each other for the first berthing opportunity, this was standard practice and not in itself his reason for turning them away.

"His fear was that the presence of a third vessel could have had serious consequences and indeed threatened the safety of all involved. 'The two steamers were neck and neck at about 20 knots,' he told our reporter this afternoon. 'Though it is hard to believe, there was a Clyde steamlighter immediately astern of the *King Edward* which, with her whistle blowing a demand to be given right of way, was clearly attempting to overtake both passenger ships at once. In the circumstances the only course of action open to me was to close the pier to all three.' "

~

I am sorry to say that Para Handy has made no effort to deny this report but, rather, has enjoyed the kudos of the qualities which certain credulous individuals now ascribe to the puffer.

My duty, I feel, is to set the record straight.

FACTNOTE

There was intense competition on the Firth at the turn of the century, the heyday of the paddlers and the first of the new generation of screw steamers on the Clyde: and of course these years were the zenith of the puffers too. Keen races for first berthing opportunities at the piers between passenger vessels operated by rival owners were commonplace — and notorious.

For the steamers, the prize was not simply the prestige of superiority in speed: it was commercial success. The faster ships attracted the greater attention and publicity and thus by reputation the greater — and more loyal — following. Of more immediate concern to the captains was that, if two steamers were closing down on a pier crowded with trippers awaiting the chance to return to Gourock or Glasgow after an excursion for the day 'doon the watter', fortune favoured the first arrival, which would scoop up the potential passengers and leave her unsuccessful rival with an empty pierhead.

A trial of speed in open water was one thing: but a high-speed convergence in the narrow confines of some isolated pier was very different and there were regular (though thankfully almost always minor) collisions: there were also frequent near-misses or, to describe them with rather more accuracy, near-hits! One collision, documented in the pages of the *Glasgow Herald*, did actually take place off the Garroch Head, in 1877, between the *Guinevere* and the *Glen Rosa*, when they side-swiped one another with consequent damage to their paddle-boxes.

The advent of the turbines inevitably sharpened the rivalries as the hitherto unchallenged crack paddlers found themselves under threat from the new upstarts.

Probably the greatest duel of all, however, was played out

on an almost daily basis between the established paddle-powered speedsters *Lord of the Isles* and *Columba*. They both ran daily services from Glasgow to Bute and on through the Kyles: the *Columba* to Tarbert and Ardrishaig, her rival continuing north to Inveraray.

Their schedules usually found them leaving Rothesay on the outward passage at exactly the same time, and from there it was a race to reach the Kyles piers (the first of these being Colintraive) ahead of the opposition. The passengers invariably took up an extremely partisan stance but, as the contemporary newspaper accounts testify, they were as ready to heap abuse on a losing Captain as they were to cheer a winner's triumph.

*TURBINE ELEGANCE — King Edward was launched from Denny Brothers' Dumbarton Yard in 1901 — the world's first turbine-powered merchant vessel — and ran the daily service from Greenock Princes Pier to Campbeltown and return. Capable of over 20 knots, she is seen here edging into the Kintyre capital's pier with a 'standing room only' crowd on board. Note the vessels on the stocks of the shipyard in the background.*

# 4

## *Trouble for the Tar*

From the deck of the *Vital Spark* the crew watched with interest as a large gaff-rigged ketch, having successfully and skilfully negotiated the deceptively narrow opening into the inner harbour at Rothesay, nosed in to the stone quayside, one of her hands standing in the bow pulpit making ready to throw a line ashore. In the capacious cockpit immediately astern of her substantial main cabin stood three elegantly turned-out men with a fourth, presumably the owner, at the wheel.

"A chentleman's life," said Para Handy, "There iss no better way to see the world than in a yat! They'll no' have problems wi' harbour-masters or ship's captains. Welcome whereffer they care to go, and steam aalways gives way to sail!"

Dan Macphail, with a watchful eye on the derrick as he swung another swaying bundle of fencing-stobs outboard to the waiting cart on the quayside, nodded agreement. "Aye, they huv it easy compared wi' the likes of us. The workers is aye the worst aff in this world, it's the gentry that comes oot best. Ah wudna say no to a poseetion on a yat!"

"Me too," cried Sunny Jim from the depths of the hold. "Just imagine no' havin' tae work wi' a cargo of coals ever again! A life of ease!"

"Mind you," said Para Handy, "even the lads on the yats have problems sometimes. Take your predecessor Jum, your kizzin Colin Turner the Tar, for instance. Crewin' on a yat nearly cost him his merriage…"

"Tell us the baur," said Jim, peering over the coaming of the hatchway. On the quayside the now fully-loaded horse-and-cart was heading for the town, and since there was as

22

yet no sign of the second cart returning, a few minutes of rest and relaxation were in prospect.

Para Handy scratched his ear reflectively. "Well, it wass like this...

~

"Ass you aal know, the Tar got merrit on wan Lucy McCallum, a Campbeltown gyurl, and left the shup soon efter the weddin'. He took a chob in a distillery in the toon ass a cooperage hand and he learnt his tred and for three years efferything went fine for the young couple. They rented a single-end chust off Main Street and Lucy had two weans, a boy and a gyurl. Mercifully it seemed they wud tak' efter her rather than their faither in character ass well ass in looks, for he wass idle, the Tar, idle — and blate wi' it.

"But it wassna his fault he lost his chob at the distillery, for it wass at a time o' sleck orders in the spurits tred and the man that owned it chust shut it doon — not for good, but for a few months till there wass demand for spurits again, and he paid off all the hands and told them to come back in 10 weeks.

"Lucy wass fair dementit when the Tar gave her the news, but she couldna blame the boy, though it wass goin' to be very hard to get ony ither work, for there were fower other distilleries layin' men off at the time and there were chust no chobs to be had in the toon.

"Her mither wass a widow-woman but she helped the young couple ass much ass she could, and it wass she who heard that there wass to be a new boat-yerd opened up at Inveraray by a kizzin o' her late husband, and she wrote and asked if he could find a chob for the Tar, chust for a few months till the distillery opened up again.

"And he wrote back and said yes, if the Tar got himself there within the week he'd tak' him on in the framin'-shed.

" 'But hoo am Ah tae get up tae Inveraray,' asked the Tar when she gave him the news. 'Me wi' no wages comin' in?'

"She had even sorted that oot for him. 'Wan o' the English chentlemen that comes up for the shootin's in September bought a yat last year and it's been lyin' at Machrihanish effer since then,' she said, 'Noo he's wantin' it taken to Tarbert to wait for him comin' up there next month.'

"Wan o' the Campbeltown fishin' skippers wass pickin'

the yat up the next mornin' and sailin' it up to Tarbert while hiss own skiff wass on the Campbeltown slup for her annual overhaul, and he'd agreed wi' her that the Tar could crew for him. And of course wance he wass in Tarbert it would be easy to tak' the two hoor trup on to Inveraray on the *Lord of the Isles* any day of the week.

"There wassna mich the Tar could do to get oot of that, so next mornin' he wass up sharp and steppin' oot the six miles ower to Machrihanish wi' his tin box on his shoulders.

"Vickery, the skipper, wass there before him and within the hour they were off. The Tar wass a bit worried when he saw who the skipper wass, for Vickery was weel-kent for his fondness for the high jinks, but he wass a successful fisherman and a good seaman. The yat wass called *Midge* but in spite of that she wass a smert boat wi' a midships cabin wi' a couple of berths and a wee punt in tow.

"They made good time round the Mull of Kintyre and chust aboot two-o-clock they had Davaar Island dead ahead, and then the mooth o' Campbeltown loch openin' up to port.

"Vickery looked at his watch. 'We've made good time, Colin,' he says to the Tar. 'What d'ye say we chust look in to the toon for an hour and I'll see how they're gettin' on wi' the repairs on the skiff?'

"There wassna anything the Tar could say, he wassna skipper, so they tacked up the loch and moored the *Midge* in the harbour and rowed ashore in the punt. Ass fate would have it they met a brither o' Vickery's who'd chust got hame from Gleska that very mornin' on the *King Edward* efter a year at sea, and before the Tar kent what was what, they wass aal ensconced in the nearest Inn at a table by the window — 'So I can chust keep wan eye on the yat', said Vickery — and the drams kept comin' ass soon ass aal the brither's friends foond oot he was back in toon and came in for a yarn.

"Five in the afternoon came and Vickery gave the Tar the keys to his hoose and sent him to fetch a gallon jar so they could tak' some refreshments back on board wi' them. And the first person he met ass he wass comin' back along the street wi' the jar wass his mither-in-law! 'What are you doin' still here, Colin,' she cried briskly, 'when you should be well on your way up Kilbrannan Sound — and whaur are ye goin' wi' that jar?'

"The Tar tried to explain in a way that wouldna incriminate him but she gave him a sharp look and reminded him that the chob at Inveraray wouldna wait for effer. 'Get you to Tarbert, Colin Turner' she said. 'Or you'll answer to me for it!'

"Here and when they left to go back to the yat did Vickery's brither and anither couple o' his cronics no' come wi' them, and wi' their ain jars, and the perty sterted aal over again. At eight o'clock Vickery consulted his watch and annoonced that it wisna worth settin' off that night, they'd wait till next mornin' and get awa' sharp: and he went back ashore wi' his brither and left the Tar in charge.

"Next morning, the Tar woke at seven and there wass no sign of Vickery at aal. But within the hour he wass back, wi' a grey face, a short temper and a heid as spiky as a bagful o' old spanners. 'Iss this Campbeltown or Cairo,' he cried, 'and am I comin or goin'? Be a good lad, Colin, and nip ashore and get a can o' mulk at the dairy and a pooder frae the chemist, and if I can find where I pit ma heid we'll mak' a start.

"Who did the Tar meet on the quayside but his wife Lucy, wi' the elder wean on her shoulder and the baby in a pram full o' dirty washin', on her way to the laandry.

" 'Colin Turner!' she shouted on him, 'You should be in Tarbert by noo. Wait till I tell my mither on you!' And though the Tar tried to explain she chust stormed off in a real tizzy but not afore she'd gi'en him the bleckest look he'd effer seen on a wumman.

"When he got back on board the *Midge* he managed to persuade Vickery to loose her from her moorin' and off they set.

"But ass luck wud have it the winds wass against them, and then when they were off Carradale at aboot fower in the afternoon, the sea haar cam' doon like cotton wool and they couldna see the tap o' the mast.

" 'It's nae use, Colin,' said Vickery. 'Ah'm no riskin' the boat in fog like this.' And he picked his way into the harbour at Carradale.

"Pretty soon the Tar foond himsel' in the Inns at the head of the pier and again efferybody seemed to know Vickery and in no time at aal there wass a spree goin'. Wan o' the company wass a Campbeltown cairter caaled McCallum, wi' the by-name o' the Twister, who wass a kizzin o' the Tar's mither-in-law, and a man wi' a dreadful reputation for a dram, so soon they wass aal in full flight.

"The poor Tar had had enough of it and he tried to get his skipper back on board. 'I will no' be long at aal, Colin,' said Vickery. 'Why don't you chust awa' ootside and streetch oot on McCallum's cairt and have a snooze? I'll gi'e ye a shout when we're ready to go and we'll be in Tarbert in no time at aal.'

"Well, the Tar went and did chust that, for he wass aalways a man wi a great capacity for sleep. If Dougie was here he would tell you himself. The cairt wass half full o' sacks o' corn so he made himsel' a comfortable bunk and snugged doon.

"So he slept and better slept.

"When he finally woke up it wass seven o'clock next mornin' and broad daylight! He sat up at wance, feart that Vickery had sailed withoot him — and foond they wassna even in Carradale at aal! The cairt was stood at the foot of Main Street in Campbeltown! They wass outside the Ferry Inn and what had woke him wass the din ass Vickery and McCallum kept bangin' on the door to get the landlord to open and gi'e them their mornin's!

"Chust then, who came roond the corner from the close leadin' to his ain single-end but his wife and his mither-in-law!

"They both clapped eyes on him at the same time and let oot a shriek that even stopped Vickery and the Twister deid in their efforts to break into the Inn.

" 'Colin Turner!!! Whaur's your sense o' responsibeelity to your wife and weans! You've mooths to feed and aal you can do iss chust cairry on wi' drink like a Cardiff stoker!'

"It wass ass well for Colin that the cairter, at least, wass chust sober enough to tell his kizzin and her dochter that the poor Tar wass innocent of ony devagation, that he and Vickery had been thrown oot o' the Inn at Carradale at midnight and, having forgot aal aboot the *Midge*, and the Tar asleep in the back of the cairt, had let the horse do the navigation and meandered doon hame to Campbeltown in the wee sma' hours.

"So the Tar neffer made it to the chob at Inveraray, and the chentleman that owned the *Midge* wass in a right tirravee for he had to send a new crew doon frae Tarbert to pick her up from Carradale.

"The only thing that saved the Tar's skin wass that the spurit trade picked up (probably lergely due to Vickery's singlehanded support) and he got his old chob back the next week when the distillery re-opened.

"So, Jum, remember it's not aalways plain sailin' on a yat!"

*FACTNOTE*

Now that the network of steamer services on the Firth of Clyde is but a distant memory, the Mull of Kintyre is unquestionably the most isolated community not just in Scotland, but in all of mainland Britain, and Campbeltown the country's most remote town. In fact in some respects it is more remote from Central Scotland now than it was 100 years ago, when daily services by fast steamer from Glasgow, 80 miles by sea, were usually faster and certainly more comfortable than today's tortuous 140 mile bus journey — which takes four-and-a-half hours each way.

The Tar's journey from Campbeltown on the eastern coast of the narrow peninsula to Machrihanish on the western side must have taken place before August 1906, for otherwise he would not have had to walk!

That month saw open to passenger traffic the splendidly-named Campbeltown and Machrihanish Light Railway Company's services on a narrow-gauge line, an extension of the track originally laid to transport coal for export across the peninsula from the Drumlemble pit to the docks of Campbeltown harbour.

Inevitably christened 'the wee train' the line remained open for passengers for 25 years, finally closing in 1931 after the shut-down of the coalmine during the 1929 depression.

Carradale lies roughly half-way between the southern-most tip of Kintyre and Tarbert, where the peninsula 'rejoins' the mainland at Knapdale, and was an established port of call for steamers on passage to Glasgow. Today it remains a popular destination for visitors in the summer months and maintains its traditional fishing industry year-round.

Discussing this storyline with a resident of Campbeltown prior to publication I suggested it was rather far-fetched that I had the horse bring the cart all the way home from Carradale by itself. "Not at all," he said: "they used to do that from the Tarbert Fair in the old days — and that was twice the distance!"

The seas around the Mull are exposed and subject to vio

lent storms. Hence the construction almost 200 years ago of the Crinan canal, which allows small vessels to move between the Clyde and the Western Highlands in sheltered conditions. The hazards of the Mull are perhaps best exemplified by the fact that in the years before the development of powerful, fast rescue vessels there were not as today, just one, but *three* lifeboat stations within a few miles of each other at its southernmost limits — Campbeltown, Southend and Machrihanish.

*DREAMLAND FOR DRINKERS* — *This panoramic view of Campbeltown and its bay shows, behind the mother and her two infants, an unbroken phalanx-in-depth of distillery after distillery. There were more than 20 in the town in the years around the turn of the century and the grain they required was a frequent cargo for the puffers, and larger vessels too.*

# 5

## *Up for the Cup*

It can be — depending on the particular circumstances
at any particular time — either an advantage, or a dis-
advantage, to be the skipper of a West Coast puffer. In
the remotest communities the arrival of the little vessel is a major event, the social (and business) highlight of
the month or, in some instances, the year. She may be
delivering the bits and pieces of the material world, from
mangles to mattresses, which the community has anxiously been waiting for: or she may have come to load a cargo,
be it timber or whinstone, barley or roofing slate, the eventual sale of which will provide the cash income necessary to
keep the village economy going for another season.

As almost the only link with the outside world, the puffer
provides often the sole opportunity such communities have
to maintain even the most basic social communication with
distant family and friends. Thus the *Vital Spark* has been
known to carry a few jars of rhubarb jam (and, most important of all, the recipe for it) from an old lady in Colonsay to
her newly-married niece in Greenock, or a border collie
pup from a farmer in Ayrshire to his cousin in Appin.

Sometimes Para Handy is flattered by such requests,
sometimes irritated by them: it depends on his mood. But,
being of a kindly disposition, most of the time he is happy
to help.

What can test his generosity to the limit, however, is
when the little extra something he is asked to carry is neither animal nor inanimate — but human.

"I've had mair trouble wi' the occasional supercargo than
ye'd hae wi' a barrowload o' monkeys," he told me when I
encountered the crew recently in a Gourock hostelry, "but

the wan we had last week wass the giddy limit. Neffer, neffer trust a man frae Colintraive. Chust ask Macphail!"

Hearing mention of his name the engineer, who had been sitting hunched over the niggardly fire in the far corner of the bar, turned round and in so doing displayed a monstrous 'shiner' on his right eye.

"How on earth did Dan come by that?" I asked in astonishment.

"Och, he didn't exactly come by it," replied Para Handy. "He didn't have to go and look for it at aal, at aal. Somebody gave it to him. Neffer, neffer trust a man from Colintraive."

And, with only a little further coaxing, he told me the tale.

~

"It wass partly Dan's own fault, of course," said the skipper with a nod in the direction of the figure at the fire. "It usually is. You ken yoursel' what he's like. Not exactly full of the milk of human kindness, no, nor exactly the soul of tact or discretion.

"It all started last Friday when we wass picking up a cargo of oak bark at Colintraive.

"You wud see in the papers that the Kyles Athletic fitba' team had managed to get to the third round of the Scottish Cup by beatin' Dunoon Rovers, and then Renfrew Thistle. And who were they drawn to play next but Gleska Rangers themselves! And at Ibrox Park!

"You can imagine the excitement all along the Kyles. The team had gone up to Gleska the day before on the *Minard Castle* and they were stayin' in wan o' they Temperance Hotels — a very wise precaution given their reputation for a spree — ass guests of the Gleska Highlanders Association. Friday afternoon, when the *Columba* called in on her way back from Ardrishaig, maist o' the men of the Kyles villages wass waitin' on Colintraive pier wi' their tin boxes in one hand, and the addresses of their Gleska cousins wrote doon on a bit o' paper in the ither.

"By the time we finished loading on Friday afternoon, the Kyles wass a deserted place indeed. We wass all doon in the fo'c'sle at wir tea when there came a shout frae the pier and Jum went up to see what wass up.

"Here wass Ferguson the innkeeper — and a quiet weekend he wass facin', what wi' all the menfolk awa' tae Ibrox and it too early in the year for ony towerists to be aboot — wi' a young fellow maybe in his early twenties scuffin' his feet beside him.

" 'I dinna think ye've met Hamish, my youngest', says he by way o' introduction.

"The upshot of it wass that Hamish had been up in Glendaruel on a chob wi' the Forestry and had got back to Colintraive too late to catch the boat to Gleska wi' the rest o' them, and him a desperate keen supporter o' the Kyles Athletics team.

"I could see which way the wind was going to blow but I owed an obleegance to Ferguson for the time he'd subbed us till the wages cam' through from the owner so before I could say eechie or ochie aboot it, young Hamish was aboard the boat and we were to gi'e him passage up river when we left at dawn the Saturday mornin'. In truth it wass no great inconvenience, for we wass to unload oor cairgo at Govan on Monday mornin' and so we'd planned to berth the shup there for the weekend ass it wass.

"Noo ye'll mind that afore Macphail moved to Plantation he'd spent all his years in Govan so, though he'd never been to a fitba' game in his life, he coonted hissel' a supporter o' the Rangers. 'Brutain's finest', he wud say when the papers showed them winnin' some new trophy or ither: 'Rangers iss the boys!'

"So he didna' take too kindly to a Kyles supporter installed in the fo'c'sle, specially wan festooned in the favours o' the Kyles team, in a kind o' roarie yellow colour like the skin of a custard and wi' a stripe or two o' purple through it.

"Dougie wass ashore visitin' a cousin so Jum and me did oor best to keep the peace but Macphail was aye needlin', needlin' at the young fellow. It wass 'At least you lot'll see fur wance whit way a real team plays fitba' tomorrow' — and — 'See in yon strup o' yours, the Kyles boys'll look like naethin' so mich as a set o' kahouchy skuttles or a cageful o' canaries!' — and — 'Whit nicht wull ye be haudin' the wake in Colintraive?'

"I tell you I wass that worried they wud come to blows then and there I took Hamish to wan side and made him promise to keep hiss hands in his pockets and off the enchineer. 'Ye'll have to mind he's an older man and you wud lose face if you laid wan on him,' says I. 'Michty,' says Hamish. 'It's him that wud lose face — and a' the component pairts o' it — if I did.' But he promised me he'd swallow the insults ass if they wass water off a wally close and sit on his hands if needs be. 'You have my word on it, Captain MacFarlane,' he says: 'I swear I'll no' lay a finger on the auld fool.'

"To be on the safe side and to keep them apart I took Macphail up to the Inns and treated him oot of my ain pocket. When we got back aboard the young man wass sound asleep in the spare bunk and I thought that was that, for we had a very early start the next mornin', and Macphail wud be snug doon in his enchines wi' the latest novelle and oot o' herm's way.

"Everythin' went sweemingly on the Saturday, we made a quick passage up the river and put in to the basin at Govan at aboot two o'clock and set the young fellow ashore within an easy walk o' Ibrox Stadium.

"His faither had promised to send a telegraph to wan o' his Gleska cousins and get him to meet him at the quayside and sure enough there wass another yellow-and-purple bedecked figure waiting for him at the dock gates.

" 'Whateffer you do, dinna' staun' behind the Kyles goal' was Macphail's parting shot. 'For there'll be that mony holes in the net in nae time that ye'll be sittin' targets like ducks in a shootin' gallery! Or canaries raither!'

"But chust two minutes later the young fellow wass back! Here and wass it no' an aal-ticket game! His cousin had chust the wan ticket so there wass nothin' for Hamish to do but drum hiss heels. 'I've arranged for cousin Gordon to come back doon here to collect me wance the game's over,' he said, and him near to greetin' wi' the disappointment of it all. 'I hope it's all right for me to wait on the boat till then?'

~

"Mercifully Macphail went aff to sulk among his enchines and the rest of us sat doon in the fo'c'sle and had a baur.

"Come five o'clock the young fellow went up on deck to look oot for his cousin comin' back. Dougie and me went up too, and began gettin' the shup ready for the unlading on Monday. Dougie started to loose the tarpaulins on the cargo hatch, and I freed the jib o' the derrick from its bracket at the fore end of the wheelhouse.

"Chust then Macphail came out on deck. 'I thocht you'd have been ashore tae get your black armband and your weepers,' he cried to Hamish. 'But at least I can gi'e ye plenty o' coaldust tae mak' yer ain!'

"I'll say this for the boy, he never stirred, chust drummed his fingers even-on on the jib-arm of the derrick.

"And then hiss cousin appeared at the gates, and walked up to the side of the quay. You chust needed to see the way that he walked to ken he certainly wassnae the bringer o' glad tidings frae Ibrox.

"Hamish looked up anxiously. 'Whit wis the score, Gordon?'

" 'Seventeen-nil.'

"Hamish said nothin', chust kept drummin' his fingers even-on on the jib-arm, but there was a great guffaw from behind him where Macphail stood on the other side of the deck by the bulwarks at the after end of the hold. 'Seventeen-nil! *Seventeen-nil!* Go on, Hamish — are you no' even goin' tae ask him — *who fur?*'

"It took just seconds. The young fellow spun round, seized hold of the jib-arm, and with a mighty shove swung it outwards and towards Macphail. It caught him chust at head-height, as you can see from the state of his eye: and knocked him overboard into the basin.

" 'I'm right sorry, Captain,' said the young fellow: 'but a man can take only so mich: and I kept my promise. I didn't lay a finger on him.'

"Since Sunny Jum wass ashore gettin' the groceries, and I'm the only wan o' the rest of the crew that can swum, it was me that had to dive in and fish him oot. And ruined my best pea-jacket in the doin' o' it.

"Like I said at the beginning: you can neffer trust a man frae Colintraive."

*FACTNOTE*

The quiet Kyles village of Colintraive has a number of particularly fine houses, many of which were originally built as summer homes by wealthy Glasgow merchants and professional men. The shortest ferry-crossing on the Clyde operates from here to Rhubodach on the island of Bute, less than five minutes away across the narrows.

The most unexpected teams can occasionally reach the later rounds of the Scottish Cup, and they can find themselves drawn to play established, senior clubs. This helps to give the Cup (at least from the point-of-view of the neutral bystander) a sometimes surreal serendipity.

In 1995, for example, a non-league Fife team called Burntisland Shipyard (named from the years long gone, when it was a 'works' team in the days when Burntisland *had* a shipyard) reached the third round of the tournament. Sadly for those whose sympathies lie with the underdogs, that was the limit of their progress.

Inevitably some of these fairy-tale teams have gone down to crashing defeats. The most notorious score-line of all dates from 1885, when Arbroath (playing at home) beat Aberdeen Bon Accord by 36 goals to nil — which was equivalent to a goal being scored every two-and-a-half minutes of playing time. The *Guinness Book of Records* account of the event comments: 'But for the lack of nets and the consequent waste of retrieval time the score must have been even higher.' Arbroath still play senior football today, though in one of the lower divisions.

Two years later the equivalent record for the English Cup was set by Preston North End with a 26 to nil victory over Hyde.

I hope that any supporters of Rangers who may read this story will excuse the placing of a totally fictional game at the very real Ibrox Stadium: I am sure they will, particularly when it involves such a convincing victory! And I doubt very much if there would have been any 'all-ticket' games in Para Handy's day, but sometimes a little anachronism becomes a must in the telling of a tale!

It has also to be admitted that the Kyles area is better known for its Shinty traditions than for any pretensions to football. Shinty is perhaps best loosely categorised, for those unaware of its finer points or even of its existence, as a version of hockey which seems to have few rules and scant consideration for the safety of the protagonists. A game with a Physical Contact Quotient which makes almost any other team-game seem a pansy pursuit, and enjoying a strong loyal and local following in the Highlands (to which area it is largely confined), it has been described by uninitiated critics as legalised mayhem. To those brought up with, and devoted to, the traditions and the finer points of the game, such a comment is as a red rag to a bull. So I unreservedly withdraw it!

# 6

## *An Inland Voyage*

On occasion, the *Vital Spark* left her familiar Clyde haunts for the sheltered waters of the Forth & Clyde Canal. Sometimes she was bound for the farther shores of the Firth of Forth to load barley for the distilleries back at Campbeltown. Sometimes she would pick up a cargo of timber from the seasoning basins at the port of Grangemouth. Sometimes her business was within the canal network itself, taking coals to the Carron foundries or uplifting pig-iron from Bonnybridge.

Whatever the reasons for her presence on the canal, Para Handy viewed such journeys with an unremitting and quite remorseless loathing.

The other members of the puffer's crew looked on these inland voyages as a welcome relief from the more demanding environment of the open waters of the Firth, and the associated problems of wind and tide. To chug effortlessly through the countryside along a smooth ribbon of never-ruffled water was sheer paradise compared with the purgatory of battering round Ardnamurchan in the teeth of a howling headwind and a steely, rolling swell.

For the skipper, though, the canal was hell: for here, in every town and village through which the little vessel passed, he was at the mercy of the unfeeling urchins who watched the approach and greeted the passage of the puffer with undisguised derision.

At least on the river and in the firth the sarcastic cries of "*Aquitania* ahoy!" from boys fishing from piers or hanging over the stern of the crack paddlers shooting past the lumbering puffer could be ignored. The puffer would eventually be out of earshot of the piers, and the paddlers would much sooner be just a dot on the distant horizon as they sped away, carrying his tormentors with them.

On the canal the taunts were ever-present. The *Vital Spark* was easily outpaced by the ragamuffins of Avondale or Twechar, who assembled on the banks in droves as she approached and then ran alongside her with their merciless, mocking cries as she wheezed her way towards the next set of locks. Her looks and her speed were compared unfavourably with the elegance and pace of renowned passenger-vessels like the *Faery Queen* or the *May Queen* and Para Handy could only escape the verbal onslaught by retiring to the wheelhouse, tightly shutting door and windows however hot the weather, and feigning a lofty disdain that he certainly did not feel.

"Man, Dougie," he would protest, as he watched the gang race ahead and line up at the parapet of the next bridge the puffer must pass under, "ye wud think their faithers and mithers wud bring them up wi' some sense of the dignity o' the sea! They've no more respect for the *Vital Spark* than if she wass a common coal scow or a cattle barge!"

∾

Thus a fine May morning found the captain in a foul mood as the puffer approached Camelon on the Forth and Clyde Canal, their destination the Rosebank Distillery on the outskirts of Falkirk with a cargo of the best Fife barley. Her progress through the locks at Grangemouth had involved running the usual gauntlet of taunt and insult and the skipper's patience was exhausted.

The *Vital Spark* nosed in to the quayside at the Rosebank basin where two horse-drawn drays stood waiting to start carting the sacks of grain to the adjacent distillery warehouse.

Para Handy, once the unloading had started to the accompaniment of the noisily hissing clatter of the puffer's temperamental steam-winch, made tracks for the distillery office to report his arrival.

"You're looking a bit out of sorts today, Peter", commented the manager, who was well acquainted with the skipper and his crew over many years.

Para Handy explained the reasons for his ill-temper and, to his surprise, found he had a sympathetic ear.

"I know exactly what you mean," said the manager. "We

have just exactly the same problems with the little terrors. Thirty years I've been here, and 30 years of splendid service we've had from generations of our Clydesdales. But now these new-fangled motor wagons are all the rage, honest horses aren't good enough for the kids of Camelon.

" 'Peep, peep! Oot o' the way!' or 'Can ye no' get them oot o' first gear then, mister?' are the least of the insults my men have to put up with when they're out on the roads with the drays."

"No respect, chust no respect at aal," agreed Para Handy. "It's a peety we couldna gi'e them a lesson they'd remember, a lesson to shut them up next time they felt like givin' lip to their elders and betters."

"Dreams, dreams, Peter," said the manager and, reaching into a drawer of his desk, produced a square bottle of the colourless straight-from-the-still whisky and poured them both a generous dram.

∼

Unloading the barley sacks took till late afternoon, and so the *Vital Spark* lay overnight at the Rosebank basin. As the crew were preparing for an early start the following morning Para Handy was surprised to see the distillery manager come running up. Behind him, two workmen were pushing along the towpath a strange-looking machine mounted on four small wheels.

"Could you do me a wee kindness, Peter? Could you put this fire engine off at our Maryhill bottling plant for me?"

Half-an-hour later the puffer cast off and headed towards Lock 16, junction with the Union Canal to Edinburgh, on her journey westwards to Glasgow and the Clyde.

Macphail the engineer was of course the only man aboard able to even begin to comprehend the workings of the machine which now perched on the hatch of the puffer's empty hold. Leaving his engines to their own devices he prowled round the little contraption, cap in hand, scratching his balding pate.

"Two horse-power," he read aloud the inscription on the brass plate riveted to the platform on which the device was mounted. "Two horse-power fire pump."

"Whit does it dae, Dan?" queried Sunny Jim.

"Ah've read aboot them," said the engineer. "It's wan o' they new-fangled petrol injins the same as they hae on caurs, but this wan's for pumpin' watter." He gesticulated to the hoses coiled round drums on opposite sides of the frame. "It's tae pit oot fires. Ye stick the end o' wan o' they hoses intae the watter, caw that haundle on the end tae get the injin sterted, and point the ither hose at the flames. The watter gets pumped up and the fire gaes oot."

"Man, man," said Para Handy in some surprise. "An infernal machine, my Chove! Whateffer will they think of next?" And he resumed his contemplation of the spring countryside as it slipped by at the rate of 4 knots.

They had a peaceful passage across the central heartland of the Forth and Clyde valley but the canal urchins appeared again as they approached Kirkintilloch.

"Would you look at that," cried the exasperated skipper as a gang of young boys raced along the towpath beside them, pulling faces and catcalling, "a skelp behind the lug's what they're sair in need o'." And he pulled up the sliding windows to shut himself into the cramped wheelhouse.

The door opened and Sunny Jim squeezed in.

"Captain," he said, "I've got an idea..."

～

Five minutes later the puffer glided into the Townhead locks in Kirkintilloch. Sunny Jim jumped for the iron ladder let into the stone walls of the lock and climbed to the towpath. Pushing his way through the assembled crowd of young boys he helped the lock-keeper to swing the wooden gates shut at the stern of the boat. The lock-keeper opened the sluice in the gates above the puffer's bow, and water started to pour into the lock to lift the little vessel up to the level of the next stretch of the canal.

Jim peered down onto the deck of the puffer 10 feet below him. There was surprising activity taking place on the hatchway.

The mate was uncoiling one of the water hoses on Para Handy's "infernal machine" and Macphail was preparing to swing the iron starting-handle. The skipper himself, with a suspicious glint in his eye, was cradling the brass nozzle at the end of the second hose in his hands.

The puffer continued to rise up the surrounding lock walls as the water flooded in from the higher level. Rows of grinning faces to either side awaited her coming as the Kirkintilloch urchins prepared to subject the hapless Para

Handy to another torrent of abuse.

Sunny Jim had a quick, whispered consultation with the keeper as the level of the water in the lock rose higher. That worthy quickly took shelter in his nearby hut, and Sunny Jim, with a last check of the levels, jumped six feet down onto the puffer's deck and shouted: "*Now!*"

Macphail swung the starting-handle, the little petrol engine fired, the water pump got down to business, and in a matter of seconds a powerful jet of water shot from the brass nozzle in Para Handy's grip.

With a whoop of triumph, he directed the jet to left and right, sweeping it across the ranks of his tormentors who, caught totally by surprise, were quickly drenched through before they hesitated, broke, and fled in disarray.

"Let that be a lesson to you," called Para Handy with a grin of triumph. "Two horse-power and an auld man, that's aal it takes to send you packing! Maybe next time ye'll think twice before you give any lip to the men who run the horses and puffers on this canal, eh?"

And, turning the pump off as the lock gates ahead of him swung open and Macphail headed for the engine-room to put some way on the little vessel, he returned to the wheel-house and began to rehearse the very satisfying story he'd have for the manager of the Rosebank distillery next time they met.

*FACTNOTE*

Only two of Scotland's canals — the Crinan and the Caledonian — remain fully navigable today, though some stretches of the Forth and Clyde, and Union, Canals have been restored and there are some pleasure sailing opportunities.

The Crinan and the Caledonian remain in use because they still fulfil the purpose for which they were built — to offer an alternative, for smaller vessels, to what would otherwise be a long and exposed sea-passage. Scotland's other major canals had provided for the convenient transportation of raw materials in bulk, such as timber, steel or coal: and the speedy and more comfortable movement of passengers.

Since both these functions were, in the course of time, better catered for by the railways and the road networks, the canals became outmoded and eventually abandoned.

THE NEW HORSEPOWER — *Here is the precursor of the juggernauts of today, an early brewer's lorry with, perched on the fence, some of the urchins whose taunts on and off the Firth could make life such a misery for the beleaguered Para Handy. But it would be 50 years before the last horse-and-cart disappeared from the streets of Glasgow.*

Thus were lost the Forth and Clyde Canal from Grangemouth to Bowling: the Union Canal which (across beautiful countryside and over some quite spectacular aqueducts) linked the centre of Edinburgh to the Forth and Clyde Canal near Falkirk: the Monkland Canal from Glasgow to the coalfields of Lanarkshire: the Paisley Canal from Glasgow to Johnstone, all that was ever completed of an ambitious project to link Glasgow by canal to Ardrossan on the Ayrshire coast: and the less-well-known Aberdeenshire Canal which ran from the Granite City northwards to Inverurie.

At the height of the canal 'boom' there were proposals for many other, smaller scale, projects throughout Scotland from the Solway in the south and as far north as the Moray Firth. Some of these, such as a two-mile cut to carry coal from the Ayrshire mines to Saltcoats harbour: a three-mile waterway, again to carry coals, across the Mull of Kintyre from the Machrihanish mines to Campbeltown: and a two-mile canal at Cupar in Fife, to convey limestone, were actually completed.

Two hugely ambitious projects came to nothing: but it is quite intriguing to speculate how the economic history of the country might have been altered if they had. One, first mooted at the beginning of the nineteenth century, proposed a cross-Scotland canal linking Dumbarton on the Clyde with Stonehaven, south of Aberdeen, by way of Stirling and Perth. The second, which was actively promoted for over 60 years and only finally buried for good in 1947, was for a canal linking the Firths of the Forth and the Clyde, a through route for ocean-going vessels, a huge waterway which would have been on the same scale as the Manchester Ship Canal in England. Several alternatives were considered: by far the most dramatic, not to say controversial proposal, would have taken the waterway from the head of Loch Long and through Loch Lomond to debouch into the Forth near the village of Fallin a mile or two east of Stirling.

# 7

## *Those in Peril on the Sea*

onditions had deteriorated throughout the October night and when the crew awoke in the morning it was obvious that there could be no question of the *Vital Spark* beginning her return journey to Glasgow. Far from her usual haunts, she lay against the wooden pier at Scarinish on the Inner Hebridean island of Tiree, where she had unloaded a cargo of winter coals.

The prospect was chill and cheerless. A south-westerly wind of storm force howled mercilessly across the treeless, blasted machair of this flattest of islands, and savaged the scattered clusters of croft houses which huddled together as if searching (in vain) for some element of shelter from the worst excesses of the weather. Occasional flurries of rain were swept across the bleak landscape in stinging horizontal sheets.

Most frightening of all, though, was the state of the sea itself. Between Tiree and Mull, 15 miles away, the ocean seemed to boil in fury as the wind whipped the tops off the steep waves: and the rocky sentinels of the tiny Treshnish islands which lay off the Mull coast at times disappeared under the cataracts of flying spray exploding from the mountainous breakers which disintegrated against their low black cliffs.

"My Cot," said Para Handy, as he slammed the fo'c'sle hatch behind him after a quick peek out to assess the situation, "I doot we're goin' nowhere today, laads: indeed I doot if even Mr MacBrayne'll be goin' anywhere. Heaven help any shup that's been caught oot in this."

Macphail — whose stock of novelettes lay out-of-reach

for the moment in the engine-room — looked up from his perusal of the only reading matter to hand, a copy of the Oban Times which the Mate had purchased the previous day in the Scarinish shop. "If the *Mountaineer* so mich as pits her nose oot o' Tobermory in this, they're askin' for trouble," he agreed. "This is aboot as bad a storm as I can mind of for mony years."

Sunny Jim, whose previous sea-going experience — as a hand on the Cluthas — stopped at Yoker, was mightily relieved to have confirmation that the puffer was not intending to venture into a storm the very sound, never mind the sight, of which had given him an apprehensive, sleepless night.

"Whit's the worst experience at sea that ye've ever had wi' the *Vital Spark*, Captain?" he asked.

Para Handy scratched his right ear reflectively.

"That would have to be a time a few years back, when we wass bringin' a cargo o' brand new herrin' boxes from a Campbeltown factory up to wan o' the fush-merchants in Oban. But it wass a bad experience not because it wass dangerous at aal, Jum, but chust because it wass so doonright vexatious.

"We had to sail to Oban roond the Mull o' Kintyre, because they wass repairin' wan o' the locks in the Crinan canal and it wass closed to aal shups for three weeks. For several days afore we set oot from Campbeltown, there wass a steady wund from the west: not a gale, you understand, but chust this constant, constant wund.

"Caairyin' a bulky, light cargo like herrin' boxes meant that even wi' the hold cham-packed wi' them we still had a lot of freeboard, so we wass able to pile up a great mass o' them as deck cargo as weel. Even then, though her stern wass doon, her bows wass still up, and there wass a wall o' the boxes aboot eight foot high streetched right across the hatchway.

"Ye couldna see a dam' thing ahead of the shup from the brudge, and the Tar had to sit on the tap o' the deck cargo to gi'e us directions.

"Effery time we roonded the Mull and the wund hit us, we chust got pushed back! Even wi' Dan's predecessor, McCulloch, pilin' on the coals and near burstin' the biler wi' the steam pressure we couldna get enough power to mak' ony headway into thon wund! The pile o' boxes wass chust like a sail and we wass doin' mair speed under wund-power

43

— but goin' astern — than we effer did under steam-power goin' ahead!

"I wass bleck-affronted. Effery mornin' for fower days we left the harbour at Campbeltown, and effery evenin' for fower days we had to turn back there to anchor overnight and try again the next day. I have neffer been so embarrassed aboot the shup even though it wass not her fault — it wass the wund. And when the fishermen in Campbeltown foond oot what wass goin' on they took a real rise oot o' us. My Chove, wan night someone cam' oot in an oarin'-boat while we wass aal asleep and pented oot the name o' the shup on the stern and pented on *Cutty Sark* instead! And the local paper printed a piece sayin' the vessel should be caalled the *Bad Penny* because she kept comin' back, and that if we stayed ony longer we'd chust as well get a Cooncil licence to give roond-the-bay trups to towerists!"

Sunny Jim turned to the engineer. "Whit about you, Dan?" he asked, "wi' you goin' foreign for so mony years you must have seen some sights!"

"The worst experience I can mind wis nothin' to dae wi' a storm either," offered Macphail. "I wis an apprentice at the time, on a Union Castle liner tae Capetoon, and we lost the propeller aff the shaft aff the Skeleton Coast. There wisnae a dam' thing we could dae aboot it. There wis no wireless in them days, of course, so we jist had tae wait till anither shup appeared, and then hope she could gi'e us a tow.

"There wisnae a breath o' wund, and the sea jist like glass, but there wis a swell ye wudnae believe unless ye saw it! The sea had a run o' thoosands o' miles frae Sooth America tae build up a swell, and it wis like a roller-coaster at Hengler's but mich, mich bigger. The taps o' the waves wis aboot a mile apart, and aboot a hundred feet high! When ye were doon in the troughs you couldnae see a thing but the slope o' the swell either side. We went up and doon and up and doon jist like a twenty thoosand ton yo-yo, and at the same time she wis daein' that, she wis rollin' like a pendulum, and the maist o' the passengers wis that ill they thocht they wis deein'.

"In fact some o' them *hoped* they wis deein'. I wis on the poop deck wan evenin' and there wis a poor cratur hingin' ower the rail, jist as green as grass, and I said to him, no' tae worry, naebody ever died o' the sea-sickness.

"He gave me a look I'll never forget, and groaned 'Dinna

say that, boy, for peety's sake: it's only the hope o' deein' that helps me tae keep goin' !'

"When we finally got a tow in, the swells wis that deep that there wis times the shup that wis pullin' us jist disappeared frae sight completely: ye couldna even see the taps o' her masts!"

Dougie, a notoriously timid sailor and a man who had spent his entire career on the puffer routes in the west, shuffled his feet and looked uncomfortable when Jim swung round and looked enquiringly in his direction.

"You needna be askin' Dougie," said Para Handy, "for he hass nothin' at aal to tell you aboot the perils o' the deep. Whiles some of us hass been stravaigin' across the oceans o' the world — I've been to Ullapool masel', and twice to Belfast — here iss a man who could be feart for hiss life crossin' on the Govan Ferry on a summer's afternoon! Iss that no' right, Dougie?

"Onyway, while you're tryin' to think up some heroic tale for the laad, I will chust tak' a dash up to Harbour House and see what my old friend the Piermaster is thinkin' the weather might be doin', for if we are to be marooned mich longer we wull have to speak nicely to his good-wife aboot the len' o' some proveesions."

And the Captain pulled on his heavy oilskin coat and clambered up the companionway and out into the wild of the storm.

"He thinks he iss very funny," said the embarrassed mate, "but I have a story for you Jum, for aal that: and by the time I've finished tellin' it Para Handy wull be sorry he needled me in the first place!

"The worst conditions that ever I experienced had nothin' at aal to do wi' the weather — but a very great deal to do wi' a certain steam-lighter Captain!

"Before oor time on the *Vital Spark*, Jum, Para Handy and I wass workin' for a man in Girvan that had a sailin' gabbart caaled the *Elizabeth Jane*. Wan time we wass in Campbeltown wi' a load o' lime from the quarry at Glenarm in Antrum, and wass due to sail back ower to Ireland for anither wan.

"The herrin' fushin' in Kilbrannan Soond and Loch Fyne wass absolutely in its prime at the time. The skiffs wass comin' in each mornin' nearly sinkin' under the weight o' the fush they had on board. There wass such a glut o' herrin', you couldna give the fresh fush away in Gleska, and the kipperin' sheds and the picklin' factories couldna keep up wi' the supply.

"Para Handy wass chust a young man, and he wass aye lookin' for ways to turn a coin. He had an uncle that wass a fush merchant in the toon and when he saw the glut o' fush there wass, Para Handy went to him wi' a proposition. The *Elizabeth Jane* would cairry a load of fresh herrin' in barrels ower to Glenarm, where there wissna mich o' a fushin', and sell them there, and the pair o' them wud split the profit on the trup.

"I didna like the soond o' it, and said so. But Para Handy wass convinced he wass aboot to mak' his fortune and he wouldna listen to reason. So off we went on Tuesday afternoon wi' aboot a hunder barrels o' fresh fush in the hold, which wass to be sold in Glenarm ass soon ass we docked the next mornin'.

"It was a bonnie day, wi' chust the right north-easterly breeze to gi'e us a good passage.

"But by mudnight, the breeze had dropped tae nothin' and we wass chust druftin' aboot wi' aal sails flappin' and us gettin' nowhere. For three whole days there wassna a breath o' wund and we lay like a piece o' druftwood, goin' a mile here and a mile there wi' the tide and the current, and the sun wass chust bakin' doon!

"We could see the hills of the Irish Coast to the sooth, and Kintyre to the north, but they could have been the mountains o' the moon for aal the chance we had to reach them. We got the sweeps oot and tried to row her, but wi' the weight of the fush we had in the hold we didna mak' a hundred yerds an hoor and we dam' near drapped wi' the effort o' it.

"By the third day the fush wass in an interestin' condeetion and there wassna mich fresh air on board, I can tell you! They wassna fresh fush at aal by noo, those herrin': they was in gey poor trum, cooped up in barrels in yon hothoose o' a hold under a bleezin' sun. By the fourth mornin' you chust tried no' to breathe, if at aal possible.

"On the fifth day, thank the Lord, the wind got up again, from the sooth-west: there wass no point in tryin' to sail against it to Glenarm, for naebody wud buy the fush noo, so Para Handy headed back for Campbeltown to dump the cairgo — before it got up and waalked ashore on its own. Ass we came in the harbour you could see the folk on the quayside stert sniffin' and then run for cover, and the piermaster wouldna let us berth the gabbart, never mind unload it!

"We had to pit oot to sea again, and spend the night wi' a scairf tied over our noses and mooths, winchin' the barrels oot o' the hold and drappin' them quick ower the side o' the boat. The smell wass chust unbelievable!

"It aal cost Para Handy a pretty penny, he had to pay for the barrels, but worse we both lost oor chobs, for the owner foond oot why we wass so late gettin' back to Glenarm and when we reached Campbeltown wi' the second load of lime there wass a new skipper and a new mate waitin' to tak' oor berths.

"And though, for all Para Handy says, I have neffer in my life been *sea-sick* I can tell you Jum, that for the maist of that particular trup I wass sick at sea. Very sick. And so wass the Captain!"

*FACTNOTE*

The Minches, those stretches of water which separate the long arm of the Outer Hebrides from the Inner Hebrides and Mainland Scotland, can be unpredictable and stormy at almost any time of the year. Littered with islets and rock skerries they were a maritime graveyard for centuries, and despite the proliferation of light-houses and automatic lights as an aid to their safe navigation they still claim the occasional victim.

The Treshnish are a group of tiny, uninhabited islands a few miles west of Mull. They cannot rival world-famous Staffa and the dramatic basalt columns of Fingal's Cave closer inshore but their dramatic silhouettes do make an unforgettable sight. One, also known as the 'Dutchman's Cap', has every appearance of the traditional 'pirate' hat made familiar to cinema-goers in all Hollywood manifestations from Treasure Island to Captain Blood. Only the skull-and-crossbones is lacking!

Tiree has a wild beauty but is also notorious as the windiest place in Scotland: and the flattest island in the Hebrides. It is less remote today than in Para Handy's time, with a regular vehicle ferry service from Oban and plane from Glasgow.

Largely due to their lack of power, and a lack of 'grip' in the water caused by their hull shape, the puffers were notoriously unmanageable when riding 'light' in even a moderate wind and the problems faced by Para Handy as he attempts to round the Mull of Kintyre are based on the actual experience of a Ross & Marshall puffer in the 1950s.

Off the west coast of South Africa the Atlantic swells running in from the Roaring Forties have been known to reach gigantic proportions in which a 10,000-ton ship can apparently, and frighteningly, 'disappear' with ease as she drops into the trough of the waves.

At the height of the herring fishing on the Clyde there could be such a glut of landings that the shore stations were unable to cope with them. I never had experience of that but when we lived in Shetland I saw at first hand just how enormous herring landings could be, given the right circumstances. In the early days of purse-netting, Icelandic and Scandinavian boats brought in quite unbelievable catches. None more so than a Reykjavik purser which came in to Lerwick harbour with only the whaleback and the poop above water: her main deck was actually submerged with the weight of fish on board. When her skipper discovered that he could only sell the catch for fish meal and not on the more lucrative processing market (I cannot remember the legal details but such was the position at the time) he then actually tried to put to sea to sail his catch home — and had to be forcibly prevented from doing so by the harbour authorities!

# 8

## Macphail to the Rescue

The *Vital Spark* had never visited Loch Etive before, but Para Handy knew enough of the reputation of the fierce tide-rip in the shadow of the railway bridge at Connel to time his arrival at the narrows to coincide with the slack of the tide, when the otherwise steeply rushing waters lay relatively at peace.

In this he succeeded: but nevertheless took the precaution of whistling down the speaking-tube to Dan Macphail in his noisy domain to ask for full power.

"Power!" a contemptuous voice echoed back: "the day there's ony power on this hooker Ah promise you'll be the very first to know aboot it! It's a miracle we've got this far but hoo the owner has the nerve tae send this tub onywhere ootside Garroch Heid is beyond me. Wan o' these days we'll jist no' get back, she'll peg oot on us and dee o' auld age."

"Chust so, Dan," said the Captain in a placatory tone, "but I am certain you will see us safe home again —" and turning to the Mate who was standing at his side he whispered "— Dan's in duvvelish bad trum this week! What iss wrong wi' the man?"

"He's no been himsel' since he visited yon spae-wife at Minard Fair last week," said Dougie, "and had his hand read."

"He should have more sense," said Para Handy, "than to pay ony attention to the ravin' of a wumman wi' nae mair knowledge o' his future than he has o' the workin's of a turbine enchine."

The Mate tactfully resisted the temptation to remind Para Handy of the occasions on which he himself had slipped into a fortune teller's candy-striped tent at country fairs, with his shilling grasped firmly in the grubby hand which he was about to present for a mystical interpretation. Such a service was usually offered by the wife of the round-about proprietor, disguised in spotted red head-kerchief and borrowed floral robe, prodigally (and deliberately) burning so much incense for atmosphere that it was almost as difficult to breathe as it was to see.

By now they had entered the wider, sheltered upper loch and the vessel was headed towards the pier at Bonawe. She was scheduled the following morning to load a cargo of granite setts from the nearby quarry for Glasgow Corporation roads department. By five o'clock the puffer was snug at the pier and the crew, with the exception of the Engineer (who refused to be persuaded to join them under any circumstances), set out to walk the mile or so inland to the inn at Taynuilt.

They had scarcely settled themselves at a corner table with glasses of beer and the landlord's best set of dominos when the outer door burst open and a worried-looking man in a yachting cap came in almost at a run. He banged the bell on the bar loudly and urgently and when the landlord appeared had a brisk and anxious exchange with him, the two of them hunched across the counter so that their heads were almost touching.

Finally the landlord straightened up, shaking his head.

"I'm sorry, Captain Forbes, but there's no' an ingineer this side o' Oban. Go you there on the next train," and here he consulted his watch, "You'll be in the toon by eight o'clock and if you're lucky in finding a man you'll be back before 10."

"Ten!" cried Forbes. "I can't leave a touring party strand-ed on the ship till then! They're due back at the Hotel for their dinners at eight!"

Para Handy cleared his throat. "Where's the shup, chentlemen," he asked, "and what seems to be the trouble? We have a sort of an enchineer wi' us — he's no' here but he's no' far away — and I am sure he would not see you stuck."

~

Half-an-hour later Captain Forbes, Para Handy and Macphail (the last still in the same ill-humoured temper) were clattering through the Pass of Brander in a pony and trap.

Forbes was indeed in a predicament.

The small Loch Awe pleasure steamer, of which he was captain and part owner, was aground at the mouth of the pass, where it opened out into the broad waters of the loch itself. "We should never have come so close in shore," he admitted ruefully "but I've done so often enough before without any trouble."

The trouble stemmed from the fact that the engine had died just as he was about to turn the little vessel back to deeper water and, drifting with the momentum of her passage, she ran gently aground 200 yards offshore. The problem was seriously compounded when all efforts to get her engine re-started failed.

"We took a new engineer on for this season," said Forbes, "and I don't think he has the experience he said he had."

The three rowed out to the little ship — imaginatively named the *Lochawe* — in the dinghy in which Forbes himself had come ashore in search of another engineer. As they clambered aboard the Captain was surrounded by a crowd of passengers, some of them curious, some anxious and some just plain angry.

"Why don't you chust tak' them below to the salong," suggested Para Handy, "and trate them to the wan wee refreshment. A man aalways feels mich better when he hass a gless o' somethin' in hiss hands! Macphail and me will have a look at your problem.

"He may not look much," he confided as his Engineer disappeared in the direction of the engine-room at the stern, "but though I would neffer tell him to hiss face, in case it would make him swoll-headed, he iss wan o' the very finest enchineers in the coastal tred!"

So it seemed.

Twenty minutes later came the gratifying sound of the shaft turning and, by dint of moving the passengers to the stern of the little boat (which was in deeper water) and calling for maximum power astern, Forbes was able to pull the grounded bows off the shoal onto which they had strayed, and the vessel was soon under way and headed for the pier at Loch Awe village, just beside the Hotel at which her passengers were staying.

"You and Mr Macphail can get the train from the village station back to Taynuilt, Captain Macfarlane," said Forbes with some warmth. "And I am sure I do not know how to thank you enough. You have saved my reputation! And probably my ship as well!"

"It wis nae problem," said Macphail, grudgingly. "Jist a broken linkage, and that on an injin gey like mah ain. Ah've telt your man whit went wrang so if it happens again, he should be able tae fix it. Else ye'd best look oot fur a new ingineer."

~

"Well, does that not make you feel better, Dan?" asked Para Handy as they sat in the Glasgow to Oban train for their short trip back to Taynuilt. "I am not referring to this ... " he waved the crisp, white Bank of England £5 note pressed on them by the grateful Forbes " ... but to the cheneral proof of your agility and your value. You have been in a foul mood for the last few days and we are aal most anxious to see you snep out of it!"

"If onything it mak's me feel worse," said Macphail miserably.

"Dan, Dan, what ails you?" asked the perplexed Captain. "We've been long enough at sea, Captain and Enchineer, that we should have no secrets."

Macphail sighed, long and deep.

"It wis yon spae-wife," he said at last. "she wisnae wan o' the usual rubbish ye get. She wis wan o' the real Gipsy Rose Lees! She telt me the names o' my wife and weans, she telt me the name o' the shup, she telt me we wis comin' tae Loch Etive for the setts.

"Worst, she telt me she saw me on a puffer wi' a brokedoon injin and an injineer no' able tae fix it, and the shup herself goin' on the rocks! Jist like whit happened tae that man this efternoon — but no' on a passenger boat like yon, on a puffer she said. That has tae be the *Vital Spark*.

"Peter, get anither injineer, at least till ye're all safe back tae Gleska, for sure as daith if ye keep me on we'll be agroond at the Connel tide-rip, or even a worse boneyerd, an' the shup'll be lost!"

"You're a haver, Dan," said the Captain, but taken aback by the Engineer's unfeigned, vehement despair. "Spaewifes! They're aal rubbish!"

"No' all," said Macphail, "No' all of them." And he turned with a heavy sigh to stare miserably across the passing countryside into the dying evening light.

～

Para Handy came back to the corner table from the bar counter at the Taynuilt Inn, with four drams perched tantalisingly and precariously on a battered tin tray featuring the advertising slogan of a long-forgotten brand of chewing tobacco: a silver mountain of change from Captain Forbes' five pound note: and a broad and quite triumphant grin.

"Dan," he said, "I have the best news you've had for days and if you don't believe me you can ask himself over there himself and he'll tell you it iss aal true": and he gestured towards the landlord, who nodded and smiled back.

"Even if your spae-wife wass the chenuine Gipsy Rose, Dan, and even if effery single thing she told you wass true, you have nothing at aal to worry aboot! It hass aal happened already!

"The *Lochawe* wass wance a puffer herself, that's what she wass built ass! They turned her into a passenger shup years ago but orichinally she wass a puffer chust like the *Vital Spark*, which is why the enchines wass so like what you were used wi'. What happened today iss what your spae-wife told you aal about — but she neffer said it wud happen to you on *your* shup, chust that it wud happen to a puffer and that you'd be there when it did. And it has happened — but tae the *Lochawe* and her enchineer!

"That means it's not going to happen to you — nor to the *Vital Spark*!

"So cheer up, Dan, and let's have no more of your nonsense. And don't you effer, effer again let me cetch you goin' onywhere near a spae-wife while you're the enchineer on my shup!"

*FACTNOTE*

The railway bridge at Connel was completed in 1903. For more than half-a-century it doubled as a toll-paying crossing for motor traffic for which exorbitant tariffs could be (and were) charged in view of the near-monopoly situation which its owners enjoyed. The only alternative route for vehicles from Oban to Benderloch or Appin or Lochaber (or vice versa) was a tortuous road journey of nearly 100 miles. Eventually, in 1966 — after the closure of the railway line to Ballachulish — it became a normal, toll-free part of the road network.

The tide-race at this point, known as the 'Falls of Lora', is most noticeable at the spring tides, when it presents a quite daunting spectacle for any small boats contemplating the passage into Loch Etive.

The first major industrial venture attempted at the Etive village of Taynuilt, in the 18th century, was an iron foundry but this had a relatively short lease of life.

For decades thereafter, however, a large granite quarry on the shores of Loch Etive opposite Bonawe was the source for many of the cobblestones or 'setts' which paved the streets of Glasgow for many generations. A few now by-passed city backstreets and cul-de-sacs survive with these original surfaces: hardwearing, impervious to almost any abuse but quite notorious hazards for two-wheeled traffic (pedalled or powered) in the wet, when they turn swiftly into treacherous, ridged skid-pans.

The Pass of Brander runs westwards from the northern shores of Loch Awe just beyond the remarkable Cruachan Hydro-Electric Power Station, built inside the mountain and completed in 1965.

The small passenger steamer *Lochawe* served on the loch for half a century, finally going to the breaker's yard in 1925. Mystery surrounds her origins. She is registered as having been *built* in 1876, but there is evidence that she was in fact *converted* in that year for passenger duties, having been originally designed and constructed some years earlier as a steam lighter of 100ft overall.

Her lines and general appearance were certainly suggestive of a cargo rather than a passenger carrying ancestry. She had a very substantial freeboard, and a cavernous saloon and dining room which gave every indication of having been created in the original hold. Like every puffer ever built — and unlike almost every purpose-designed passenger vessel of the time — she had her engines aft. The Pointhouse yard of A & J Inglis was responsible for her conversion (or construction) in 1876, and she was then dismantled and transported in sections to Loch Awe for assembly on a lochside slip.

# 9

## *The Kist o' Whustles*

It was several weeks since the paths of my own peregrinations had crossed with the passages of the *Vital Spark*, and I was out of touch with the latest news of the doings of her Captain and crew when I came across them loading a cargo at the factory pier of the fireclay works on the river Cart.

"It's drainage pipes for Cowal," acknowledged Para Handy with a deprecatory shrug, meeting me as I strolled up the quayside just outside Paisley, "and given the amount of rain they've been havin' on the peninsula this last week or two, it iss mebbe not before time."

Using a contraption consisting of a complex rectangle of netting made from webbing-straps the puffer was loading a cargo of ochre-coloured pipes of quite startlingly large diameter.

"They are going to Kilmun," continued the Captain, "for that Mr Younger, the chentleman that mak's his money from the beer: he iss puttin' mair gairdens into hiss Benmore Estate and with the amount of rain watter that comes pourin' off the hill, he needs aal the drains he can get, poor man.

"Macphail wass suggestin' that mebbe he iss goin' to divert the watter to the brewery but then Dan iss of the opeenion that aal beer hass been wattered, exceptin' perhaps when it's his favourite stout."

"They look an awkward cargo to handle," I suggested, watching as another dangling, precariously-secured bundle came swinging inboard, and ducking instinctively as it passed just a few feet above my head.

"There iss worse," said the Captain agreeably, "though at

the moment I wud find it very dufficult to say chust what. But at least they are clean.

"And in any case, it's aal chust in the day's work for the shup. Drain-pipes for Kilmun: or whusky from wan or ither o' the distilleries," he added emphatically and hopefully, — but I did not even offer to take the hint: "we can cope wi' it aal. If Dougie wass here…"

～

The Holy Loch cuts into the Cowal Hills just two miles north of Dunoon, the salt-water arm of a geological fault-line linking the estuary to Strachur on the upper reaches of Loch Fyne to the west. Between the Holy Loch and Strachur lies narrow Loch Eck, mirroring the steep and wooded hills which rise around it.

That freshwater loch, renowned as among the most beautifully situated of any in the country, also mirrors (in miniature) the attributes of its larger saltwater neighbours, for it boasts a modest passenger steamer service, provided for excursionists and round-trippers, by the *Fairy Queen*, a screw steamer little larger — though with much finer lines — than an ordinary Clyde puffer.

I was reminded of this on the occasion, some months after my encounter with Para Handy at the Paisley docks, when I came across the *Vital Spark* and the captain and his crew at Kilmun pier, where I had arrived aboard the steamer *Redgauntlet* on a Saturday morning, invited to spend the weekend on the coast with old friends who had taken a house for the summer.

Laid against the north side of the pier, the puffer was busily unloading a series of plywood boxes, little more than two feet square but as much as 12 or 15 feet in length. Dougie the Mate was operating the steam-winch with very considerable care, not to say delicacy, of movement. Sunny Jim, standing on a flat-bodied dray on the pier, guided the boxes as the jib swung them towards him, lowering and stacking them on the cart with as much concentration as if they had contained the very finest of bone china.

More surprisingly still, there was a goodly crowd on the pier to watch this process including, huddled together in a group, a number of distinguished-looking gentlemen — one even sporting gaiters — dressed in clerical clothing.

"My goodness, what sort of cargo is it you have today,

then, Captain?" I enquired as Para Handy came over to pass the time of day, "for I'm sure the ship is as much at the centre of attention as if it was the Crown Jewels themselves, and the crew are taking as much care of it as if it was eggs!"

"Well," he said, "conseederin' what the last cargo you saw us wi' wass, and that it wass consigned for Kilmun too, you could surely guess that it would be pipes. Chust pipes," he said, and then added mysteriously, "but mebbe a raither special sort of a pipes."

"Well, it's the first time I've ever seen pipes boxed up like that," I said. "so it's not drain-pipes for sure. Lead pipes for a plumbing contractor, is it? They must be very particular about where they buy their raw materials."

"Goodness me," said Para Handy, "it iss not plain water pipes we have in the boxes, Mister Munro. For wance the owner hass managed to get the contract for a dacent cairgo worthy o' the shup. Wan that iss mair in keepin' wi' her style and her cheneral abilities.

"These here iss organ pipes — sent doon from Gleska, for the new unstriment they're puttin' in at the Kilmun Kirk along the road there.

"We brought down the wud and the metal and aal the rest o' the materials for the insides of it last week, alang wi' two men that are buildin' it, and then last night we came back wi' aal these fancy bits!"

It was a pleasure to see how the Captain glowed with pride at the distinctive cargo which had been in his care: and to reflect that, given the enthusiasm of all on board the puffer for what the engineer would have called a "good tune", and the modest but nonetheless accomplished musical talents of Dougie and Sunny Jim, they were perhaps the most appropriate crew on the river to be entrusted with it.

"Ass weel ass these pipes for the front, and fancy carved wud screen-frame to hold them," continued the Captain, "there iss two keyboards, I'm tellin' you no lee, two o' them nae less. It seems chust a waste o' time to me for I have neffer yet seen an organist wi' fower airms. But that iss not aal! For then there iss what the men that's buildin' it tell me are pedals for the man that plays it to use his feet on to get a choon!

"If they were to pit it in a side-show in wan o' the fairs you would surely get the public-at-lerge to pay their saxpences chust to watch it in operation: for the man that plays it must have aal the agility and cheneral sagiocity o' the India Rubber Man at Hengler's Circus and Carnival!

"Obviously none o' yer common-or-gairden harmoniums iss good enough for the folk at Kilmun. This is a proper fantoosh organ, the like o' them that you wud find mebbe in St Mungo's where the Gleska chentry go, or in Paisley Abbey where the Coatses come from, or in a Kirk that's beholden to Mister Carnegie for the occasional contribution."

"Well, Captain," I said. "You must remember that Kilmun Church has been under some patronage from the Dukes of Argyll for many years, and so maybe it is His Grace that is paying for it as a present for the congregation!"

And, reflecting that it was perhaps just as well that the crew of the *Vital Spark* were not of the persuasion of the Free Church of the Western Highlands, (for then the care bestowed on the instrument in their charge might have been somewhat less painstaking) I shook the Captain's hand and headed off towards my friends' lochside retreat.

~

I had the pleasure of attending the recital given a couple of months later in Kilmun Church on the occasion of the official inauguration of the new organ.

The historic little kirk was packed and the instrument, safely installed in the choir gallery above the main door of the building, was resplendent with its banks of gleaming pipes, its rich wood carvings and fretwork.

What I think nobody was prepared for — or could have even begun to be prepared for — was the splendid sound quality and sheer magnificence of the organ itself.

The audience sat in rapt silence as the church filled with the most sublime harmonies and melodies, the sheer power and depth of the bass pipes almost outshone by the daring virtuosity of the contrasting melodic stops, brilliant in their cascading ripples, their soaring scales and shimmering arpeggios.

After two hours in which the listeners were transported, as it were, to another world, the concert concluded — fittingly and properly — with the singing of that most inspiring of all the master-works of the Scottish Psalter, 'Ye gates, lift up your heads on high' to the tune *St George's, Edinburgh*.

~

As the hushed crowd left the church and passed into the cool darkness, a sense of the infinite hung about the churchyard and the last soaring, triumphant notes of the great organ crescendo which had closed the evening seemed to hang on, still, in the silent night.

As I picked my way along the shore side of the churchyard wall, a dark silhouette — a familiar dark silhouette — detached itself from the trunk of a venerable tree which overhung the path, three other figures just discernible beyond it.

"I am gled they feenished with *St Chorge's*," said Para Handy quietly. "Anything else would chust have been a let-doon."

"I had not expected to see you here, Captain," I said. "Why did you not come into the kirk?"

"I do not think that wud have been right, Mister Munro, for we are chust Brutain's hardy sons, straight from a day's work perambulatin' aboot the river, and in no' fit state to be seen in among the Kilmun congregation alang wi' aal the chentry.

"But we were prood to have brought the new kist o' whustles doon here, and happy to have had the chance to hear it played. There iss some chobs we value more than ithers..."

"...and there are some men to whom we owe a debt of gratitude for the care and devotion with which they carry out those jobs," said a voice from behind us, and the Kilmun minister clapped Para Handy on the shoulder.

"We would all be very pleased, Captain, if you and your crew would come up to the Hall right now, and join us all for supper so that we can thank you properly."

*FACTNOTE*

The Loch Eck steamer was for decades an integral and essential link in one the most popular of all the 'round trips' on the Firth. Passengers sailed from Bridge Wharf down river and through the Kyles, then on to Strachur on Loch Fyne whence they transferred by coach or (later) charabanc to the head of Loch Eck, and thence back to the Holy Loch or Ardentinny piers for their return passage to Glasgow.

*PADDLE POWER — This splendid picture captures the drama of a crowded paddler at full stretch. The steamer is one of the North British Steam Packet Company's Craigendoran fleet — Redgauntlet — referred to in the story about the Kilmun organ. She was built at Barclay Curle's Scotstoun yard and launched in 1895. She is listing to port as the crowds line that rail to watch the steamer from which this photo was taken vanish astern. Note too the huge diameter of the steering-wheel on her open bridge, requiring two helmsmen to handle it.*

The *Fairy Queen*, an 80ft vessel with generous saloon facilities for her patrons, was built in the upper reaches of the Clyde at Seath's Rutherglen Yard in 1878 and gave almost half-a-century of service before she went to the breakers in 1926.

Such excursions are a distant memory but the gardens at Benmore between the Holy Loch and Loch Eck remain one of Argyllshire's greatest treasures. The millionaire Edinburgh brewing family, the Youngers, gifted the estate to the nation in 1925. As well as being a spectacular attraction and an asset for visitors and locals alike, Benmore — managed nowadays as an adjunct to the Royal Botanic Gardens in Edinburgh — has an outstanding flora and is also a major research station, especially renowned for a rhododendron collection of 250 different species.

The church at Kilmun stands on the site of the oldest Christian foundation in this part of the country, established in the early seventh century by St Munn, an Irish monk who had previously served in the Columban community on Iona.

The present building, completed in 1841, is the third to have been erected on the site looking out across the Holy Loch. It is unusual in many respects, particularly for the way it has been constructed to encompass and shelter, on its north-eastern corner, the mausoleum built in 1795 as the resting-place of the Campbell Dukes of Argyll, whose ancestors used Kilmun as their burial-ground, and most of whose descendants are interred here.

The church is of great beauty and considerable interest: many thousands of visitors come to see it each summer. The stained glass and the woodwork are particularly fine. So is its organ, installed in 1909 and unique in being powered by a hydraulic pump — operated by the local mains water supply — the last such in the country. It is, quite simply, a splendid instrument, the unexpected jewel of a tiny kirk, and one which would not be out of place in any of the larger churches in the land. It was a gift to the congregation from the Youngers of Benmore.

How the organ and all its works was first brought to Kilmun I do not know: but it is perfectly possible that transportation was indeed provided by a puffer, for it could certainly not have arrived in any way other than by sea.

# 10

## *Hurricane at the Helm*

I had arrived in Oban by train late one September afternoon on my way to Lochboisdale in South Uist. The MacBrayne steamer *Mountaineer* sets out on the 10 hour crossing three days a week — at 6.00 in the morning. I had reserved a sleeping-berth so that I could pass a comfortable night on board and avoid an unconscionably early rise in the morning, waking instead in time for breakfast as we approached Tobermory.

As I climbed up the gangway from the South Pier I happened to glance across the bay and, to my considerable surprise, saw a familiar but totally unexpected maritime silhouette. So it was that, a short while later, with my baggage safely stowed aboard the paddler, I made my way along an esplanade thronged with a great crowd of visitors enjoying an early evening stroll before dinner, and out onto the town's North Pier.

Para Handy was seated on the hatchcover of the *Vital Spark* with his pipe in one hand and a mug of tea in the other, studying the toes of his boots with apparent interest.

"Good evening, Captain," I said. "You are about the last person I expected to find in Oban."

"Well, well," he said, looking up with a start. "It's yourself then. This writing business must be doing well, eh, if you can afford a nice wee holiday at this time of year? Not that it's any of my business...

"Ah well then," he continued after a few moments, once he realised that I had no intention of unburdening myself of any confidences about my present financial condition, "yes, we are chust here perambulating aboot the Sound of Mull for a week or thereby. The owner has got a contract to tak' in the winter coals to some lighthooses and so here we are.

"I wish I could offer you something but would you credit there iss nothing on the shup…"

It was not too difficult to persuade the Captain to join me in making the short journey to the bar of the Argyll Hotel.

~

"This iss not familiar watters for the *Vital Spark*," he said a few minutes later as we settled to a table near the fire, "but I have Hurricane Jeck with us on this trup and it iss certainly familiar to him."

I remarked that I had not been aware that that intrepid mariner had had much experience in the islands trade.

"Cot bless you, yes" said Para Handy. "For aboot eight months he wass aal over the Hebrides for Mr MacBrayne, chust after his spell as master of the clupper *Port Jackson*.

"Jeck had a hankerin' to settle doon, for that wass the time he wass walkin' oot wi' the widow MacLachlan from Oban, before the problem he had at the Gleska Mull and Iona Soiree, Concert and Ball wi' her and Lucy Cameron.

"Nothin' worked oot for him, he had the very duvvle's own luck ass usual, he lost the gyurl and then he lost the shup and in chust a matter of months he wass back goin' foreign again, this time on the *Dora Young*."

I indicated that I would be more than interested in the story by calling for the Captain's glass to be refilled.

"It wass this way," he continued, sniffing the amber liquid with some satisfaction. "Mr MacBrayne took him on ass skipper on the *Handa* when she wass on the Oban to Tiree service.

"You'll mind she wiss aal hold, very broad in the beam and she carries only a couple o' dozen passengers, but Jeck ran her ass if she wass the *Columba* and his manners wass that sublime that folk thocht it a rare preevilege chust to be allowed on board the shup.

"Wheneffer Jeck took the pier at Tobermory he'd be oot on the wing o' the brudge, wi' his kep on three hairs and wi' a cheery wave for aal the world. When he had docked her he wud sweep off the kep wi' a most dapper bow to the gyurls on the quayside and it soon wass that the maist o' the weemenfolk o' Tobermory wud come doon each mornin' chust to waatch the *Handa* berthin'.

"It wassna chust his manners that wass sublime, it wass his cheneral agility ass well. Ass he came into Tobermory Bay he'd be leanin' maist elegant ower the enchine-room telegraph on the wing o' the brudge, and he'd run her in at full speed, headin' straight for the pier, and leave it till the very last moment afore he'd ring doon for full speed astern, and caal to the helmsman to birl the wheel, and lay her alangside ass delicate ass if she wass an egg.

"It wass a performance that became namely wi' visitors ass weel and efter a month or two of Jeck bein' on the run the pier wass bleck wi' folk each mornin' aal come to see the show. And he wass that dapper, and such a perfect chentleman, that it wass a preevilege to watch it aal, though Jeck's critics (maist of them ither captains who was chust jealous for his success) said he wud get his come-uppance wan o' these days.

"You probably ken that the *Handa* is no chicken. She wass built in 1878 at Port Gleska, and ass the years went on she has needed mair and mair upkeep.

"That wass Jeck's undoin'. Wan mornin' he wass oot on the wing of the brudge ass usual, waitin' till the last meenit to ring for full power astern, and when he chudged the last meenit had come and pulled on the telegraph lever, did the dam' thing no come awa' in his hands, the base of it aal rusted to nothin', and wi' the force o' the pull Jeck went tumblin' backwards doon the brudge ladder and landed sprauchled oot on the main deck.

"It wass aal of a half-meenit afore the folk on the pier realised that the *Handa* wassna goin' to pull up in time that mornin' and there wass wan richt clamjamfrey ass they aal struggled to get out o' the path of the shup!

"She rammed the pierhead bow first, and embedded hersel' eight feet into it! It wass two days afore they could get her pulled oot and two weeks till the pier wass fully repaired!"

"Mr MacBrayne would be none too pleased," I ventured.

"He wass really quite reasonable," said the Captain. "It had to be admutted that if the telegraph-handle had stayed in the wan piece the accident would never have happened, so part of the blame had to be wi' the shup.

"Forbye, the reputation o' the man had reached Gleska and the clerks in the Heid Office wass able to see that the *Handa* wass earnin' more money than ever for Mr MacBrayne, what wi' aal the folk thinkin' it wass a privilege to sail wi' sich a chentleman for Captain.

"So while the *Handa* wass awa' bein' repaired, Mr MacBrayne made Jeck First Officer on the *Flowerdale* on the Outer Isles service. Though she wassna his own command, she wass a much bigger shup wi' a lot o' prestige, and Jeck took to her to the manner born.

"Pretty soon he wass enchoyin' the same sort of reputation wi' the *Flowerdale* in Castlebay ass wi' the *Handa* in Tobermory. She used to lie over at Barra from six in the evening till early the followin' mornin' and Jeck wass aye welcome in the hooses in Castlebay, for he wass a fine cheerie chap and carried a perty aboot wi' him whereffer he went. There wass many a gyurl in Castlebay had her kep set on Jeck but he wass havin' too mich of a spree to be thinkin' o' settlin' doon, and mony's the hert he broke in the months that followed.

"The trouble came at the year's end. The *Flowerdale* tied up at Castlebay on Hogmanay evenin' and since she wassna sailin' till fower o'clock next mornin' Jeck went ashore to tak' a ne'erday dram or two with a wheen o' his Barra friends. He took the enchineers wi' him, for Jeck wass aye verra considerate of the boys who made possible aal the speed he could get oot o' the shup, and aal the manoeuvrability she had, for Jeck could turn her on a postage stamp, her havin' two propellers.

"He could caal for full astern port, full ahead starboard, and spin her roon' in her ain length like a peerie in a close. Jeck took great pleasure in showin' his agility wi' the shup and it's a good thing that Captain McKissock was fast asleep in his cabin when Jeck wass in cherge, for he wass a true chentleman of the old school and would not have looked kindly on Jeck's high-jinks and cheneral frivolity.

"Onyway, that Hogmanay nicht, Jeck and the enchineers got back on board chust before sailing time. Jeck wass in fine trum, but he could carry his dram like a chentleman and nobody wud have known it. The enchineers wass feelin' no pain either, but since they were oot o' sight o' the cheneral public it didna really matter what they looked like.

"Jeck headed for the brudge, the enchineers for their control room, and at fower o'clock off they set like hey-ma-nanny for Coll and Tiree.

"For more than three hoors *Flowerdale* tore through the watter like a greyhound, Jeck hummin' a whole repertaree

of Gaelic song to himsel' in the wheelhouse and the helmsman on watch tap-tappin' the time wi' his feet.

"Chust gone half past seven in the mornin', wi the dawn
comin' up fast over the hills of Ardnamurchan, Jeck wass
connin' her into the bay at Arinagour on Coll at near on 18
knots, a beautiful sight for the folk launchin' the passenger
flit-boat aff the beach, as the shup came hurtlin' roon' the
headland wi' a rake on her like Jeck's kep on a Setturday
night.

"The lads in the flit-boat had seen the sheer poetry and
drama o' Jeck's arrivals at Arinagour often enough in the
past weeks but it wass aalways an impressive performance.
He wud head her straight for the beach and wait till the
very last possible moment on the brudge wing afore he rang
doon for full astern port, full ahead starboard, and spun her
roond in her length and dropped the anchor.

"He wass determined to get the New Year aff wi' a bang
and he hung on and on, draped casual across the brudge
wing and never movin', till even the boys in the flit-boat
began to get anxious: but then he snapped to like a sodger,
rang his instructions to the enchine room, and gave the flit-
boat a smert naval salute.

"And nothin' happened. She kept racin' for the beach at
a good 18 knots. Jeck rang and better rang on the telegraph
till he wass near demented, but there wass neffer a cheep
frae doon below.

"He ran into the brudge-hoose and grabbed the wheel,
and spun it desperate-like to starboard to try and steer the
*Flowerdale* oot the bay. It wass too late. She had too much
pace and he had too little space to mak' it work, and he ran
her straight onto the sandbar at the eastern headland at full
speed. Mercifully it wass a chentle slope, and she slowed
doon ass sweetly ass if she wass under control. Nobody
wass hurt and there wass no real damage to the hull, either.
But they had to wait three days before the tides wass right
for the *Fusilier* and the *Chevalier* to be able to tow her
back into deep water.

"By that time, Jeck wass lookin' for another chob.

"Tuppical of the man's ill-fortune. You wud have thocht it
wass *his* fault, the way MacBrayne treated him.

"It wass the enchineers should have got the seck. There
wassna a man jack o' them sober doon below. There wassna wan o' them awake either, come to that. They'd all had
mair nor they could tak' at Castlebay, and they wass aal fast

asleep in the enchine room. Jeck could huv rung the telegraph till he wass black in the face!

"He's neffer had a good word to say for enchineers till
this day: I think that's why he's often so nippy wi' Macphail.
But he still has the hert of a child, and the chenerosity of
Mr Carnegie!"

At which hint, I felt it incumbent on me to arrange for
the Captain's glass to be replenished.

*FACTNOTE*

Fact can sometimes be stranger than fiction — or maybe
simply mirror it. Whatever the truth of the matter, the two
incidents which provided me with the idea for this story
were reputed to have happened to real-life MacBrayne ships
and were told to me some years ago by a former MacBrayne
seaman as historical fact.

The collision with Tobermory pier was said to have taken
place in the early 1930s, exactly as described. The vessel
involved was the regular Sound of Mull steamer *Lochinvar*,
which had been built in 1908: and was fully refurbished in
1934.

She was a strange-looking ship, and a strangely-powered
one as well. Only 145ft overall, she was originally constructed with three six-cylinder paraffin engines driving
three screws: in 1926 these were replaced by four-cylinder
diesel engines. The engine-room was placed at the stern,
with her cargo hold immediately forward of it: and the passenger accommodation and bridge forward of that again.
Cargo was loaded and unloaded by a jib-crane and her only
mast was a simple pole mast on the foredeck. As built, she
had one very thin, very tall smokestack later replaced by
the complete opposite — one very short, very squat funnel.
In either guise she looked something of an ugly duckling,
though her actual hull was finely proportioned.

The incident at Arinagour is reputed to have occurred in
the 1960s and there must be witnesses who could confirm
if it did really take place. The vessel was the *Claymore*,
mainstay of the thrice-weekly link from Oban to
Lochboisdale, the second ship to carry that name. Her predecessor gave nearly 50 years service to MacBrayne, mostly on the Glasgow to Stornoway run.

The second *Claymore* was commissioned in 1955, a
handsome ship with comfortable accommodation in two

classes — the last of her kind in that respect. However, she was notoriously tender in heavy weather. She had the fatal combination of substantial top-hamper (thanks to the generous public space offered in her lounges, dining-saloons and bars): linked to a shallow draft (necessary for access to island piers at all states of the tide, and to places like Coll which in those days had no pier but relied on flit-boats to attend ships — which came as close in shore as they could).

I can vouch for her lack of sea-going qualities! Blessed with the happy fortune to have been born a good sailor, I sympathise strongly with those who are not so lucky. I remember with wry amusement the throwaway line from the skipper of the *Claymore* to a passenger enquiring as we left Oban what the weather ahead was likely to be. "Well I hope you like rock-and-roll," he said, "for you're certainly going to get it today!" And indeed we did — not just on that occasion but on many others too.

MACBRAYNE'S GLADSTONE BAG — *Such, thanks to her carrying capacity, was the nickname bestowed on the little Handa, seen here at an unidentified pier somewhere on the West Coast. Though they lacked the glamour of the big paddlers such vessels were the workhorses of the Highlands and provided the crucial link to the outside world. The engine-room telegraph on the port wing of the bridge, and the ladder behind it, can be clearly seen!*

# 11

## *The Vital Spark at the Games*

I t was a fine August morning and the *Vital Spark*, having made an early start from Colintraive where she had
spent the last two days unloading a cargo of roadstone,
was punching round Toward Point into a light northerly breeze.

There was something of a holiday atmosphere aboard,
what with the sun glinting on the spray of her (modest) bow
wave: but more particularly because the crew had succeeded in selling a few sacks of the owner's coal to the
Colintraive merchant, and were planning a clandestine
spree once they were docked at the Broomielaw and before
heading for their weekends at home.

"Rothesay's gey quiet the day, Peter," said the mate, gesturing towards the curving esplanade and phalanx of boarding houses of Rothesay Bay in the middle distance. "No'
mony steamers there at aal this mornin'."

Indeed, the usually bustling pier of the capital of Bute
was all but deserted. Only the diminutive *Texa* lay alongside, her derrick swinging the crates of a mixed cargo to the
quay, while MacBrayne's majestic *Columba* was edging out
on her daily mail run to Ardrishaig.

"Well, Dougie," replied the Captain, " whit else wud ye
expect on the last Setturday of August? Aal the boats'll be
runnin' in and out o' Dunoon right noo, and since you've
reminded me o' that, I've a good mind that we should
maybe chust go to join them. What d'ye think yourself?"

"Mercy, I'd clean forgot what day it wass," said Dougie.
"But aye — why not, why not indeed!

"Then that's what we'll do," said Para Handy: and after
making a great show of whistling through the speaking tube

to an engine room and an engineer he could have bent down and touched, he called down it: "Richt, Macphail, if for wance you can get that neb o' yours oot o' they novelles for a meenit, ye could maybe get up some steam and see if we can get to Dunoon sometime this month!"

~

"What's the great attraction aboot Dunoon?" asked Sunny Jim curiously, looking up from the forehatch, where he sat peeling an enormous potful of potatos which, with salt herring to encourage the thirst, had been planned for dinner prior to berthing in Glasgow.

"We're goin' to see Cowal Gaithering," replied the skipper.

"Cowal?" queried Jim with a puzzled expression. "Wha's Cowal? And whit's he gaitherin'?"

"Man, Jum," said the skipper. "There iss times when I think you are nothin' but an ignorant lowland neep to be sure: but of course I blame your time on the Cluthas. Your world ends at the Yoker Ferry. You havna the advantage nor the concept o' the great traditions of the west. Cowal's no' a person — it's yon whole lump o' land" — he pointed towards the hills on the port side — "and a Gaitherin's a Games. D'ye tell me ye never heard of the Cowal Hieland Gaitherin? It's namely aal over the world ass the snappiest Games of them aal, bar nane. Iss that not so, Dougie?"

"Whateffer you say, Peter," observed the mate agreeably. "For they're certainly the snappiest for a dram. Every time you find your gless iss empty there's aye somewhere fine and handy to get it refilled. If you've the coin."

"And that we have," rejoined the skipper, "for ye'll mind o' the wee deal we struck wi' Mackintosh in Colintraive, eh? But not a cheep tae the owner!" And he laid an index finger along the side of his nose with a conspiratorial grin.

"But whit happens at a Games," queried Sunny Jim, ignoring the snort of disgust which came echoing up from the engine-room. "Is it like the fitba'?"

"Jum, Jum, I despair o' ye. A Games iss what has made us Brutain's hardy sons. It's the very bedrock o' the nation, the true tradition o' the Hielan's. Bonnie lasses in tartan skirts louping aboot like things possessed: laddies skirling the pipes: big fellas, that well built they wud mak' Hurricane Jeck look like a skelf, tossin' tree-trunks aboot chust the same ass if they were matchsticks: pipe baun's merchin' up and doon the streets: an' grown men that should ken better sneakin' off from their wives and weans to hae a few drams mair nor's guid for them."

"What he means," cried Macphail from the sooty depths of the boiler-room, "is that it's jist a lot of weel-oiled tumshies a' dressed up like kahouchy balls cavortin' through the toon, and frichtening the lieges: an' a bunch of wee nyaffs jumpin through girrs an' that."

"Ye're a leear, Macphail," cried the affronted skipper, "chust the nearest thing tae a Sassenach, ye should be right ashamed tae call yerself a Scot!"

"But I thocht a' these Games things wiz jist somethin' invented for the towerists," said Jim, "naethin' but chaps in hired kilts wi' the wrang legs for them and their behinds stickin' oot, and accents ye could saw wud wi'?"

"Naw Jum," said the Captain. "In Braemar maybe, or even Inverness forbye, for they're a' saft in the heid up there and the countryside's fair stuffed wi' toffs and sich. But no' at Cowal. Cowal's aal chust for the people. Brutain's hardy sons! Chust wait till ye see!"

And — the puffer by then being off Bullwood with the Gantocks rocks dead ahead — Para Handy concentrated on navigating safely through the twin hazards of the reef and the constant stream of paddle-steamers depositing their quota of revellers on the main Dunoon pier, till he coaxed the *Vital Spark* into the very last remaining space at the puffers' traditional berth, the little Coal Pier in the East Bay.

≈

The misanthropic engineer was more than pleased to nominate himself as the unanimous choice for shore watchman. Wild horses would not have dragged him to the festivities as he settled back into his bunk — for all that it was but mid-day — with the latest penny dreadful, an unread novelette, and a quarter of candy-striped balls.

The remainder of the crew, with Sunny Jim under the skipper's patient tutelage, fought their way through the colourful crowds on Argyll Street and on up to the Dunoon stadium: paid their admission moneys (with some reluctance) and spent the next few hours enthralled by a harlequinade of sight and sound as the very finest of Scottish music, dance and athletic prowess was put through its paces.

Frequent forays to the beer tent while funds lasted, and then a desperate but unsuccessful search for the 'Committee' when they ran out, kept them in the best of spirits in more ways than one.

When the Gathering climaxed with the traditional assembly and march past of more than 2000 pipes and drums even the normally taciturn Mate was observed to wipe a surreptitious sleeve across his eyes, Sunny Jim stood gawping at a spectacle so splendid, so sonorous and so stirring, and Para Handy himself was with some difficulty dissuaded from climbing onto a nearby cart and delivering 'Hielan' Laddie' in an enthusiastic but tuneless baritone.

It was dark by the time the throngs from the stadium made their way back to the esplanade. Across the water the lights of Gourock beckoned and at the pier the paddlers were banked three deep for the evacuation to come.

But one final ritual remained.

As the clock on the Parish Kirk on Castle Hill struck 10, the night exploded into a blinding light that would have challenged the mid-day sun, and a noise that would have shamed the opening barrage at Waterloo.

The last tradition of the Cowal Highland Gathering, the Grand Fireworks display, ran its tumultuous course for 20 minutes. Then the crew of the *Vital Spark* picked their way through the crowds, and across the smouldering detritus of the display, back to the ship.

Spreadeagled on his back on the hatchway of the hold, with his hands pressed hard against his ears, his feet drumming on the planking, and his mouth open in a soundless scream, they found the engineer — bellowing, once he was able to speak again, that a world war had begun.

~

"Man, Macphail, ye' re an ignorant gowk so ye are," said Para Handy unsympathetically half-an-hour later, when they finally calmed him down enough to allow the administration of a stiff medicinal dram from the jealously-guarded bottle kept (with some exercise of willpower) solely for such emergencies.

"Surely ye knew what wass up when ye saw the ither puffer crews leave their boats and get awa' from the pier ass

soon ass the darkness fell? Surely ye knew that the fireworks display iss aalways set up on the very Coal Pier
itself?

"No wonder ye got the fright o' yer life an' thought ye
were in an explodin' munitions factory. But let this be a lesson to you Dan! If you'd come ashore wi' the rest o' us ye
might have had to pit your hand in your pocket — but at
least ye wouldn't have pit your hert in your mooth!'"

*FACTNOTE*

Traditional Highland games are held in communities
large and small throughout both the Highlands and
Lowlands of Scotland and the Cowal Highland Gathering,
which celebrated its Centenary in 1994, is the largest and
most spectacular of them all. To Scots the name of Cowal is
probably the best known but English visitors are perhaps
more likely to be aware of the Braemar Games thanks largely to the 'Royal' connection. Senior members of the Royal
family attend every year, as the event coincides with their
holiday in nearby Balmoral Castle.

Similar games are held throughout the world, wherever
there is a strong Scottish community or connection, and
many overseas competitors take part in the games in
Scotland — particularly at Cowal, which hosts the official
world championship events in Highland dancing as well as
prestigious solo piping and pipe band competitions. Other
attractions at any self-respecting games will include the traditional heavy athletic events (the tossing of the caber in
particular) without which no Highland event would be
deemed complete — and most certainly not by any visitors
from south of the border!

Dunoon's wooden steamer pier still stands, though it is
today a somewhat depressing mockery of its past glories,
reminiscent of a Hollywood film-set: all facade and no sub-
stance. Much of its splendidly colourful and overstated
Victorian superstructure of tea-rooms, towers and turrets
lies sadly unused and some — most regrettably part of its
long viewing-gallery — has been demolished. It is the terminal for CalMac's work-horse vehicle ferry service from
Gourock and, in summer months, an occasional port of call
for the *Waverley,* the only operational sea-going paddle
steamer left in the world.

Old photographs from the turn of the century show a

THE GENERATION GAP — *The great tradition of Highland games continues unabated — the wardrobe of the participants might be unrecognisably different, but the programme of Highland dancing, pipes and drums and heavy athletics celebrated every August in Dunoon Stadium today is the same as it was in the days when the* Vital Spark *sailed the Firth. Para Handy would be as much at home at the Cowal Games in 1995 as he was in 1905, though the outfits worn by today's dancers and pipers would seem as strange to his eyes as those in this photograph are to ours.*

different world — paddlers queuing up to come alongside, passengers streaming on and off in their hundreds (they still do, though now from the far-from-glamorous ro-ro ferries) and files of charabancs and horse-buggies awaiting them on the shore side of the pier gates. Even into the fifties Dunoon remained a steamer 'cross-roads', with day-long activity to watch, and many holiday-makers passed hours on the pier (with interludes in its tea-room or its bar according to taste!) enjoying the varied pageant of shipping on the Firth.

A few hundred yards north east of the steamer pier is the still older stone jetty which was used by generations of puffers, and their predecessors. Though it is decades now since there was last a cargo boat of any description calling at Dunoon this is still known locally as the "Coal Pier" — and the displays of pyrotechnics which climax the last night of Cowal Gathering are indeed constructed on this convenient platform.

# 12

## A Spirited Performance

At once one of the most popular and the most frustrating tasks the puffer crews can be asked to perform is to carry cargos to or from the highly-reputed malt whisky distilleries dotted around Argyll and the Inner Hebrides.

Popular, because a puffer with its hold full of barley for the malting loft, or of oak staves for the cooperage, is a welcome visitor with a badly-needed cargo: and skipper and crew are traditionally treated to a generous dram or two of clear spirit straight from the stills, and with a proof content which make the commercial blends seem like spring water by comparison.

Frustrating, because sometimes puffers are contracted to carry a load of whisky in cask from the remote distilleries to the bottling and blending plants in the upper reaches of the Clyde or in Glasgow itself. The agony of sailing atop a cargo ample enough to guarantee a lifetime of high-jinks, but guarded by Customs Seals and (sometimes) by Customs Officers in person and thus as unattainable as if it had been on the far side of the moon, is a frustration adequate to torture Tantalus himself.

The *Vital Spark* and her crew were in just that situation one fine summer's evening as the vessel lay moored alongside the private jetty of one of Islay's most respected distilleries.

On her arrival that afternoon in ballast the resident Customs Officers had boarded the puffer and all but stripped her from stem to stern.

"What on earth are they daein'?" spluttered an aggrieved Sunny Jim as he was summarily aroused from his comfortable cat-nap in the fo'c'sle and unceremoniously bundled on deck.

"Chust checkin' on us, Jum," said the skipper, "to see if we've a place somewhere handy for hidin' a barrel or two. I'm bleck affronted they should even think it of us. The *Vital Spark* hass something of a reputation in the coastal trade..."

"You can say that again!" boomed a sonorous voice from the echoing depths of the engine-room. "And some reputation it is, tae."

"Pay no heed to Macphail, Jum," said the skipper, raising his voice to ensure that that worthy would miss nothing of what he was about to say. "He's chust embarrassed because wan o' the Officers found his secret store of novelles under that loose deckboard in the fo'c'sle and called all his colleagues down to have a good laugh at them."

The engine-room did not respond to that sally.

"And have any puffer crews ever managed to steal something from a cargo of whisky?" asked Sunny Jim.

"I don't care for your language, Jum," said the captain. "Not steal, for sure and it wass neffer for selling that any spurits wass taken, but chust for drinking. Liberate would be a better word for it.

"Myself, I don't think there iss the same imagination in the puffer crews nooadays ass there wass when I wass a young man your age. Not the same spurit of adventure, you micht say. The modern sailors iss timid, chust timid. They're feared o' bein' caught, for a stert: and they're feared o' the Customs — not that I exactly blame them for that. Put a man intae a uniform nooadays and he behaves like an enemy sodger, all aggravation and aggression. Time wass when the Customs offeecials would use their mental agility tae ootfox the crews: today they chust come on board like this efternoon and kick the boat to pieces whether they've ony reason to or no'. There iss no subtlety left in what aye used to be a chenuine battle of wuts, when whicheffer side won, the ither respected them for it and swore to get even next time roond.

"I mind servin' ass an apprentice wi' a skipper caaled Forbes who had his ain boat: a sailin' gabbert it wass, and him and the mate and me wass the only crew on board her. Wan time we loaded wi' whusky in casks at Campbeltown and the Customs men came on board and pit their seals all round the hatch covers.

"You'll understand that these were inspected when we docked at the blenders in Gleska, and if the seals wass tampered wi' in any way, then it wass the high jump for aal the crew.

"We were hardly oot the harbour when Forbes grabbed me by the lug and pulled me to the fore end of the cargo hatch. Wan o' the planks in the hatch side-coaming wass a false plank — it had no tongue and groove to it, so it could chust slide oot leavin' a wee square hole into the cargo hold.

" 'In ye go, Peter,' says Forbes. 'This iss whit we employed ye for: ye're the only wan o' us small enough to get in through there. Tak' this wi' ye' — and he handed me a piece of rubber tubing — 'and when ye've prised the bung frae the top o' wan o' the whusky casks, siphon the spurits and pass us oot the end o this tube so we can start filling oor ain barrel up here.'

"I telt him I couldn't do that, it would be the jyle for me if I did, for sure.

" 'It'll be the jyle for you if ye don't,' says he. 'For ye're an apprentice disobeyin' the command of a superior officer on a shup at sea an' I'll hae ye up tae the docks polis in Gleska so fast your feet'll nae touch the ground.'

"And would you believe, Jim, I wass that feared of him I went and did it, though for weeks efter I didna sleep properly for fear the polis were comin' to get me.

"There was another gabbart, the *Amelia Ann*, that wass namely among the longshoremen for the quantity of whusky her skipper could liberate on a trup from Islay to Gleska: the Customs men was fair demented for, no matter hoo mony ropes and wax seals they put on the hatchway, there were aye two or three barrels less in Gleska than the manifest showed: but the wax seals wass neffer broken and the ropes wass always whole. The skipper of the *Amelia Ann* swore blind that there wass a Customs Officer at the loading berth in Islay who simply couldn't coont, and they'd no way of disproving it for the seals wass aye intact and they could neffer find ony trace of spurits on the boat.

"What none o' the authorities knew wass that the skipper had a brither that worked at the forge where the brass master seals for the Customs wass made, and the man chust cast wan extra set for his brither. And ass for the disappearing barrels, well, he simply hung them ower the side from what looked chust like an ordinary fender rope, and hauled them back in again when the inspectors had given up and gone home in disgust.

~

"Of them aal, though, there wass nobody could touch my old friend Hurricane Jeck for sheer agility when it came to liberating a drop of good British spurits.

"I mind fine wance when him and me wass crewin' on a puffer caaled the *Mingulay* that belonged tae a Brodick man. Thanks to Jeck she had the duvvle's own reputation at the distilleries and wi' the Customs men, and they always swore they'd catch us sooner or later and really put us through the girrs when we came into a distillery pier.

"Wan time we came into a jetty in Islay late one evening ready to load up a cargo of the very best malt spurits in cask the following mornin'.

"Well, they thocht they had the better of Jeck this time. The distillery had already waggoned the casks down to the pier, and they'd put an eight foot high wire and metal-framed fence not chust at the landward end, but right roond the other three sides of it: and they'd two security guards inside it, sittin' on top of the stacks of casks.

" 'Let's see ye get somethin' oot o' that, MacLachlan,' said the heid Customs man wi' a smug grin. Jeck said nothin', but chust shook his head sadly.

"At two o'clock in the mornin', when the tide was fully out and the *Mingulay* was dwarfed by the jetty now rising high above her hull, Jeck shook me awake.

" 'Come on Peter, let's get oor share o' the spurits!'

" 'You're no' canny, Jeck,' says I. 'We'll get nothin' here. The spurits iss all fenced in and the guards iss still awake for I can hear them talking.'

" 'So much the better,' says he: 'the more noise they make, the easier for us.'

"And would you believe it, he produced an empty barrel and a big brace-and-bit. We climbed over the puffer's bulwarks onto the horizontal trusses on the framework of the jetty and worked the barrel till it wass under wan o' the gaps between the planks that made up the surface of the pier, right at the very middle of it. Then Jeck used the gap to drill a hole into the base o' wan o' the whusky casks from below, and ass the spurits poured oot he caught them in the barrel we'd brought with us.

"It wass much harder to get the full barrel back on board the boat — but we managed it efter a bit o' a struggle.

"Next morning we loaded the cargo on board in netting slings, the Customs men roped and sealed the hatches tight, and it wass long efter we'd unloaded in Gleska before the empty cask wass discovered. By that time it wass too late to blame anyone, and the Customs people finally decided it must have been liberated by someone at the blenders. They never jaloused that it would have been possible for Jeck and me to do what we did."

"What I don't understand," said Sunny Jim, "is where you got the empty barrel from — and where you hid it on board?"

Para Handy grinned. "Well, Jum, let's say that we didn't drink any tea on the way hame from Islay, long trup though it was. We had chust used the *Mingulay's* own water-barrel for the chob!"

"Happy days and high-jinks," said Jim a little despondently. "I wish we could enjoy some o' that sort of spree these days, but with these foxy Customs men that's jist a daydream."

Para Handy stood up from where he'd been sitting, hunched on the corner of the cargo hatch.

He looked round to ensure no unwanted ears were within eavesdropping range.

"What were you planning for supper the night, Jum?" he asked.

"Salt herring, I thocht," said Sunny Jim.

The captain grimaced.

"No, Jum, for peety's sake no. Naethin' salty, whatever you do. Naethin' to provoke a thirst. And, a word of advice — don't be tempted to drink ony of oor ain watter." He nodded towards the wooden waterbreaker lashed to the mast.

Sunny Jim stared in disbelief. "You don't mean...?"

Para Handy laid a forefinger against the side of his nose. "But how on earth...?" Sunny Jim began.

"Wheesht, Jum," said the skipper anxiously. "Wheesht. That's for me to know: and for them neffer to find oot!" And he turned and waved to the three Customs men standing in animated conversation on the quayside.

*FACTNOTE*

Many puffers called upon to transport whisky really did

regard the operation as something of a challenge to their ingenuity and all of the subterfuges described in this tale were actually employed at one time or another by different crews!

There are about 100 whisky distilleries in Scotland today, a far cry from earlier days before rationalisation, take-over and the economies of scale saw mergers and buy-outs which decimated the numbers of individual enterprises. In Para Handy's time there were more than 20 distilleries in Campbeltown alone!

The majority of whisky is used for blending, with whiskies from a variety of other distilleries, to create the best-known proprietary brands. The blender's art is the most highly prized of skills, and the secret of the blending processes jealously guarded.

Only a minority of distilleries produce a whisky which will be bottled and marketed as a 'single': that is, unblended with the product of other manufacturers. Almost without exception those whiskies which are branded and sold as sin-

*THE AGONY AND THE ECSTASY — Two puffers waiting at the Caol Ila Distillery pier, Islay, for the most frustrating cargo in the world — casks of malt whisky straight from the bond. Though this photograph dates from the 1940s, the agony of proximity to such temptation (and the ecstasy of the generous dram which was the crew's expected bonus from the manager) were the same then as they had been 40 years previously.*

gles are malt whiskies, distilled from malted barley in copper pot stills, rather than grain whiskies which are the chief ingredient of the blends, made from maize and unmalted barley in a continuous distillation process.

The character and quality of the familiar commercial blends is generally dictated partly by the quantity, but above all by the quality, of the malt whiskies which they contain.

As a rule of thumb, grain whisky is bland but malt whiskies are full-flavoured: most important of all, each malt has its own unique character which the experiment of centuries has proved impossible to duplicate. On Speyside, the major centre of malt whisky production, adjacent distilleries drawing their water from the same river and buying their barley from the same grower will produce totally different whiskies. And nobody knows why.

Some of the finest singles would have been as familiar to Para Handy as they are to the whisky connoisseurs of today — like the world-renowned Islay malts, product of that fertile island lying west of the Kintyre peninsula. They are among the very greatest, the most distinctive (and, for many English or overseas visitors anxious to sample them in public house or off-licence, among the most unpronounceable) names in whisky lore and legend.

Lagavulin. Laphroaig. Bruichladdich. Bunnahabhain. Names to conjure with!

# 13

## *Things to Come*

T he whole of Arran seemed to be asleep this
Saturday afternoon in August. An air of somno-
lence as heavy as the unexpected heatwave, now
entering its second week, hung across the island
and Brodick pier was deserted, but for a solitary black-
hulled puffer lying, empty of any cargo, against its inner
face.

A line of washing stretched from a hook on the forward
face of the wheelhouse to the mast of the *Vital Spark* and
water dripped spasmodically onto the tarpaulin covering
her hold. As befitted a vessel on which all men were "chust
Jock Tamson's bairns, wan effery bit as good as the next" as
her Captain put it, it was a very democratic line on which
Para Handy's best jersey jostled for space with Macphail's
socks, these latter having more holes in them than a
gruyere cheese.

From the fo'c'sle chimney a thin column of smoke drifted upward and in the bows of the puffer Sunny Jim was
rinsing the crew's dinner-plates in a bucket of sea-water.
Replete with herring and potatos, the three other members
of the ship's company sat on upturned fishing-boxes on the
pier with mugs of thick sweet tea, and contemplated the
view in companionable silence.

"There is nothin' in the world beats the Clyde," said Para
Handy conclusively, "when the weather is in the right
trum! You could not ask for a finer sight than Brodick Bay
and the Goat Fell on an efternoon like this! You could be
sellin' tickets to towerists chust for a look at the view!"

Macphail snorted. "Towerists is wantin' mair than jist a
view nooadays," he said. "Wi' them it's all go! Jist look at

whit's happened in Bute! Tram-caurs, an' sweemin' baths, an' concert halls, an' baun'staun's, an' gowf, an' boats an' yats tae hire, an' an aqua room."

"Aquarium," corrected Sunny Jim, as he clambered up the ladder and onto the pier.

"Or whatever," conceded the engineer, "but Ah'm sure it gi'es a richt fleg tae veesitors: there's plenty Glesga fowk think a fush is somethin' only tae be foond in cans, they dinna realise it's a wild animal that swums aboot in the watter jist as free as a burd!

"And besides, if it's scenery ye're wantin', Scotland's got a long way to go to be upsides on some o' the places Ah've seen when I went foreign." Macphail's much-aired experience of the world was at once an irritation and a challenge to the crew and in particular the Captain, who never knew whether to give total credence to the engineer's pronouncements in that area. Indeed Hurricane Jack had, on occasion, been known to hint darkly that he for one didn't believe the engineer had ever been furth of the Irish Sea.

"I wouldna be sure on that, Dan," offered the Mate who, though normally of a peaceful not to say diffident disposition, took umbrage at any criticism — whether direct or implied — of his West Highland homeland. "You would go far to find a finer sight than the view from Oban of a sunset over Mull."

"Or Brodick and Goatfell," repeated Para Handy.

"Mull! Goatfell! Ye've nae idea o' the world, neither the pair o' ye. If ye'd seen Capetoon an' Table Moontain, or New York an' the Statue o' Luberty, or Rio de Janwario and the Sugar Lump, ye'd no' be blawin' aboot yer ain kail-yerd."

"Rio," mused the Captain. "Jeck wass there wance: he said it wass awful over-crooded wi' foreigners o' every description and neffer a wan o' them spoke a word o' English and there wassna a dacent gless of whusky to be had! He thocht New York wass chust much aboot the same, for none o' the Americans he met could speak much English either!

"Go to ony o' those places indeed! I'd ass soon go to — iss it Spain? — onyway, where aal the Onion Chonnies come from, chust aal garlic and chokers and berets and bicycles! No: we are Brutain's hardy sons, livin' in the land o' the free, here we are and here we stay!"

"Man, Captain, you're jist a richt stick-in-the-mud," protested Sunny Jim. "Whit way d'ye think Brutain got the

Empire in the first place? It wisnae thanks to auld fogeys that widnae stir frae their ain firesides. If it had been left up tae the likes o' you, we widnae ha'e colonised the Cumbraes yet!"

~

The topic came up again the following week as the puffer lay at Inveraray waiting for its cargo of oak-bark to be carted down from Glenshira.

Captain and crew were seated on deck enjoying the last of the evening sunshine, and studying the latest crop of Inveraray tourists with covert interest, in continuing good weather. The fine spell, indeed, had now lasted so long that local worthies seated on benches outside the Inns with a schooner of beer were talking of record temperatures, and local farmers nursing a whisky at the bar were complaining endlessly to anyone who was prepared to listen about the lack of rain.

It did seem, however, as if the weather might be on the change for the clouds were gathering over the hills at the head of Glenaray, and the drivers of tourist charabancs waiting on the seafront were rigging their canvas awnings — just in case.

Among the full house of summer visitors staying at the Argyll Arms Hotel, which stood within sight of the pier, and just across the road from the driveway leading to the impressive castle seat of the Dukes of Argyll, was an American family comprising father, mother — and two very slender, very tall and very blonde daughters in their early twenties.

The parents were a conspicuous addition to the attractions of Inveraray with their — by the standards of that douce Highland town — garish and unfamiliar clothes, nasal conversation never delivered at any level under a shout, and a predilection for hiring boats or carriages at the drop of a hat and tipping with a reckless generosity that had the townspeople lost for words.

The girls in particular had made an immediate and overwhelming impact on the community — or at least on its young men, many of whom took to hanging around the fore shore opposite the hotel at all hours of the day in the hope of catching just a glimpse of the objects of their admiration as the family went about its peregrinations.

Jim, who had lost no time in calling at the public bar of the hotel in search of further information about the visitors, was able to report that the paterfamilias was originally of Scots extraction — a Campbell, no less — and that he had made his fortune in the United States steel industry.

"He'll have come back to Inveraray in search of hiss fam-ily's roots," suggested the Mate, digesting this snippet.

"Naw," said Jim who, seemingly seeking any escape from the pervading heat, had been soaking his head under the ship's pump and was now vigorously towelling it, "for he didnae stert oot as a toff, his roots is in Glesga, in the Gorbals accordin' tae the barman. He's come tae Inveraray tae try an' buy a piece of land frae the Jook, tae build a hoose tae use on his holidays, for the barman says the man's fair determint tae come back tae Scotland year on year frae noo on." And with that he stood up, stretching, and clambered down into the fo'c'sle.

"Neffer!" said Para Handy as Jim disappeared. "Think o' the expense, think o' aal the discomfort o' the journey."

"Havers!" chipped in the engineer. "For a stert, money's nae object wi' a millionaire: and the journey's a dawdle nooadays, since they built the *Lusitania*. You could jist as weel be in a hotel! We're no' talkin' aboot tryin' tae cross the Atlantic in a tarry auld tub the like o' the *Vital Spark*. We're talkin' aboot real shups!"

"She's aalways real enough for you when you iss col-lectin' your wages at the end of the week, anyway," said Para Handy with some anger. "That's no way to talk aboot a shup that's kept you and your femily in the way they iss accustomed to for mony a year!"

"She'll never be an ocean greyhound, that's for sure," replied Macphail heatedly. "Ocean tortoise, mair like!"

"Weel," said the Captain, "since you're the man that's supposed to be in cherge o' the enchines, dinna look to fault me on that score! Look to your own laurels iss my advice to you!"

"All Ah'm sayin'," retorted Macphail, "is that we'll be seein' mair and mair American veesitors in the future, wi' the fancy new ways o' travel that's aboot the noo. Wait you and see! The maist o' the towerists on the Clyde'll be frae overseas, and the Glesga fowk wull stert traivellin' abroad!"

"Away with you," said Dougie incredulously. "Where would they go? Spain, I suppose, to save the Onion Johnnies a journey?"

"And why not?" asked the engineer. "Ah've been tae Spain when I wis deep sea: there's mullions o' fowk livin' there so it canna be a' that bad a place. Lord knows, it's usually hot enough."

"It's hot enough here for anyone," replied the Captain. "I doot the average Gleska faimily wud have more sense than to trevel to a country that's chust choc-a-bloc wi' foreigners who canna even speak English — even if they had the money for it."

"You'll see," said Macphail darkly. "The Americans is comin' and the boardin' hooses on the river'll hae tae set oot mair than jist a fush tea fur them, and the resorts mair nor a penny peep-show and a hurdy-gurdy man, if they want tae stay on in business."

"So what are they to do, then?" asked the Captain with heavy sarcasm. "I suppose you think restrongs'll stert dishin' out curries and rice and aal the other fancy gew-gaws you're aye blawin' that you ate when you wass on yon tramp-shup in the Indian jute trade? And that the Chook'll open up the castle doors at sixpence a time for folk to troop through and gawp at him and herself takin' their teas?"

As Macphail was flexing his thoughts in search of a suit-ably vitriolic response there came the most horrendous crash of thunder, which echoed off the watch-tower hill of Duniquaich and round the bay.

Within seconds the skies had opened and raindrops the size of pan-drops were bouncing off the parched ground: within minutes there was not a soul to be seen anywhere out of doors, puddles gathered on roads and paths, and the grassy area in front of the Argyll Arms Hotel was like a quagmire.

"My Chove," gasped Para Handy from the safety of the fo'c'sle, "that's some thunderbust! Check the diary, Dougie, and see if this iss no' the day o' the Argyllshire Gaitherin', for if it iss we should have known fine what wass comin'. It aalways rains for them in Oban, puir souls!"

"Which," said Macphail, resuming the thread of his earli-er argument, "is exactly why the Glesga fowk wull soon be awa' abroad for the Ferr: sunshine guaranteed, no' like Loch Fyne. The only things guaranteed here is rain and mudges!"

"At least the Americans'll no' come back, wance they see rain like this," observed Dougie. "And when the word gets round, aal the foreigners'll bide at hame."

"That's jist where ye're a' wrang," said Sunny Jim, pulling on his jacket and picking up his melodeon from the shelf at the head of his berth. "Mandy and Carrie tell me that they come tae Scotland tae get awa' frae the constant heat o' their own place in Texas. And they dinna caal it rain, lads: they jist caal it Scotch Mist: and they love it!"

"Stop you a meenit," said Para Handy in surprise as Jim made his way towards the companionway. "Where are you goin'? And who are Mandy and Carrie?"

"Jist the American lasses at the Argyll Arms," said Jim: "I had a word wi' the family when I was up there earlier the day and I've been invited to gi'e them and their faither and mither a recital o' reels and strathspeys on the melodeon.

"Their faither says they fair tak' him back tae his youth and he particularly asked me tae jine them tonight, for their havin' a ceilidh before they leave tomorrow."

"But...but what about the rest of us?" spluttered the Captain. "Are we chust to be left here like lost sheeps?"

"Naw," said Jim. "A'body's welcome: but jist leave me a clear road wi' the lasses.

"You could fill in yer time mair better in fact, for the Jook wudnae sell Mr Campbell ony land: maybe ye could persuade him that the *Vital Spark* is a yat — and get him to buy her tae use her each time he comes back hame!"

*FACTNOTE*

It goes without saying that tourism as we know it today had not been invented in Para Handy's time — and that the weather on the Firth remains as unpredictable today as ever!

Patrons of the Clyde resorts at the turn of the century fell into two categories. Most day-trippers were from the 'working class' areas around Glasgow. Longer-stay visitors ranged from factory workers to professional men and came for anything from a weekend to a month, some in hotels or boarding-houses: some, the first self-catering holidaymakers, in rented property.

Many Glasgow business-barons, however, either rented a house for the entire summer, or built their own: and, while their families enjoyed the sea and summer air, they commuted daily to their office using the efficient, speedy steamer network.

Few tourists came from farther afield: Scotland was not

*Technology, Edwardian-style — A Kintyre Motor Company charabanc arrives at the Campbeltown quayside, about 1910. This one has a solid roof, but many had canvas hoods which were folded down in fine weather. One lad runs alongside, the feet of another chasing the vehicle can be seen to the rear, behind the back wheel. Hanging onto the back of buses or lorries for a free ride was a popular, if highly risky, pursuit!*

yet established as a holiday 'destination' for the English, never mind the overseas market. Long-distance travel was confined to the wealthy. Most English visitors and most of the very few from foreign countries, were 'gentry' coming either to their own estates, or those of their friends. Society moved north in season for the highly specialised pursuits of fishing and shooting, and to a lesser degree, yachting as well.

Macphail was right in seeing that increasing speed and comfort on the Atlantic passage would bring Americans over in growing numbers. There was fierce rivalry between the shipping lines of Britain, France and Germany to capture their share of the profits to be had in catering for the travel whims of wealthy Americans. Para Handy, however, could never have imagined that air-travel would open up Europe, and then the world, to all his countrymen, whatever their social or economic background.

'Onion Johnnies' usually came from the Basque country in the foothills of the Pyrenees and were a common sight throughout rural Scotland well into the second half of this century. They would travel as a group but then work as individuals, sharing a central base where they could store their stock-in-trade: and criss-cross the country on bicycles so festooned with strings of Spanish onions that they could hardly push them, never mind ride them, at the beginning of each circuit.

The Dukes of Argyll, so far as I am aware, have never hosted expensive ticket-only dinner-parties for socially-hungry American or Japanese tourists, though some of their opposite numbers in the English aristocracy certainly have. However, in common with almost every stately home everywhere, only by opening its doors each summer to the curious tourist has Inveraray Castle been able to finance the repairs, upkeep and general investment essential to the maintenance and enhancement of its structure.

# 14

## *Look Back in Agony*

The *Vital Spark*, all way off her, almost at a standstill, was drifting the last few feet onto the fendered face of Rothesay pier when there came the most spine-chilling, ear-piercing howl from the engine-room under the wheelhouse.

Startled by-standers jumped in alarm, and heads swivelled towards the source of the banshee tocsin which sounded for all the world like the puffer's own steam whistle but set an octave higher and with a far greater capacity to discomfit the hearer.

"My Cot, Dan," shouted the Captain, bending down to peer into the stokehold at his feet, "if you've been and stubbed your big toe or whacked your foot wi' the shuvvle again, wull you for peety's sake keep the noise doon to a dull roar, for the Ro'say folk'll be thinkin' we've come to deliver aal the de'ils o' hell to the island instead o' chust a cargo o' coals!"

"It's no' ma toe, ye clown," howled the Engineer, "it's mah back: talk aboot white-hot pokers gaun' through it — Ah cannae move a muscle."

Some five minutes later, with the vessel safely secured at her berth, the crew assembled in the cramped engine-room to examine the stricken engineer, diagnose his problem, and offer their consensus advice.

Macphail was on his feet, but bent forward from the waist at a right angle so that the upper part of his body was virtually parallel to the deck, and his arms dangled loosely in a posture reminiscent of the ape in Hengler's Menagerie.

"Man, Dan," said Para Handy at length: "this is a fine to-do to be sure. How did you effcr contrive to get in such a fix?"

"Ah'm sure an' Ah didnae contrive it," said Macphail with some exasperation, "d'ye think Ah'm enjoyin' masel'? Every meenit's jist agony an' Ah cannae budge! Ah'm stuck!"

"Well you cannot chust bide there for ever," said the unfeeling Mate, "it's your shout for the refreshments up at the Harbour Inn for a start and, besides, we need a fourth for dominos."

~

However it soon became clear that the Engineer really seemed quite unable to straighten up and Para Handy's attempts to free him from his predicament by forced manipulation — "Chust the wan wee tug, Dan, and you'll be ass straight ass a ramrod again!" — had the effect of producing blood-curdling shrieks of protest compared with which the Engineer's earlier howling was as birdsong at evening.

Thus by-standers and passers-by on Rothesay pier, and on the esplanade itself, were treated to the remarkable spectacle of one adult male, body locked into a kind of inverted L-shape, being pushed along the pavement standing in a small wheelbarrow propelled by one, young, man while two older men, one at either flank of the barrow, held the stooped man by the arms to stop him from falling out of the conveyance to one side or another.

In due course, and not a moment too soon for any of those involved in it, the little tableau reached the chemist's in Montague Street.

Para Handy held the shop door open, and Sunny Jim heaved the barrow over the shallow lip of the step into the narrow gas-lit interior of the pharmacy. A low counter displayed a range of toiletries of every description and a stock of specifics for virtually every known ailment, real or imagined, which might afflict the citizenry of Bute. The wall behind the counter was lined with rows of small mahogany-fronted drawers to shoulder height, each with a lettered and gilded glass plate proclaiming its contents. The wall on the other side of the pharmacy was shelved from floor to ceiling and the light glinted on porcelain canisters and ribbed specie jars and bottles lettered in Latin and in gilt.

"Well, well, it's yourself then Mr Maxwell," said the Captain as the white-jacketed figure of the pharmacist appeared from behind the frosted-glass screen which concealed the dispensary at the far end of the shop. "You're keepin' weel, I hope?"

"Can't complain, Captain," said Maxwell genially, pushing his horn-rimmed spectacles up onto his high forehead: "and yourself too, I hope. What can I do for you all?"

Sunny Jim pushed forward past the barrow and its teetering occupant. "Ah'll hae twa pennyworth o' cinnamon," he asked, fishing in his trouser pocket for the coppers. The chemist opened one of the drawers behind him, took out half-a-dozen of the brittle brown sticks and wrapped them in a screw of paper.

"And I'll have chust a smaal bottle of Bay Rum," said the mate, "seein' ass we're aal here onyway," and handed his sixpence to the proprietor.

A croak of protest from behind them suddenly reminded the crew of the real reason for their presence in the pharmacy.

"Well," said Para Handy, "we have got ourselves chust a wee bit of a problem wi' the enchineer here."

"It's no' you that's got the problem, you eejit," protested Macphail through clenched teeth. "It's me that's got it, for peety's sake, and if it wis you staundin' where Ah'm staundin' ye'd no' be callin' it a wee problem either."

"Whateffer," said Para Handy, "but we wass efter wonderin', Mr Maxwell, if you have onythin' for a sore beck. The poor man can scarcely move."

"An' there's a lot of coals needin' shuvvled afore this day's oot," interrupted Sunny Jim pointedly, "an' Ah'm no' gaun tae shuvvle them, that's for sure."

"There's not really a lot I can give him for a bad back," said the chemist, "except maybe some laudanum if he's in pain. Are you in pain?" he asked, turning to Macphail.

"Naw, naw," said the Engineer with heavy sarcasm. "Ah dae this for the fun o' the whole thing: ye can surely see jist hoo mich Ah'm enjoyin' masel'?

"Pain? Of course Ah'm in pain! Or in purgatory, mair like!"

"Have you tried ironing it?" Maxwell enquired of the Captain. "Often a hot iron will simply lift the cramps out of the pulled muscles, or ease any twisted tendons back into place..."

"There's nane o' this lot comin' near me wi' an iron, hot or cauld!" spluttered Macphail. "Ah wudna trust ony wan o' them for it. They'd be sure to scar me for life, or maybe drap it on my fit forbye, or whatever.

"See's yer laudanum, an' let's get oot o' here!"

～

"If you would just try to straighten up, Mr Macphail," said the Doctor, "I think you would find that once you'd done so, your problems would be over."

The Engineer, his shirt pushed up to his neck and his back laid bare as he clung to the top of the examination couch in the High Street surgery, said nothing.

"You've pulled a tendon," the Doctor continued, "just below the right shoulder-blade here..." he scarcely touched the spot with the tip of his finger but Macphail let out a yell which made the hairs on the back of the necks of his audience stand up to be counted. The crew jumped but the Doctor carried on just as if there had been no interruption "...but if you could force yourself to jerk upright, I am certain it would slip back and you would be right as ninepence."

Macphail turned his head slowly, cautiously, as if fearful of putting any sort of strain on neck or back, and favoured the Doctor with the sort of look that an early martyr might have reserved for his persecutors.

"We can only thank you for your time, Doctor," said the Captain apologetically, as they manhandled Macphail back onto the barrow with the sort of level of difficulty that might have been expected had rigor mortis already set in, "but I'm afraid Dan is thrawn, thrawn when it comes to his health."

～

"I am getting chust sick and tired of aal this," complained the Captain an hour later as he, Dougie and Sunny Jim leaned reflectively on the bar counter of the Harbour Inn. Macphail they had left outside, despite his protests, the wheelbarrow leant up against the Inn wall alongside a couple of push-bikes, a knifegrinder's hand-cart and a (sold out) stop-me-and-buy-one trike, the owners of all of which were now playing four-handed cribbage at a corner table.

Since leaving the Surgery they had been along to the Glenburn Hydropathic in a vain attempt to have Macphail admitted to its salt-water hot spa baths (they had been unceremoniously ejected from the hotel foyer by an outraged duty manager) and then spent 20 fruitless minutes trying to persuade the Engineer that a donkey-ride along the sands of the west bay might just shoogle the twisted tendon back into place.

Ignoring the occasional calls of protest from their shipmate in the street outside, and the now less-frequent and, it must be said, rather less-convincing howls of anguish as well, Para Handy called for beer and scratched his head in some perplexity.

"What in bleezes are we goin' to do wi' the man?" he enquired of nobody in particular. "I am thinkin' the Doctor iss probably right, if we could chust persuade him to move his beck, then it wud aal fall into place. But he'll no' do it, the duvvle."

His voice tailed off in mid-sentence and a sudden gleam came into his eye.

"Lads!" he cried: "I think I see the light! Drink up, and we shall see what we can do…"

∾

"We will chust have to take you back to the shup, Dan," said the Captain two minutes later as they wheeled their ungainly cargo down towards the quayside.

At the Square beside the Esplanade the barrow dunted across the cobblestones and the gleaming metal rails of the double-track of the Rothesay tramway, each such tremor producing a croak of protest from the Engineer.

Then, at a signal from the Captain, Sunny Jim lowered the handles at the rear of the barrow and let it stand, supported by its front wheel and rear legs, right between the rails of one of the tramway tracks at the very corner where the trams came hurtling round from the Esplanade and into the terminus.

The three men backed away, leaving Macphail teetering on the barrow, gazing after them beseechingly. From the near-distance and getting nearer all the time could be heard the distinctive and imperious clang of the bell of a fast-approaching tram.

"The Doctor said somethin' had to mak' you move, Dan, for your ain good!" shouted Para Handy. "And if you don't look lively and chump oot o' that barrow like a good laad, I think that wan o' the skoosh-caurs is goin' to fetch you a right dunt — ony meenit noo!"

There was the teeth-gritting screech of metal on metal as the still-unseen tram flung itself into the turn and the wheels bit at the rails in protest as it took the 90 degree curve. Just as the blunt nose of the speeding vehicle appeared round the corner, Macphail gave an agonised yell, an agonised leap — and threw himself out of the barrow in a desperate flurry of limbs and sprinted for the safety of the pavement, as swift and as supple as an athlete.

Within seconds he was at the side of his fellows, all his back problems forgotten, heaving with rage.

"Ye left me to dee!" he roared, wagging an accusing finger.

"Not really, Dan," said the skipper. "For a start I knew fine that hearin' the skoosh-caur comin' wud mak' you leap for your life, if you were fit. And if you weren't fit then I knew what you obviously don't — that the wee bitty track we left you on hasn't been used for years, ever since they brought in the electric caurs to replace the auld horse yins! It's as deid as the dodo! They only use a single-track nooadays, no' the two, and the caur wud have passed ye on the ither side!"

*FACTNOTE*

It was only after I had finished writing this story that I recalled an episode in the TV series with Roddy MacMillan as Para Handy in which Macphail had a back problem (in Arran) and rolled off the pier on a luggage trolley. I remember no other details. I apologise for any unconscious plagiarism but I have kept this story in as I think it is sufficiently different, and above all since there is too much personal nostalgia in it for me to abandon it.

If there are any old-fashioned pharmacies left, I would be glad to hear of them. My father was a chemist with his own business in the village of Kilmacolm, Renfrewshire. He died very suddenly in 1962 and at that time the premises had been little altered since the turn of the century: certainly after he acquired the business as a young man in the 1930s he changed nothing. The interior was much as I have described the Rothesay pharmacy. Though not gas-lit, it had a small gas jet, used to melt the scarlet wax by which every prescription he dispensed, each wrapped meticulously in

*An Edwardian Legacy — I was unable to trace any 'untouched' pharmacies which might resemble my late father's shop in Kilmacolm or the pharmacy in Rothesay described in 'Look back in Agony', but the MacGrory collection includes this photograph — taken, presumably, on the occasion of the formal opening of the business — of Campbeltown grocer Eaglesome. It is still there in Reform Square, virtually unaltered in 90 years. The photographer and camera can be seen, reflected in the glass of the doorway.*

shining white paper, was sealed using a metal monogram stamp. He was pleasingly old-fashioned in other ways too, sported a watch-and-chain daily and was most probably one of the last men in Scotland to wear spats — which he did, in winter at least, till the day he died.

He also devised and sold many specifics of his own, as did many pharmacists of that generation. I am told this would be illegal nowadays. More's the pity. My father's hand lotion, headache powder, midge repellent, cough mixture and many more were much in demand in the village, and were mailed to customers not just in this country but overseas as well. Sadly, the secrets of all of them died with him.

Kilmacolm was once well-known for its Hydropathic or spa hotel sited on a prominent hill on.the northern edge of the Parish. After it closed there was a brief unsuccessful attempt to turn the building into a Casino in the 1960s before it was torn down and houses built on the site.

Rothesay's Glenburn Hydropathic was the most palatial of all the Clyde hotels, built in 1892 to replace an earlier version which had been destroyed by fire, and it is still in business today though no longer as a Hydropathic: the last hotels to carry that name, to the best of my knowledge, are Dunblane and Crieff Hydros in Perthshire and Peebles Hydro in the Borders.

I'm not sure if Rothesay had donkey-rides in Para Handy's day but it had everything else! It was the premier Clyde resort and as well as a huge range of boarding-houses and hotels for all tastes and pockets, it offered a yacht club, boat hire, water sports, bathing both indoor and out, tennis, golf, cricket, an aquarium, camera obscura, concert halls and much more.

# 15

## *The Incident at Tarbert*

There is a very genuine camaraderie amongst the vessels which crowd the Clyde. In part it stems from the struggle with the common enemy, the sea, which unites all those who go about their living upon it, whether on a crack transatlantic liner or an inshore fishing dorey.

What particularly binds the puffer crews on the Firth, however, is an even deeper tie than that.

It is the need to show solidarity against the slings and arrows of outrageous disdain to which they are all too often subjected by those 'establishment' figures who see their own calling or their own position in the marine hierarchy as being inherently superior to the humbler workhorses of the river.

Such solidarity has rarely been better demonstrated than by an episode which occurred recently in East Loch Tarbert and news of which has now filtered through to Glasgow. The *Vital Spark*, of course, was well and truly involved in events, although Para Handy insists that her role was that of supporter rather than instigator.

Given her reputation, coupled with Hurricane Jack's presence on board in Dougie's absence on leave (his wife was on the point of presenting him with their twelfth child), I have my doubts about that.

～

The Tarbert piermaster is notorious for his brusque treatment of the puffers which are such regular visitors to the busy harbour. The huge local fishing-fleet he will tolerate (but only just) because on its activities is much of the wealth of the community founded. For him, though, the proudest moment of every day comes with the arrival of the *Columba*, unmatched jewel of the MacBrayne fleet, on her Glasgow to Ardrishaig run.

Her posted berthing time on her outward passage — and rarely does she deviate from it by more than a minute or so — is five minutes before midday. By that time the pier is thronged with bystanders and sightseers, and traps and carriages stand at the pierhead ready to whisk those passengers bound for Islay or Jura across the narrow isthmus to the waiting steamer at West Loch Tarbert.

On a recent Friday morning the *Vital Spark* lay at the small stone jetty in the innermost recesses of the East Loch, in company with three other Glasgow-registered puffers, unloading building materials for a local contractor.

"Would you look at that," Para Handy suddenly exclaimed, "where does the *Tuscan* think she's goin'? McSporran will no' be at aal pleased when he sees this!" McSporran was the notoriously high-handed piermaster who presided over maritime proceedings at Tarbert.

Another puffer had appeared in the harbour and was edging her way alongside the main steamer pier with the obvious intention of berthing in an area normally reserved exclusively for the passenger vessels and, on occasion, larger cargo carriers such as the *Minard Castle*.

"No, Peter," said Hurricane Jack, joining Para Handy at the rail and shading his eyes against the morning sun to stare across the water at the new arrival. "She's aal right, she's cairryin' a flittin'."

There was an unwritten concession, usually honoured by all the piermasters in the large Firth ports, that a puffer carrying a domestic as opposed to a commercial cargo would be allowed to use the main piers. Sure enough, the *Tuscan's* deck was covered with a jumble of wardrobes, bedsteads, chairs and the like, and a horse and cart were waiting to receive them at the inner corner of the pier, where their unloading would not interfere with the berthing arrangements of the *Columba*, expected within the next half hour.

Since the new arrival's skipper was a cousin of Para Handy's whom he had not seen for some months, he and Hurricane Jack strolled round towards the steamer pier to exchange the gossip of the river.

They got there just in time to witness the events which

transpired as the *Columba* appeared round the protecting Tarbert headland, her decks thronged with passengers.

The unloading of the puffer was in full swing when McSporran came rushing out onto the pier from his office at the turnstiles, waving the silver-topped ebony stick which was his unofficial staff-of-office.

"MacFarlane," he shouted to the skipper of the *Tuscan*, "will you get this rust-bucket aff my pier at once, and away to where she belongs, ower there wi' the rest of the screp-yard fleet!"

Para Handy bristled.

"There's no call for language like that, Mr McSporran," he protested before his cousin Tommy could get a word in. "Besides she's cerryin' a flittin' and it is chenerally agreed that the coal piers iss no place for hoosehold goods."

"You keep oot o' this, Para Handy," roared McSporran. "Besides this is the Royal Route, and what may be good enough for the likes o' Wemyss Bay or Brodick is certainly not good enough for Tarbert.

"Get that thing shufted — and this dam' cart as weel!"

Before anyone could stop him, or take evasive action, he lifted his stick and struck the patient Clydesdale, waiting in the shafts of the cart, smartly across the rump. The horse kicked out once and careered off up the pier, the cart buck-eting in its wake and spilling its contents onto the quayside.

Ignoring the rumpus which that created, McSporran loosed from their bollards first the forward and then the stern ropes securing the *Tuscan* to the pier, and threw them contemptuously onto her deck.

"Get oot of this, MacFarlane. And from noo on stick to where ye belong. This pier is for the gentry. The Coal Pier is for the likes o' you. And that's the way I intend to run this harbour!"

~

"Somethin's goin' to have to be done aboot that man," said Para Handy half-an-hour later as the crews of the two puffers stood lined up along the bar of a shoreside hostelry.

"You can say that, Peter," said Tommy MacFarlane. "He's cost me a lot of money today, wi' the damage to the flittin' and me no' insured for it. Not to say the damage to my rep-utation at the same time."

"I know he's an awkward duvvlc, boys," said the barman,

101

wiping the wooden counter with a damp cloth, "but he's under a lot of pressure because of what's happenin' the morn."

"Eh?" said Para Handy. "What's that, then?"

"Hiv ye no heard? The Chook o' Hamilton's taken a shootings on Islay for the month, and he's chartered the *Duchess of Fife* from Ardrossan to Tarbert first thing tomorrow, en route for Port Askaig, wi' a whole gang o' toffs.

"Ass weel ass a wheen o' Bruttish gentry there's a couple o' Princes frae Chermany or somewhere. Every carriage and trap in the coonty seems to have been hired to meet the steamer and take them ower to the West Loch chust after breakfast, and auld McSporran's up to high doh aboot the whole thing."

"Iss that so indeed," said Hurricane Jack. "Well, well" — and he drained his glass. "Boys, I think we should awa' and have a considered word with our colleagues at the Coal Pier..."

~

Anyone up and about in Tarbert at three o'clock the following morning would have been aware of mysterious goings-on in the darkness of the harbour. The silhouettes of the steam-lighters moored at the Coal Pier seemed to be moving, though the engines were silent. Closer examination would have revealed that the dinghy of each puffer had been lowered into the water and, with two men heaving at the oars, was painfully towing its parent puffer across the water — apparently toward the steamer pier a couple of hundred yards away.

~

When McSporran strode onto the pier just after eight o'clock to inspect the arrangements for the arrival of the *Duchess of Fife* and her very special passengers, he could not believe his eyes.

Its entire length was occupied by a row of five puffers moored stem to stern. A skiff could not have been manoeuvred in to the jetty.

As for the expected steamer...

McSporran spent 30 frantic minutes trying to get the puffers shifted. But the crews had all mysteriously disappeared and, though he could cast off the mooring lines, he could do nothing to move the boats for not only were their anchors down (but no steam up to allow them to be raised again), they were also chained tightly together.

"It's naethin' to do wi' me, Mr McSporran," said the Tarbert policeman to whom the piermaster had appealed for help. "The boats iss chust berthed: they're no' breaking ony law that I'm aware of."

∾

At nine o'clock, with the *Duchess of Fife* due in just 15 minutes, he admitted defeat.

The waiting conveyances were moved round to the only available berth in the harbour.

The coal pier.

From their vantage point on a hill above the town, the crews of the five puffers watched with some considerable relish as the chartered paddler approached the steamer pier, her captain plainly in ill-humour as he leaned from the wing of the bridge to hear a shouted apology from McSporran, and his instructions about berthing against the tiny, grimy puffer quay.

They watched the dozens of gentry on their way to Islay pick their way down the gangways and across the littered, coal-rimed jetty towards the waiting carriages.

They watched the retinues of servants who followed with all the massed paraphernalia of an Edwardian shooting-party at its grandest.

And, above all, they watched the mortification, embarrassment and humiliation of the snobbiest piermaster on the whole of the Firth.

"Weel, that's set his gas at a peep" said Hurricane Jack with some satisfaction. "I think it'll be some time afore McSporran kicks the *Tuscan* — or any ither puffer come tae that — from its berth again!"

*FACTNOTE*

The Glasgow to Ardrishaig service was jealously guarded and promoted by David MacBrayne as the paramount Clyde route, as indeed it was. An end in itself for round-trip passengers on a day excursion, it was much more than that. It was the major water-borne through-route to the Western

*THE OVERLAND CONNECTION — Although the town was very much the crossroads for passengers going west and north, there never were any scheduled steamer services from Tarbert to Campbeltown and intending passengers faced an uncomfortable, clattering coach journey over much of the length of the Kintyre peninsula. The 40-mile trip would have taken almost a whole day by horse-drawn omnibus. The first motor buses appeared in the area in 1907 — needless to say in MacBrayne livery!*

and Northern Highlands and Islands and many of its patrons were the wealthy landowners and gentry (and their guests) who lived most of the year in city homes — in London as often as Glasgow — but spent much of the summer months on the Highland estates.

It truly was an express service. Despite requiring to make nine intermediate stops, *Columba* reached Tarbert after a 90-mile passage from Glasgow in less than five hours and arrived at her terminus and turning point, Ardrishaig, 40 minutes later.

Those bound for Islay or Jura disembarked at Tarbert while those headed further North or West — to Oban or Mull, Inverness or Skye — stayed on board till Ardrishaig and then transferred to the Crinan Canal packet.

The dovetailing with MacBrayne's West Highland fleets meant that a passenger leaving London on the overnight train could be in Islay in time for tea the next afternoon, a time-scale only possible today by air. Those travelling north from Ardrishaig could reach Oban for high tea, Fort William for dinner.

Excursionists were an increasingly important market and it can be said that David MacBrayne almost invented the concept of the inclusive tour — and assiduously promoted it. The full day trip from Glasgow to Ardrishaig and return cost in 1899 only 12/- (60p!) in first class and 7/- (35p) in second: both inclusive of a meals package consisting of breakfast, lunch and tea!

Demand on the route was such that as well as *Columba's* daily service there was an additional sailing in the peak months by her consort *Iona*, which left Glasgow at 1.30 p.m. and reached Ardrishaig at 7.15: here she lay overnight before returning to Glasgow first thing the following morning.

Sadly, there were harbours where the puffers and their ilk were treated very much as poor relations, with their own designated berths in some hidden corner, and with officials anxious to keep the main pier as the preserve of the steamers, the yachts and the occasional scheduled cargo service.

One has the distinct impression that Para Handy and his crew were always happier in the smaller communities where they were assured of a warm welcome at any time of the year!

# 16

## *The March of the Women*

Para Handy consulted the tin alarm clock which hung
on a string from a nail driven into the fo'c'sle bulk-
head. "Nearly six o'clock: Jeck iss late," he
announced. It was a Saturday afternoon in August
and the *Vital Spark* was lying at Anderston Quay, loaded to
the plimsoll line with steel plates for the shipyard at
Campbeltown.

She was ready to sail and, indeed, Para Handy had
planned to be half way to Greenock by this time. But
Hurricane Jack, learning on their arrival in Glasgow the
previous evening that his old command — the clipper *Port
Jackson* — was docked at Leith, had taken the train to
Edinburgh then and there to see his former colleagues, with
the promise to return by early afternoon the following day.

"Ye cannae trust that man at all," said Macphail with
some asperity, "he's a mountebank! We've missed the tide
noo and we micht as weel wait till the morn'."

Before the Captain could leap to the defence of his oldest
friend there came the clatter of boots on the deck overhead
and the man himself came bursting down into the fo'c'sle.

"Sorry, shipmates," he said, "but it's chust been wan o'
those days and my head's aal spinnin' wi' the stramash of it
aal."

"Wass it a heavy night wi' your friends, then, Jeck?"
asked the Captain solicitously. "Jum will run up to the dairy
and get a bottle o' milk to settle you."

"It iss not last night that is the problem," replied Jack
with great vehemence, "and my head iss fine, thank you.

"No, I got back to Glasgow as planned, just before dinner
time. The trouble started when I came oot o' Queen Street

Station."

"Trouble?" Dougie put in anxiously. "What trouble?"

"He'll hae met a friend that owed him and they've been on the ran-dan for the last five hoors," chipped in the Engineer with rancour.

"Pay no attention, Jeck," soothed Para Handy. "Chust tak' your time and tell us exactly what went wrong and where, and whether you want anything done aboot it."

"George Square, my boys," said Jack, "that's where it's aal happening: but nothing went wrong! Everything went right! When I came doon the steps from the Station, the Square was chust packed wi' wummin: nothin' but wummin and gyurls ass far ass the eye could see!

"There wass some sort of a wudden platform put up at the far end o' the square, chust in front o' the Toon Hall, and there wass a wheen o' older wummin stood on it, wi' wan o' them aye rantin' on aboot somethin'. I wisna' much carin', so I paid no attention to yon.

"But aal the pavements at the station end o' the square wass chust choc-a-bloc wi' gyurls: red-heads and brunettes and fair haired gyurls that would stop a tram in its trecks they wass that bonnie." He sighed with pleasure at the memory. "Dozens o' them! Hundreds o' them! I have never in aal my life seen sich a tempting array o' feminine beauty aal in the wan place at the wan time!"

Macphail the misogynist snorted: "And Ah'm sure you made their day too, and they wis jist speechless wi' excitement at seein' you," he said dismissively, "bein' the fine figure o' a man you maybe used tae be — aboot 20 years ago. Your courtin' days is done, Maclachlan, and it's high time you admutted it and acted your age!"

"Pay no attention, Jeck," said the Captain. "He is chust jealous. Go on! Who were they aal?"

"Suffry-jets," said Jack. "Ye'll have read aboot them. Gyurls and wummin wantin' the vote."

"Wantin' the vote?" said Sunny Jim incredulously. "Whitever will they think o' next. Votes for wummin? Fat chance!"

That dyed-in-the-wool anti-feminist, the Engineer, nodded in vigorous agreement.

"Well, I don't know," began the Mate, who was notoriously (and unceasingly) henpecked. "Maybe they have a point..."

"When are you goin' tae hae the courage tae start wearin'

the breeks in your ain hoose?" demanded Macphail trucu-
lently and it was only the Captain's timely intervention that
prevented a trading of insults between the two.

"Go on Jeck," he repeated firmly: "and tell us aal aboot
these suffry-jets."

~

The suffragette movement, till now largely directed
towards the thinking women of the London area, had
embarked on promoting a more national support, and
Hurricane Jack had by chance debouched onto George
Square in the midst of their first ever rally in Glasgow.
There had been a considerable degree of local interest gen-
erated by the placing of a series of advertisements in local
papers, bills posted everywhere proclaiming the place and
time of the event, and a discreet but fervent word-of-mouth
campaign.

Holding the rally on a Saturday had been something of a
stroke of genius since it made it possible for the factory girls
of Glasgow to attend in droves, alongside the middle-class
women who had been the main target of much suffragette
proselytising till then.

While most of the Glaswegian males who came upon the
scene passed by, as it were, very firmly indeed on the other
side, it was not in Jack's character as a devoted ladies' man
of many decades devotion to pass up the opportunity to
mingle with such a vast number of members of the opposite
sex.

So, setting his cap at a jaunty angle, and regretting bitterly that he lacked a brass-mounted telescope tucked
authoritatively under one arm, he had infiltrated the
crowds of young girls on the square opposite the station.

After so many rebuffs, and frequent rudenesses, from the
male sex, the young ladies surged eagerly and winningly
around their new-found supporter and soon Jack was in his
element.

He accepted the leaflets they thrust into his hands: "I
have aalways had a very high opeenion o' gyurls chenerally," said he gallantly: "and I wush you every success in your
endeavours. I chust wush I wass able to be of some help..."
and he bowed and touched his cap to every side.

"We are planning to demonstrate forcibly, Mr
MacLachlan," cried one particularly stunning red-haired

girl with a wide-brimmed white hat and an enormous parasol, "we will show our sisters in London that we are prepared to follow their example."

There was a chorus of approval.

"We would be chaining ourselves to the very buffers of the trains," she continued, "but they will not even let us into the station. Or to the railings of the City Chambers: but the Council has placed guards in front of them."

Once they had established that Jack was a sea-faring man, they showed particular interest in his ship and the unfortunate Hurricane, carried away somewhat by the heady glamour of his surroundings, gave into the temptation of gilding the lily somewhat both in his description of the puffer: and in regard to his position on board her.

"The finest vessel on the Firth," he said firmly, with a pride and enthusiasm of which Para Handy would have most thoroughly approved, "sailing tonight for distant seas and far horizons under the command of yours truly."

And when, reluctantly, he dragged himself from their midst on the plea that he must return to his ship, the redhaired girl insisted on walking with him to Anderston Quay.

"Not as big as I would have wished," she said mysteriously when they reached the *Vital Spark* at her berth. "But she will do." And resisting Jack's clumsy attempt to place a farewell kiss on her cheek she jumped nimbly aboard a city-bound tram and waved him goodbye from its upper, open deck.

∽

"So there you have it, shipmates," said Jack, beaming on the company. "Bonnie gyurls and a friendly atmosphere! D'ye think they wud have *me* for a suffry-jet for I would enlist tomorrow chust for the sake of the cheneral frivolity?"

"You're some man for the high jinks," said Para Handy enviously and the crew climbed on deck and started to prepare for their delayed departure.

Macphail scurried into his den to stoke up the boiler fires and Sunny Jim and Dougie lashed the puffer's dinghy firmly across the hatch of the hold.

As Para Handy, Hurricane Jack just behind him, opened the door of the wheelhouse, they were all suddenly aware of the music of a brass band a few streets away — but coming rapidly nearer. It sounded too as if a crowd was singing along with the playing of the band, and there were periodic excited whoops and cries.

Then the clash and crash of the band and its followers became overwhelming, as the head of a substantial procession appeared round the corner of one of the warehouses and headed straight towards the *Vital Spark*.

There were several hundred women trailing the band, singing enthusiastically at the tops of their voices, and a handful, all bearing suffragette placards, heading it. In the very van was a tall, red-haired girl wearing a broad-brimmed white hat and twirling a parasol on her shoulder.

The song died away as the band came to a halt on the dockside immediately alongside the puffer. The marchers massed behind it in a semi-circle and a repeated staccato chant went up: "Votes For Women! Votes For Women! Votes For Women!"

With a smile and a wave to the perplexed Hurricane Jack, the red-haired girl and two others stepped forwards and suddenly producing sets of hand-cuffs from, it seemed, thin air, they attached themselves to the hawsers holding the puffer fore and aft onto the quayside and threw the keys into the water.

"Jum," said Para Handy glumly, "wull ye go an' tell Macphail he needna bother gettin' up steam: and Jeck, seein' you got us into aal this, wull you go and fetch a polisman? You know where I'll be if you need me."

And, turning his back on the triumphant, chanting crowd, he made his way slowly along the deck and vanished down into the fo'c'sle.

*FACTNOTE*

Glasgow's George Square has for generations been 'centre stage' for rallies, protests and public meetings ranging from the sublime to the ridiculous. It thankfully escaped the worst ravages of the city's post-war architectural vandalism and is still overlooked by the magnificent Victorian facades of the City Chambers, the General Post Office, and other properties in keeping with its scale and character: but one doesn't need to look further than the adjacent skyline to see the philistine treatment which parts of the city received in the fifties and sixties.

The Queen Street and Central Stations have survived

*A FORMIDABLE MATRIARCHY — The sole man in this family group looks appropriately worried about the encroaching feminism! Victorians were still getting used to the whole idea of photography and the only member of this particular group who looks at all happy about having a picture taken is the dog!*

more or less intact but long gone, and much lamented, are the more modest but characterful Buchanan Street: and the most imposing of them all, St Enoch's, with its sweeping carriageway and the towering gothic frontage of its integral hotel.

The Suffragette Movement was at its zenith in the first decade of the century, spurred on by the leadership of Emmeline Pankhurst. As well as political protest and pressure, it relied on less peaceful means of promoting the cause and what we would now call publicity stunts ranged from the relative innocence of protestors chaining themselves to railings at the Houses of Parliament, Buckingham Palace or anywhere else where they felt attention would be focussed upon them: to the tragedy of the Derby of 1912, at which the Suffragette Emily Davidson threw herself under the hooves of King George V's horse, brought it down, and was herself trampled to death.

Many historians feel that the public revulsion stimulated by such activities was counter-productive to the cause, and that what in a sense 'saved' the Movement was the First World War, in which women played an incalculably valuable role. Indeed some commentators see the easing of suffrage restrictions which followed that holocaust as the country's way of recognising the service of the nation's womanhood.

One of the more colourful, though less high-profile, supporters of the Movement was the composer Ethel Smyth, who joined the suffragettes in 1911 and in the same year composed for them what became their battle hymn — the splendidly up-beat and instantly memorable 'March of the Women'.

It is one of the few of her compositions recorded and marketed today. But she merits a much wider audience for such stirring programme music as the overture to her opera *The Wreckers* and above all for her magnificent and moving mass, written in 1891 and first performed in 1893 — but not heard again for more than 30 years. Now available on CD it memorably deserves acclaim and recognition.

# 17

## *The Missing Link*

Para Handy looked up from his perusal of the *Glasgow Herald* with considerable surprise. "My Chove," he said, "did you read this piece in the paper aboot the Piltdown Man, Dougie?"

Captain and Mate were alone in the fo'c'sle: Macphail was carrying out some running repairs with, to judge from the baffled curses which could occasionally be heard even from the forefoot of the vessel, scant success. Sunny Jim had been sent ashore with a long shopping list, for this brief stop-over at Partick would be their last chance to stock up the provisions cupboard for some days.

The puffer was on her way from Rutherglen, where she had loaded a farm flitting, and would shortly be sailing for the remote clachan of Bellochantuy on the western shores of the Kintyre peninsula. It would be some days before they were within hailing distance of a shop again.

"Piltdoon Man?" asked the mate: "and who might he be when he iss at hame?"

"He iss not at hame any longer," said the Captain, "for he hass been dead now this many thoosands o' years: but he used to live in the sooth of England and some professor or somethin' hass been and dug him up again, and says he iss the 'Missing Link', whateffer that might be.

"Chust look you at this picture, Dougie," he commanded, handing over the paper, opened at the page carrying the story of the Piltdown discovery under a banner headline, and bearing beneath that an artist's impression of what the 'Link' was thought to have looked like.

"It is quite uncanny!" continued the Captain with con- siderable conviction. "Did you effer in your naitural, if you were chust to shut the wan eye and look at it sidey-ways, see onythin' that pit ye mair in mind o' Macphail on wan o' his aff days?"

The Mate peered quizzically at the sketch.

"He certainly disna look too healthy," he said at last: "but iss he not raither mair like thon English chentleman that wass up for the shootings at St Catherine's last year, and shot himsel' in the foot, and we had to gi'e him a hurl across the loch in the punt, ower to the doctor's at Inveraray?

"I think it iss a wee bit unkind o' ye to be comparing him wi' poor Macphail, Peter. Even after 30 years shuvveling coal Dan's airms iss no' quite ass long ass that."

"Whateffer you think yoursel', Dougie," said the Captain: and carefully folded the paper before placing it on top of the mess table: "but I will be interested to have Jum's opeenion when he gets back wi' the proveesions."

~

At that very moment Sunny Jim was coming to the end of a longish grocery list in a branch of the Glasgow Co-operative on Dumbarton Road.

"And six pounds o' best pork sausage," he concluded.

"Links or Lorne?" asked the grocer.

Jim thought for a moment. "Mak' it links," he said at length "and a couple of black puddin's, and twa mealie wans too, jist for a wee divershun tae go alang wi' the sausages."

The grocer weighed out the goods, wrapped them in grease-proof paper and perched them on the top of the large cardboard box into which a full week's supplies for the crew of the *Vital Spark* had now been consigned.

"Onything mair?"

"Seein' I'm here, Wullie," said Jim, "you could jist open me a screw-tap o' Worthington and I'll get ootside that while you're doin' the sums."

And he leant sociably on the brass-edged counter pulling at his beer while the Co-op man, licking the point of his pencil at intervals with a sigh of fierce concentration, totted up a long column of figures once, then twice to check it, and finally a third time — apparently for luck.

"That'll be five pund fifteen and saxpence," he said at length, straightening up and handing the document to Jim: "and anither saxpence for the ale."

"Mercy! Near on six pound! I'm sure I didna think I wis

buyin' the premises when I cam' in." said Jim. "And a tan-
ner for the beer! Are you no' throwin' that in for the good
wull o' the hoose?"

"Ah canna dae that," said the grocer. "For it's nae ma
hoose and the chentlemen in Morrison Street wud soon be
throwin' me oot of it if they foond Ah'd sterted tae gi'e the
goods awa' on a whum.

"Whit Ah can dae for ye is send wan o' the delivery lads
doon wi' the box on a bike tae the boat. That'll save ye a
pech. And I'll gi'e ye a nip o' my ain whusky."

And on that offer the bargain was struck. Sunny Jim paid
with six crumpled pound notes, pocketed his change, swallowed a generous dram poured from the bottle gifted to the
grocer by one of his suppliers, and saw the box safely
loaded onto the metal cradle at the front of the delivery
bike.

"See and no' cowp it," he admonished the youngster who
was to pedal it, "for there's eggs in there, and as we dinna
like them scrambled you'd best get them tae the shup in
wan piece. Put the meats in the wire safe on the foredeck,
and the rest o' the stuff in the fo'c'sle. And tell the Captain
I'm on my way."

~

The puffer slipped down-river in the gloaming with
Dougie at the wheel: Para Handy passed the article about
the Piltdown Man to Sunny Jim as the two of them sat on
the stern gunwale.

"Dan to the life," he said in a deliberately loud voice:
"but when I showed it to the man himsel' an hoor ago, he
wass not at aal amused. You wud think he wud be prood tae
be taken for onythin' ass important ass a 'Missing Link', but
no. He chust ran awa' from the suggestion: he iss like the
Gabardine Swine in the Scruptures, that had the pearls o'
wusdom thrown tae them, but chust went dashin' awa' into
the wilderness!"

A furious clang of metal from the engine-room at their
feet indicated that the unfortunate engineer was reduced to
taking out his feelings on a pile of coals.

"We wull put in to Bowling for the night," Para Handy
added pointedly, "and mebbe Dan wull obleege the
company by givin' us aal a Piltdoon performance at the
Inns!" But, despite their cajoling, Macphail huffily refused

to join the rest of the crew when they went ashore after a herring supper to quench the thirst it had given them.

When they returned on board, though, he was in his bunk and fast asleep — with a somehow satisfied-looking grin on his face which made Para Handy bristle with suspicion. "He's been up to something: wait you and we wull see!"

~

The *Vital Spark* continued down the Firth after an early start the following morning and mid-day found her just off the south end of Bute.

Sunny Jim went below to make a start on preparing dinner for the crew. With the potatos peeled and set on the stove to boil in a pan of sea water, he went up on deck, opened the door of the meat safe and reached for the link sausages.

They were not there.

Cursing the delivery boy for his perfidy, Jim made the best of a meal he could from the black and mealie puddings.

"Ah'm sorry, boys," he said: "but yon wee duvvle has pinched the sausages on us, and there's nae mair I can do by way o' a meat dinner."

Para Handy and the Mate accepted the situation, grudgingly, but Macphail refused to eat any of the fare on offer and retired in high dudgeon to his stokehold.

"To bleezes!" said the Captain: "The man's still in an upset over the ribbin' we gave him yestreen: well, aal I can say iss that he'll be hungry afore we are," and he tucked into a forkful of mealie pudding with apparent relish.

~

In fact, Macphail refused to join them for any meal over the next two days, surfacing only to butter a few slices of bread and make himself a cup of tea at regular intervals, as they rounded the Mull, beached just off the farm to which the flitting was consigned, and unloaded the strangely mixed cargo into the new tenant's waiting horse and dray.

Then, on the morning they were due to sail for home, Sunny Jim squeezed his way into Macphail's domain, anxious to make peace with the engineer for the air of gloom and doom which hung over the little ship went quite contrary to Jim's nature.

And he found Macphail frying a pound or thereby of finest pork sausages on the back of a shovel held over the glowing ashes in his fire-pan!

His yell of outrage brought Para Handy and the Mate dashing to the engine-room.

"You're a duvvle, Dan!" Para Handy protested. "Can you no' tak' a bit o' a joke wi'oot complainin', or at least wi'oot losing the heid and stealin' from your shupmates!"

"Ah'm no' complainin' noo," said the engineer: "that's been the best grub Ah've ever had on this decrepit auld hooker. Two solid days o' meat meals and I'll say wan thing fur ye, Jum, ye ken a good sausage when you see it.

"Ah'm fair vexed that's the last o' them — or Ah'd offer you all a taste.

"Mebbe that'll teach you a lesson. Never mind aboot the Missin' Link: it's the missin' *links* that you should all be a lot mair concerned aboot!"

And with a satisfied laugh to himself, he swallowed the last morsel of sausage with evident, if exaggerated, relish.

~

A few minutes later, the farmer appeared with his cheque-book to pay for the flitting and as he perched on the seat of his cart to sign it, he had his first sight of Macphail (who had been seated unseen in the engine-room throughout the unloading process of the previous hours) as that worthy came on deck to get a breath of air.

The farmer stared at him, transfixed, and was so put off his stride that he smudged the signature badly and had to start all over again and write a fresh cheque.

"My heavens, Captain," he confided to Para Handy in an awed whisper, "it's none o' my business, but that's some man you have as your engineer! You ken, he's the very double o' that 'Missing Link' that had his likeness in the Gleska Herald a day or two back.

"I hope I'm no' offending you saying that…"

FACTNOTE

The discovery of Piltdown Man was one of the great news stories of 1912, and one of the supreme academic hoaxes in history. For sheer audacity and confident theatricality it ranks with such classics of the genre as America's Cardiff Giant or the Berners Street prank in London, Scotland's 18th-century 'Ossian' literary imposture: or the hoax that went so infamously wrong when what had been intended as a slightly scarey leg-pull turned to near-tragedy when Orson Welles' radio play, based on the H. G. Wells novel *War of the Worlds*, was believed by many of the listening American audience to be an accurate news broadcast, with whole families panicking and fleeing their homes.

Charles Dawson was an amateur antiquarian and archaeologist who announced to a startled academic world in 1912 the discovery of the 'Missing Link', the hominid which spanned the physical and intellectual gap between ape and man. For about two generations thereafter the skull and jawbone which he had 'excavated' to prove that theory held an honoured place in the pantheon of the British Museum and the site of his 'discovery' — a chalk pit in the Sussex Downs — became a place of pilgrimage for earnest and enthusiastic antiquarians both professional and amateur in the quest of further, momentous 'finds'.

All of which doesn't just help prove the truth of the old adage that 'There's a sucker born every minute'. It also demonstrates quite gratifyingly — at least to the layman — that as often as not the 'sucker' is a loudly self-proclaimed 'expert'.

Only in 1953 was the hoax finally exposed as what it was though even then (and, who knows, perhaps still today) there were voices raised in defence and protest against the destruction of a myth so dearly-held. The skull of the 'Missing Link' was proved, by dating techniques, to be that of a 20th-century man and the jawbone that of a 20th-century orang-outang, both cunningly stained to simulate great age.

I think the only individual involved in the whole scam who came out of it with honour intact was the orang-outang!

Scottish pork butchers, on the other hand, inherit a long and honourable tradition. Glasgow firms like McKeans, established in the 1870s, built up a worldwide reputation, winning awards and medals at food exhibitions (of which the Victorians were so fond) as far afield as Canada, and still trade today, changed beyond recognition by the demands of an evolving market.

Lorne sausage, for the uninitiated, is a coarse-chopped,

sliced sausage-meat in block form. The origin of the name is unknown (the first maker perhaps?) but, when it is well made and spiced to perfection, it is tastily addictive.

# 18

## *The Cadger*

Macphail and Sunny Jim watched the Mate come disconsolately towards them along the quayside at Lamlash, his head down, and his hands deep in his pockets.

"Ah doot it's no' good news," said the Engineer. "We'll be here a week at the least afore the man's weel enough mended tae come back. A week in Lamlash! It shouldnae happen tae a dug!"

The accident had happened the previous afternoon, as they were unloading fencing-stobs for the Duke of Hamilton's estates. As a bundle of the posts was being swung upwards and outwards from the hold the knot on the rope binding them together had slipped and the stobs had come tumbling onto the deck. One caught Para Handy a hefty blow across the head, sending him flying across the hatch-coaming and into the depths of the hold.

The doctor, when he eventually arrived in a pony-and-trap from Brodick, was less concerned with the broken wrist which the Captain sustained in the fall than with the large area of contusion on the side of his head.

"I can strap the wrist no problem," he pronounced, "but I can give no guarantees about your the effects of that blow to your head, Captain MacFarlane. I'm not happy about it at all."

Macphail restrained himself with considerable difficulty from offering his own opinion on that matter, but the upshot was that Para Handy was removed within the hour by horse-drawn ambulance and taken the three miles over the hill to the Cottage Hospital at Brodick 'for observation'. Dougie went with him, partly to keep him company and see him safely installed, partly in order to telegraph the owner in Glasgow to advise him of developments.

"Whit's the news then?" asked Macphail as the Mate scrambled aboard. "Is he deleerious?"

"No, nor hileerious: but he's ass carnaptious ass a wagonload o' pensioners for they're sayin' they want to keep him in for a week, and there's a nurse yonder built like a dreadnought wha's in cherge o' the ward and he's feart for her already, chust feart. No' that I blame him: if they'd had her at the Crimea it wud have been in the front line trenches and no' Florence's hospital they'd have pit her."

"So we're tae lie here for a week!" exploded Macphail. "A week in Lamlash in October! Nae wonder ye're lookin' as miserable as an innkeeper at a Rechabites meeting. We'll be oot o' wir minds wi' boredom, and here's me wi' naethin' Ah hivnae read, an' nae mair chance o' buyin' onything mair here than I hae o' gettin' a transfer tae the *Columba*."

"No," said Dougie, "it's worse nor that. I telegraphed Gleska and they said there iss a cargo o' scrap iron waitin' for us at Ardrishaig that's urchently needed up at Pointhoose so the shup hass to go and load it. Peter iss to choin us at Pointhoose ass soon ass they let him oot."

"Thank the Lord," said Macphail emphatically. "At least we get oot o' here. So whit are ye lookin' so miserable aboot then Dougie? I thocht ye always wanted a chance tae skipper the boat yersel'?"

"Indeed I did, Dan," replied the disconsolate Mate: "but the Gleska office will not let me do it! They say that for the insurance we have to have an experienced Captain and they're sending wan down to Brodick on board the *King Edward* tomorrow morning."

"Well, Ah'm vexed for ye," said the Engineer generously, "but at least we'll no hae to drum wir heels in Lamlash for a week. So why are ye lookin' like a wet December funeral?"

"For the same reason ass you will be in a meenit," responded the Mate dolefully. "Wance I tell you who the relief skipper iss goin' to be. They're sendin' doon Cadger Campbell."

Macphail blenched visibly. "Ye're jokin' Ah hope!"

"I wish I wass," said the Mate. "But I would not joke aboot ass serious a matter ass Cadger Campbell."

"Ah should hope not indeed," said the Engineer. "It wud be jist temptin' providunce if ye did!"

"For sure," agreed Dougie miserably.

Sunny Jim had been growing increasingly restive during this (to him) totally incomprehensible and infuriatingly repetitive exchange.

"And just exactly who," he managed to get in at last, "is this Cadger Campbell?"

"Dinna tell me that ye've never ever even heard o' the Cadger..." began Macphail.

"Look," said Jim in total exasperation, "if I had heard o' the man I wudna need tae be askin' who he wis, wud I? Noo are ye gaun' tae tell me, or no'?"

"He's wan o' the most notorious skippers that ever had command on the river," said Dougie. "He's lost wan chob after anither through drink an' fightin' an' he's been in the courts three times on a cherge o' wreckin' boats for the insurance only they could neffer prove it. What they did prove more nor wance though wass that he's a fist on him like a menagerie gorilla an' he's quite prepared to use it. The man's done fower spells at least in Barlinnie for assault. He's got a tongue on him as acid as a soor-plum and aal he can come by in the way o' work nooadays iss an occasional berth when the regular skipper's no' weel and there's an urchent chob to be done. Like noo, wi' us."

"By comparison wi' the Cadger," added Macphail, "Hurricane Jack is a teetotal pacifist wha kens every Moodey and Sankey hymn by hert an' sings them tae himsel' a' the day lang. Need I say ony mair?"

~

The Cadger came aboard at half-past-eleven the following morning, bearing about him like a miasma an aroma reminiscent of a distillery and a brewery rolled into one, and carrying a grubby canvas hold-all which clanked noisily, as of bottles, when he placed it down on deck in the wheelhouse.

He was more than six feet in height, a hugely-built man in his early forties with more hair in his ears and nose than most men have on their beards, and a lived-in face the colour of a side of raw bacon and the texture of a pebble-dash wall.

He picked on Sunny Jim at once.

"And who the bleezes are you?" he asked, pulling the cork from a half-flask of whisky retrieved from the hold-all.

"Ah ken your shupmates fine — yon lanky streak o' a mate wi' the reputation o' bein' the most tumid man that ever set fit on a boat, an' the ither yin hidin' doon there pretendin' tae be a proper ingineer when he cudna even wind up a waggity-wa' nock wi'oot breakin' the spring.

"But you, Ah've never clapped eyes on you."

Sunny Jim explained himself as best and as briefly as he could.

The Cadger's eyes lit up. "The Cluthas, eh! Weel, there's hope for ye yet: at least they wis boats wi' a turn of speed and a bit o' class aboot them. A bit o' a come-doon for ye tae finish up on this rust-bucket, though."

Gesturing to Jim to cast off the mooring ropes fore and aft, he pushed the unhappy Dougie unceremoniously out of the wheelhouse and, without granting him the dignity of employing the whistle and speaking-tube for the purpose, he bellowed his instructions to Macphail, grabbed the wheel, steered the puffer out from the pier and set a course which would clear the northern promontory of the sheltering Holy Isle, and move towards the open waters of the Firth.

$\sim$

Four hours later the *Vital Spark* was well into Loch Fyne with the entrance to East Loch Tarbert just off the port bow, and their destination — Ardrishaig — only 12 miles ahead.

The atmosphere aboard was thick enough to cut with a knife. The Cadger, tipsy when he arrived off the *King Edward*, had been steadily demolishing firstly the half-flask of whisky, and then when it was finished the three quart bottles of stout which appeared to be the sole contents of the hold-all. Dan Macphail, hidden among his engines, had missed the worst of the relief skipper's verbal assaults and Jim, on the excuse of preparing the crew's dinner, had retired to the fo'c'sle — safely out of ear-shot, and out of sight as well: in fact though, so sudden and so unexpected had been the Cadger's departure from Lamlash that he had had no chance to replenish the ship's stores and the crew would go hungry till he could go ashore and stock up once they reached Ardrishaig.

The unfortunate Dougie, unable to make his escape, had suffered the brunt of the Cadger's unrelieved torrent of abuse, directed first at the boat, then at her ship's company one-by-one. Even the mild-mannered Mate was at breaking-point when the Cadger suddenly swung the wheel violently to port and headed into Tarbert harbour.

"It's no' Tarbert oor cargo iss at," Dougie protested, "but at Ardrishaig. We've near two hours to go."

"We're gaun nowhere wi' a dry shup," growled the Cadger with some menace, pitching his empty bottles overboard. "Unless you want tae go the same way as ma deid men, get intae the bows and get ready tae pit a line ashore when we come alangside."

Sunny Jim was summoned from the fo'c'sle, given a crumpled pound note taken from the Cadger's back pocket, and sent up to the village Inn to buy two bottles of whisky.

"What the blazes kept ye," roared the Cadger when Jim returned 10 minutes later carrying not just the whisky, but two plain loaves, a bag of potatos and a couple of pounds of sausages as well, "and whit the hell d'ye mean by wastin' ma time and your money buyin' a' that breid and stuff?

"Never in a' ma life hiv I seen sich a bunch o' useless shilpit nyaffs as the three o' you. Macfarlane must be saft in the heid richt enough tae pit up wi' it: nae wonder the fenceposts did him sich a mischief at Lamlash!"

~

Para Handy came down the road to the jetty beside the Inglis brothers' Pointhouse Shipyard in the late afternoon of the following Wednesday, a bandage round his head and his left arm in a sling.

The crew welcomed him, like a long lost brother, with literally open arms.

"Now, now," he cried, retreating in some embarrassment, "I am chust fine, chust sublime, stop this fuss this instant and tell me how you got on with Mr Campbell, for I'm sure he's the only reason you are so pleased to see me back again! Iss he still here?"

"He never actually got here," said Sunny Jim. "Dougie brought her home frae Ardrishaig an' a right good job he made of it an' a'." Whereat the mate blushed like a young girl. "Naw, Campbell the Cadger is probably still somewhere on Fyneside, and lookin' for a cargo o' scrap — and his crew.

"By the time we got tae Ardrishaig he wis jist destroyed

wi' a' the whusky he'd been drinkin' an' he went oot like a light.

"We were to lift the cargo o' scrap that the auld Hay's puffer *Aztec* wis bringin' hame frae Furnace when her biler blew aff Lochgair. They've decided she's no' worth the repairs an' she's tae be scrapped hersel' wance they can fix a tow tae Faslane.

"So wance we'd shifted the cargo, we jist cairried the Cadger over tae the *Aztec* 'n' dumped him on a bunk in her fo'c'sle and changed the lifebelt wi' her name on for the wan wi' oors. Then Dougie brocht the shup tae Gleska.

"When Campbell finally woke he wud believe he wis still on the *Vital Spark*: he's probably huntin' through Ardrishaig for his crew richt noo!"

*FACTNOTE*

The Island of Arran, 165 square miles in area, and about 20 miles in length and 10 in width, has often been referred to and (in tourist terms) promoted as 'Scotland in miniature'.

There is a logic to the claim. The island contains dramatic mountain scenery, fertile rolling farm country — both grazing uplands and arable lowlands — and a dramatic coastline from beetling cliffs to gentle beaches.

For generations Arran was a popular retreat for Glaswegians rich and poor and though the great days of doon-the-water sailing have gone, and though more and more we desert our own land for sunnier shores when it comes to holidays, the island retains an immensely loyal following and maintains a mystique all its own.

The village of Lamlash was the first port-of-call for the steamers after the island capital, Brodick, and was a particularly popular haunt for break-takers during Glasgow's 'September Weekend' — always the last weekend of that month and the (unofficial) end of the holiday season.

Holy Isle, which shelters the bay of Lamlash, takes its name from the monastery founded there in the early middle ages. That tradition of sanctity is maintained today by the Tibetan Samye Ling Buddhist community who purchased the island in 1992, have renovated the farmhouse and lighthouse, and plan to build two new centres as refuges for interdenominational retreats at those sites.

The 'Pointhouse' to which the puffer's cargo of scrap-iron

was consigned was the famous yard of A & J Inglis, builders of many generations of the most renowned of the Clyde steamers as well as whole families of ships great and small created for other owners, other waters and other purposes. The yard (sadly, like virtually every other Clyde ship-builder, long gone) stood on the north bank of the river Kelvin at the point where it joined the Clyde opposite Govan.

The character of Cadger Campbell is of course purely fictitious but it has to be said that there were always some notorious individuals on and around the river Clyde, as there were in any industrial environment anywhere! When researching background material for my factual study of Para Handy and his world (*In the Wake of the Vital Spark*, Johnston & Bacon, 1994) I was given much information which, even a generation or more after the event, I felt it unwise to specify. One snippet concerned a puffer captain reputed to have ingeniously 'lost' at sea not just three (as in Cadger's case) but *four* puffers in pursuit of fraudulent insurance scams!

# 19

## *The Blizzard and the Bear*

The frost had scarcely lifted all the February day and now at three in the afternoon, with only a couple of hours of daylight left, the first flurries of snow began to tumble from a steely grey sky which seemed suspended only a few feet above the tip of the puffer's mast. From the engine-room came the clang of the furnace-door being thrust open and the rattle of Macphail's shovel in the bunker as he prepared to spread another layer of coal onto the glowing fire.

The three other members of the crew were squeezed into the wheelhouse in a vain effort to keep warm by dint of numbers but the only effect of their combined presence in that confined space was that their breath, condensing on the windows, had almost completed misted the glass.

The Captain wiped the pane in front of him with an oily rag and peered vainly into the gloom of the dying day. The curtain of falling snow now made it virtually impossible to see anything beyond the bows, which were rising and falling smoothly on an oily swell. Fully laden with a cargo of slate from the quarries at Ballachulish and en route to Port Ellen in Islay, the *Vital Spark* was in the unfamiliar territory of Loch Linnhe and Para Handy had intended to put into Oban for the night.

"Dougie," he now said: "I am thinking we would maybe be better chust to put her in somewhere close at hand and wait for this snow to blow over rather than risk the shup."

"Whatever you think yoursel', Peter." said the mate, who had been increasingly uneasy about the prospect of picking a blind course through the boneyard of the Lynn of Lorn when the only navigational aid on board for these strange waters was a school atlas Para Handy had bought second-hand from a Glasgow book barrow prior to their departure from the Broomielaw three days earlier.

And so, with the lights on the northern end of Lismore faintly visible as a guide on the starboard bow, and Sunny Jim perched reluctantly in the bows as a shivering look-out, they picked their way into the tiny harbour at Port Appin and tied up at the stone pier. There was not a breath of wind and a silence as of the grave lay on a landscape rendered all but invisible by the snow, which fell more thickly than ever. The crew prepared to make the best of a bad job by creating as much comfort as possible in the cramped fo'c'sle. Macphail carefully carried a shovelful of red-hot coals from the engine-room furnace to get the stove going: Dougie carefully trimmed and lit the two oil lamps hanging from the deck-beams: Sunny Jim filled a basin with water and began to peel potatos for their evening meal.

"I have neffer seen weather like it!" said the Captain, "The snow we get on the Clyde is chust a handful of confetti compared wi' this."

"You call this snaw!" derisively snorted Macphail, who had 'gone foreign' before returning to Glasgow and his berth on the puffer several years previously. "You should see the winter in the Baltic. The Rooshians get that much snaw the hooses get totally buried in it: it's only the lums sticking oot and smokin' that let folk ken whaur their hooses is at."

"That's a bit of a whopper, surely, Dan" said Sunny Jim. "Whit wye could they get in and oot o' them?"

"The hooses is all built wi' special doors in the roofs beside the lums, of course," said Macphail. "And I know for a fact for I've seen it that they can build railway lines ower some of the lakes in winter, the ice gets froze that deep. So if Para Handy wants tae conseeder some real winter weather then he shouldna be greetin' aboot a puckle snow in Appin, but raither remember whit things can be like for the Tsar and his weans and a' the ither folk at St Petersburg: it isnae all snowmen and sledges there, that's for sure."

"Is that so," said the skipper with heavy sarcasm. "Weel, that sounds like a spring mornin' compared wi' the conditions that Hurricane Jeck had to put up wi' wan year when he wass on the cluppers.

"He wass first mate on the *City of Lisbon*, wan o' they nitrate shups, and they wass on a voyage home to Liverpool from Chile wi' a cargo o' phosphates. Efferything wass

smooth enough till they came to Cape Horn and here they
wass hit by the most terrible storms for you should know,
Jum, that this iss a place most weel-thocht-of for wund and
waves the like of which you'll no' see anywhere else in aal
the seven seas. Dougie himself will tell you."

"Right enough, Peter, right enough," affirmed the mate
with alacrity, though he had never been further west than
Barra nor further south than Belfast all his days at sea. "It
iss a most terrible place, to be sure."

"For six days and nights they wass forced to run under
bare poles, they daurna' show a scrap o' canvas, and the
men on the wheel wass lashed to it for fear they would be
washed awa' wi' the seas that wass sweepin' her from stem
to stern. And aal the while they was bein' blown sooth, way
off their course and aye nearer and nearer to the Sooth
Pole.

"Then wan night the wund stopped chust ass sudden ass
when it started, and there wass a deathly silence, and a
night chust as black ass the Earl o' Hell's weskit. In the
mornin' when the daylight came they foond to their horror
they wass becalmed in the mudst of a whole fleet of ice-
bergs, effery wan of them as big ass a land o' hooses.

"It wass so cold you would not credit it. The riggin' wass
ass hard and ass brittle ass icicles, and if you made the mistake of knocking against ony pairt of it, it wud just snap in
twa like a stick o' seaside rock. The men off-watch below
wass aal frozen solid into their hammocks and had to be
chipped oot o' them by the men on watch. If you would try
to tak' a billy of tea from the galley to the fo'c'sle it wass
chust a lump of ice by the time you got it there and in the
officers' salong the rum froze in their glasses afore they
could drink it, and they had to sook it chust ass if it wass a
cinnamon ball.

"Worst of all, the compass wass froze in the binnacle and
they couldnae tell north from sooth so that even if the ice
let up a bit, and a wind cam' up and they had the chance to
pit some sail on her, they would have had no wye of knowin'
which road to tak'."

"Ye're a haver, Para Handy," cried Macphail. "Whether
the leear iss yourself, or whether it wass MacLachlan, I
dinna ken: but wan o' ye is talkin' nonsense and it's wrang
tae pit sich daft notions in young Jum's heid."

Para Handy paid no attention. "Jeck said," he continued,
"that the only thing that saved them wass a perty of

Eskimos oot huntin' polar bears who happened by in their kayaks, and wass able to point oot where north wass tae them, so that when…"

"Eskimos!!!" shouted Macphail. "Eskimos at the Sooth Pole! And polar bears forbye! Ye done it noo, even Jum must know that you only get Eskimos and Polar Bears in the Arctic."

"Whit d'ye mean 'Even Jum'?" cried Sunny Jim angrily. "Are you makin' oot I'm some sort of eejit or somethin'? Of course I ken the whole story's rubbish — but it's gey entertaining rubbish and it wis whilin' the time awa' very nicely.

"Why not get back tae wan o' your novelles, Dan, and leave the rest of us tae enjoy a harmless baur if we want tae…" And the enraged Jim picked up the potato knife and took his feelings out on a half stone of Kerr's Pinks.

~

Once their supper was finished, the engineer retired to his bunk, while the rest of the crew played a good-natured game of pontoon for matches.

After about half-an-hour, with the harsh sound of Macphail's stentorian snoring echoing through the dimly-lit fo'c'sle, Para Handy climbed up the ladder and opened the hatch to have a look at the weather.

The frost was harder than ever, but the snow had stopped and a crescent yellow moon hung in an inky black sky peppered with stars. For the first time it was possible to see something of the tiny harbour in which they had taken refuge. The village, and the village Inn, lay less than a hundred yards away but were totally hidden by an intervening hillock. Indeed there was not a single house to be seen anywhere from the deck of the puffer.

Even the shallow sea-water in the harbour was covered with a layer of ice, such was the severity of the frost: and the further harbour wall was so blanketed and smothered in snow that it was unrecognisable as a man-made object but looked more like a floating mass of ice.

At the edge of the jetty against which the puffer was moored there stood — coated with snow — a wooden tripod about six feet in height, surmounted by a round ball which, when aligned with the ball on a similar construction just visible half-way up the hill behind the harbour, would form a guide-mark for incoming vessels.

The tripod had two wooden arms projecting to either side about five feet off the ground. From each there hung a life-belt.

Para Handy tiptoed back down the ladder into the fo'c'sle and beckoned to Dougie and Sunny Jim.

"I'll treat you both to a dram," he said. "But come up quiet and dinna wake Macphail. Will you, Dougie, set the alarum clock to go off an hour from now: and Jum, bring yon shovel Dan used to bring the coals from the enchine-room. There iss a wee chob to do before we go up to the Inn..."

~

Ten minutes later he stood back to admire their handi-work. The lifebelts had been removed from the arms of the tripod and snow had been built up round it in a rough cone shape as far as the ball which topped it.

Snow had been carefully moulded onto the horizontal arms, and five short twigs of wood added claw-like at their tips. Around the ball at the top a muzzle-like shape had been created on the side facing the boat. Two large ear-like pieces projected from the top of it and three pieces of coal had been set into the head so created — one for a black snout at the front of the muzzle, two for eyes at its top.

"Not bad," said the Captain. "Not bad at aal. Enough to give Dan a bit of a fleg when that alarum goes off and he decides to come up on deck to find out why he's alone on the shup. Wi' an icebound landscape like this aal roond him I've no doot he'll wonder for a moment chust where he iss...

"He'll see then that there's polar bears in ither places than the North Pole — and maybe that'll teach him no' to be sich an auld misery next time, when aal we are havin' is a harmless baur!"

And with a spring in their step the three set off across the snow towards the companionship and warmth of the Appin Inn.

### FACTNOTE

There are two villages carrying the name of Ballachulish, the North and the South, one at either side of the narrows where Loch Leven enters Loch Linnhe.

South Ballachulish was, until the middle of this century, the unlikely venue for a major industry. It was largely to cater for that industry's needs that the isolated branch-line railway from the main Oban to Glasgow route (involving the construction of a cantilever bridge across the fierce rapids at Connel just north of Oban) was laid through the difficult Appin terrain and first opened for business in 1903. Passenger services on the line offered a faster route to link with connections from North Ballachulish onwards to Fort William and Inverness.

Freight services took Ballachulish's industrial output to markets UK wide. But eventually more efficient road haulage facilities, and the growth of car ownership, precipitated an inevitable decline in demand and led to the closure of the line. Freight services ended in 1965 and the very last passenger train pulled out of the village the following year.

The industry which had spawned it all in the first instance was a slate-quarry, the highly-esteemed materials from which were exported not just throughout this country, but worldwide. First opened in 1761, it remained in full-scale production for two centuries. The scars which its operations inflicted on the West Highland landscape are only now beginning to mellow.

The Ballachulish narrows were one of the great natural divides between the North and the South. For generations there was a ferry between the two villages which saved travellers the inconvenience of a 15-mile detour round the roller-coaster road which followed the shore of Loch Leven. In the post-war years, the tiny vehicle-ferries with a capacity.of just half-a-dozen cars were wholly unable to cope with the growth in traffic and delays of two hours or more became commonplace in the summer months. At long last a road bridge was built across the narrows, and opened for business in 1976.

Puffers did indeed carry slate from the quarries, and could be quite regular visitors to Loch Linnhe for other reasons. They operated on and through the Caledonian Canal, usually with cargos of timber. Sometimes it was newly-felled from forestry plantations in and around the Great Glen and ferried south: on other occasions after it was processed and manufactured, it returned north as telegraph poles or fencing stobs.

But these Highland waterways would be unfamiliar territory to skippers who were more at home on the Clyde, where they could boast that they knew every one of its rocks, shallows and shoals (if not by name) at least by reputation!

# 20

## *The Launch of the Vital Spark*

The hard work of the day was done, and a peaceful stillness lay across the *Vital Spark* like a balm. The only sound was the faint hiss of escaping steam from the derrick engine, abandoned and cooling itself down now after several strenuous hours spent loading timber from the nearby Forestry estate.

The crew were strewn across the deck-cargo of rough-cut planks in the late evening sunlight, in a companionable silence.

Dan Macphail was engrossed in a new paperback romance, dipping absent-mindedly now and again into a handily-placed bag of humbugs. Para Handy was sitting deep in thought, Sunny Jim was just sitting. Dougie was thumbing idly through the pages of a week-old Glasgow paper which he had acquired from the Forestry Manager.

"Mercy!" said the mate suddenly, "Would you credit this! Here's an Eyetalian liner sunk the very meenit she wass launched frae the slipway."

"Awa' ye go, Dougie, someone's chust makin' mischief wi' a bit o' a baur," said the incredulous Captain.

"Naw, naw, Peter: it's a fact," said the mate. "It chust proves that Clyde-built iss the only guarantee of quality in a shup. Listen to this!"

And, spreading the paper across his knees, he read aloud "Our Rome correspondent reports that the new Italian liner *Pri ... Princip ... Principesa Jolanda* sank within minutes of her launch in Genoa yesterday. The vessel had been fitted out with her masts and funnels rigged while still on the slip, as is the common practice in Italy, and was a proud sight as she slid down the ways. But within minutes of taking to the water she began to list to port and to the consternation of those aboard her, and of the thousands of spectators, she heeled right over and sank in the shallow water of the harbour, leaving only the plates of her starboard superstructure still showing above the surface ..."

"My Chove," said the Captain. "Consternation's the word! Wass there ony casualties, Dougie?"

"Naw," replied the mate. "They wass aal rescued by the tugs that wass standing by her."

"Well," said Para Handy, "it'll no' be the first time, nor the last, that someone's had to fish folk oot o' the watter at a launchin' perty."

Sunny Jim sensed a story. "Go on, Captain" he prompted.

Para Handy scratched the lobe of his right ear reflectively for a moment or two.

"Well," he said at length, "it was like this ...

~

"Ass Dougie knows, I've been on the *Vital Spark* since the day she wass launched, first ass mate, when Hurricane Jeck wass the skipper of her, then ass Captain when he — er — retired, ass you might say. But that's another story," he said hastily, "of no consequence at all right now.

"Jeck and I had been hired by the owner chust a couple of days before the shup was due to be launched, and we were to stay on board her and oversee the riggin' of her and, (wi' an enchineer by the name of McCulloch from Clynder), the fittin' o' the biler and the machinery. Ass yet the owner had not decided which of us wass to be captain, and which wass to be mate. He had said he would put us through oor paces wance the vessel wass feenished.

"Now ass you can imagine, for aal that we wass the best of friends, both Jeck and I wass very anxious tae get the position for wirselves, and I think Jeck wass particularly keen for this wass no' long efter he'd lost his master's berth on the *Dora Young*, a Liverpool grain clupper. No' by way of ony shenanigans on his pairt, mind: chust the sort of bad luck the man could neffer seem to escape.

"So on the mornin' set for the launchin' of the shup, the three of us took a train from Gleska Buchanan Street Station oot tae Kirkintilloch."

"What on earth were you goin' there fur?" put in Sunny Jim.

"Where else would we go for her launchin'," asked a mystified Para Handy, "except the yerd she'd been built in?"

"She surely wisnae built in Kirkintilloch!" cried Jim. "That's miles frae the river, there's naethin' there except the canal and there's nae room tae launch a shup intae a canal!"

"Jum, I despair o' ye. Maist of the puffers have aye been built in either John Hay's or Peter McGregor's yerds at Kirkintilloch and they still are, on a slup parallel wi' the canal. They slide doon sidey-ways, wi' chains on them to stop them duntin' into the bank on the ither side.

"When we got to Kirkintilloch there wass a real cheery holiday atmosphere in the vullage, for the launch of a shup is always an excuse for a celebration. You'll understand though that the *Vital Spark* herself wass not then the handsome sight she is noo. She wass chust aal hull, wi' not even the wheelhouse on her, never mind a bonny bleck-topped scarlet lum, nor a gold bead, nor a smert boot-topping.

"For aal that, she was a splendid specimen o' the builder's skill, and Jeck and I were fair proud when we climbed the wooden ladder onto the deck ready for the ceremony.

"There wass a crowd like an execution to see her launched and the banks o' the canal, and the brudge ower it, were bleck wi' people, and there was ass many more hangin' oot the windows of effery building that gave a view of the yerd and the shup.

"There wass a wee wooden platform built up at the bow of the vessel to chust below deck level and on this wass the heid shupwright, and the owner of the *Vital Spark*: and his dochter, a bonnie gyurl of about 20 or thereby who wass goin' to name her and break the bottle on her bows.

"On the far bank wass aal the pupils from the local school who'd been brocht to see the launchin' and the teachers wass havin' some chob keeping them back from the edge, which aye got swamped wi' a sort of tidal wave whenever a shup wass slupped.

"The lassie said her wee speech and named the shup, and the men wi' the axes cut the last twa ropes holdin' her on the slup and doon she went. There wass twa chains attached to her at the bow and the stern, and from there to rings on the slup, so that they would bring her up short o' the far bank.

"Suddenly there wass a terrible cracking sound frae the

bows and afore Jeck or I or McCulloch could move, the wee platform sterted to fall ower, wi' the gyurl and her faither and the yerd's man on it. I found oot later that some fool had fankled the drag chain roond wan o' the legs o' the platform and when the shup went oot wi' the chain, it pulled the leg aff like snappin' a twig.

"Well, the owner and the man frae the yerd chumped for the deck o' the shup, but the lassie never thocht to do that and she wass thrown into the watter.

"The rest of us wass so ta'en aback wi' aal this we chust stood and gawped, but Jeck moved like lightnin'. Quick ass a flash he threw his jecket off and dived into the canal, and caught hold of the gyurl and swum ashore wi' her.

"Aal the croods wass cheerin' by this time, and ass he cam' up the slup cerryin' the gyurl in his arms it wass chust like a scene oot of wan o' Macphail's novelles. The gyurl's mither ran to hug the lassie and her faither wass shakin' Jeck's hand ass if he wass pumpin' beer, and clappin' him on the back.

"The upshot wass that the actual launch o' the boat wass herdly noticed in the papers, but they wass aal full o' the exploits o' Jeck, and his photie wass on maist of the front pages under headlines like 'Hero of Canal Rescue' and 'Seaman Risks Life to Save Drowning Girl'. Oh aye, he wass the man of the moment in Gleska all right.

"So it cam' as no surprise at aal when the next day Jeck wass summoned to the owner's office in Gleska, and told that he had been chosen to be Captain o' the *Vital Spark*, wi' me ass his mate."

"That wass a lucky break for Jeck," said Dougie.

"There wass little enough luck aboot it," said Para Handy, "ass I found oot soon enough.

"I had my suspicions at the time, but it wass the next weekend that I walked into wan o' the Kirkintilloch pubs and found Jack in very close conversation wi' wan o' the riveters frae the yerd. Neither o' them saw me: but I saw Jeck slip the man a pound note, and thank him roundly. I knew then chust what had happened, Jeck had got the man to fankle the chain round the leg o' the platform. And stood by either to catch the gyurl, if she chumped: or dive in to save her if she didn't: reckonin' — and he wass right — that her faither would be that grateful he wouldna look past Jeck for the skipper's chob.'

"Whit a cheatin' rascal," cried Sunny Jim. "Could ye no'

hae telt the owner the truth?"

Para Handy pursed his lips, and then sighed. "Och no, Jum. It wass a ploy that wass chust typical o' Jeck's natural agility at the time — and you couldna grudge him that it had the outcome he wass hopin' for when he'd had the imachination and the foresight to pit the whole thing in place.

"Besides, if ye must know, I had plans o' my ain along similar lines.

"I'd arranged wi' McCulloch the engineer to fake a biler explosion when we wass givin' the owner his first trial run on the vessel efter the launch so that I could play the hero by divin' below tae rescue him.

"Jeck chust beat me to it, that was aal. Ass I should have known aal along he would, for you must mind he has aalways been a man of the greatest sagacity and deviosity — not tae mention sheer dam' umpidence as weel!"

*FACTNOTE*

The majority of the puffers were indeed built in the smaller, specialised yards established on the banks of the Forth and Clyde Canal. As well as those at Kirkintilloch there were others at Maryhill and Port Dundas.

The puffers were derived from canal-based craft and were originally built to operate on the canals, hence the restriction on their size dictated by the maximum dimensions of the locks through which they would have to pass. Even when they were intended for a working life on the Firth, there was still a limit on overall length — at about 75ft — for the boats which were actually built on the canal, as they had to navigate 13 locks between Maryhill and Bowling in order to reach the river.

Of the two Kirkintilloch builders, Hay's was the older, and also had a longer life-span. The first steam vessel from that yard was launched in 1869: the last, the puffer *Chindit*, in 1945. All but a handful of the dozens of vessels built by the yard over three quarters of a century were for the Hay family themselves, in their 'other' role as by far the largest owners and operators of puffers.

Some licence has been taken in the description of the launching of the *Vital Spark*. Though it is probable that the very first boats built on the canal were indeed built on its banks and then launched directly into it, very soon Hay's (and their rivals, McGregor's) had excavated basins and slips accessed from the canal: and future construction and launch took place there. However, the puffers (and other vessels) built in the yards were indeed sent down the slips sideways: and a launch was always something of an 'event' for the community, drawing large crowds to every vantage point.

No licence has been taken, however, in referring to the story of the unfortunate *Principesa Jolanda*. She was a two-funnelled liner of 9200 tons gross, 486ft in length, and (intended to operate a scheduled service on the Genoa to Buenos Aires run for Lloyd Italiano) she was launched on September 21st 1907. With masts and funnels in place, and dressed overall with flags and bunting, she slid majestically down the launch-ways, took the water with some aplomb, slewed 90 degrees off course, listed heavily and dramatically to starboard: and sank. In Williams and Kerbech's *Damned by Destiny* (Teredo Books, 1982) there is a splendid series of photographs capturing the whole sorry episode, from the confidence of the naming ceremony to her final, inglorious submersion.

No attempt was made to salvage her. At low tides, she was broken up for scrap where she lay.

# 21

## *Rock of Ages*

Para Handy looked up at the great wall of rock towering above the little puffer with an expression of admiration mixed with wonder. "My Chove," he said, "she's a whupper, iss she not! It's only when you're in this close that you realise chust how big she really iss! From scenes like these ..."

The *Vital Spark* was edging in under the looming shadow of Ailsa Craig, the great granite rock which stands sentinel at the entrance to the Firth of Clyde. 'Paddy's Milestone' has been for centuries the welcome confirmation of safe arrival at the estuary not merely for the seamen from Ireland who originally bestowed its nickname upon it, but for mariners from every country in the world.

However, though the puffer had often had Ailsa Craig in plain sight as she rounded the Mull of Kintyre on her journeys to and from Islay, or coughed her way into Girvan harbour for a load of Ayrshire coal, this was the first time she had had occasion to be so close to the remarkable monolith. Only three quarters of a mile in length, it soared to a 1100ft peak: sheer cliffs on the western side, but with a spit of rock and shingle on the east where the *Vital Spark* now found herself.

Her destination was the small jetty which served the rock's tiny permanent population, and periodic visitors. The residents were the lighthouse keepers and their families, and a tenant crofter who raised a handful of cattle and sheep, and grew a few vegetables. The occasional visitors, whose presence on the island right now were the reason for the puffer's visit, were the Ayrshire quarrymen who were from time to time contracted to extract a quantity of the fine granite for which the islet was world-famous.

~

Two of them were standing on the jetty as the *Vital Spark* came alongside, one wearing the traditional badge-of-office of the foreman, a rather battered bowler hat.

"You're late," said this worthy, without preamble. "We expected ye twa hoors ago."

"Chust so," replied Para Handy without rancour, "but what you contracted for wass the *Vital Spark*, no' the *Glen Sannox*. We are not exactly runnin' to a schedule."

"In fact," came a voice from the engine-room at his feet, "wi' the state o' this machinery it's a miracle we're runnin' at all!"

"Pay no attention to Macphail, chentlemen," said the Captain, unperturbed, "for bein' cooped up in that cubby-hole aal hoors of the day would turn anybody soft in the head."

Four hours later, her cargo of granite blocks in place, the puffer cast off from the jetty at Ailsa Craig and headed north towards Arran and her ultimate destination, the James Watt dock in Greenock.

"That's gey fantoosh stane tae be used for buildin' hooses in Greenock," observed Sunny Jim.

"Good heavens, it iss not going to be used to build anything at aal, Jum," exclaimed the Captain. "Surely you ken that Ailsa granite iss the nameliest there iss for makin' curlin' stanes, and they're sent aal over the world!"

"They must be weel thocht of stanes, then," said Jim, "if it's worth the labour o' folk tae go cairtin' them aboot the place like that. Who foond oot aboot them in the first case, oot on the Ailsa rock like that?"

"It will have been wan o' they gee-oligists, Jum. Like the man we saw last week at Furnace, the Englishman that wass stayin' at the Inn, and had thae sacks o' rock samples stored in the cellars, and him oot first thing every mornin' wi' his wee hammer and awa' along tae the quarries, afore they sterted blastin' for the day, to knock more lumps oot o' them."

"Whit's the point o' it all," asked Sunny Jim. "Whit dae they dae wi' the rocks when they've got them tae wherever they're takin' them?"

"Tae judge from the quality of coals we're gettin' on this

shup nooadays," observed Macphail, appearing at the wheelhouse door wiping his hands with an oily rag, "Ah doot they sell them aff cheap tae the coal yards, and whenever the merchants get an order frae the Glesga office tae fill the bunkers on the *Vital Spark* then they jist pit wan sack o' rocks in the cairt for every wan sack o' coals."

"There's times I think you could be right at that, Dan," said the Captain. "When I saw the rubbish we wass being given last week by MacFadyen's man at Craigendoran, I wass nearly sendin' for the local polisman to put MacFadyen on a cherge. There wass mair rock in it than I've seen in many of the shup's cargoes of roadstone!

"What they really do wi' it, Jum, iss to tak' it awa' and study it."

"Study it!" cried Sunny Jim. "Why dae folk want tae study a bit o' rock for guidness sake!"

"I don't know aal the ins and oots of it," admitted Para Handy with a shrug, "but it'll be for museums and the like. Then again maybe that's how they cam' to find oot in the first place that there iss good slate at Ballachulish and Seil Island, and tip-top granite at Ailsa Craig and at Furnace, and roadstone at Alexandria and aal the rest. Wee men in plus-fowers and sonsy bunnets crawlin' aal ower the country and chust chip-chippin' awa wi' their hammers, and takin' great lumps of Scotland hame in their luggage when they're done. Nae wonder folk are aalways sayin' the country's no' half whit it was fufty years ago!

"Hurricane Jeck met up wi' wan o' them when we wass laid over in Portree for a day or two a few years ago, and sent him home wi' aal the wrang ideas aboot Skye, that's for sure …

～

"It wass this way," he continued in a moment, once his pipe was going to his satisfaction, and the puffer had run the cheeky gauntlet of half-a-dozen youths in hired rowing-boats off Millport Bay. "Jeck and me wass crewin' a puffer that belonged to a man in Brodick, and we had gone to Skye wi' a cargo of early Arran potatos, and to pick up a load of peats for wan o' the Campbeltown distilleries.

"There wass a delay in gettin' the cargo in. I think mebbe it wass a deleeberate delay, for the skipper wass a Skye man and he chust went off hame for a few days, leavin' Jeck and me and the boy in the harbour at Portree.

"Jeck and I spent some time in the inns at Portree till oor money ran oot and it wass there that we met wi' this English gee-oligist. He was a hermless enough fellow, but there wass nothin' to him, he wass aboot five foot two in hiss stockin' soles and ass skinny ass a Tiree chicken. Effery mornin' he'd be off first thing wi' a hammer and an empty sack and effery evenin' he'd come staggerin' back into Portree bent double wi' the weight of whateffer he'd pit in it that day.

"It wass peetiful! There wass times you wud think he wud drop on the spot!

"Wan night he wass that trauchled that Jeck went up from the boat and gave him a hand to get the sack to his Hotel, and pit it in the cellar wi' aal the rest he'd collected. There wass mair than a dozen of them, aal whuppers, wi' big labels roond their necks sayin' where the rocks in them were from, and whit day he'd foond them.

"The upshot wass that he offered Jeck a chob for the next day to go out with him and help fill his samples and then, come the evenin', cairry them back to Portree. Five shullings he offered and Jeck chumped at it, for we wass oot of money except for a couple of coppers and some foreign coins the Portree Inns wudna take. 'I'll split the money wi' you, Peter', says Jeck: 'You stay here and keep an eye oot for our peats comin', and I'll go and help the mannie.'

"Next mornin' Jeck wass up at the crack o' dawn and up to the Hotel, and I saw the two of them headin' off, the mannie wi' a wee knapsack and his hammers, and Jeck wi' two huge empty sacks draped ower his shoulders.

"Six o'clock at night, Jeck appeared on the quayside and you wud not think he had walked a yard nor cairried a pound for he wass as fresh ass a daisy: but you must remember he wass at the height of his powers at the time, full of natural sagacity and energy, built like a brick oothoose and with the strength of three.

" 'You're lookin' quite jocko, Jeck,' says I, ass we made oor way along the harbour towards the Inns. 'It wass not too hard a day then?'

" 'It could have been,' says Jeck. 'Wud ye believe we went aal the way to Sligachan, a good eight miles along the main road, and then off we go into the hills and he leaps aboot the rocks wi' thon hammer hammerin' awa', and he fills the sacks till I could scarce lift them off the ground. He says it makes sich a difference havin' a fine strong chap to do the cairryin', and for sure he took advantage of it!

" 'When it comes to dinner-time and I'm thinkin' the least he can do iss tak' me and treat me at the Sligachan Inn, here he ups and opens the wee knapsack and brings oot some bread and cheese and two bottles of milk. *Milk*!

" 'Towards fower o'clock, when the sacks are full to the very top wi' lumps o' rock of effery shape and size and description, he thanks me very politely for my services, and gives me the five shullin's we'd agreed on for the feein'.

" 'Then he says that he'll go back to Portree the long way roond, takin' the track that runs along the coast beside the Sound of Raasay: but that I can chust tak' the main road hame for the sake of speed and comfort. So I did, and so here I am. There's no sign of him back at the Hotel yet but his sacks is aal safely snugged doon and labelled in his cellar.'

" 'You look very fit on it, onyway,' says I. 'The sacks couldna have been aal that heavy for you look chust ass fresh ass when you set off and there iss no' ass much ass an ounce of perspiration on you.'

" 'There would have been, if I'd let it,' said Jeck. 'But did ye think I wass goin' to be daft enough to hump half of Sligachan eight miles up the road to Portree? Wan stane is like any ither stane ass far ass I can tell, so I chust waited till he wass well oot o' sight and then I emptied the sacks oot at the roadside at Sligachan, hung them round my neck, and when I got back to the town I filled them up again wi' rocks from yon big pile of roadstone lyin' at the pierhead.

" 'He'll neffer ken the difference ...' "

*FACTNOTE*

Lying at the mouth of the Firth nine miles west of Girvan Bay, Ailsa Craig has become familiar to anyone in the UK who has ever watched transmission of the Open Golf Tournament from the nearby Turnberry links. Cameras make a habit of zooming in on the dramatic silhouette of the rock when there is not much happening on the course!

For decades the very best curling stones were indeed regarded as those made from Ailsa granite. There was little else of any material value on the islet, though it was tenanted from the Earls of Cassilis, into whose estates it fell, for a tiny rental which, at least till the beginning of last cen-

THE ARRAN CONNECTION — *Here in all her late Victorian, splendour is the Glasgow and South Western Railway Company's* Glen Sannox, *which gave 33 years service on the Ardrossan to Brodick crossing, her speed helping to reduce the Glasgow to Arran journey to under 90 minutes. She ran her trials on 1st June 1892 and it is probable that this photograph was taken then. This is obviously a 'new' vessel, and there are no members of the public on board.*

tury, was paid in kind — young gannets for the table, and seabird feathers and down for bedding and cushions. It was still tenanted just a generation or so ago, but the fisherman's summer bothies, the remains of which can still be seen on the north-east coast, have been deserted for much longer.

Most of the eminent travellers in Scotland, from Monro in the 16th century onwards, have visited and been overawed by the rock. Many of them, coincidentally, were geologists — though their travels were not solely motivated by that specialised branch of science. John McCulloch, who criss-crossed the Western Highlands and Islands in the first two decades of the 19th century, has left the most comprehensive account. Much of it may be almost unreadably turgid but nobody, not even Pennant in the late 18th or Muir in the late 19th centuries, covered so much ground. McCulloch visited virtually every rock and atoll in the north west and left a unique account of their society as well as their geology in four volumes published in 1820.

It is interesting how early travellers in Scotland seemed to come in surprisingly well-defined categories in an evolutionary progression.

The enquiring — such as Monro or Martin. The curious — Johnson or Boswell. The polymaths — Pennant or Garnett. The geologists — Jamieson or McCulloch. The antiquarians — Cordiner or Grose. The economists — Newte or Anderson. The historians — Selkirk or Logan. The natural historians — Kearton or Harvie-Brown.

And (at regular intervals) the downright eccentric, such as the formidable Englishwoman, the Honourable Mrs Murray Aust of Kensington, who undertook a journey through the Highlands which included the crossing of the notorious 2,200 feet Corrieyairack pass from the Spey Valley to the Great Glen *in a post-chaise carriage and pair*, and wrote a two volume account (published in 1810) to prove it!

# 22

## *Taking the Needle*

Para Handy stared, fascinated, at the approaching figure of the *Vital Spark's* engineer. "My Chove boys,
come and take a look at this! What on earth hass
Dan been up to?" The *Vital Spark* was berthed in
Campbeltown, and Macphail had just appeared in sight
staggering along the quayside with a large square wooden
contraption cradled in both arms, his face only just visible
peering over the top of it. Behind him came a man carrying
in one hand what looked like an oversize megaphone and in
the other a large brown suitcase.

"It looks like he went to that hoose sale right enough,"
Dougie observed, "and it looks ass if he bought the half of it
ass well."

Indeed, his eye caught by an advertisement in that
week's issue of the *Campbeltown Courier*, Macphail had at
breakfast announced his intention of attending a roup taking place that morning, at which the effects of a recently-
deceased citizen of the burgh were to be sold at auction.
Para Handy and Dougie had had enough of auctions for the
time being, following a couple of unfortunate experiences at
such occasions in the recent past and Sunny Jim was, as
usual, suffering from a chronic shortage of funds. So the
engineer had gone off on his own, announcing that he
would stay just a few minutes "for the entertainment
value".

"It seems you got more than chust entertainment then,
Dan," the Captain observed as the engineer puffed his way
on board and, with a sigh of relief, laid his burden on the
hatch-cover of the hold. His companion did the same, and
then, after a short consultation during which a few coins

changed hands, scrambled up onto the quayside and made off.

"What on earth is aal this?" Dougie asked as Macphail picked up the giant 'megaphone' and inserted its narrow end into a metal-rimmed hole in the top of the wooden box. This itself had, let into one side, a brass handle which was in shape something like a miniature version of the handle on the puffer's anchor winch and on the top, a circular plate with a convoluted brass contraption alongside it.

"What d'ye think," asked Macphail sharply. "It's a grammyphone, of course."

"And what might that be when it's at hame?" asked Para Handy.

"For peety's sake," said the exasperated Macphail. "D'ye live in the Erk or somethin'? Grammyphones is a' the rage in the big hooses nooadays. Listen and I'll show ye!"

And opening the leather case to reveal a stack of black shellac records, he pulled one out, set it on the turntable on top of the instrument, birled the handle to wind up the spring-driven motor, swung the playing arm over and carefully lowered the needle into its groove.

A tinny version of *Rule Britannia*, sung by an enthusiastic but breathless soprano who sounded as if somebody was standing on her foot, blared from the horn of the gramophone and across the harbour. Heads turned to stare at the *Vital Spark* from all directions.

Para Handy, Dougie and Sunny Jim retreated towards the puffer's bow.

"My Cot," said the Captain. "Whateffer wull they think of next? How on earth do they get the wumman to fit into the box — never mind the baun'!"

"Very funny," said Macphail sarcastically. "Ye ken fine hoo it works, ye've seen them aften enough in the shops.

"It's the thing o' the future! A concert hall in every hoose! A few years frae noo the harmonium and the piano wull be things o' the past. Nae mair frien's an' relations makin' eejits o' themselves tryin' tae play choons they cannae play and wraxin' tae sing sangs their voices wisnae built for. Instead a'body can hae entertainment tae suit every taste at their command jist so lang as they hiv plenty o' these!" And reaching into a small recess on the top of the machine beside the turntable, he held up a small, fancily-decorated tin full of tiny needles.

Sunny Jim, meanwhile, was picking through the selection of records in the leather case.

"There's no mich here for the likes o' us, Dan," he said. "This all looks gey highbrow stuff tae me. Who's Dame Nellie Melba and whit's an operetta when it's at hame? Whit aboot Dan Leno or Marie Lloyd, or even some Harry Lauder? And I dinna see onythin' that wid be suitable for a baal or a soiree. Nae Gay Gordons, nae Dashing White Sergeant: jist waltzes and polkas an' that."

"Exactly," said Macphail, whose ideas of the appropriate sort of musical taste for a gentleman to assume had been honed and moulded by many years acquaintance with the glamorous world of his penny novelettes. "That's the point! None o' this popular trash, jist class, class at yer fingertips!"

"Cless!" said Dougie pointedly. "I've no' had a cless since I left the school and I'm no' stertin' noo! Jum's right, this iss aal right for the chentry, but it's no' the same as a good birl on the melodeon, when Jum's in good trum."

"Nor better nor yoursel' on the trump," conceded Para Handy generously. "Mony's the spree we've had with them both."

"Jist wait you and see," said Macphail defensively. "Every hoose in the land will hae yin o' these afore lang. And besides ye can get every type o' music ye care tae think of for it, so if ye wantit onything at a', from the Hokey Cokey to the Reel o' Tulloch, ye wud jist awa' oot and buy it."

"Fair enough," said Jim, "if ye could afford it! But there'll aye be a place for the melodeon, and the trump come tae that."

~

Over the next few days, though, the Mate and Sunny Jim became more enamoured of the new-fangled plaything and for most of the time the puffer was on passage, the instrument sat on the hatch-way and blared out a selection chosen from a collection of records which proved, if nothing else, that their departed owner had been a man of eclectic, not to say strange, tastes.

Only Para Handy remained aloof, and lost no opportunity to play down the worth of the new acquisition, and stress the value of having available for entertainment purposes on board any vessel such extempore live musicians as Dougie and Jim.

The performances of Macphail's travelling open air

concert-hall received what the newspaper columnists would have referred to as 'mixed reviews'. Some of the river traffic detoured towards the puffer in search of the source of the mysterious sounds but others beat a very hasty retreat to distance themselves as much as possible from it.

Which reaction occurred, and how quickly, usually depended on what particular record was in concert at the time. Italian opera did not, as a general rule, go down very well with either mariners or yachtsmen on the Firth: American brass band music on the other hand was very much more popular — and nothing more so than *Liberty Bell*, which acted like a magnet for approaching vessels and which, as a result, Macphail aired so frequently and repeatedly that Para Handy remarked that in no time at all the groove would be worn right through to the other side of the gramophone record.

Matters came to a head at Arrochar, where the *Vital Spark* arrived one Saturday afternoon to discover that a dance was being held that evening in the village hall. Jim was sent ashore to acquire tickets for all, and the senior members of the ship's company spent a couple of hours on a toilet as elaborate as it was unusual.

"Look at the three o' ye," said Jim sardonically, "three merrit men that should ken better gettin' all spruced up tae dance wi' lassies young enough tae be yer ain dochters! You should tak' shame at it!"

"What you should take shame at, Jum, iss the way you aalways cairry yon melodeon wi' you to the country soirees, for you ken fine that you'll aye be asked to perform when the band iss at its refreshments, and it gives you a shameless chance to flirt wi' aal the gyurls and impress them wi' your general agility on the unstriment!" retorted the Captain. And sure enough, Jim had already looked his melodeon out and was wiping it with a cloth to bring out the shine on its brass fittings.

"Not," continued the skipper, "that I aaltogether begrudge you that, Jum, for you're a better player than maist of the bands and I fair enchoy a good selection on the melodeon myself!"

~

The crew's consternation, therefore, when they reached the Hall to find that the band which had been booked had not arrived on the steamer from Helensburgh, and that the organisers were thus intending to cancel the event, may be imagined.

Macphail was the first to recover his composure.

"There is no need for that at all," he said. "For on the shup Ah've got a cracker o' a grammyphone, wi' a fine selection o' music. Jist gi'e me the len' o' a couple o' your chaps tae get it up here and this'll be the best soiree Arrochar ever had!"

And so, indeed, it seemed.

The vaunted instrument — or 'implement' as Para Handy had now christened it — was indeed a great hit with the folk of the village, and Macphail found himself the unaccustomed centre of attention of a flattering coterie of ladies — young, and not so young.

Sunny Jim, who had taken his melodeon back down to the puffer in despair earlier in the evening, looked on in disgust.

"Stole my thunder, so he has," he complained. "And him a merrit man that age! Arrochar's aye taken kindly to my melodeon in the past but the nicht, they never even wantit it!"

And he went to sulk at the far end of the hall and sat with his back to the posturing engineer.

~

Five minutes later Para Handy tapped him on the shoulder and winked in conspiratorial fashion.

"Jum, I think it would be no' a bad idea if you wass to go on doon to the shup and retrieve your melodeon. You could bring Dougie's trump at the same time, for there's goin' to be a demand for some real music here in a few minutes, and it wudna be fair if you had to play aal night. You should be allowed to enchoy the dancin' too, and I know fine that Dougie wull be only too pleased to spell you every noo and then so that you can have a circuit or two o' the floor wi' some o' the gyurls."

"Chance wud be a fine thing," said Jim. "Naebody wants the trump or the melodeon so long as Dan's holdin' court wi' thon portable concert-hall."

"Ah," said Para Handy, "but that's the whole point, Jum. I have a feelin' that Dan's reign is chust aboot drawin' to a close and that we'll no' be hearin' much more from his band-box the night."

"Whit way?" asked the mystified Jim. "Is it broken?"

"No, nor broken," said Para Handy. "But I think he is chust on the point of runnin' oot o' these ..." And he thrust his opened right hand under Jim's nose. On the palm rested the brightly coloured tin of gramophone needles.

"Look lively then, Jum. Fortune favours the bold!"

*FACTNOTE*

Edison registered his patent for a 'sound-recording' machine in August 1877, yet for the next 20 years the invention was regarded as little more than a curiosity and little effort was made to commercialise it.

During this period, the cylindrical record was superseded by the new disc record, carried on a turntable: the earliest of these were a mere seven inches in diameter. Not till 1904 was the first machine with an 'internal' loudspeaker manufactured. Till then, all instruments were of the type immortalised in HMV's famous logo of a horn gramophone and a listening dog.

Grove's *Dictionary of Music and Musicians* affirms that in those early years 'various well-known musicians played or sang into the instrument, but they did so more or less for the fun of the thing: there was no attempt to market or duplicate their efforts.' Then when commercial production started in the early years of this century 'it was found that powerful notes caused trouble with the primitive instruments of the day' and that 'the grooves in which such notes occurred were liable to rapid wear'. So Para Handy wasn't altogether mistaken in his comments with regard to the possible foibles of Macphail's machine!

Puffer crews often carried their own entertainment, in the form of musical instruments. Melodeons were a popular smaller version of accordions — both of which were relatively recent creations. The humbler 'trump' or 'Jew's Harp', to give it its proper name, was by contrast an instrument of very considerable antiquity and surprising universality as well. There were many and various forms of this small, horseshoe-shaped gadget with its vibrating metallic tongue, held between the teeth and played by striking with the fingers and using the lips to create notes of a different pitch. Almost unheard-of in this country today, forms of the 'trump' have been known throughout Europe, Asia, and the

Far East for centuries, and it can be seen depicted in Chinese illuminated manuscripts of 900 years ago. It briefly ranked as a serious orchestral instrument in Europe in the early 1800s with acclaimed soloists performing recitals — and even a concerto — on the orchestral platform.

Harry Lauder, born in 1870, was enjoying a worldwide reputation by the early years of this century which, given the lack of any seriously-marketed gramophone records, was quite remarkable — a reputation built up, literally, by word of mouth. Originally a miner, he quickly established himself — both as singer and as raconteur — as the archetypal 'pawky Scot' and toured the world from the USA to Australia, with considerable and constant success. He died in Strathaven, Lanarkshire in 1950.

# 23

## *High Life at Hunter's Quay*

Low tide at Sandbank often produces a spectacle which is most unlikely to conjure thoughts of a glamorous maritime career in the imaginations of any passing landlubber.

The world-renowned boatyards of the Holy Loch village may be the cradle of some of the finest racing yachts ever constructed but the men working on the sleek speedsters taking shape on the slipways are treated almost daily to a timely reminder of the more mundane side of life at sea.

When the tide ebbs it exposes, at the head of the loch, a far from romantic stretch of sandflats (from which the village of course takes its name) to which the puffers are regular visitors. Slipping in at high tide, they are left high and dry as the water recedes, lying throughout the ebb period like stranded whales, their steam winches busy as the crews employ specially-designed grabs to load a cargo of sand before the tide creeps back in.

The value of such a cargo is slight — but the cost of acquiring it (apart from the aching backs and blistered hands of the crews) is nil, and there are always builders and contractors in need of large quantities of coarse sand for construction projects up and down the Firth.

~

The crew of the *Vital Spark* loathed coming into Holy Loch. The job of loading the cargo of sand was hard and dirty work and had to be carried out at speed if it was to be completed in time to the movement of the tide. Worse, the Sandbank Inn was tantalisingly close at hand but quite unreachable, for if you were to stroll across to it on the dried-out sand of the ebb, then by the time you were ready to return, you would need a dinghy to take you back to your boat across the flooding tide.

One June afternoon the puffer, after unloading 50 tons of coal at Ardnadam, came up to the head of the loch on the flood and, as the tide neared the foot of the ebb, got ready to take on board a cargo of sand for delivery to Bowling.

Macphail attended to the steam-winch, Dougie attached the steel sand-grab to the pulley of the crane, and Sunny Jim took the boards off the main hatch. Para Handy, as befitted the status of Captain, surveyed all these preparations from the relative comfort of the wheelhouse.

There were three other puffers beached close to hand and soon the clatter of steam-winches and clang of sand-grabs echoed off the hillsides. As the day drew on a change in the weather was plainly imminent: a breeze got up, the clouds closed in and there was a hint of rain in the air. By the time the job was done, it was gone seven o'clock: as the *Vital Spark* began to lift off the sea-bed on the incoming tide, Para Handy came to a decision he he had been contemplating for some time.

"Boys, " he said, "we will chust stay in the cheneral area for the night. I dinna much care for the idea of pickin' oor way up river wi' no freeboard on her in dreich-lookin' conditions like this. We'll go back doon to Hunter's Quay and tie up overnight after the last steamer hass been in, and mak' a snappy start in the mornin' to get hame by dinner time."

A shouted consultation with the skippers of the other three boats ended with them all agreeing to do the same, and at eight o'clock the four puffers weighed anchor and headed in convoy towards the mouth of the loch.

∽

The paddler *Madge Wildfire* had just made the final call of the day and was pulling away from Hunter's Quay pier as the little flotilla of puffers came hiccupping round the point from Hafton House.

On the beach to the west of the pier were jetties serving the Royal Clyde Yachting Club, whose imposing clubhouse towered above the shore road and gave broad panoramas up river. Half a dozen racing yachts rode at their moorings in the bay and on any normal day would themselves have been a fine and imposing sight. But this evening they were dwarfed into insignificance by a vessel anchored just beyond them in the mouth of the loch.

"My Chove," said Para Handy in admiration. "Issn't that the beauty! She's a whupper and no mistake!"

The vessel in question was indeed magnificent. Almost as big as the *Madge Wildfire*, she actually managed to look bigger, thanks to the optical illusion provided by her soaring masts. She was a white-hulled, three-masted, topsail schooner, with a bright yellow funnel proclaiming her auxiliary steam power.

Macphail stuck his head out of the engine-room. "That's the *Sunbeam*," he said. "Earl Brassey's yat. I read in the paper she wis comin' intae the Clyde. She's on a roond-the-world cruise."

"Chust so," said the Captain. "Well then, we wull go and tak' a roond-the-yat cruise, for I want a closer peek at her." And he spun the wheel to port and headed for the anchored ship. The three other puffers, their crews apparently more interested in the attractions of the Hunter's Quay Inn than those of the sailing ship, kept on course for the pier.

As the *Vital Spark* approached the yacht, a small steam launch was being lowered from her davits and a party of what looked to be very important people indeed was descending the companionway slung over the starboard side. "That'll be Earl Brassey himself," Para Handy surmised, "and the chentry that's sailin' wi' him."

To his considerable surprise, as he circled the *Sunbeam* at a respectable distance, the yacht's steam tender chuffed over to the puffer and began to circle round it. Para Handy was first bashful, then flattered, to realise the *Vital Spark* was under scrutiny through binoculars by the gentry seated in the launch.

"Man Dougie," he said. "Haven't I aalways say that the shup iss too good for the tred the owner hass her in? They think we're the *King Edward* and they want to tak' a look at turbine power in action!"

After a couple of circuits round the puffer, the launch pulled away and headed off at high speed for the shore, throwing out a gleaming bow wave and kicking up a great wake as she did so.

Para Handy gazed after the little boat with a somewhat wistful expression. "Or then again," he said resignedly, "maybe they were chust amusin' themselves at oor expense!"

~

The *Vital Spark* approached the main quay to find something of a confrontation in progress. The other puffers were bobbing in a semi-circle about a hundred yards off the pierhead, whence a uniformed figure, with a megaphone to his mouth, was bellowing something (Para Handy was just too far away to catch the words) to the skipper of the *Cretan*.

"Wha's yon eejit?" Macphail queried, "and whit's he bangin' on aboot tae puir Ogilvie?"

"I canna chust mak' it oot, Dan," said the Captain. "The man's the Chief Steward at the Yat Club, wan McCutcheon, I ken him by his face, but I doot he's no' givin' us aal an eenvitation to the Clubhoose for oor dinners."

A surmise which was confirmed seconds later, when the other puffers could be seen turning away from the pier and heading slowly towards the open Firth, their crews indicating their anger at the Club Steward in one or other of a variety of tried and trusted ways of so doing by means of explicit hand-signals traditional to the West of Scotland.

"You too, Para Handy" yelled the megaphone-bearer, swinging that implement towards the approaching *Vital Spark*. "This is a gentleman's club and a gentleman's pier and I'll no' have trash like you littering the quay and the foreshore. Clear aff!"

Catching sight, out of the corner of his eye, of the *Sunbeam's* launch gently manoeuvring alongside the steps at the innermost wall of the stone quay, he rushed over to catch the line thrown ashore by a white-clad crewman: shouting, as he did "Get tae blazes oot o' this, Para Handy" in the one direction, followed immediately by an obsequious "Allow me to be of service, Earl Brassey!" in the other.

"My Chove," said Para Handy from the door of the wheelhouse, "there's a man that dearly loves a Lord, and is sore in need of bein' taken doon a peg or two. But to be honest, it hass been a long day and I am no' in trum for an altercation wi' McCutcheon right noo, hiss turn wull come! Dan! Let's head for home!"

But, as he turned back and seized the wheel, he was astonished to hear a conciliatory, one could almost say a grovelling voice on the megaphone.

"Er, Captain Macfarlane," enunciated McCutcheon in the strangulated voice with which he tried to impress people, and which he reserved for his dealings with the gentry: "would you be so kind as to lay your ship alongside the pier? Earl Brassey would like to have a word..."

Sure enough, while the main party from the yacht waited at the top of the stairs, the moustachiod peer strolled across to the head of the quay accompanied by a tall, angular man with a mane of white hair, and a smaller, sturdy man with a huge plate camera slung across his shoulder and a large wooden box full of its paraphernalia clutched in one hand.

~

An hour later the crew were sat round a table in the bar of the Hunter's Quay Hotel. On it, as well as four dram glasses and four beer glasses (all appropriately filled), were two golden sovereigns, glinting in the light of the tilley-lamps.

"My Chove," said the Captain. "Now there wass a true chentleman and no mistake.

"But what for did he want all those photies? Yon man wass snap snap-snappin' awa' for the best part of an hoor aal over the shup. Wheelhoose, hold, enchine-room, the fo'c'sle — above aal, the fo'c'sle. You would think we wass savidges on a sooth sea island rather than chust some o' Brutain's hardy sons gaun' aboot their daily business...

"And ass for the questions thon white haired mannie asked? Whit a cheek! And in any case, whit's an anthro...anthripolijist when it's at hame? Whit did the Earl mean when he said tae him that there wass mair to wonder at on yer ain front doorstep than there wass in the farthest outposts o' cuvileesation? And why did Brassey keep sayin' — the impertinunce o' it — that the shup was chust junk in British watters and shud be preserved for posterity or folk wudna believe it?"

"Not 'chust junk', Peter, 'chust *like* a junk', whateffer he meant by that," said Dougie.

"Onyway," said Macphail. "They wis real toffs richt enough. Twa whole sov'rins for wir trouble!"

"Aye," agreed Para Handy. "But best of aal wass the expression on McCutcheon's face when Brassey shook

hands with us aal — but ignored him!
"Some things are chust beyond price!"

Today there are few vessels in private ownership capable of worldwide deep-water cruising. Most large yachts are based in the Mediterranean, Caribbean or, rather more exotically, such fashionable Pacific islands as New Caledonia or Hawaii. But there they seem to stay, doing little more time at sea than some occasional island-hopping, as often as not used more as holiday homes and entertainment venues than as ships.

By contrast, the years at the turn of this century were the zenith of the great privately-owned ocean-going yachts, whose owners used them for ambitious voyages of many months duration to remote and inaccessible destinations as well as to the more expected or established ports-of-call worldwide. Very often places on them were available to zoologists and those of other scientific disciplines who must otherwise have had scant chance of visiting the distant islands which were their common goal.

Largest of them all was the Earl of Crawford's towering 245ft *Valhalla*, the only ship-rigged yacht in the world. Brassey's *Sunbeam*, though, was certainly the best known. For almost 40 years she spent much of her time at sea traversing the oceans of the world on an extraordinary series of voyages chronicled in her owner's book *Sunbeam RYS*, first published in 1917. His wife, who accompanied him on most of his travels, wrote her own account of them in *The Voyage of the Sunbeam*. in most years the yacht did indeed spend some time in Scottish waters either at the beginning or end of a longer voyage, or as a destination in itself.

*Sunbeam* was launched at Seacombe in Cheshire in 1875. She was 170ft overall and with all sail set carried 16,000 square yards of canvas! Lairds of Liverpool installed a 70hp auxiliary steam engine for which her bunkers carried 80 tons of coal.

The human history of the remote destinations he visited and the way of life of the (then) virtually unknown peoples and tribes he met, were a constant fascination to Brassey and his book gives many valuable accounts of strange societies, unfamiliar communities and unexpected life-styles.

The imposing clubhouse for the Royal Clyde Yacht Club

was built above the bay at Hunter's Quay in 1888, a splendid psuedo-Tudor construction totally out of character for its location. With half-timbered gables and balconies, stone tower and parapet, it is about as 'un-Scottish' as it could be yet sits magnificently in its prominent location.

Today it enjoys new life as the popular Royal Marine Hotel and is thus a social as well as an architectural landmark in the Cowal community.

*SUNBEAM, RYS — By an astonishing coincidence, the MacGrory collection contains this photo of Brassey's Sunbeam in Campbeltown Bay. Initially filed as a Naval archive (for obvious reasons) this is beyond doubt that remarkable ocean-traveller, as a comparison with a plate in the Earl's own book confirms. The crew of the launch are not in naval uniform but the yacht's own issue, and were this a naval scene the launch would be flying an ensign. The Sunbeam was in Scottish waters 10 times between 1897 and 1909.*

# 24

## *Flags of Convenience*

I
t was one of the puffer's periodic visits to Bridge Wharf
in the centre of the city of Glasgow, and an urchin
appeared at the quayside with a letter in his hand, the
envelope carefully addressed to 'The Captain, Steam
Lighter *Vital Spark*, Glasgow' on one of the new typing
machines which were sweeping all before them in the city
offices.

"My Chove," said Para Handy, perusing the contents with
an increasingly puzzled expression, "whit a fine kettle of
fush!"

"What is it, Peter," asked the Mate anxiously. "Is it from
the owner? He surely hassna been and sold the boat over
oor heads?"

"Sold the boat!" came a splutter from the engine-room,
where Dan Macphail was busy with oil-can and wrench trying to make good a leaking joint in the shaft-casing. "Of
course he's no' sold the boat: he couldnae gi'e it awa' as a
prize for a Good Templar's raffle!"

"Pay no attention to him, Dougie: he's been in a paddy
ever since John Hay's *Spartan* overtook us at Bowling this
mornin' chust after he'd been blawin' aboot the difference
he'd made to our speed since he'd cleaned oot the tubes o'
the biler.

"No, the letter iss not from the owner, though he iss the
cause of it, it's from the Board of Tred. They are holdin'
some sort of classes aboot — how do they cry it?" IIe
opened the letter up again, " 'signalling procedures'. The
owner hass volunteered me to go to them. The Board iss
sayin' that the coastal tred iss no keepin' up wi' new methods and there have been too many accidents caused by

poor signals at sea, or by shups that dinna understand them at aal.

"The upshot of it aal iss that he iss buying a complete set of signal flags for the *Vital Spark*, and I have to learn how to use them, and then they say I must teach you laads the whole whigmaleerie ass weel!"

"It iss a liberty!" exclaimed the Mate. "The *Vital Spark* hass never been in any trouble! You've aalways had a grand voice for bellowin' wi', Peter, and that's all the signals we've needed aal oor years at sea."

～

Liberty or not the owner's instructions had to be complied with and Para Handy duly presented himself the following morning at the Glasgow offices of the Maritime branch of the Board of Trade, unaccustomedly scrubbed and shaved, and kitted out in his one good pea-jacket.

"I don't like it, boys," he said as he left the puffer. "But I will not let the vessel down. A MacFarlane will neffer disgrace himself or tak' the easy way oot when it comes to representing the reputation and the good name of his shup!"

The class itself was held in an empty bay of a warehouse at the Stobcross Quay on the north bank of the river — a dusty, drab, dreich and draughty venue where were assembled some two dozen unhappy seamen, almost all skippers of steam lighters and quite without exception as resentful as Para Handy about the liberty taken in inflicting the classes upon them. Their tempers were not improved when they discovered that they would be introduced to the new mysteries, not by some veteran old salt, but by a fresh-faced youth in a grey suit and a white shirt with an Eton collar and a flower in his button-hole.

There were few of his fellow-sufferers with whom Para Handy was not well-acquainted. One however — the skipper of Hay's puffer *Spartan* whom the *Vital Spark* had by coincidence encountered on her way up river the previous day — was a particular bete-noire of the usually placid Captain.

～

"The side of the man!" complained Para Handy to his crew when he returned to the puffer for his dinner at the end of the morning session. "Aye noddin' and makin' oot he knows it aal already, and then runnin' errands for the young whipper-snapper that's takin' the cless when he needs new flags or whateffer.

"I always thought John Hay made a big mistake when he put Alec Bain in cherge o' the *Spartan* and my Chove now I know I wass right!"

"But whit aboot the class, Captain?" asked Sunny Jim. "Whit d'ye huv tae do?"

"You may well ask, Jum. Jumpin' through girrs! They have wan flag for each letter o' the elphabet but of course if you wass to use them to spell oot ony messages it wud take foreffer, so they have devised a sort of a code. You put chust two of the flags up the halyard at wance and effery pair means a different message to aal the ither pairs, and you find oot whit it is by lookin' it up in this list." At that point the Captain pulled a closely-printed sheet of paper from his jacket pocket and waved it in the air. "It's aal so unnecessary! We have managed chust fine for years withoot ony o' this rubbish!"

Sunny Jim still looked mystified.

"Let me try to explain the way of it, Jum," continued Para Handy. "If we were runnin' oot of coal, for example, what would we do aboot it at present?"

"It all depends on the cargo we're cairryin' at the time," said Jim, puzzled but trying to be helpful. "Ah mean, if it's coals we're cairryin' then ye jist send me tae the hold wi' a few sacks tae fill, for neither the merchant nor the owner'll ever fin' oot aboot it an'…"

"No, no Jum," said the Captain hastily, "that's not what I mean at aal. What do we do if we're gettin' short and we're at sea and we're not cairryin' coals…?"

"Weel, then ye'd jist bellow on the next puffer we meet and get the len' o' a bag or twa that wud see us safe to the nearest harbour," said Jim.

Para Handy beamed. "Precisely, Jim," he said. "But these dam' Board o' Trade regulations want us to put up flags for aal the world to see." He consulted the printed sheet: "The two flags you wud need fur that situation are the G and the Y — and they mean *Can you spare me coal?*"

"Whit genius thocht yon up!" snorted Macphail. "I can jist see Williamson stoppin' the *King Edward* in her tracks tae gi'e me a few shuvvles of the best Ayrshire nutty slack somewhere between Lochranza and Campbeltown, in the middle of the Gleska Trades weekend!"

"Chust so, Dan," said Para Handy. "But —" burrowing once again into the mysteries of the leaflet, "— we could maybe try flyin' the R and the H — *Can you supply me with anyone to take charge as engineer?* It wud make a pleasant change to have wan! Or maybe we wud put up the B with the J which accordin' to the list wud mean: *Engine broken down, I am disabled.* Not too unlikely for the *Vital Spark* on the days you're in bad trum, eh Dan?"

～

For the sake of peace and harmony it was probably just as well that that was the point at which Para Handy had to leave the boat to attend the afternoon session at Stobcross.

It was nearly seven o'clock before he returned, trudging along the wharf with his head down in dejection and his hands in his pockets. "Don't ask me a dam' thing till I've had my tea," he said as he stepped aboard. "I'm chust at the end my tether!"

"If I thought this mornin' was bad, boys, you should have seen this afternoon!" he commented quarter of an hour later after having disposed of a plate of fried herrings and two mugs of tea sweetened with condensed milk.

"I chust hope that the owner hass more sense than he hass money and iss not thinkin' of puttin' wan of these godless wireless contraptions on the shup, for that iss what yon young fella wass tellin' us aal about this afternoon. I do not like the sound of it aal, boys, it mean the end of the independence we aal enchoy in the coasting tred!"

"What is it, then?" asked Sunny Jim, who had heard the word bandied around in the past two or three years without having any real idea of what was involved.

"It iss almost impossible to believe," said the Captain, "but it iss chust like the telegraph, except there iss no wires to it, and your shup could be in the muddle of the Minch and the office could send you orders ass nate as anything."

"But how..." began the Mate.

"Dougie, I do not know, that's the plain truth of it. But it iss two boxes filled wi' electricity, wan for pittin' messages oot and wan for bringin' them in. It iss chust ass if you have a collie dug that big its tail iss in the office and its heid iss on the shup. So if you stand on the tail in Gleska, the heid will howl on the vessel: and if you pat its heid on board the

*Vital Spark*, its tail wags in Gleska.

"I'm tellin' you, I will have nothin' to do wi' it. If he tries to put wan of them things on the *Vital Spark* then I am takin' a chob ashore."

~

Fortunately, things did not come to this pass. The following morning, half an hour before the puffer left Glasgow bound for Skipness in Kintyre, a horse-drawn van clattered onto the quay and delivered a large black tin box addressed simply to 'Steam Lighter *Vital Spark*'.

On examination this was found to contain a complete set of 26 individual flags, one standing for each letter of the alphabet, complete with halyards and cleats for the mast together with a hard-bound copy of the printed set of codes from which Para Handy had quoted the previous day.

"No wireless, thank Cott!" exclaimed the skipper with some relief, "though these dam' things iss bad enough. Jum!! Put up the new halyards seein' they're here, and take all the rest of this rubbish to the fo'c'sle. We'll maybe peruse it at our leisure some ither time," he concluded dismissively, and the crew thought that they had probably seen and heard the last of the hated signal flags.

Not quite.

Two days later, as they were returning to Bowling having delivered their cargo of roadstone to Skipness, the *Vital Spark* came through the narrows at Colintraive and Para Handy spotted the *Spartan* in the middle distance, headed towards them, and very low in the water with a full cargo of unknown identity.

"Jum!" shouted the Captain. "Away you down to the fo'c'sle and bring oot the flags for S and P, and K and Z: and run them up the signal halyard ass fast as you can!"

"What's that aal aboot, Peter?" asked the Mate, puzzled, as the mysterious signal fluttered in the breeze.

"Och, chust a chance to get back at that man Bain and his fancy ways at the cless the ither day.

"It'll gi'e him somethin' to pause and consider aboot if no more than that — but maybe he'll be late goin' to wherever he's goin' — and serve him right! You see, I ken fine that he hassna the wireless, for he said Hay's wass not puttin' them in aal the shups because of the cost. But he doesna ken whether we have the wireless or not.

"S and P means *Have received orders for you not to proceed without further instructions*: and K and Z means *Anchor instantly*.

"If we're lucky, he may well do chust that — and I'd like to be in John Hay's office if Bain goes ashore at Colintraive and telegraphs to get those instructions."

Noticing with impish delight, as the two boats converged, that the unfortunate *Spartan* was indeed preparing to let go her anchor, Para Handy doffed his cap and waved cheerily to Bain, ignoring the other man's efforts to shout questions with a polite tap on his ear and an apologetic shrug.

The *Vital Spark* passed her at Macphail's best seven knots, and swung westwards round the tip of Bute and out of sight.

FACTNOTE

I picked up a copy of the 1904 edition of *Signalling for Board of Trade Examinations* for a few pence in a second-hand bookshop a few years ago. The little handbook, produced by the nautical publishers James Brown & Son of Glasgow, dates from the time of the watershed between the old and new ways of communication at sea.

There is a whole range of coded flag messages and those given in the story are all genuine. However, in 1899 Marconi had presented his paper on *Wireless Telegraphy* to the Institution of Electrical Engineers. It too is reprinted in the handbook and as it was published, the very first wirelesses were being installed in ships — though needless to say not in the humble puffers!

There were six shore telegraph stations set up by the Marconi Company to handle wireless communication to and from ships in the Atlantic, and 10 shipping companies including the 'big names' such as Cunard, Norddeutscher Lloyd, American Line and the French CTG, had specified wireless facilities on at least some of their passenger liners. Nevertheless, the total number of ships in the world's merchant and naval fleets so equipped (according to Marconi's own list in 1904) was still less than 50 though, of course, it would soon be being added to daily as first the convenience and then the necessity of the new technology became understood.

The James Brown handbook also details methods of ship-to-ship and ship-to-shore signalling using lamps, semaphores and quite complex (but widely understood) combinations of other masthead paraphernalia — cones, balls, cubes, coloured lights etc. The messages conveyed in signal code ranged from the banal to the dramatic and all points in between.

Thus inconsequential communications such as *Pay attention!* or *Has the mail arrived?* or *My chronometer has run down* appear in Brown's handbook alongside rather more pressing messages which include *War has been declared, I must abandon the vessel, Beware of torpedos* and *We are dying for want of water* — all conveyed by a pre-arranged combination of flags.

Puffers, even at the end of their long career on the Clyde, were rarely fitted with wireless transmitters. Skippers in West Highland ports had to telephone their Glasgow head offices for further instructions about their next ports of call. Inevitably this could lead to some hilarious interchanges when a city clerk, looking out of his office window at a calm, clear and cloudless sky, refused to believe the circumstances reported by some beleaguered skipper trapped perhaps in Stornoway by severe gales, or else marooned in Campbeltown in a thick fog.

# 25

## *Hogmanay on the Vital Spark*

It was mid-day on Hogmanay, and in the front bar of the
inn at Lochgoilhead the crew of the finest vessel in the
coastal trade were being 'treated' by the local merchant
whose consignment of best Ayrshire coal they had just
finished unloading.

Para Handy put his empty glass down on the bar counter
with unnecessary ostentation, peering into it as if incredulous that it could have held such a small and quickly-taken
dram.

"My Chove, I wass needin' that," he said with some conviction. "Coupin' a cargo of coalss iss no' the best of chobs
in weather like this." Indeed a snell north-easterly wind
was sending a thin flurry of snow drifting across the windows that looked out onto the loch, and the aspect was of
unrelieved shades of grey.

"Best respects to you Mr Carmichael, and the compliments of the season," the skipper continued, "but if there's
nae mair business to be attended to" — fiddling with his
empty glass as he spoke, more in hope than anything else
— "I think the lads and me should be getting on our way,
for it'll be a long cold trup, bitter cold, before we're in
Glasgow tonight!"

"All right Peter," smiled Carmichael, signalling to the
barman. "I can take a hint. Set them up again, Wullie!"

Surprisingly, given the day it was, the party had the bar
to themselves, with one exception.

If the small man at the table in the far corner, nursing
what looked suspiciously like a glass of ginger beer, was
aware that he was the object of the crew's curiosity, he gave
no sign of it but could not have been surprised. Strangers in

Lochgoilhead at this time of year were as unexpected as a snowflake in June.

"He's no' a traiveller, for sure," offered Dougie when Para Handy, in a very audible stage whisper, invited ideas about the identity of the mysterious stranger. "For he's got no cases and you never yet saw a traiveller withoot his samples."

"And he's no' a towerist," affirmed Sunny Jim, "for they all go away tae hibernate efter the September weekend."

The barman leaned across the counter. "I was going to speak to you about him, Peter, to see if you could do me a sort of a favour wi' yon man. He's no' exactly a towerist, chust a sort of an Englishman that's been biding here for the past week and he's desperate keen to get back to Glasgow noo — but wi' the ice and that, Mackinnon's trap couldnae get up the hill to connect him wi' the charibang at the top of the Rest this mornin', and there's no a steamer till efter the New Year. So he's kind of stuck."

"What d'ye mean 'no exactly a towerist'?" asked the captain.

"Nothin' really, Peter," said the barman: "chust that at this time o' year ye dinna expect ony o' them." And reaching to the shelves behind him for the bottle, he poured another generous dram into the skipper's glass. "It would be a great kindness if ye could tak' him wi' ye on the *Vital Spark.*"

"My Chove, Wullie," said Para Handy, eyeing his refilled glass suspiciously. "You're surely awfu' anxious tae get rid o' him. Whit's wrang wi' him?"

"Not a thing, Peter, not a thing: chust tryin' to do him a kindness, it bein' the time o' year it is."

"That's right," chipped in Carmichael. "He'll pay his passage – and I'll donate a bottle to keep you warm on the way up river."

Para Handy studied the little man surreptitiously. He looked harmless enough, but this was Hogmanay, not Christmas, and the generosity of both barman and merchant were uncharacteristic to say the least.

"What d'ye think, Dougie?"

"Whatever you think yoursel', Peter," said the mate agreeably.

"Just dinna let Mr MacBrayne find out you're in opposition for he'd be sair vexed wi' you," snorted Macphail — but the bargain was struck, and the little man was beckoned to join the group.

"Mr Clement, this is Captain Macfarlane," said Carmichael, "and he's agreed to take you to Glasgow. On the conditions that you and I discussed earlier," he added with some emphasis. "So remember to keep to them."

~

Two hours later the *Vital Spark*, riding light and making her best speed with a following tide, had Kilcreggan to port with every chance of making her berth at the Broomielaw before darkness fell. To speed their getaway from Lochgoilhead they had not taken time to stow the puffer's dinghy, which was now bobbing in her wake at the end of a tow-line.

Carmichael's bottle stood — unopened — on the top of the wheelhouse cubby pending their arrival in Glasgow: and their passenger, who had not uttered a word since leaving the bar at Lochgoilhead, other than to agree his passage fare of a florin with the skipper, was perched shivering in the bows, seated on top of his sole piece of baggage — a large tin trunk — with his coat collar vainly turned up against the cold.

"Jum," said Para Handy, "Go and tell that man tae come in oot o' the cauld: he can come in here wi' us, or doon tae the engine-room wi' Macphail, but I'll no be responsible for him catching his daith by stayin' oot there."

"Ye'll no' send him doon here," protested a voice from beneath Para Handy's feet, but the problem did not arise, as the Englishman squeezed into the wheelhouse two minutes later having, with the help of Sunny Jim, moved his tin trunk from the bows to the stern.

"Yon trunk's some weight," protested Jim. "What have ye got in there — it's no' a keg of whusky, eh, this bein' Hogmanay?"

"Whisky!" cried the man, "I would sooner carry dynamite about with me for it's a sight less harmful than that devilish drink!" And throwing back the lid of the trunk he revealed a great stack of leaflets, seized a handful and thrust one into the skipper's hands. "Whisky! It's an abomination and a curse, fountain of all the evil in this wicked world!"

"My Cot," said Para Handy. "He's wan o' they teetotallisers so he iss!"

Sure enough, the leaflet proclaimed in large print 'Clement's Campaign: Down With The Demon Drink!!!' and went on to describe in gory detail the horrors apparently attendant on the consumption of the merest drop of alcohol in any form.

"Nae wonder they wanted rid o' him at Lochgoilhead," said the mate.

"A godless place," cried Clement dramatically. "But I have seen worse in my travels across Scotland these past months. I was making some progress there. When I stood at the doors of the Inn and harangued the poor, blind sheep who were being lured to its wicked temptations, some of them turned aside from the path of sin and went their way."

"I'll bet they did," said Para Handy. "The sight and sound of you and your damn' nonsense would turn milk soor, never mind put any man off his drink: it's a miracle you got out of there in wan piece. If my friend Hurricane Jeck had come across you he'd have thrown you and your tin trunk intae the loch."

As the Skipper turned back to the wheel, Clement caught sight of Carmichael's bottle and, before Sunny Jim or Dougie could stop him, he had seized it and, stepping out on deck, hurled it over the stern into the gathering dusk.

"That settles it..." cried Para Handy. "We're putting you off at Bowling, but ye'll pay for that whusky if you want to walk ashore dry-shod, otherwise you'll be swimmin' for it, and your trunk wi' ye."

Banished back to the deck, and five shillings the poorer after meeting the Captain's demands for recompense, Clement stood in aggrieved silence as the puffer edged her way into the little harbour where the Forth and Clyde Canal joined the river.

"Peter, ye can't do this to the good folk at Bowling," Dougie protested. "Many a fine spree we've had here. Now he'll be goin' round all the pubs and makin' a'body's Hogmanay a misery. Can ye no' tak' him up tae Gleska and let him loose there? He can't do mich herm in a city."

"Naw," said Para Handy. "He's goin' ashore here. But, Dougie, you've given me an idea. Tak' the wheel a meenit while I have a word wi' the man."

~

Bowling was unusually busy, even for Hogmanay, with

the little passenger boats loading for the journey up the canal to Glasgow and beyond. Clement was unceremoniously dumped on the quayside with his precious trunk, and was last seen making his way not to the nearest Inns, but towards one of the canal vessels.

"Where's he awa' to noo?" asked Dougie as the *Vital Spark* resumed her journey up-river and Sunny Jim went to check on the dinghy's tow-line.

"Well, Dougie," said the skipper. "I think he might be on his way to Kirkintilloch: for I telt him that it was namely ass the most drouthy village in the whole country, and sair in need of some temperancising."

"Kirkintilloch!" cried the mate. "Peter, there's no' a pub in the place. It's wan o' the few 'dry' villages this side of the river ever since they had that stupid vote." His voice tailed off as realisation dawned.

"Chust so," said Para Handy. "Chust so. They do they're drinkin' at hame in Kirkintilloch. Mr Clement'll no manage to ruin onybody's Hogmanay up there!"

"And he's no' ruined ours either," a delighted Sunny Jim called from the stern, and a moment later bounced into the wheelhouse with Carmichael's bottle in his hands. "When he threw oor whusky overboard it went straight intae the dinghy. And didnae' break!"

"Well, well," said Para Handy. "It chust goes to show you, Jim, that as Mr Clement might put it — the duvvle looks after his own! Away you and get the mugs fae the fo'c'sle and we'll have chust the wan wee nip tae keep the cold out between here and the Broomielaw!"

*Factnote*

Scotland has had some pretty arcane rules and regulations with regard to the sale and consumption of alcohol. This may have been the legacy of the somewhat ambivalent attitude towards drink which prevailed in Victorian times.

On the one hand, the 'upper' classes deplored the 'excesses' of the 'lower' classes while themselves showing a healthy appetite for brandy, port and claret. On the other, the working-class quarters of towns and cities were well-endowed with temperance societies — counterbalanced by the proliferation of all manner of shebeens and drinking dens.

Periodically therefore some odd pieces of legislation

(unique to Scotland within the United Kingdom) have been in force.

Glasgow had a ban on licensed premises in all municipally-owned properties, including housing developments, for three quarters of a century: a ban which was lifted only in 1966. There is little doubt that the absence of well-run public houses as community focal points in the new peripheral re-housing projects, into which so many families were reluctantly decanted from the inner city in the post-war years, was one factor in the problem of building a sense of local pride and purpose to replace that which had been left behind with the move.

Till the early 1960s, on Sundays no public house could open and Hotels could only sell drink to so-called *bona fide* travellers who had to enter name, address and destination in a book kept specially for that purpose, and open to police inspection, not to say public ridicule. The number of occasions on which the books revealed that Mickey Mouse had passed through en route to Hollywood was legendary!

More draconian still was the Temperance Act of 1913 which made provision for 'Veto Polls' in each and every community whereby a small number of electors could enforce a vote as to whether or not pubs should be licensed within it. Kirkintilloch was one of a number of villages voted 'dry' for more than 50 years as a result. Its near-neighbour Kilsyth was another. On the south side of the Clyde the rural Renfrewshire parish of Kilmacolm, in which I was born and brought up, was without a pub from 1913 till 1989 despite having had no fewer than seven before the veto was invoked!

There were also many real life equivalents of the Mr Clements of the story: peripatetic temperance campaigners were a common enough hazard in rural areas in which the population was too small, too scattered or simply too uninterested to establish a permanent Rechabite Lodge or a Good Templar's Hall.

# 26

## *A Girl in Every Port*

The long wet winter was over, and the cheery touches of a green and cheerful spring were at last appearing on the hills and in the fields and gardens on either shore of the Firth. The pleasant effects of the change of the seasons were not lost on the crew of the *Vital Spark* as she went about her business and the welcome May weeks rolled past.

Para Handy, as befitted a man of his position, deployed his energies and his natural enthusiasm with yet more bounce than usual. Even Dougie's lugubrious countenance positively beamed and Dan Macphail, interred in the stygian gloom of the echoing stokehold, whistled at his work.

It was Sunny Jim's behaviour, however, which at once manifested in very practical terms the joy of the returning spring, but at the same time gave the crew in general, and Para Handy in particular, cause for concern. In spring they say a young man's fancy turns to thoughts of love: but in Jim's case it was his deeds rather than his thoughts which were in evidence.

No matter where the puffer tied up overnight, or how late, her young hand seemed to have an assignation ashore — and an assignation that simply would not wait.

~

"There he goes again," complained Dougie as they lay one sunny evening at Millport, watching Jim marching smartly up the quay towards the town, his hair uncharacteristically combed and dressed, his cap at a jaunty angle, and his face and hands shiny with scrubbing at the pump.

"And what did we get for oor tea tonight? Tinned sardines again. 'Quick and easy, shupmates for Ah huv tae go ashore, but jist rammed fu' o aal the goodness o' the sea!' " he mimicked disgustedly. "Huh! I'll ram him full o' somethin' and it won't be goodness, unless things improve — and soon."

"Dougie's richt," said Macphail emphatically. "It's aboot time ye dusciplined the boy before we all starve! Who's in charge on this boat, that's what Ah ask masel' — a whipper-snapper of a laddie or a man auld enough to be his grand-faither?"

Para Handy, ignoring the disparaging suggestion as to his age, explained that his concern about Jim's misdemeanours was based more on an ethical than a nutritional consideration.

"The way things iss turnin' oot noo it's the laad's morals I am more worried aboot than I am aboot oor stomachs," said the Captain. "He iss tryin' to run when he can scarcely walk. I had expected him to be content wi' chust the wan gyurl in hiss life, maybe a sensible Bowlin' lassie that he could see every time we are in there. But that iss not good enough for oor Jum!

"It is wan thing for a man wi' the sagacity and devagation o' Hurricane Jeck — or indeed mysel' when I wass in my prime — to be on caalin' terms wi a gyurl here or a gyurl there ass we wass peregrinatin' aboot the river: it iss a very different matter for a young fellow such ass Jum, who hassna had the chance to learn aal the niceties of dealin' wi' the fair sex, for that sort of experience only comes wi' practice."

"Well, he's gettin' plenty of practice the noo, that's for sure," interjected the engineer. "The baker's dochter last week when we wis in Fairlie: yon dairymaid in Largs: the lassie frae the goon shop in Wemyss Bay. Ah'm tellin' ye Peter, if he parades anither yin past us the nicht to show aff hoo smert he is like he's done up till noo, Ah've a dam' guid mind tae remind her whit he really is — jist oor deckie, and no' the flash dandy he likes tae think! Ah wonder who it's gaun tae be in Millport?"

~

Dan Macphail's question was answered half-an-hour later when the object of their criticism sashayed by on the quay-side with his topcoat hanging on one arm and a tall red-haired girl in a blue silk gown hanging on the other, an opened floral-patterned parasol twirling across her left shoulder.

"What ho, shipmates!" called the errant deck-hand, making the introductions to his latest conquest with some bravura. "Why dinna ye come oot for a stroll instead o' hunkerin' doon there on the deck as if ye wis naethin' but the maritime equivilunt o' they Chelsea Pensioners! It's a richt bonny evenin' for a perambulation and me an' Liza is jist gettin' up an appetite for a McCallum at the Shore Cafe afore we look in on the Hielan' Night at the Quay Hotel, for it would be a shame if I kept the belle-of-the-ball away from the ball!"

"Chust so, Jum, a bonny gyurl and no mistake! Complements of the evenin' to you, Miss Liza" said Para Handy gallantly, "but I doot oor perambulatin' days iss done, ass you say. Unless it wass perhaps to look for a bite to eat," he added pointedly.

"Aye, weel," said Jim, reddening slightly. "There's a grand selection of restrongs in Millport for ye to choose from. The pick o' the Clyde!"

And with that he touched the tip of his cap with a cheery grin and swung away from the quayside and headed back towards the esplanade.

"That boy needs took doon a peg or two," grumbled the engineer as soon as the pair were out of earshot.

"What I canna understand," said Dougie, "iss how Jum thinks he can keep stringin' aal these lassies along. I mean, it would be bad enough if he wass chust takin' them oot and then forgettin' aal aboot them: but here he iss sendin' them aal cairds and letters frae every corner o' the Clyde, ass if he wass the faithful swain and they wass the only girl in the world for him! It's no' fair on them, it's chust no' right. He collects them chust the same ass if they wass cigarette cards."

"Aye, sure enough," agreed the Captain. "He hass no respect for the gyurls at aal, and that iss aal wrong. Jum iss not a chentleman when it comes to hiss dealin's with the lasses."

"Indeed no," affirmed Macphail, "and he needs to be taught a lesson, so he does."

"Aye, Dan: maybe so. And maybe I can see chust how it might be done."

~

Three days later the puffer was moored at the Coal Pier in Dunoon. Arriving late the previous evening, she had discharged her cargo in the morning and the crew now had the prospect of a pleasantly lazy afternoon. She was due to take a flitting back over to Millport the following day — Saturday — but for the meantime there was nothing to be done. Para Handy's hints about freshening up the paintwork had fallen on deaf ears.

"Can ye no' leave a man in peace instead o' breakin' yer neck tryin' tae find him some work tae do?" Macphail protested, and the normally placid mate was equally adamant that he wanted nothing to do with any painting projects. Sunny Jim was already busy at the pump with soap and flannel, and did not even deign to reply.

Somewhat to their surprise, the skipper did not press the point and 10 minutes later, not long after Sunny Jim had left the puffer with a hunter's gleam in his eye, Para Handy himself went ashore.

"I chust have a little business to see to," he said, "and I'll be back in aboot an hoor." And he set off in the direction of the steamer pier, where the *Queen Alexandra* was just berthing.

He returned to the puffer in under the hour with a strangely smug look on his face.

~

As the puffer approached the north end of Cumbrae the following afternoon, her hold chock-full of all the higgledy-piggledy merchandise of a household flitting, Para Handy scrutinised the Ayrshire coast and consulted his watch. Then, to that worthy's total astonishment (for normally he was the butt of constant complaints about inadequacies of his engines) he asked the engineer to slow down.

The *Vital Spark* continued slowly down the eastern shore of the island. Across the sound Para Handy watched as the paddler *Galatea*, on her way from Greenock and Wemyss Bay, called in at Largs and then headed on towards Fairlie.

At the same leisurely pace the puffer steamed on, eventually arriving at the entrance to Millport bay just as the *Galatea* was berthing at the steamer pier, where she would lie over for a couple of hours before retracing her route back to Greenock.

"Jum," called the Captain, "go doon and put the kettle on, like a good laad, and we'll aal have a cuppa before we stert gettin' this flittin' unloaded."

Sunny Jim, who had been busy writing a series of 'wish you were here' cards of Dunoon to his coterie of lady-friends, put his pencil and his correspondence in his pocket and disappeared down the fore-hatch to the fo'c'sle.

"Now, Dougie," said Para Handy, "away you and see that you keep the laad below deck till I give you a couple of toots on the whustle: then bring him up."

"What are you up to, Peter?" asked the mystified mate.

"You'll see soon enough," said the Captain enigmatically. "But if my plan hass worked oot then I think we'll see a change in the way Jum treats the gyurls from noo on."

As the *Vital Spark* edged in towards her berth at the cargo quay four conspicuous and attractive figures standing there watched the progress of the puffer with interest, and eyed each other suspiciously at the same time.

Dan Macphail scrambled up from the engine-room, in response to Para Handy's call, to throw a heaving-line to one of the pier staff and caught sight of the waiting group as he did so.

"Here!" he turned to Para Handy in astonishment. "Is that no' some o' Jum's conquests lined up up there?"

"Chust so," said the skipper. "That's Liza from Millport, and Ellen from Fairlie, and Bella from Largs, and Jean from Wemyss Bay.

"I thought mebbe Jum would forget to let them aal know he wass comin' back to Millport this efternoon. Ass I've a friend who's assistant purser on the *Queen Alexandra*, when I saw her lyin' at Dunoon yesterday efternoon afore she left for Wemyss Bay and aal points sooth, I went and asked a wee favour from him by way o' deliverin' some correspondence for me. I took the liberty of sendin' the gyurls a caird each on Jum's behalf, askin' them if they wud like to meet him here at fower o'clock today for a wee daunder, and their teas and mebbe a McCallum, before the *Galatea* took them back hame at six.

"It'll mebbe be a bit o' an upset for the lasses, but they'll soon get over it and it's better that they should see Jum for what he iss, raither than let him break their hearts. And it's no' his heart they'll want to break when they realise what's what.

"I doot he'll learn to treat a gyurl wi' a bit mair respect from noo on."

And, with a cheery wave to the colourful bevy of beauties on the quayside, Para Handy reached for the lanyard and gave a couple of short blasts on the puffer's steam whistle.

He watched with some satisfaction, and a considerable sense of anticipation, as the fore-hatch swung open and an unsuspecting Sunny Jim climbed up onto the fore-deck.

*FACTNOTE*

Though the island of Cumbrae, with its capital Millport, was never able to rival the premier Clyde resort destinations such as Dunoon or Rothesay, or the more distant and much larger Isle of Arran, it enjoyed a remarkably loyal and strong following among Clyde trippers and holidaymakers and indeed does so to this day. Excursions to the Millport 'illuminations', the only such attraction on the Firth, remain a popular September destination for *Waverley*, last surviving paddler on the river.

Millport was just not big enough to compete on equal terms with the largest resorts. The island's total population at the turn of the century was less than 2000. With an area of just five square miles and an unspectacular topography (its highest hill less than 500ft in height) it was dwarfed by Arran, with 30 times the area and mountains rising to over 2800 feet. Yet the tenacity and determination of the islanders, and their easy proximity to the Ayrshire coast a couple of miles to the east, have made it a prized destination for its *aficionados* who — quite rightly! — will not hear a word against it.

The town enjoyed the unique distinction of having two piers to serve it — the Old Pier and the Keppel Pier — and a complex and competitive steamer service to no fewer than three mainland railway towns, namely Wemyss Bay, Largs and Fairlie. For many years too there was a direct steamer service into the centre of Glasgow.

The *Galatea* was built as the new 'flagship' for the Caledonian Steam Packet Company fleet by Caird's of Greenock in 1890 and though she was a most handsome, two-funnelled paddler with a reasonable turn of speed at just over 17 knots, her owners were never satisfied about either her performance or her appeal. Her time on the Clyde was as a result relatively brief and she was sold to

Italian owners just 14 years later.

The *Queen Alexandra*, launched in 1902, had an even shorter career on the Firth. Badly damaged by fire at Greenock in 1912 she was repaired — but then sold to owners in Vancouver, which she reached by sailing round Cape Horn because, of course, the Panama Canal was still under construction! She was replaced by a new vessel of the same name which distinguished herself by ramming and sinking a submarine in the Channel in World War I and later by emerging from a refit in 1935 as MacBrayne's three funnelled *St Columba*.

A 'McCallum' was a popular West of Scotland courting delicacy for many decades and consisted of a sundae-glass of vanilla ice-cream smothered in raspberry syrup. Just who invented it, and who gave it the name, and why, can still be the subject of debate among enthusiasts!

THE HIGHLAND GATEWAY — *Only Rothesay pier was ever as busy as Dunoon. The Cowal pier is seen here at the height of its dominance as the 'Gateway to the Highlands' as well as an important destination in its own right. Here the paths of the North British steamers from their Craigendoran base crisscrossed (among others) those of the Caledonian Railway Company and MacBrayne, from Gourock, and of Captain Buchanan, from Glasgow. In this photograph, Eagle III to the left and, ahead of her, the first Lord of the Isles.*

# 27

## Going off the Rails

Once her cargo of pit-props had been unloaded at Ardrossan harbour, the Captain of the *Vital Spark* went off as usual to the Post Office to wire back to the Glasgow office for news about their next assignment. The crew relaxed on deck in the early May sunshine, the mate perusing a copy of the previous week's People's Friend, Macphail poring over a new novelle.

Sunny Jim sat idly on the hatch coaming with a piece of tarry string with which he played cat's cradle while humming a tuneless, wordless song to the eventual, inevitable irritation of the other two.

Before too many harsh words could be said, fortunately, Para Handy was seen coming back down the quayside towards the puffer with the usual yellow telegram in his hands, and speculation replaced altercation on deck.

"Knowin' oor luck," said Macphail, "the office'll be sendin' us tae Glenarm for lime." That Northern Ireland port, serving a nearby limestone quarry, was the crew's most hated destination of all, for working that particular cargo was an especially foul job. "Whit Macfarlane has done tae offend them a' up at the Gleska office I dinna ken," continued the engineer: "but if there's ever ony dirty work tae be done it's aye the *Vital Spark* that gets tae dae it!

"I doot it's that, or even worse, by the look of the man," he concluded. And sure enough there was a puzzled frown on Para Handy's face as he jumped down onto the deck.

"Don't tell us it's Glenarm again," said Dougie disgustedly. Para Handy shook his head.

"Whateffer it iss, it's a misprint," he said. "There hass been some sort of a stoorie on the telegraph line and the message hass come oot wrong at this end. Listen to this, lads, and see if you can mak' ony sense of it. 'Rendezvous with puffer *Saxon* at Bowling and proceed together to Bridge Wharf to load cargo of trams for Rothesay.' Trams? *Trams??* Whit are they on aboot?"

"It should maybe be *Drams*, Captain," suggested Sunny Jim with some enthusiasm. "We're tae tak' a cargo o' whusky for the Rothesay Inns maybe?"

"Naw, Jum," said the Mate. "They aalways get their supplies wi' the *Texa* effery second Thursday. And even at the Fair Fortnight you wudna need a pair o' puffers tae tak' the necessary supplies for the visiting Glaswegians doon tae Bute.

"Could it no' be *Rams* they mean, Peter? Or *Lambs* maybe? For there's a wheen sheep on the island already."

"Aye Dougie," said the Captain, "but they're usually bein' sent oot, no' brocht in! It's beyond me. *Prams?* — there's no that mony weans in Bute. *Hams?* — they cure their ain.

"Cot knows whit it iss — but there's only wan way to find oot! Mr Macphail! If you can get your lang face oot o' that trash and get some steam up, we can maybe get awa' tae Bowling and see if Wullie Jardine on the *Saxon* kens ony mair aboot this than we do!"

∾

The two puffers met up at Bowling harbour the following morning when the *Saxon* came in from completing a run up the Forth and Clyde Canal to Grangemouth, collecting timber which she had then delivered to McGregor's yard at Kirkintilloch.

"It's gobbledegook tae me tae, Peter," volunteered Jardine when the two Captains met. "We'd best get up there and fin' oot the worst. Ah wush Ah cud think whit way they're wantin' the twa boats thegither: that's the real mystery."

They found out soon enough.

Standing on the quayside at Bridge Wharf there were indeed two *trams*: two of the newly perfected electrical variety: and their destination was indeed to be Bute, as replacements on the 20-year-old Rothesay to Port Bannatyne tramway for the smaller horse-drawn vehicles which had served it till now.

The only means of getting them to their destination was

by the use of a pair of puffers, lashed together to form a broad square platform onto which the two trams could then be lowered gently by crane, laid transversely across the cargo hatchways of the boats, and secured with wire hawsers and ropes to cleats and eye-bolts on the decks and gunwales.

The delicate operation took the most of the day to complete and the two crews went ashore in the late afternoon for a badly needed refreshment at the Auld Toll Vaults.

Para Handy and Jardine looked back at the strange silhouette at the quayside.

"Skoosh-caurs!" exclaimed Para Handy. "Skoosh-caurs! I do not believe it, Wullie, I neffer, neffer in aal my born days thocht to see the smertest boat in the coasting tred (no offence meant Wullie, you understand) aal higgledy-piggledy wi' a cargo the like of yon. It looks chust like a tinker's flittin', it iss makin' a fool o' the shup!"

He changed his mind half-an-hour later when a raincoated figure with a snap-brim hat put a head round the doorway of the snug at the Auld Toll to enquire: "Is there a Captain MacFarlane here?"

"Aye, that's me," said Para Handy.

"Ah, Captain: my name is Farquharson. I'm a reporter from the *Glasgow News*. Your friend Mr Neil Munro sent me to see you, he thought I might find you here. You see we would like to write a piece about you — and about you too of course, Captain Jardine," he added hastily as Wullie swung round to give him a long hard look, "since you're both in the news, as it were, on account of the cargo you're taking down to Rothesay. The first of the new electric trams for the island! The first cargo of its kind ever on the Clyde, and carried by steam lighters! Our readers will be very interested to read all about it in tomorrow morning's paper."

Para Handy positively swelled with pride. "In the news, eh? Well, what else wud you expect when dealing wi' the smertest ..." Tactfully realising, just in time, that that particular line of thought was best left unspoken, he said no more.

"Well, well," he smiled, "please sit doon and mak' yoursel' at hame, Mr Farquharson, and speir awa'. Jum! give the chentleman that seat, and get a stool for yoursel'.

"I am chust sorry I cannot offer you a refreshment, but we only came in for the wan wee gless of sherbet to clear oor throats and my money iss aal on the shup."

The reporter, well forewarned by Neil Munro, took the hint with no further prompting.

～

Sunny Jim was sent ashore first thing next day to buy a copy of the paper before the strange hybrid creation set off on its journey down the Firth.

There was a long article on page two of the *News* congratulating the Directors of the Rothesay Tramway Company on their 'brave investment in the remarkable new technology which would shortly revolutionise transport on both land and sea', as the writer put it: and complementing the shippers on their ingenuity in creating 'the first set of nautical Siamese Twins ever to have been seen on the Firth' to accomplish the task of transporting the cargo safe to its destination.

Only Macphail remained jaundiced about the whole enterprise and scathingly critical of the indignities heaped on the puffer.

"It's just a shambles!" he protested. "Wud ye tak' a look at whit we look like for peety's sake! Jist a broken-doon penny ride frae Hengler's Circus and Carnival, jist makin' a richt bauchle o' the boat."

Para Handy, on the other hand, once he had had the chance to study the piece in search of any hidden, unflattering innuendos (explaining to the mystified Sunny Jim, in the meantime, just what was meant by the allusion to Siamese Twins) and finding none that he could see, was quite delighted by the notice (or notoriety) which was, at last, attaching to his command — even if he had to share the glory with Wullie Jardine.

It was as well that the Captain of the *Saxon* was an old friend, for the actual passage down-river was fraught with considerable difficulty, and demanded considerable tact on the part of both Captains and both crews.

Which skipper was to be in overall command?

Which engineer and which set of engines was to dictate the speed at which the floating tangle of glass and steel should be progressed?

Which helmsman was to establish the headings to be steered, and how — when neither wheelhouse gave a view of anything other than the side of a tramcar three feet in front?

Para Handy was just about to broach these delicate questions with Wullie Jardine when the latter, following an earnest discussion with his engineer in the wheelhouse, approached the Captain of the *Vital Spark* with the unexpectedly generous suggestion that Para Handy, as the more experienced man, should have overall charge: that Macphail, as a former deep-sea engineer, should set the pace for the voyage: and that Dougie, being taller than the mate of the *Saxon* and therefore better able to see where they were all heading, should be navigator-in-chief.

"My Chove, that's very gracious of you, Wullie," said Para Handy, and the two shook hands on the agreement, and gave orders for the lines to be cast off.

The twin-decked carrier moved slowly into the middle of the river.

∽

The twin-decked carrier continued to move slowly, very slowly indeed, all the way down the Firth.

"I neffer thought it wud tak' so long," said Para Handy with some exasperation as at last they came abreast of Toward Point and within sight of their destination. "The *Saxon* chust iss not in the same class ass we are for speed. I shall neffer, neffer be rude to Dan aboot the enchines again!"

The Directors of the Tramway Company, together with all the great and the good of Bute, were awaiting their arrival at Rothesay and for the first time in her long career the *Vital Spark* (and of course the *Saxon*) came alongside a flag-bedecked jetty to the cheers of a large crowd.

∽

"My Chove, Wullie," said Para Handy an hour later, as they sat in the bar of the Commercial Hotel, "I thocht we wass neffer goin' to get here. I chust hope we can make better progress back up river to Gleska!"

"I wudna bet on that, Peter," said Jardine guiltily. "Ye see, ye'll hae tae gi'e us a piggie-back again."

"A piggie-back? Again? Whit are you on aboot?"

"Well, it's like this. We cracked wir biler this mornin' jist as we were gettin' steam up at Bridge Wharf and had tae shut it doon. That's what the ingineer wis tellin' me aboot in the wheelhoose. But I wisnae goin' to miss the spree and the glory of it a' so I kept ma peace! The *Vital Spark* wis the only shup wi' ony power on the way doon river, and I'd be obleeged if ye'd just keep us lashed by ye for the trup back hame.

"We'd baith look awfu' schoopit if this got intae the papers Peter, wudn't we?"

*FACTNOTE*

The Bute Tramway was in existence for more than half-a-century, the first two miles of track being opened in 1882 between Rothesay and Port Bannatyne. For the first 20 years of its operations the service was provided by horse-drawn vehicles which took about an hour on the round trip. Though the initial impetus for its construction came from its role as a tourist attraction (Rothesay was then just about to enter its zenith years as the number one tourism mecca on the Firth) the service ran year round.

In due course, the winter operations were being provided by specially constructed enclosed vehicles, whereas the summer service (somewhat optimistically!) was always maintained by open-top carriages.

In 1902, the service was electrified. This involved closing it down completely for a few months to allow the necessary conversion to be carried out, before the new tramway opened for business in May of that year. Some three-quarters of a million passengers were carried annually at its peak, and there were 22 trams in service.

In 1905, following years of planning and discussion, the line was extended to provide a summer season service to the fine sands of Ettrick Bay on the south side of the island and though there was occasional talk of further extensions, none actually came to reality.

The tramway finally closed down in 1936, the victim of the expansion of more comfortable and reliable coach and charabanc service.

Most of the vehicles for the Rothesay tramway were indeed brought to Bute by pairs of puffers or lighters lashed together to provide the necessary beam, this being the most practical and above all the most economical way of transporting such a bulky and awkward cargo.

The limestone cargoes referred to earlier were confirmed by most puffer crews as their real bete-noir. The loading and unloading process kicked up a positive stour of clinging dust which got into clothes, hair, lungs, and pervaded every nook and cranny aboard the boats.

By comparison, carrying a couple of tramcars down river really must have seemed like a relaxing holiday — especially since it would not have involved any back-breaking work with the steam winch or the shovel!

*ROTHESAY TRAM TERMINUS — Here is the town terminus for the Bute Tramways at Guildford Square, Rothesay, with one of the new electric vehicles loading holidaymakers for Port Bannatyne and Ettrick Bay. To the left lies the inner harbour, destination and berthing place for the numerous puffers which served the island community, but it was unfortunately empty of shipping the day this photograph was taken.*

# 28

## *The Cargo of Cement*

Sunny Jim had been sent up on deck to bring back a
report about the weather as soon as the battered old
alarm clock (the only item of any ornamental pre-
tension in the fo'c'sle) had gone off as usual at seven
o'clock.

"Sorry boys," he said as he returned. "It's rainin' as hard
as ever, and no sign of a break in the sky at all."

The *Vital Spark* had lain at Berry's Pier on Loch Striven
for four days now and, though the month was May, the rain
had been unrelenting for nearly 96 solid hours. The tops of
the hills in Cowal to the north and on the Kyles to the south
were embedded head first, as it were, in the base of low grey
clouds which pressed down to within a few hundred feet of
the surface of the loch.

"Still rainin' on!" complained Para Handy, swinging his
feet out of his bunk and reaching for his shirt. "I have neffer known weather like it and I am fair at the end of my
tether wi' it aal.

"I shall go and talk to the builders again. We cannot lie
here for effer and a day. What the owner must be thinkin' I
hate to imachine. With there bein' no telephone in the big
hoose for us to get a message to him, he'll be thinkin' that
we iss aal lost at sea, and his shup wi' us!"

～

Their enforced idleness had been caused by a combination of the constant rain, the nature of their cargo — and a
very cautious clerk-of-works. The 'big house' at Glenstriven
was in process of having some amenities added before the

annual summer visit of its owners, a Glasgow merchant and his family.

Chief amongst these was the building of a large new boathouse beside the pier which served the estate: and the construction of a substantial flagstoned terrace at the front of the house, as a necessary adjunct to the quite unheard-of extravagance of the small outdoor swimming pool which had been installed there only the previous year.

The paving stones, bricks, tiles and miscellaneous items of hardware for these works had been delivered by the puffer the previous Thursday — together with the building squad, who had spent the weekend carting sand and pebbles from the nearby beaches to the site of operations. On Monday, the puffer had returned from the Broomielaw with the last and most important ingredient in the recipe — the bags of the cement itself.

And that, so far as the supervising agent of the contract was concerned, was the problem.

Cement.

Despite the skipper's assurances that they had trans-shipped such a cargo successfully many times in the past and that the specially-treated bags were rain-proof, the clerk-of-works, terrified of the effects of such an unending downpour on his precious cement, had refused point-blank to countenance its unloading till the rain had stopped. That was Monday. And today was Friday.

Thus the hatch on the puffer's hold was undisturbed. The heavy tarpaulin across it was still fastened down tightly, and the bag of rope netting which would transfer the cargo to a waiting horse and cart on the pier hung idle from the derrick.

On the puffer, the crew sat fuming in the fo'c'sle and getting ever more short-tempered with each other: ashore, the builders huddled under the leaking canvas roof of their ramshackle bothy and wished they were back in Glasgow.

And both sets of disgruntled and frustrated men individually and collectively cursed the clerk-of-works — who was himself safely ensconced in the considerable comfort of the staff wing at the big house, courtesy of the estate factor, though to the dismay of the domestic staff who were expected to look after his needs.

~

"He still insists that the bags would chust turn ass solid ass a rock," Para Handy protested as he climbed back down into the fo'c'sle and hung his dipping oilskins over a line stretched across the deck-beams next to the chimney of the iron stove in the fore-peak.

"To the duvvle," said Macphail with feeling. "Is your word no' good enough for the man, Peter?"

"He wuddna' believe it even if it wass written in the Good Book itself," said the skipper bitterly. "He iss that nervous for his chob. We must chust thole it oot for another day, boys, and see what comes.

"At least though we can get a wee break, for when I telt him we wass low on proveesions, instead of offerin' food from the big hoose, ass any Chrustian wud do, he chust said we could tak' a trup ower to Rothesay and stock up."

Within a short space of time, Macphail had steam up, and the puffer eased out from Berry's Pier for the crossing to the capital of Bute. Though the rain still swept mercilessly out of a grey sky, the prospect of a change of scenery, the chance of some company, and the promise of a quiet dram, went a long way to brightening the day for the crew.

For once, their optimism was not to be disappointed.

The owner, when Para Handy telegraphed his office to report on their problems and their whereabouts, was sufficiently moved by their plight to wire some money to them at once, care of the Rothesay Post Office.

Though this was probably through a sense of relief at learning that his investment was not lost with all hands somewhere off the Cumbraes, it at least made possible a re-stocking of the *Vital Spark*'s larder, and a welcome refreshment for the crew before they re-embarked for the return crossing to their berth in Loch Striven.

∾

As the puffer edged in to Berry's Pier, two things immediately became apparent.

Firstly, the clerk-of-works was to be seen, waiting for them on the pier — and in a very agitated state.

Secondly, the rain had stopped for the first time in four days and though it seemed that the respite would be brief (for dark, laden clouds were rolling in from the south west) it was at least a break from the monotonous deluge which they had tholed for so long.

The reason for the clerk-of-work's agitation was soon made clear. Dunoon Telegraph Office had delivered a wire from the owner of the big house, advising the factor and the steward that his three sons, with a dozen or more of their friends, would be arriving at Berry's Pier on a chartered steam launch at six o'clock that evening, intending to spend the weekend at the house.

"You'll have to move the boat immediately," cried the frantic clerk-of-works. "They will need to berth the launch here and, besides, we cannot have the loch frontage of Glenstriven marred by the spectacle of a steam-gabbart at the pier."

Para Handy was with some difficulty restrained by the engineer and eventually was able to point out that he had a cargo for delivery here, it was still aboard, and he had no intention of leaving until it was safely ashore.

"The fact that it iss not," he concluded, "iss entirely your own fault, Mr Patullo, and I would be grateful if you would chust remember that before you miscall the shup!"

The wretched Patullo wrung his hands. "But we've got to get the boat away — and my gang, too, if you'll give them passage back to Glasgow. The gentry will want the place to themselves for the weekend."

"Well," said Para Handy. "Get my cargo off the shup, and we'll can do that for you. But so long ass my cargo iss aboard — here I stay!"

"But how can I do that," protested the clerk-of-works. "It may be dry enough to unload ye noo — but the weather for the weekend looks set to continue wet, and I've no place to store the cement under cover.

"Captain," said Sunny Jim suddenly. "I think we can maybe sort this all oot..."

~

Two hours later the *Vital Spark*, on passage to Glasgow in ballast with her cargo of cement safely ashore at Glenstriven and the builder's gang sheltering down in the fo'c'sle from the rain (which had returned with a vengeance), met a smart steam yacht rounding Toward Point and heading westwards past Ardyne.

"That'll be the chentry," said Para Handy. "Och, they'll neffer know we wass there."

Sunny Jim's idea had been ingenuity personified. The

sacks of cement had been hurried ashore by every manner
of means while the rain held off: most slung onto the waiting cart but others taken by wheelbarrow and a few, the last
few, even manhandled, up to the waterless swimming-pool.

Mr Patullo had supervised their careful stacking in the
empty pool. To clean it out and prepare it for the summer
was one of the jobs for which he had been contracted — a
job which would have to wait until the work on the new terrace had been completed, hopefully next week when he and
his men returned on Monday after the young gentlemen
and their friends had gone back to Glasgow.

Meantime the sacks were safe under cover: Para Handy
had been happy to lend one of the puffer's heavy hatchway
tarpaulins and this was now stretched across the pool,
weighted down on four sides by heavy flagstones.

"I'll can get that back from you next week sometime Mr
Patullo, for we'll be passing through the Kyles on our way to
Furnace sometime afore next Thursday."

~

It was, however, a stoney-faced estate factor who met the
*Vital Spark* when she arrived at Berry's Pier early the following Wednesday afternoon to recover her property.

"Is Mr Patullo no' weel, then?" asked the Captain from
the wheelhouse window, as the crew lashed the heavy tarpaulin to the eye-bolts at the fore end of the main hatchway.

"Not ill, Captain. Just — shall we say — in disgrace. I
don't think you'll be seeing him in Glenstriven again.

"It probably was not entirely his fault, but the master can
be very unforgiving at times. You see, the weather turned
better on Saturday and the young gentlemen decided they
would have a swim. So they opened the stop-cock to fill the
pool — without looking under the tarpaulin first.

"I'm afraid we now need a new pool, as well as a new terrace."

And he inclined his head solemnly, pivoted on his heels
and walked away.

Para Handy turned towards the deck below him with an
agonised expression: "Jum!" he shouted: "Jum!!! I need to
talk to ye!"

The deck was deserted, but the fo'c'sle hatchway had just
crashed shut with an echoing thud.

FACTNOTE

Duncan Cameron Kennedy of Glenstriven ordered the building of the 'big house' on the estate in 1868. It enjoys a magnificent setting high above the loch, looking due south across the sheltered waters. I must confess that it has never had a swimming pool — though there were plenty of them in the resorts such as Rothesay, whose first 'salt water swimming baths' were opened in the 1870s.

In 1872 Walter Berry, a Leith merchant, acquired Glenstriven estate and it was he who commissioned the construction of the pier which bore his name. There were more than 80 piers on the Firth at the height of the steamer and puffer traffic. Most of those on the Renfrewshire and Ayrshire side of the Firth were built by the Railway or Shipping Companies: most of those on the Argyll coastline either by the local community or for it by a wealthy landowner — such as, for instance, the wooden pier erected at Lamlash by the Duke of Hamilton in 1888.

There were some wholly privately built and owned piers of which Berry's was one: it was one of the very few, however, which were large enough to accommodate steamers. Most of the private facilities constructed for the big houses, or for the isolated farms and estates, were merely jetties or slips designed to allow goods, livestock or passengers to be ferried to or from the shore on a flit-boat.

Of the original Berry's pier nothing now remains except a few stumps of the old uprights. It was never used for scheduled services, but as a destination for occasional special excursion or charter parties and there is a splendid photograph of one such group, coming alongside aboard the paddler *Diana Vernon*, in the book *Clyde Piers* published by Inverclyde District Libraries. Though it is difficult to be categorically certain (the photograph is a little indistinct as to detail) it seems as if all passengers aboard the steamer are men, and most look to be wearing some sort of uniform. There is a small welcoming party at the head of the pier, including a number of ladies.

The pier at Otter Ferry on the east side of Loch Fyne was also originally built as a private facility for the large house which stands at the shore end. There was an established local ferry service across to Lochgair from a stone jetty at the tiny hamlet of Otter Ferry a few hundred yards to the south — a service which had been running for many years before the pier was built in 1900. In contrast to the pier at Loch Striven however, that at Otter Ferry was for some years a port-of-call for steamers on scheduled services. Even today the structure seems to remain remarkably intact, though the last cargo was unloaded there just after the Second World War and the last passenger steamer called in 1914!

# 29

## *The Pride of the Clyde*

Daybreak always has a hushed, cathedral-like quality about it but this particular dawn had broken in a spectacular silence accentuated by the visual crescendo of light streaming in from the east: first a delicate bluey rose, then a brightening but still pale off-white, and finally a dramatic, blinding golden sunburst which chased the last vestiges of the retreating night across the western horizon and into oblivion.

Seen from the uninterrupted vastness of the ocean that palette of colour would have been quite overwhelming. Even from the upper reaches of the Clyde, where it was set against the gaunt silhouettes of the stone tenements of Govan and Plantation, it was unforgettable.

The Captain and crew of the steam-lighter coasting quietly down river with the current after an early start from Windmillcroft Quay were not unappreciative of this natural wonder unfolding before their eyes.

"Man, Dougie," said Para Handy reflectively: "if only it wass possible to tak' a picture of that and pit it in the paper, to let folk ken what they wass missin', the world and his wife wud be oot their beds betimes, and you wudna be able to move on the river for the crowds come to see it!"

It was June, and the *Vital Spark* was headed for the Kyles with a mixed cargo consisting of assorted building materials for Colintraive, hotel furnishings for Tighnabruaich, and fencing wire for Kaimes.

A mile or so past Renfrew Ferry an immaculately-groomed launch of the river pilot service, speeding upstream, closed in on the puffer.

"Steam lighter ahoy! Where on earth do you think you're

off to?" shouted a uniformed figure, leaning from her wheelhouse window and gesticulating frantically. "The river's closed at Clydebank: you can't go any further downstream now till the afternoon! D'you puffer captains never even bother to read the navigation bulletins posted on the quays, or published in the *Glasgow Herald*?"

"No," replied Para Handy, with commendable but (in the present circumstances) ill-advised candour. "Never. Why?"

The master of the cutter turned an interesting purple colour.

"Because if you did, you'd have known that this is the morning the *Lusitania's* being launched from John Brown's yard. The river's closed to all traffic between the Cart and Dalmuir from eight o'clock till two o'clock! Now get in to the bank and stay there! Or do you want me to arrest the boat?"

"I wudna put you to the bother," replied Para Handy in a rather more placatory tone, and he put the wheel over and headed the puffer for the Renfrewshire shore.

The towering cranes of the world-famous Clydebank yard were now in sight, poised above the monstrous hull which had been growing beneath them for the past 15 months. Here had taken shape, and today was now ready for launching, the largest and most luxurious ship ever yet conceived by the designers, or created by the craftsmen, who between them had made the name of the Clyde and the reputation of its workers synonymous with shipbuilding perfection.

The river bank on the Renfrewshire side opposite the yard was black with crowds come to see the spectacle. From their modest vantage point actually on the water, however, the crew of the puffer had a grandstand view of the whole proceedings, and once the *Vital Spark* had been made fast to a convenient marker post they settled on the hatch-coaming with hastily-brewed mugs of tea and an early dinner of bread and cheese.

Stands "for the chentry", as Para Handy put it, had been placed facing the bow of the ship, immediately behind the platform for the launch-party. The men who had built her were crowded along the slipway the whole length of her hull, with a favoured few perched on the foredeck and as yet unfinished superstructure of the new liner.

The slip on which her foundation keel had been laid down and on which she had then been painstakingly raised over the preceding months — vertical rib-upon-rib, riveted plate-upon-plate — was placed at an acute angle to the river channel.

The Clyde itself was an artificial creation, a once sluggish stream dredged and broadened to its status as a birthplace for ships, a mecca for trade. At this point on its journey towards the sea it ran, despite the work of generations who had made it fit for an international commerce on which it depended, through a channel which was narrower, bank-to-bank, than the length of the hull which was about to slide into it.

Only the subterfuge of that angled slipway made the very launch possible and even with that heavy drag chains would have to be deployed to bring the enormous hull quickly to a stop, in order to prevent her running ashore on the opposite bank.

A small flotilla of tugs stood by to capture the vessel and then to manoeuvre her into the adjacent fitting-out basin where she would be transformed from an impressive but inanimate hulk into a living being, a ship (like all ships) with a personality and indeed a soul.

"Brutain's hardy sons," said Para Handy with some emotion when at 12.30 precisely Lady Inverclyde christened the ship in the traditional manner. To the roaring approval of tens of thousands of spectators, drawn from all walks of life but united by a pride in what had been achieved, the majestic hull took spectacularly to the water. In the process *Lusitania*, just as every ship before and since has always done, curtseyed sweetly and gracefully to the lady who had named her, and sent her forth to fulfil her destiny.

∾

Fourteen months later the *Vital Spark* was lying against the easternmost extremity of Greenock's Princes Pier, ready to load a flitting for Furnace once the scheduled steamers had left.

In their more favoured berths ahead of her the *King Edward* and the *Lord of the Isles* impatiently awaited the arrival of the train from Glasgow St Enoch station and their cargo of on-going passengers for Campbeltown and Inveraray respectively.

Anchored in the middle reaches of the Firth at the Tail o' the Bank, however, was a vessel which commanded the attention and the respect of everyone within eyesight, to the total exclusion of everything else that lay or moved upon the firth.

*Lusitania* had, just the previous day, come down river from the fitting-out berth at John Brown's Clydebank yard: and was next morning to embark upon her speed trial over the measured mile at Skelmorlie, and her general proving, before being officially and formally handed over to Cunard.

The crowds massed on Greenock promenade and further along the western shores of the Firth towards Gourock almost matched those which had witnessed her launch the previous summer.

In due course the train, an inconsequential minute and a half late, came in from St Enoch: the Campbeltown and Inveraray steamers loaded, and departed.

Para Handy rose from the pierside bollard from which he had been watching the world go by and stretched luxuriously.

"Boys," he said. "let us chust warp her up to the railway yerd chetty, and get this fluttin' aboard: and then we can go..."

"Excuse me," came a quiet voice from behind the Captain, "but I wonder if I could ask a favour of you ?"

∽

As the puffer eased alongside the liner, edging in towards the floating pontoon at the foot of the companionway stairs which soared, seemingly into space, towards the entry port umpteen decks above them, the *Lusitania's* hull was like a wall of sheer black cliff, dwarfing them into total insignificance.

Their passenger smiled his thanks.

"The least I can do," he said, "is invite you to have a quick look through the ship before she sails. If you'd like to."

An authoritative nod sent two seamen scurrying from their posts on the floating jetty at the ship's side to take up watch on the puffer's deck and secure her safely, bow and stern. With the First Officer of the *Lusitania* — for it was he — leading the way, the crew of the *Vital Spark*, moving as if in a dream, began to climb the companionway towards the upper decks of the liner.

"I can't thank you enough," said the First Officer to Para

Handy as they stepped through the portway and into the First Class Reception Foyer. "Most embarrassing if I'd been stranded on the pier at Greenock! They knew I was due off that train and there should have been a launch to meet me.

"There should be a lot of people in a great deal of trouble...

"But it has been such a pleasure for me to meet you gentlemen and be reminded of my own beginnings as a hand on the old Hay's puffer *Inca* all those years ago..."

Even Para Handy was — almost — speechless, as wonder after wonder unfolded in front of their eyes.

The First Class Smoking Room, panelled in walnut with an open fireplace and an ivory ceiling: the First Class Lounge with its intricate carving and stained-glass domed roof: the Foyer, magnificent in wrought iron and with the gates of the first electric lift ever installed on a ship at sea: staterooms with marble baths en suite, carpets into which the feet sank at each step: works of art crowding every wall, carvings and statuary featuring on stairways and in corridors.

And, towards the stern of the great ship, spacious Third Class accommodation for the emigrant traffic which made the facility offered on board the poor *Vital Spark* seem like the very worst deprivation on the most notorious slaver in maritime history.

"Dinna you daur touch a thing," Para Handy commanded Sunny Jim in a piercing stage whisper, "for I'm sure I dinna ken when you last washed your haun's. At least we got rid o' Macphail!"

Indeed the Engineer, in a paradise all his own, was on a tour of the ship's pioneering high-pressure turbines and her 25 boilers, courtesy of the Fourth Engineer, commandeered for such duty by their considerate host.

"I wish I could thank you properly," said that gentleman 20 minutes later as he ushered the crew back towards the waiting puffer: and reached instinctively for his notecase.

Para Handy was affronted.

"No, Cot bless you sir, no! Don't you even be thinking of such a thing. But there iss chust the wan wee favour, if you could see your way to obleege us with it, that wud mean more than we could effer say."

~

Which is why, if you should find yourself aboard the *Vital Spark* at the right time of the day: if the crew have taken kindly to you: if the prognostications are right: and if the Captain is in good trim: if all of these imponderables have fallen into place then you might, just might, be offered a mug of tea in the fo'c'sle of the finest vessel in the coasting trade.

Tea prepared in a very, very special tea-pot to be found on no other puffer, or indeed other vessel of any description, on the Firth.

A tea-pot, polished to blinding brilliance and handled with due ceremony and respect, bearing a proud legend: *RMS Lusitania.*

FACTNOTE

In the early years of the twentieth century supremacy on the lucrative and prestigious North Atlantic passenger services lay with the two German companies Norddeutscher Lloyd and HamburgAmerika (Hapag).

Ships like the *Kaiser Willhelm der Grosse*, the *Kronprinzessen Cecilie* and the *Deutschland* provided standards of luxury and levels of comfort and service hitherto undreamt-of, and helped the German shipping companies to capture more than half of the Transatlantic passenger business.

Cunard replied with two stunning sister ships (built with the help of government loans and subsidies), one — *Lusitania* — from John Brown of Clydebank: the second — *Mauretania* — from Swan Hunter on the Tyne.

With a length of 762ft and a beam of 88ft these vessels were the largest ships yet built. *Lusitania* was ready for launching three months before her sister. Her launch weight of more than 20,000 tons represented the greatest mass which man had ever tried to move. She came down the Clydebank yard's slip on June 7th 1906 and sailed from Southampton on her maiden voyage 15 months later — recapturing the Blue Riband from the Germans in the process.

*Lusitania,* as everyone knows too well, was treacherously and tragically torpedoed off the Irish coast by a German U-Boat in 1915 with appalling loss of civilian life. *Mauretania* survived the war and stayed in service (ending her days as a precursor of today's Caribbean cruise liners) before finally going to the breaker's yard in 1935.

Because of her short life-span and tragic end, *Lusitania* has tended to be overshadowed by her sister ship in the litany and legend of the North Atlantic. In fact she started as the more famous of the two ships — really by virtue of being the first into service. The Americans in particular adored the *Lusitania* and though *Mauretania* has been called, with some justification, the most famous and best-loved ship of all time, it has to be remembered that this was only because of the sad and early end of the Clyde-built vessel.

Had she survived, the two ships would undoubtedly have shared the honour, the esteem and the affection which they both — equally — deserved.

*The Fastest Way to Cross — Blue Riband holder* Lusitania *at speed was an impressive sight as the largest ship in the world thrust her 31,000 gross tonnes through the seas as fast as a family car. As well as a quicker crossing, she also brought to the passage standards of comfort and cosseting beyond the most sanguine expectations of her 2000 passengers as she wrested transatlantic supremacy back from the German fleets.*

# 30

## *The Downfall of Hurricane Jack*

I had always been intrigued by the chequered career of
Para Handy's oldest and dearest friend, Hurricane Jack,
who had for long been on a seemingly irreversible downward spiral from the heights of his time as the revered
Captain of a record-breaking wool-clipper, then a temporary officer with MacBrayne's, and by way of the skipper's
berth on the *Vital Spark* in her early days on the Firth, to
his present state-of-affairs as occasional odd-job man on
any vessel prepared to give him a part-time berth.

Para Handy would occasionally make some oblique reference to Hurricane Jack's departure from the puffer, usually in terms of 'Jeck's doonfall' but all my efforts to elicit
more information about the circumstances of it were to no
avail, and led merely to a swift change of subject.

Then one morning, as I was changing steamers at
Rothesay on my way from Helensburgh to Inveraray, I
came across the *Vital Spark* in a corner of the inner harbour with her skipper seated on an upturned fishing box on
deck, and studying a copy of the *Glasgow Herald*. The
intermittent sound of heavy hammering and the occasional muffled curses which came from the engine-room were
evidence that Dan Macphail was struggling as usual with
more running repairs to that temperamental piece of
machinery, but of the Mate and Sunny Jim there was no
sign.

I coughed politely from the edge of the quay and the
Captain. looked up from his paper.

"Why, it's yourself then," he said. "What a surprise to see
you in Rothesay: what brings you to Bute at this time o'
year?"

I explained that I was merely killing an hour till the arrival of the *Lord of the Isles* from Glasgow on her way to Inveraray where I was to spend a few days with old family friends.

"The *Lord of the Isles*, eh? Well, now there iss something of a coincidence," said Para Handy. "for here I am chust readin' in the paper aboot that very boat, where I see tell that she is changin' owners, and thinkin' back to the time when it wass her that wass lergely to blame for the circumstances that led to poor Hurricane Jeck losin' his berth on the *Vital Spark*."

"You know I've always wanted to know more about that sorry event, Captain," I prompted hopefully.

"Well," he said hesitantly: "I suppose there would be no much herm in tellin' you aboot it after aal these years for it wass a long time ago."

I scrambled down the iron ladder bolted into the quay wall and jumped onto the deck of the puffer and sat down on the coaming beside him before before he had time to change his mind. "Go on, Captain," I said encouragingly: "I'm listening."

∽

"Ass you probably have realised," he began, "Jeck wassna the kind of a man that wud suffer fools gledly, so at times he could occasionally be chust a little bit impatient … "

"Impatient!" came a protesting voice from the engine-room. "He wisnae impatient at all! He wis the maist argimentative and pugnacious man on the Firth, and wis never happier than when he had his dander up and wis thrang pittin' the frighteners on some puir innocent body that jist had the sheer misfortune tae be passin'! His temper wis aye on a hair-trigger, he wis the sort of chap that if ye gi'ed him hauf a chance he could start a fight in an empty room!"

Para Handy paid no heed.

" … but at the same time," he continued, as if there had been no interruption, "he had the hert of a child and wass aalways happy to do a kindness to ony o' his fellow bein's wheneffer he had a chance: aalways anxious to introduce a ray of sunshine into a gloomy day and gi'e folk somethin' to enchoy at the time and talk aboot later. It wass that very spurit of goodwull that cost him his chob when he wass skipper on the *Vital Spark*.

"Wan time we wass lyin' at the Albert Harbour basin in Greenock waitin' for instructions from the owner. Jeck went ashore to go up to the telegraph office to see if there wass any message but ass he came oot onto the shore road he wass chust in time to see a smash between wan o' the Greenock to Gourock skoosh-caurs and a hackney cab. The caur had caught wan wheel o' the cab wi' its step-board ass it cam' roond the corner and though the horse, and the cabman, wass chust fine, the passenger had been thrown onto the street and it wass clear the puir duvvle had broke his leg.

"He wass a ship's officer by his uniform so Jeck rushed over to see if he could help. It turned oot the man wass a Captain Fairlie, and he had been on his way to Princes Pier station to catch the Gleska train, for he wass to take ower next mornin' ass a relief skipper on the *Lord of the Isles*. He wass pleased to see anither sailor and of course for aal he knew Jeck could have been master o' the *Oceanic,* no' chust a steam-lighter, he wass aalways so smertly turned oot.

" 'If ye could jist send a telegraph for me to the Inveraray Shuppin' Company's Gleska office and tell them whit's happened to me,' he asked Jeck anxiously ass he wass bein' strapped to a stretcher by the ambulance men, 'I'd be mich obleeged. I'm no' wan o' the regular reliefs, in fact I wis engaged through their Greenock Agents so they only know me by reputation and I dinna want tae let them doon first time.'

"Jeck told him to relax, efferything would be chust fine, but ass soon ass the poor fellow wass off to the Infirmary he didna go near the telegraph office, he chust came back to the shup and told us he had to go to Gleska, the owner wanted to see him, but he'd be back the followin' night.

"If I had known whit wass goin' on I'd have told him no' to be sich a fool … "

"And ye'd have been at the Unfirmary yersel', gettin' a lesson in emergency repairs o' the human anatomy resulting from an aggravated assault," shouted Macphail from the engine-room.

" … but nane o' us had ony idea whit wass whit, and so off he went. He spent the night wi' a kizzin o' his in Yoker and at half past six the next mornin' he presented himsel' on board the *Lord of the Isles* at the Brudge Wharf and let on his name wass Fairlie and that he wass the relief skipper.

"Naebody asked eechie or ochie aboot that at aal, he wass chust accepted ass bein' who he said he wass, for they wass aal expecting a new man and why should they jalouse that there wass shenannigans goin' on?

"Jeck wass in Paradise! He'd had plenty of high-jinks in the Hebrides two years earlier wi' Mr MacBrayne's *Flowerdale*, what wi' her twin screws and her cheneral mobility, but she wass ass an ageing cairthorse to a young thoroughbred compared wi' the *Lord of the Isles*, which wass less than a year old and chust at the height o' her powers! She wass one-third again ass big ass the *Flowerdale*, wi' enchines to match and, bein' a paddler, she wass chust ass lissom ass a greyhound and you could turn and spin her like a young gyurl dancin' the Gay Gordons!

"At 20 meenits past seven, Jeck gave the order to raise the gangplank, cast off the bow and stern ropes, and rang doon for half speed ahead, and off they went. The regulations on the river stopped him givin' her her heid till she wass past Clydebank, but then he whustled doon to the enchineers and promised them aal a dram from the first-class salong bar when they got to Inveraray if they made the trup in six hours, which wass 10 meenits less than her best time ever, and anither wan for effery extra five meenits they could knock off that!

"Jeck stayed on the brudge till efter they wass through the Kyles for they wass callin' in at maist o' the piers and he wanted to be sure they were in good trum on each occasion, but wance they had cast off from Tighnabruaich, wi' the next stop no' till Crarae, he left the First Officer in cherge on the brudge and went into the Captain's day cabin. There he found some oh-de-colong and macassar oil belonging to the regular captain, spruced himself up, set his kep on three hairs, then went perambulating through the first-cless salongs and the dining room.

"You know how gallant Jeck aalways iss wi' the ladies, and he wass at his best form that day, bowin' to aal the young gyurls and sweepin' his kep off nearly to the ground in a gracious manner it wass a privilege to behold, givin' the grups to their faithers, and kissin' the backs o' their mithers' hands ass if they had been royalty.

"He wass a great success wi' aal the chentry on board and by the time the shup reached Inveraray — which she did in a record time o' chust under five hours and fufty meenits — the maist of them was wishin' they didna have to go ashore

to choin the Chook on a shootin party, or trevel on up to
Loch Awe for the fushin', but could chust bide aboard for
the return trup to Gleska in sich distinguished hands and
stylish company!

"It wass that return trup — and Jeck's fondness for fun
and his pleasure in bringin' high-jinks to his fellow man,
whateffer the cost to himsel' — that wass his doonfall!

"They left Inveraray right on time and, since Jeck knew
fine that he daurna reach Brudge Wharf earlier than the
printed schedule or there would be questions asked, he
took things easy on the trup back through the Kyles and
then on by Rothesay and Dunoon.

"Their last caal before the run up-river to Bridge Wharf
wass at Greenock Princes Pier, which wass chust a couple
of hundred yerds from the basin at Albert Harbour where
we wass waitin' for the man to return from Gleska where,
you'll mind, we thought he wass in confabulation wi' the
owner.

"Jeck chust couldna resist it. Ass he said to me after it
wass aal over, 'Peter, I had to show ye whit wis whit, and let
ye join in the fun! It would have been a poor hert that
couldna rejoice and share the spree that wass on, given
whit I had at my haun's that day!'

"What he did — instead of headin' oot into the up-river
channel when he cast off from Princes Pier — wass to bring
the *Lord of the Isles* through the narrow entrance into
Albert Harbour at ass good a speed ass he could get up, and
then throw her into full astern. By jinkin' from ahead to
astern wi' the helm hard over he spun her roond in a tight
pirouette not chust the wance but no less than three times
in the muddle of the dock, whiles he wass oot on the brudge
wing wi' the steam-whustle lanyard in his hands, givin us
aal a cheery wave and blastin' oot on the shup's whustle like
the early mornin' hooter at Singers's!

"You can imachine that the officers and crew, neffer
mind the passengers, were taken aback wi' this: there wass
somethin' of a commotion aboard the shup: and there wass
proper uproar on the quayside ass well.

"The out-turn wass that somebody telegraphed the
shup's owners in Gleska and when Jeck docked her at
Brudge Wharf — which he did bang on time, and ass nice
ass ninepence, like efferything else he did — the polis wass
waitin' wi' the Directors o' the Company, and it wass the
high chump for Jeck.

" 'My fault entirely, Peter,' he said when we met up the next day efter he'd been let oot on bail. 'If I had chust taken her up to Gleska and then disappeared, naebody would have been ony the wiser about who took Fairlie's place and there would have been no trouble at aal. That wass what I meant to do. But when it came to it, there wass no way I wassna goin' to share it wi' you! I'd been given the very best toy and the very biggest toy I ever had to play wi' in my whole life, so I chust had to let my oldest friend get at least a flavour o' the sheer joy and happiness of bein' a bairn again!'

"So that wass how Jeck took a tumble, and how I got the command of the shup, for the owner sacked him on the spot.

"But I wush it had never happened that way, for Jeck didna deserve such a fate when aal he wass tryin' to do, as aal he ever tries to do, wass to bring some sunshine into the lives of his fellow men."

*FACTNOTE*

Two Clyde steamers carried the name *Lord of the Isles*. The first was launched from D&W Henderson's Meadowside Yard in 1877 for the Glasgow & Inveraray Steamboat Company Ltd. She was from the first locked in rivalry with the *Columba* and that has been well-captured in John Nicholson's dramatic painting of the race between them.

It was something of a shock when the Company sold the paddler to English owners just 13 years later, in the autumn of 1890, and though she was replaced by the launch the following Spring of the second *Lord of the Isles* from the same builders it still remains a little mysterious that the changeover took place when it did.

The two ships were almost identical in dimensions, the second being just nine feet longer at 245ft: had similar machinery, though of slightly greater power in the 'new' *Lord*, giving her marginally more speed and (with a newly-developed steam steering gear in place) greater manoeuvrability: and they were of broadly the same appearance.

The main difference, and probable reason for the change, was that the saloons on the new ship ran the full width of her hull and thus gave significantly enhanced passenger space. As she had to compete with the *Columba*, whose onboard facilities were legendary, this may have been the logic behind the whole project, for the *Lord of the Isles* on the Inveraray run and her great rival on the Ardrishaig run were catering for the wealthy tourist, not the Scottish working class family on holiday.

Hurricane Jack's imaginary 'day out' is set in 1892: and the ship really did change hands — twice: firstly in 1909 when she was sold to the Lochgoil and Inveraray Steamship Co: and again in 1912 when they went out of business and the ship was bought by the pioneers of the new generation of civil marine power not just on the Clyde but worldwide, Turbine Steamers Ltd, who had come into being to operate the then brand-new *King Edward* just 11 years earlier.

Paddlers were, generally speaking, more manoeuvrable than their screw-steamer sisters, particularly in a confined space, partly thanks to a significantly shallower draft which allowed them to be 'spun' rather more easily through the resistance of the water: partly because the larger surfaces of the paddle-blades could more quickly bring the vessel to a standstill and get her moving again in the opposite direction.

And yes, I have grossly exaggerated their sprightliness but as any storyteller might claim, a tall tale should be a tall tale!

# 31

## Pushing the Boat Out

The possession of a sturdy, seaworthy dinghy of one sort or another is an essential prerequisite on board a steam-lighter. There are occasions when the vessel must anchor off outlying communities where either there is no jetty at all, or else such facility as does exist is too small and in waters too shallow to allow the parent puffer to berth: thus if the crew are in need of provisions, or a refreshment, the puffer's dinghy is their sole means of communication with the shore.

I am sorry to have to place on record, though, that in the case of the *Vital Spark* the role of its dinghy is frequently a more nefarious one, for no other vessel in the coasting trade on the west coast has a more infamous reputation for the poaching activities of its crew.

Neither her Captain nor any of his shipmates have yet featured in the case-lists at any of the District or Sheriff Courts in the West Highlands, nor have their misdeeds been recounted in the columns of the *Oban Times*, *Campbeltown Courier* or *Argyllshire Standard*. But nobody who knows the *Vital Spark* can be under any misapprehension about the nature or purpose of the night-time excursions of her crew when salmon and sea-trout are running in the mouths of the Aray or the Shira, the Ruel or the Eachaig, or any other of a dozen rivers in reach of wherever the puffer happens to be lying overnight.

I previously recounted an earlier incident in which Para Handy was forced to abandon the puffer's dinghy to the water bailiffs in order to make his escape back to the ship and I am afraid that this was not an isolated occurrence. On two further occasions the Captain has had to make this

209

ultimate sacrifice in order to preserve (at least in official quarters) his own reputation, and that of the *Vital Spark* as well.

While not exactly condoning the activity which has led to such avoiding action being required, I admit to a certain sneaking sympathy with the Captain, for surely there are more salmon in their waters than the Duke or the Marquess or the Earl and their households could ever consume, and many Scotsmen would regard their freedom to take a stag from the hill or a fish from the river as an inviolable, inherited right.

The whole subject was brought to mind again last month. I was in St Catherines, bound for Inveraray, having come through Cowal on the 'overland' route by way of Loch Eck, and had an hour to pass before the next posted passage of the sturdy skiff which provides a periodic ferry service across Loch Fyne to the Campbell capital from that village. A poster advertising a displenishing sale at an adjacent farm caught my eye and when I wandered into the yard where various items for auction were on display, I was surprised to encounter Para Handy himself.

"Boats," said that mariner in answer to my enquiry as to what he might have his eye on at the sale. "Chust boats. I am afraid we had a bit of a calamity last weekend at Loch Gair, and the shup iss withoot a dinghy again."

"Not *another* poaching debacle, Captain!" I exclaimed. "Surely you have learned your lesson on that score by now."

Para Handy winced.

"I do not like your lenguage, Mr Munro," he protested, "who said onything aboot poaching? We wass chust looking for a fush for our teas, ass iss the right of any man, when here and does the Asknish gamekeeper and his cronies no' come burstin' through the undergrowth and into the shallows, wi' torches and dugs and cheneral aggravation. There wass nothing else we could do but abandon shup so to speak for the dinghy iss a heavy boat and slow under the oars, and make the best of our way three miles over the hill to Loch Gilp, where we had left the vessel.

"This is the first opportunity that I have had since then to do something aboot replacing the lost boat."

There was a choice of two small craft lying in the yard — one a heavily built, broad-beamed, flat-bottomed rowing-boat of the traditional type, about 16 feet in length: the other was a very narrow, shallow, delicately-constructed skiff which gave every indication that she would be a very fast boat under oars, light and easily manoeuvrable.

"Not that I in any way approve your nefarious nocturnal doings you must understand, Captain," I said, pointing towards this craft, "but I would suggest that this is the boat for you. Look at the lines of her! I don't think any water bailiff would have much chance of catching you in a flier like that!"

Para Handy shook his head sadly.

"I am afraid she chust would not do, Mr Munro," said he. "You are quite right, of course, she would be chust the chob for the poachin', but I am afraid that we need a boat on the shup that can do more than chust make a getaway from the gamekeepers of Argyll.

"Blame the owner for that! If he wass using the shup the way she should be used, caairyin' excursionists or shootin' perties or nice clean cairgos like whusky or firkins o' butter aal the time, then it would be a dufferent matter. But wi' some of the terrible contracts he makes the shup work to, we need a dinghy that can carry a cairgo chust ass readily as it could carry a fushin' expedition.

"That iss a bonnie wee skiff, sure enough. But she would neffer do for the *Vital Spark*."

Ten minutes later, the two boats came up for sale. The skiff went for £4-10s to a sharp-faced man who announced his bids loudly and almost threateningly in the unmistakeable vernacular of the East End of Glasgow. ("A professional!" whispered Para Handy sadly, "That iss the kind of man who iss spoilin' aal the fushin's for us amateurs!") The stout dinghy was knocked down to the Captain for £2-12s, a price with which he seemed quite content.

Since the *Vital Spark* was berthed at Inveraray (from whence the Captain had come by the same ferry service which I had intended to take in reverse) he would of course row his new acquisition over and, in accepting his invitation to cross with him, I responded by inviting him to join me at the St Catherines Inn for a refreshment before we set off.

"What did you mean a few minutes ago," I asked as we carried our glasses to a corner table, "when you said the *Vital Spark* had to have a dinghy that was capable of carrying a cargo? I thought you were always able to beach or berth the puffer for loading or unloading?"

"It iss neffer loading that iss the problem," said Para Handy, "but there iss times — not many, you understand, but we have to be able to cope wi' aal emerchencies — there iss times when we have to unload the shup usin' the dinghy, and a right fouter it is too, ass well ass a beck-breakin' business."

And, lifting his dram, he gave me good health in the Gaelic and disposed of the contents in one gulp, optimistically shaking the empty glass upside-down over the tumbler of pale ale with which I had complemented its purchase, lest even one solitary drop of the precious golden liquid should be carelessly lost.

"What sort of cargos are those, then?" I prompted. "I mean the ones that give you the trouble of needing a big dinghy like the one you've just bought?"

"It iss not so much the cairgo ass its destination that iss the problem," replied Para Handy. "For instance, wance a year we have a contract to tak' the winter coals to a wheen o' the west coast lighthooses, and there are some of them that have no sort of a jetty at aal, nor any sandy ground where you can beach the shup, and that means that effery drop o' their coals hass to be manhandled ashore usin' the dinghy.

"That chob is a richt scunner, I can tell you. No problem at Oban, of course, where we load the coal wi' a sling: but the coal iss all bagged, no' loose like the way we usually cairry it, and at lighthooses like Eilean Musdile off the sooth end o' Lismore, or Rhudagan Gall on Mull, we have to lie off the rocks, load the secks into the dinghy wi' the winch, row her in to a convenient flet rock — and then unload effery demned seck one by one by hand.

"It iss a nightmare, for we are not funished even then, for the contract iss to deliver the coal to the keeper's hooses or to the light tower itself. Sometimes, if we are lucky, there iss a sort of a path up to the station and mebbe the keepers will have a barrow or a sort of a truck. But maist o' the time we chust have to carry the secks on our becks, one at a time.

"It's no way to be treatin' a fine shup like the *Vital Spark*, or her crew come to that. What I say iss, if the owner wants to do business o' that kind then he should have bought himself a coal gabbart for it in the furst place, no' a vessel that wass aalways meant for better things.

"It is demeanin' and a disgrace, and I am bleck-affrontit

that we have to do work like that. But we canna avoid it if we want to keep oor chobs, so I canna think to buy ony-thing other than a strong wee boat like the one I bought today."

The Captain cheered up considerably when he saw me signal to the barman for another gill of whisky.

"Could you not think to have another, smaller dinghy as well then," I suggested, "so that you have the best of both worlds with a boat for work and a boat for, er, the fishing too?"

"It would be an expense," said the Captain, "but I could make the second boat pay for itself, right enough" — I did not press Para Handy for more detail on this point — "but the problem iss there iss no space on deck. The shup is a fine, smert boat but she iss no' awful big, and what wi' the hetches and the steam winch and the capstans and the ven-tilators and aal, there chust would not be the room for two boats on board her."

"Well," I suggested, "have you considered one of these new folding boats. I understand they are…"

Para Handy nearly choked on his beer, and broke into a paroxysm of coughing from which I was only able to release him by dint of several hefty smacks on the back.

"Folding boats!" he declared with some vehemence once he was able to articulate again. "Do not speak to me aboot folding boats. They're nothin' but a snare and delusion for the unwary: if Dougie wass here he would tell you himself. Chust ask Wullie Jardine on the *Saxon*. The poor duvvle wass near drooned, thanks to one o' your precious folding boats, and it's purely thanks to it too that his name iss now on the Court records at Dunoon.

"Wullie had the same idea ass yourself, he went and bought one o' these new-fangled Berthon dinghies. She packed up flet, the sides kind of tucked in and there wass hinges on her keel and gunwales so that she folded up in half and back on herself like you wass closin' the blades of a scissors. The first moonless night — they were in the Holy Loch at the time — Wullie and his Mate opened her oot and put her together, slupped her ower the side o' the *Saxon*, took a wee bit o' a splash net wi' them, and off to the mooth of the Eachaig like hey-ma-nanny.

"Efferything wass going chust dandy at first, and Wullie had a half-a-dozen wee salmons in the boat in no time at aal, they belonged to nobody, they didna have ony labels on them, when suddenly there's a bellowin' from the bank chust below Ardbeg, and out shoots wan o' the Benmore Estate boats wi' Mr Younger's gamekeeper and a wheen o' his men.

"It wass a mile to where the *Saxon* was anchored off Kilmun pier but there wass several other puffers there and Wullie reckoned that if they could get a lead on the keeper's boat, then they could lose her in the derk and Mr Younger's men wouldna be able to tell which shup the poaching-perty had come from.

"So Wullie and his Mate fair threw themselves at the oars, and a good speed they made too, till efter aboot a half-a-mile or so there wass an awful crackin' sound like wud spluttin' in two and the boat chust folded up on itself in less than a second, the bows came oot the watter and the stern came oot at the same time and they snapped together in the air like the chaws o' a sherk, and trapped Wullie and his Mate inside the hull.

"It wass a mercy they didna droon! She toppled over, but then floated chust long enough for the keeper and his men to come alongside and open her up and take poor Wullie and his Mate oot, and then it wass off to the polis for them, and up to the Sheriff in the mornin'.

" 'I'm gled I didna droon, Peter,' Wullie said the next time I met him. 'And I kinda ken noo whit Jonah must have felt like yon time he wass in thon whale. But I think it wass a luberty o' the *Argyllshire Standard* to carry the story under the headline SKEDADDLING SKIPPER SCUTTLES SKIFF.

" 'It made me a laughing-stock on the river for weeks!' "

*FACTNOTE*

The puffers did indeed undertake contracts which involved their crews in some truly back-breaking labour, and the delivery of coal to the more isolated lighthouses was one of the most hated of these. I had a first-hand account of a Ross and Marshall puffer which supplied coal to the cliff and rock stations in and around Mull in the 1940s: even listening to the tale made the muscles ache at the mere thought of the physical hardships.

Folding or collapsible boats are no myth, either.

The 'Berthon' boats were possibly the best known of these. They were the invention of Edward Lyon Berthon, a

*A NEW LIFEBOAT — The MacGrorys captured every detail of Campbeltown's 'great day' in the summer of 1912 when the town's first powered lifeboat the* William Macpherson *was handed over. It is shown being manoeuvred out of the builder's (onshore) yard, carted through the streets of the town amidst a great throng of people, formally named down at the harbour, and then finally launched — as shown here — with considerable aplomb. I wonder who the lady was?*

man who deserves to be better known if only for the bizarre circumstances of his life and career. Born in 1813, he died in 1899 and in the years between charted, with mixed success, a strangely diverse and various voyage through life. He originally studied medicine but in his mid-30s he returned to university to read theology and served as a curate in several parishes in the South of England.

Throughout all these years however, invention, and specifically marine invention, seems to have been his great interest though it was pursued with scant success — and even less luck. For in 1835, and a full year before Pettit-Smith registered the first patent for a screw propellor for ships, Berthon submitted plans for just such a device to the British Admiralty — who rejected them.

His next invention, a nautical log, was also thrown out by the Admiralty. A trier, if nothing else, he then developed a design for a folding boat and this, too, was submitted to the powers-that-be in Whitehall. Once again (and with a regular monotony which hints at a lack of imagination somewhere within official circles) the Navy did not want to know — though in this case they did at least give a prototype a 'trial run'.

It says much for Mr Berthon's perseverance that he returned to the fray some years later and this time his improved design for a folding boat was accepted and endorsed by the Admiralty.

The boats which were finally manufactured were usually of small size and were popular for some years with yacht-owners, as when not in use they stowed more easily and occupied less space. But they could — and sometimes did — fold up on themselves without warning when in use!

More serious attempts to develop larger versions of what were now being intended as collapsible ship's lifeboats were made early this century: the Englehardt design was the best known. There were four boats of this type on the *Titanic* though only two were assembled in time to launch before the ship sank.

# 32

## *The Umburella Men*

ara Handy pushed open the brightly-coloured stained-glass door of MacGrory's double-fronted drapery store on Campbeltown Main Street and shut it smartly behind him against the biting cold southeasterly March wind. In response to the tinkle from the bell set above the door, the curtain at the rear of the shop which led to the fitting rooms was swept aside, and one of the two brothers who owned the business appeared, a tape-measure round his neck and a pair of serrated cutting-scissors in his right hand.

"Ah, Captain MacFarlane," he said jovially when he saw who his customer was. " Pleased to see you as always. What may we do for you today?"

"No' much to be worth your trouble, Mr MacGrory," said Para Handy. "But I am after a new woollen comforter. I lost my auld wan overboard yestreen, what wi' the wund, and it no' properly tucked in, and it's a cauld spell o' weather to be withoot."

The draper pulled down a glass-fronted drawer from the wall of such drawers behind the counter and in a matter of moments Para Handy had selected a bright red scarf and wrapped it securely round his neck.

"There iss no need to be makin' a parcel of it. I will chust wear it straight aff", he said, and bringing a handful of coins from his pocket he paid for his purchase and moved towards the door.

"Before you go, Peter," called MacGrory, "could I ask a favour of you? I hear you're off to Glasgow tomorrow morning with a load of whisky and then straight back in a couple of days with a cargo of barley. Is that right?"

"Chust so," said the Captain.

"Well," said MacGrory. "It's like this…"

His tale was soon told.

Campbeltown, standing in splendid isolation at the foot of the Kintyre peninsula a hundred miles or so from Glasgow, has too small a population to make possible the provision within the town of all the services which modern life expects. Thus it is that the MacGrory brothers, though *purveyors* of umbrellas, are unable to offer a repair service for broken ribs or torn panels from their own resources.

Umbrellas brought in for repair are kept within the premises and then at regular intervals conveyed to Glasgow to the workshops of the reputed wholesale house of Messrs Campbell and MacDonald, courtesy of their representative Mr James Swan, when he visits Campbeltown on one of his regular journeys in the West. They are returned, once repaired, courtesy of that same gentleman, who sees this service as being the very least he can do for one of the most valued and valuable customers on his entire circuit.

"Mr Swan was here just three weeks ago, Peter, and took a stack of umbrellas to Glasgow with him. I've now had a telegram from Campbell and MacDonald to tell me they are repaired and ready for my customers, but Mr Swan has broke a leg wi' a fall on icy cobbles, and won't be back to Campbeltown for at least another month.

"I was wondering if you would be good enough to collect them for me when you're in Glasgow and fetch them back doon later this week…?"

～

The *Vital Spark* edged in to the private quay at the distiller's Partick bottling plant late the following afternoon and for the next three hours the puffer's steam-winch spluttered and coughed as the precious cargo of finest Campbeltown Malt Whisky was swung ashore under the watchful scrutiny of the plant's own security men, a pair of bleak-eyed Customs Officers — and Para Handy and his frustrated crew.

"Chust imagine," said the Captain with some rancour later the same evening as he grudgingly slapped his sixpence onto the bar counter at the nearby Auld Toll Vaults and picked up the glass containing his diminutive dram, "chust imagine here and we've been and delivered enough whusky to keep the whole o' Partick in drams for a twelve-month and we are expected to pay for chust the wan wee taste o' the cratur.

"There's nae justice at aal in this world."

Dougie, Sunny Jim and MacPhail could only shake their heads sadly in silent, sympathetic agreement.

~

Next morning the puffer made the short crossing over to the southern shores of the river and tied up at the jetty serving a Govan grain-merchant's yard. Once the loading process was under way with MacPhail on the winch, and Sunny Jim — and a couple of the merchant's warehouse-men — ready to stack the sacks as they came juddering down into the hold in netting bags, Captain and Mate headed ashore.

"Dougie and I will away into the town and collect Mr MacGrory's umburellas, boys," said Para Handy as he scrambled up the iron ladder bolted to the quayside: "and we'll see that you have a share of the bottle the man has promised us for the favour."

And the two set out to walk to Govan Cross Subway Station from whence one of the much-admired new underground trains would whisk them, in just a matter of minutes, to St Enoch Square and the warehouse of Messrs Campbell and MacDonald.

They had only walked a couple of hundred yards, however, when there was a sudden flash of lightning followed by a crashing peal of thunder, and in a matter of seconds raindrops the size of pan-drops were bouncing violently off the cobbled street. In even fewer seconds Captain and Mate instinctively searched for, identified, and raced towards, the nearest public house.

"My Chove, Dougie," said the Captain as they supped a glass of pale ale in the snug bar. "That iss some cloudburst to be sure. We will chust sit here and let it aal roll by before we go any further. Indeed we could be doing with having Mr McGrory's umburellas with us right now, for here we are without so much ass a coat or a kep between us."

However, the rainstorm showed no sign of moving on. An hour later it was as heavy as ever, and Para Handy pulled his watch out to check the time.

"The boys will be wondering what has become of us,

Dougie," he said. "We should have been there and back before this and I do not want them to be thinking we iss malingering on them or that we have maybe bumped into Hurricane Jeck and gone off on a spree and forgotten them. I am thinking we must chust face the rain and make a dash for it to Govan Cross. What do you think yourself, Dougie?"

For answer, Dougie tugged on Para Handy's sleeve and pointed surreptitiously in the direction of the outer door of the snug bar. Beside it, there stood a battered umbrella-stand which had seen better days. Resting within it, however, was one solitary umbrella — shinily new, neatly rolled up, and quite bone-dry. A quick glance round the other occupants of the bar revealed nobody who looked even remotely like the possible owner of such a fine and expensive accoutrement.

"Some toff must have set it there and forgotten aboot it days ago, Peter," whispered the Mate. "For sure and it has not been out in the rain today. Aal I am suggesting is that we *borrow* it. We wull can put it back on our way back to the shup..."

Para Handy again looked round the company. Nobody was looking in their direction. The other occupants were variously grouped in animated conversation. The landlord had his back to them as he reached up to a high shelf for a bottle of port.

As the two sailors reached the door Para Handy casually reached across and quickly — too quickly — tried to scoop the umbrella out of the stand. It was bad enough that it rattled on the side of the stand: much worse that it caught on it, tipped it over, and sent it crashing to the floor.

"Hoy! You pair! Where the blazes d'ye think ye're aff to wi' my best brolly?"

Para Handy, the umbrella clutched guiltily in his hand, turned to see the landlord leaning halfway across the mahogany counter of the bar, gesticulating furiously with the bottle of port and being restrained with some difficulty (by two of his customers) from hurling it in the Captain's direction.

"My mistake, my mistake," gabbled Para Handy. "I thought it wass my own umburella, for it iss the very spit of it, but you are right, I completely forgot that I left mine on the shup."

"A likely story," howled the landlord. "Thieves! That's whit ye are! And me wi' a funeral to go to up in toon this afternoon. A richt clown I'd ha'e looked wi'oot my brolly! Get oot, the pair o' ye. And never let me see either wan o' ye in this pub ever again. This is an honest hoose!"

∼

It was a shamefaced pair who, all thoughts of the promise to the MacGrory emporium temporarily forgotten, scuttled through the teeming rain to the nearby quayside — and the comparative haven of the *Vital Spark*.

"We will wait on board, Dougie," said Para Handy, "and go up to the toon when the rain is past."

It was almost four o'clock before the downpour finally fizzled out as suddenly as it had begun, and the chastened mariners headed again for the Govan Cross Subway. This time they reached it without incident.

Less than half-an-hour later they emerged from Campbell and MacDonald's capacious St Enoch's Square premises, each of them clutching, with both arms in front of their chests, the awkward burden of a substantial bundle of umbrellas of every size and description, ladies' and gentlemen's alike, secured with a couple of rope ties.

At the ticket office Para Handy fumbled in his pocket with some difficulty to extract the coppers for their fares, and the two clattered down the stone steps onto the subway platform.

In a minute or so the two bright red carriages of the train came looming out of the tunnel mouth and into the station with a distinctive whoosh of disturbed air — and an unmistakable but indescribable, warm smell: an aroma of mystery and of quite unfathomable depths which — when once first encountered — would never be forgotten by succeeding generations of patrons of the Glasgow Underground.

Para Handy and Dougie took their seats on one of the slatted wooden banquettes which ran down each side of the carriage.

Opposite them, someone was hidden behind an opened copy of the *Evening Times* and Para Handy leaned forward curiously to read the day's headlines.

As he did so, the paper was lowered — and the Captain found himself looking into the eyes of the landlord of the Govan pub, dressed now in a dark suit, wearing a black tie, a mourning band on his arm, and with his rolled-up umbrella across his knees. The two men stared at each other for some moments in silence. Finally the landlord, having glanced several times in bewildered disbelief from the strangely-assorted bundle on Para Handy's knee to that on Dougie's and back again, leaned forward and said with heavy sarcasm and in a penetrating stage-whisper:

"Well, I'm glad to see that you've had a good day..."

FACTNOTE

The MacGrory Brothers, as well as owning Campbeltown's leading drapers at the turn of the century, were enthusiastic amateur photographers and the illustrations in this book are taken from the substantial archive of their original glass plate negatives which is now in the safe hands of Argyll and Bute Libraries.

Campbeltown was probably the most prosperous community on the outer edges of the Firth at the time, and certainly one which had founded its wealth on industry rather than tourism.

As well as a substantial fishing fleet, with its ancillary boat building yards, net and rope factories and — of course — curing stations, the town had a rich agricultural hinterland. Within the burgh there were more than twenty whisky distilleries and other industrial activity included coal-mining, salt-pans, shipyards, cooperages and shipping companies.

Glasgow's underground railway is a 6-mile circular route with clockwise and anti-clockwise tracks sharing a common, central platform at each of 15 stations. The line twice passes under the Clyde, linking the city centre north and south. First cable-driven, it opened in 1896: and ran virtually unchanged for 80 years, though it was electrified in the mid-1930s. Some of the original rolling stock was still in use when the system closed down in 1977 for a three-year modernisation programme from which it emerged with the scarlet Victorian passenger carriages replaced by equipment of a gaudier hue, which quickly earned the facility its new sobriquet of *The Clockwork Orange*.

Known to generations of commuters as the Subway (never the Underground — London terminology eschewed by Glaswegians) there have been proposals down the years for extending the network but these have come to nothing. The simple circle has served efficiently, effectively and economically as a mover of people for exactly one hundred years.

The old Subway did indeed have an odoriferous atmosphere all its own, lost for ever in the process of modernisation. Warm, damp, musty, primeval (yet not unpleasant) it was pushed in front of the carriages as they threaded the dark tunnels: spilt out into the stations as the trains arrived: and percolated up the escalators to the streets above. Nobody knew what caused or created it but it was unique to the Glasgow system — and sadly missed by those who remember it with affectionate nostalgia.

Devotees of Neil Munro's tales of the adventures of 'Jimmy Swan the Joy Traveller' will recognise in this episode the shadowy figures both of Mr Swan himself, and of the Glasgow Wholesale House whose kenspeckle representative he so successfully was.

*RING A RING OF ROSES — One of the most appealing features of the MacGrory archive is that so many of its pictures are natural and spontaneous though most other surviving photographs of the age were carefully and predictably posed. This lively picture of schoolgirls at play is a delight and, given the ponderous equipment and the slow shutter-speeds of the time, a remarkably crisp action shot.*

# 33

## A Naval Occasion

The puffer had spent the last two days at Salen, on the island of Mull, unloading the mixed paraphernalia of a farm flitting and was now bound for Oban where a cargo of whisky in cask from one of the local distilleries awaited her on the town's North Pier, scheduled for delivery to a blending and bottling plant in Dumbarton.

It was ten o'clock on a glorious July morning as the *Vital Spark* passed out of the Sound of Mull, leaving Duart Castle on the starboard beam, and the panorama of the Lynn of Lorne and the sheltered stretch of water between the islands of Lismore and Kerrera came into view.

At least a dozen navy vessels ranging in size from dreadnoughts to torpedo-boat destroyers were at anchor outside Oban harbour to the west of Ganavan Bay. Furthest from the shore, towering over the other ships of the flotilla, lay the giant dreadnought battleship *Bellerophon* and inshore from her a scattering of smaller vessels including the venerable cruisers *Theseus* and *Grafton*, several light cruisers, and two modern destroyers, the *Cossack* and the four-funnelled *Teviot*.

Para Handy, at the wheel, guided the puffer to pass as closely as commonsense dictated beneath the soaring grey bows of the *Bellerophon* and gazed admiringly at her towering upperworks and huge twelve-inch guns.

"Brutain's hardy sons," he said with some emotion, watching the ratings drilling on the quarterdeck as the *Vital Spark* crawled the length of the battleship's hull.

The squadron, part of Britain's Atlantic fleet, was in Scottish waters on an inshore training excercise and had anchored just a matter of three hours previously, having entered the Firth of Lorne after negotiating the sound between the Torran Rocks off the south-west corner of Mull, and the island of Colonsay.

The signal halyards were busy as the fleet exchanged messages and instructions, and a number of cutters and motor launches manned by immaculate ratings sped between ships carrying men and materials.

Very conscious of the uncomfortable contrast between his own command and the naval elegance so openly on display, Para Handy rounded the northernmost point of Kerrera with — almost — some sense of relief and some recognition of the shortcomings of his beloved *Vital Spark*. Even here, though, he could not escape the presence of naval supremacy for one ship had been deployed into Oban Bay itself and was now the centre of attraction for the summer holiday crowds thronging the esplanades and the piers of the popular summer resort.

Moored some 300 yards off-shore and approximately equi-distant from the South and North Steamer Piers was the cruiser *Shannon*, the equal of the *Bellerophon* in over-all length though not, of course, in bulk or armament. Ratings were swarming over her decks erecting white sun-awnings, and a mahogany companionway ladder was being deployed from the midships entry port on her starboard side (facing the South Pier) onto a floating pontoon against which two motor pinnaces were tied up. On the port side of the cruiser a more modest Jacob's Ladder hung from the rails of the quarter-deck.

The *Vital Spark* bumped gently against the timber uprights of the cargo berth on the North Pier and Sunny Jim leapt ashore with the bight of the bow mooring rope in his hand.

Ten minutes later, with the puffer safely secured and the crew now perched up on her main hatch watching the passing show as a veritable fleet of dinghies and small yachts circled the anchored cruiser, Para Handy presented himself at the dingy dockside office — little more, in truth, than a small wooden hut — of his owner's local agent.

"I'm afraid I have to tell you that your cargo is still up at the distillery, Captain," said that worthy, somewhat shame-faced and flustered. "What with the fleet coming in and all, the town has declared an unoffical holiday and there is just no way that I can get even one carter today, never mind a squad.

"Why don't you just regard it as a holiday for yourselves

and take the day off? I can promise you a top-notch team
to fetch your cargo at first light tomorrow."

~

"Well, at least we couldna get a better day for it,"
conceded the Captain as he, Dougie and Macphail settled
down on a bench outside the Lorne Arms with a glass of ale
apiece. Sunny Jim had gone to take a stroll about the town,
no doubt — as his somewhat envious older colleagues
correctly surmised — to see what young ladies in their
summer finery had been attracted onto the Oban esplanade
by the fine weather and by the occasion.

"Better day for what?" snapped Macphail ill-temperedly.
"Better day for drummin' wir heels in this back-o'-beyond
towerist trap for near enough twenty fower hours? Ah can
think of mony places Ah'd raither be and mony things Ah'd
raither be daeing."

Para Handy shrugged but maintained diplomatic silence
while Dougie went off in search of one of the Bar's sets of
dominos in the hope that a test of skill and chance at a half-
penny each game might help to pass the time in a
pleasanter atmosphere.

Macphail, however, was in no frame of mind to be fobbed
off with such an inadequate palliative as a game of 'the
bones', as he disparagingly described it, and tensions were
again mounting when Sunny Jim rejoined the party, just
before one o'clock, and in a state of some excitement.

"Ah've been roond on the Sooth Pier," he announced
breathlessly and without preamble, "and it's fair hotching
wi' folk. The Navy's openin' the shup to the public-at-large
this afternoon and layin' on twa pinnaces to tak' them oot
and back."

"Bully for the Navy," said Macphail caustically. "What's
that tae us?"

"Simple," said Jim. "There's money to be made on it."

The recollection of some of Sunny Jim's previous money-
making schemes, from the successful but nearly catastrophic affair of the Tobermory Whale to the totally
unrewarding scam involving a purported marathon swim
the length of Kilbrannan Sound, lurched uncomfortably
through the memories of his audience.

Para Handy was the first to recover his composure.

"How?" he asked bluntly.

"Easy!" said Jim. "The pinnaces is runnin' to the shup from the Sooth Pier only. There's nothin' to prevent us takin' oot a hired rowing-boat for the afternoon and ferryin' the towerists oot to the shup from the *North* Pier at saxpence a time, and landin' them onto the Jacob's Ladder on the port side where the Officers and that'll no' see them, for they'll be too busy on the starboard helpin' the young lasses aboard and then tryin' to tempt them wi' the offer of a tour of the shup's engines."

There was a moment's silence, until:

"Capital, Jum, capital!" cried Para Handy. "You aalways have the eye for a bit of business wheneffer the opportunity arises and you have excelled yourself this time. The towerists from the North Esplanade hotels will be chust delighted that they do not have to walk aal the way to the Sooth Pier, and how are they to know that the service there iss for free?"

Even Macphail was grudgingly, cautiously welcoming of the idea and it was Dougie who spotted a possible flaw in the management of the operation.

"There iss chust wan wee thing," he pointed out. "How are we to bring them back again? It's one thing to slup them on board on the quiet side of the shup but another thing entirely if they start queueing at the head of the ladder and looking for us."

That had not been thought of, and for some time the four sat wordlessly, exploring the possibilities of overcoming what now seemed an intransigent problem.

"Got it!" Sunny Jim cried excitedly after some minutes. "We jist dinna tak' them back at all! We tell them it's a roond trup and they're to go back to the Sooth Pier in the pinnaces.

"Once they're on board, we can forget all aboot them. They're no' oor problem then, they're someone else's. The Navy's, and they'll jist huv tae tak' care of it."

~

The afternoon, even by the most exacting standards, could only be judged an outstanding financial success.

Such was the popularity of the passage by rowing-boat from the North Pier that the crew — who had intended to take it in turns to row as pairs (Para Handy teamed with Sunny Jim, Dougie with Macphail) — found themselves forced to hire a second boat from McGrouther's slip, and provide a non-stop shuttle service to the unsuspecting *Shannon* for more than two solid hours.

Sunny Jim's surmise — that the Officers and crew would be much too busy appraising the young ladies attracted to the *official* point-of-entry on the starboard side — proved to be perfectly accurate and the crew of the *Vital Spark* landed their own contraband consignments throughout the afternoon without any trouble whatsoever.

By half-past-four the crowd on the North Pier had thinned to an unrewarding trickle and, in any case, the crew by that time were exhausted by their unbroken exertions in the heat of the day. Sending the last handful of their prospective passengers, some of them protesting querulously, to walk their way to the South Pier, Para Handy and his crew returned their hired boats and settled with their owner.

After meeting all expenses (which had had to include recruiting a local youth to marshal the queues on the Pier while the boats were on the water) a substantial surplus remained. Sunny Jim was despatched to the nearest butcher's shop to buy steaks: the Mate went in search of a green-grocer's from which he returned burdened with punnets of wild mushrooms and fresh strawberries: Macphail staggered back from the Argyll Arms bearing two very large canisters of ale: and Para Handy negotiated a 'favoured friend' price for two bottles of finest malt whisky from the Manager of the distillery whose wares they were to load the next morning.

As the sun sank slowly towards the mountain ridges of Mull the crew sprawled across the main hatch in the cooler, evening glow and sighed with satisfaction. They had been fed and watered in such luxury as could, all too easily, have become a habit — but for the fact that the opportunity of raising the cash to fund such an epicurean existence came their way but once in a blue moon.

Para Handy lit his pipe (a fresh supply of finest tobacco had also been a part of their shopping-list) and surveyed the world about him with the greatest contentment. He had no quarrels to make with anyone. Not even Macphail.

~

Aboard the *Shannon*, the wardroom was hazy with cigar-smoke as her officers relaxed with coffee and brandy after a sumptuous dinner which for them was more or less a matter of routine.

Her captain, however, had one lingering doubt as he leaned back in his chair at the head of the long, highly-polished table and studied his fingernails with a puzzled frown.

"All involved in today's operation deserve our congratulations and thanks," he said at length: "and I will ensure that the men enjoy some well-earned shore leave tomorrow.

"There is, though, just one thing that puzzles me greatly and I wonder if any of you can shed any light on it.

"Why is it, I ask myself, that the head-counts taken by the officers on the pinnaces show — beyond all doubt — that while we landed exactly 317 visitors onto the *ship*, we then managed to return no fewer than 453 to the *shore*?

"Has anyone any idea how this could happen?"

*FACTNOTE*

Ships of the Royal Navy were indeed frequent visitors to Oban and to the waters of the west coast in the early years of this century and of course the numerical strength of that Edwardian Navy was measured in the hundreds. Nowadays in all probability the entire British fleet could be very comfortably accommodated within the area of the Firth of Lorne — and with room to spare.

Para Handy and his crew were going about their business in and around the Clyde at the time of what was probably the greatest period of change in naval history. The turbine engine, first tested in a Clyde steamer, was but a part of that revolution.

Underwater the submarine was coming into its own as a practical and very lethal piece of military machinery. Indeed there were arguments about the very ethics of deploying such an invisible aggressor possessed of such a deadly strike-rate, and against which current defensive and offensive strategy by surface ships was virtually impotent.

Surface strategy itself had been revolutionised by Britain's development of the Dreadnought class of battleship. These ships were not necessarily any larger in their dimensions than their predecessors had been: but their armaments and construction heralded and belonged to a new generation of naval technology.

First of them all was the eponymous *Dreadnought*, which came into service in February 1906. She was swiftly followed by more vessels of the new specifications so that at the outbreak of the First World War the British Navy had

*RULING THE WAVES — Here is one of the nine 15,000 ton, 400ft battleships of the Majestic class (it is not possible to identify precisely which one) at anchor in Campbeltown Loch. They were completed between December 1894 and November 1896 which says something both about the naval finances and the shipyard capacity of the age: but by the time this picture was taken they had been outgunned and outperformed by the new Dreadnought class.*

more than twenty ships of this category in service. The *Bellerophon* was one of these, launched from the Admiralty's Portsmouth yard in 1907 but engined and boilered from the Clyde by Fairfield and Babcock respectively.

The four-funnelled cruiser *Shannon*, which came into service in March 1908, was of almost identical size to the dreadnoughts of the *Bellerophon* class, but of a much lighter construction and with a much less potent ordnance. With a top speed of 23 knots she was one of three sisters which were designed to post a significant improvement over their immediate predecessors — the four vessels of the *Warrior* class commissioned in 1905.

Sadly, despite their enhanced design speed they never delivered what they promised and were therefore generally regarded as something of a disappointment on most counts in comparison to the *Warrior* and her kin.

This class was among the last to be built for the British Navy with a distinctive and steeply-angled ramming prow.

# 34

## *The Centenarian*

On this occasion there was no doubt. The mishap could not in any way have been perpetrated or contributed to by the *Vital Spark*, her Captain or her crew. The puffer, as she had every right to be, lay moored alongside the Albert Harbour basin in Greenock. Para Handy and his crew were sound asleep in their bunks, having had an early night and retired to rest before midnight. First thing next morning they were due to begin loading the cargo of bricks (consigned to a Rothesay builder) which awaited them on the quayside.

The night was cloudy, but calm: and the clock on Greenock Town Hall had not long struck two when a small coaster began to pick her way with hesitant manoeuvres through the narrow entrance to the Harbour. The *Glen Affric* was heavily-laden with slates from the Eisdale Island quarries, and she was very late in arriving at her destination. From the moment she left the Crinan Canal she had suffered intermittent engine-failure and her passage down Loch Fyne, through the Kyles, and up-river to Greenock had been erratic, spasmodic and painfully slow. Her long-suffering crew were irritable, irritated — and very tired.

That, probably, was what caused the accident. But for whatever reason the coaster, as she swung into the basin with plenty of space for her length to be comfortably accommodated immediately for'ard of the *Vital Spark*, failed to nudge her way into that waiting berth but, instead, cannoned fiercely against the hull of the puffer with a crunching noise and a reverberating shock which echoed through its stubby hull and awakened instantly all the sleepers in the fo'c'sle.

Para Handy was the first to scramble into trousers and guernsey and stumble bleary-eyed onto the deck to see what had happened.

The bulk of the coaster loomed large across the puffer's bow and her navigation lights cast a faint illumination upon the scene. From her bridge at the stern came sounds of angry altercation, abuse and accusation, and finally a gruff voice which commanded that 'Wullie' should get ready to leap for the quay with the bow rope readied to moor her, while 'Callum' was ordered ashore to see if there was any immediately apparent damage done to the coaster, or to whichever vessel it was that she had struck.

Ten minutes later the crews of both vessels had made as full an inspection as circumstances — and the darkness — would allow and at that point had found nothing obviously amiss. It was then agreed by the two skippers that no further progress could be made that night, and that a detailed and more searching examination would be made at first light.

All concerned then retired to their bunks, and peace fell again across the Albert Harbour.

Next morning Para Handy and the Mate opened the main-hatch to inspect the puffer's empty hold, and found more than a foot of water in it.

"Bless me!" said the Captain. "I certainly thought that that was one terrible dunt we took last night, and sure enough, here and we have gone and sprung a plate, by the look of her, chust see the watter that she's takin' in! A plate gone, I am sure"

This was also the diagnosis of the diver employed by the owner of the *Vital Spark* (as soon as he was advised by telegraph of the events of the previous night) to carry out a thorough underwater examination of her hull.

By lunchtime the owner himself was at the quayside and — while the lawyer he had brought with him from Glasgow went off with a bulging briefcase and a grim expression to open the preliminary parley with the skipper of the *Glen Affric* — he took Para Handy up to the nearest chop-house.

"You have nothing to reproach yourself with, Peter" he said firmly, to the Captain's considerable relief, "and the pump is coping with the leak. But she will have to go into dry-dock for repair before you can think of sailing. Now, I cannot get her a berth anywhere in Greenock: the nearest available space is at Ferguson's Graving-Dock in Port

Glasgow, but you'll be able to sail her there with no problems, just keep the pump running and don't be tempted to look for too much speed from her and you will be all right. What I must ask you to do is stay aboard to keep an eye on operations but the crew can take some leave if they want it: this job is going to take a week at the least."

And, pushing away his plate of lamb cutlets, reduced now to but a collection of well-picked bones, he signalled to one of the pot-men to replenish their tankards of beer.

~

Para Handy and Macphail brought the *Vital Spark* up-river to the Port Glasgow Yard of the Ferguson Brothers later that same afternoon, having seen Dougie and Sunny Jim safely aboard a Glasgow train and off on an unexpected (and, it must be said, unpaid) week of leave.

"There surely iss no point in keeping the boys, Dan," he had suggested to the Engineer with some apprehension, lest that worthy had thrown a tirravee at the very idea of being delayed in harness while others holidayed. "I need an enchineer, but it only takes the one man on deck to run her to Port Gleska."

Dwarfed by the mighty ocean vessels under construction in the Greenock and Port Glasgow Yards as she hugged the shore on her way upstream, the puffer finally reached Ferguson's, the last yard on that stretch of the Renfrewshire coast of the river between Port Glasgow and the Cart at Paisley.

The graving-dock had been excavated on the open foreshore beyond the high brick walls of the yard, to the eastwards of and parallel to the builder's construction slips, and it was entered by way of a lock gate very similar to those with which Para Handy was familiar on the canals. Guided by one of the yard's foremen, and with three of his men operating the gates, the puffer was directed into the dry-dock and, as the water was drained off, settled onto the massive blocks on its floor.

Macphail, once he had damped down the fire, came up on the deck wiping his hands on a piece of rag and stared about him in some awe. The dry-dock had been designed to accommodate the largest cargo-vessels using the Clyde and the *Vital Spark* lay within it as insignificant as a child's toy boat. From the dock floor the surrounding walls soared above them, cranes to either hand soaring even higher. A flight of concrete steps was let into the walls to right and left and down one of these came a gang of men, two carrying a long wooden ladder which they propped up against the hull of the puffer so that the Captain and Engineer could disembark.

As the docks squad swarmed round the *Vital Spark* and began to construct a scaffolding frame around her hull, Para Handy and Macphail climbed the stairway and headed for the town centre.

Port Glasgow was in festive mood. Everywhere bunting was draped across the streets and flags and banners hung from windows. The sound of a distant brass band could be heard even above the din of the riveters' hammers and the screech of a passing tram.

Para Handy and Macphail made their way to the railway station where the Engineer established the time of the next train to Glasgow and bought a single ticket. With half-an-hour to pass the pair went into the bar of the Station Hotel.

"The toon is fairly hotchin' today," Macphail observed to the barman as he ordered two beers. "Whit's up? Is't a wedding?"

"Naw", replied the barman, "it's jist pairt o' the celebrations for the *Comet* — the auld shup, ye ken, it is just exactly wan hundred years since she wis launched at Woods's yerd and the Cooncil is havin' all sorts of hootenannies to mark the occasion. This is party-time at the Port. I hear there's even to be a replica o' the shup herself arriving on the river tomorrow!"

～

"Well," said Macphail as he boarded his train and leaned out of the carriage window to take farewell of Para Handy, "at least ye'll no' want for company or cheer by the look o' Port Glesga, but Ah'm vexed ye have to be watchman on your own shup!"

"No problem at aal," said the Captain: "there iss plenty I can do to pass my time. She could be doing do with a lick or two of paint for a stert."

And on his way back to the ship, after waving the Engineer's train out of the station, Para Handy called into a conveniently placed ship chandler's and bought a tin of black paint, a tin of white paint, and two brushes. That evening, after the dockyard squad had packed up for the day and gone home, he climbed onto the planked scaffolding surrounding the ship and began to apply a fresh coat of black paint to her bulwarks.

That job of refurbishment took longer than expected as it had to be abandoned during working hours, when the dockyard gang was busy about the puffer, and therefore it was the following evening before it was finished. At seven o'clock Para Handy put the paint and brush away and climbed the dock stairway, heading towards town for a deserved refreshment. At the top of the stairs he paused to look down on his handywork, admiring with some satisfaction the gleaming band of black which encircled the hull. Tomorrow he would use the white paint to restore the puffer's name at bow and stern, which had of necessity been overpainted as he applied the fresh coats of black and then — if there was time — he promised himself that he would give her just a touch of gold beading to set her off to perfection.

~

Half-an-hour in the Clune Bar was more than enough for the Captain. The saloon was crowded and noisy, and the talk was of nothing but the *Comet* celebrations, and the expected arrival of the replica, which was discussed at considerable length with excited anticipation.

As the Captain made his way back to the foreshore in the bright evening sunshine he was aware of greater-than-expected numbers on the street ahead of him, and of a constant stream of people hurrying past in the direction of the river.

There was an air of excitement about, and he caught frequent references to the *Comet* and cries of "She's here!" and "She's arrived!" and "Come on, let's have a look at her!"

He was quite astonished to find, as he came round the corner of the high brick wall surrounding the shipyard and within sight of the graving-dock in which the puffer was lying, to see a huge crowd lining it on all sides, men, women and children leaning over the parapet and pointing excitedly into the depths of the dock.

"My Chove," he said to himself, "they must have put the *Comet* in beside the shup! I wonder chust what she looks like? Well, her crew will be company for me." And he quickened his steps.

There were complaints as he pushed his way through the press of people but when he protested indignantly: "My shup iss in there, you must let me through!" a respectful hush fell on the assembled crowd and they drew back to leave a passage for him.

Para Handy reached the parapet and leaned over in anticipation, eager to see this fabled replica of the world's first succesful steamship.

There was nothing in the dry dock — nothing except the *Vital Spark*. Not of course that anyone else would have known that that was her name — not since her Captain had overpainted it with gleaming black.

Para Handy was dimly aware of the cries and questions from the crowds around him.

"My Lord, imagine anyone having the courage to sail in *that!*"

"Where's her nameboard?"

"They're probably fitting it in the morning."

"She's even smaller than I would have believed!"

"Did you ever see anything like that in your life! It's come straight out of the Ark!"

Drawing himself up with dignity, Para Handy paused at the top of the stairway leading down to the dock-floor.

"Ye're a bunch of ignorant gowks," he shouted, "that issna able to recognise wan o' the finest examples o' modern shup-building on the whole river! And when the *Vital Spark* celebrates *her* centenary, you'll no' need to build a replica to celebrate. She will still be aroond herself."

And with his back ramrod-straight and his chest puffed out with determined pride, he made his way down the stairway and clambered aboard the smartest vessel in the coasting trade.

*FACTNOTE*

The incident in the Albert Harbour was suggested by the more serious accident which befell the three-man estuary puffer *Craigielea* in 1952. She was side-swiped in the hours of darkness by an incoming, heavily-laden coaster and was in fact sunk (though later refloated). Fortunately, her crew were all asleep at home in Greenock.

Henry Bell's *Comet* was the first succesful attempt to

provide a regular passenger service by steamer in Europe and, like so many other great Scottish 'firsts' it came about in spite of and not because of the attitudes of the Government and established commercial interests of the day. Bell had been an apprentice in a shipyard on the Forth, worked in a London engineering workshop, and studied both theory and practice when he tried, in the early years of the 19th century, to obtain government backing for experimental work to develop the application of practical steam-power to shipping.

The government was totally uninterested. Bell moved on to other things, and ten years later was owner of a large and prosperous hotel business in Helensburgh. The difficulties he experienced in finding comfortable and reliable transportation from Glasgow for his customers provided the incentive for a return to his earlier experimentation with steam. The result was the *Comet*. Bell designed not just her hull, but her engine as well. She was 50ft overall, with a 4 h.p. engine driving two tiny paddle wheels on either side of the hull and steering was by tiller.

This very first of the 'Clyde Steamers' had a top speed of just 5 knots — reduced to almost nothing against wind or tide. She offered accommodation in two classes — 'Best Cabin' at 4/- and Second at 3/-. These were astonishingly high fares at that time and there was indeed a small cabin for passengers paying the higher fare, shoe-horned in astern of the engines. The tiny vessel was built at the Port Glasgow yard of John Wood, and launched in July 1812. She gave eight years of generally reliable service before being stranded at Crinan in mid-winter 1820. Just what she was doing up there I do not know. The boat was broken up but her engine was rescued and today sits in the South Kensington Science Museum. Why *there* instead of Glasgow's superb Transport Museum I do not know either.

I have cheated shamelessly over the question of the replica for although one *was* built (by Lithgows Port Glasgow) for the 150th anniversary of 1962, the only manifestation of the little ship which was featured in the otherwise lavish and extensive centenary celebrations in 1912 was the 'conversion' into the *Comet* of one of the town's electric trams, which ran as an illuminated replica.

# 35

## *High Teas on the High Seas*

Macphail squeezed into his place at the apex of the triangular table in the forepeak of the fo'c'sle and studied with quite unconcealed disgust the plate which had just been placed before him.

On it a couple of rashers of half-raw streaky bacon sat in a pool of fat next to three black, smoking objects which could with some difficulty be identified as sausages. At the side of the plate two eggs demonstrated their cook's ability to achieve what most would have deemed impossible: the yolks were startlingly hued in a bilious green and of the consistency of an india-rubber, while the whites were transparent, glutinous and virtually uncooked save for their ragged edges which were charred to an intense black.

With a heavy sigh, the Engineer slowly raised his face from its contemplation of this culinary feast and, with a shake of the head and a prolonged sigh, stared with narrowed and unfriendly eyes at its perpetrator.

The Mate — for he it was — shuffled uncomfortably and avoided the Engineer's steely stare.

"I'm sorry, Dan," he said apologetically: "I chust havna got the knack of the stove yet, it's aalways either too hot or too cold wi' me: but I wull can only get better."

"Which is mair than I can say is likely for ony of the rest of us," said the Engineer unfeelingly. "Whaur the bleezes did *you* learn tae haundle a frying-pan? The try-hoose on a whaler?"

"Now, Dan," said Para Handy in a placatory tone, "Poor Dougie iss makin' the best chob of it he canm in the conditions, for he signed on ass the Mate of the vessel remember, no' as its held cook and bottle-washer. He iss chust ass much a victim of the circumstances ass we are."

～

The circumstances, in a nutshell, were that the *Vital Spark*'s cheerful resident *chef de cuisine*, Sunny Jim, had taken a few days leave of absence to attend a wedding in Kirkcudbright — "a notorious toon for jollification and high-jinks," he had warned Para Handy: "no weddin' ever lasts less than three days there so Ah'm likely to be gone a week." Para Handy's dismay at this pronouncement was only slightly mollified when Jim added that he had arranged, as replacement, that his cousin Colin Turner, the Tar (he of mixed memory for the crew of the puffer) would officiate as relief deckhand and cook during the week of his absence.

Given the Tar's past reputation, it was perhaps not altogether surprising (though nonetheless annoying) that, on the morning of the vessel's scheduled departure from Bowling, he simply failed to appear as promised.

"Whit else wud ye expect frae Colin Turner?" was Macphail's unsurprised comment: but the patient Captain gave the missing crewman the benefit of the doubt until early afternoon before he accepted that the Tar just was not going to turn up, and gave orders for the puffer to slip her moorings and set off for her destination which, on this occasion, was a forestry pier on the Sound of Mull.

Though the Tar would be sorely missed on their arrival at that pier to take on a cargo of sawn timber — a backbreaking job loading this at any time, but most especially when three-handed instead of fully crewed, and with little help expected from the forestry men — there was a more immediate problem, namely the question of the catering arrangements on board, which must be resolved.

The larder was well-stocked for the outward jorney — Sunny Jim had seen to that before he left: but it would have to be fully replenished, probably at Oban, for the return trip. But even a well-stocked larder requires somebody to prepare its contents for the table and this was the subject of a great debate as the *Vital Spark* sailed slowly down-river in the late afternoon.

Nobody on board wanted the responsibilities of acting-cook.

Though the argument was debated loud and long for an hour or more, there was really no doubt in the mind of any of the three protagonists, from the very outset, as to what the outcome of it would be.

Para Handy would be able to argue that, as Captain with overall responsibility for the navigation and the general maritime integrity of the vessel, he could not possibly be distracted from those duties by the mundane requirements of making cups of tea or frying sausages — particularly in a location from which he would have no view whatsoever of the outside world and the circumstances and whereabouts of his command.

Macphail would advance similar pleading for his role in the hierarchy of the running and management of the ship, pointing out also that where the Captain and Mate could to a degree be interchangeable in respect of their duties as navigators and helmsmen, *nobody* on board could deputise for the engineer of the vessel, who must plainly be sidelined totally when it came to a decision on responsibilities for the commisariat.

The engineer also had the distinct advantage of knowing that however much the other two were anxious to avoid the role of ship's cook for themselves, neither would view with equanimity the prospects of food-preparation being (quite literally) in the hands of somebody who had just finished shovelling a load of nutty slack into the furnace and then topped that activity off with an application of the oil-can and its accompanying oil-rag to a tangle of greasy engine parts.

The unfortunate Mate realised from the very first that he was a doomed man, placed by fate in circumstances over which he could have no control. Though it was with ill-grace, when the debate was at last concluded, that he made his way to the fo'c'sle to study the contents of the larder and plan his menus, it was also with a condemned man's recognition of the inevitable.

His offering that first evening was mince and tatties.

Unhappily, he was unaware of the important role played in such a delicacy by the introduction of finely-chopped onions to the mince: nor that the best way to cook mince was not to *boil* it fiercely in a large pan of seawater: nor that potatos required more time to cook through than the few moments it took to bring to boil the pan of water in which *they* had been placed. Nor did condiments play any part in his cuisine.

Most of what was served to his shipmates on the enamelled metal plates of the puffer's only dinner-service finished up over the side of the vessel, and Para Handy and Macphail made the best of a meal they could from bread, cheese, and (eaten raw) the onions which the Mate had ommitted from the mince.

The three retired to their bunks, with the *Vital Spark* moored at Kilchattan Bay, in a frosty silence.

The Mate slept but fitfully: dreams of the acclaim of his shipmates as he served them five-star meals and basked in their warm compliments were interrupted by nightmares in which they rose in horror against the culinary disasters placed before them, and threw their perpetrator over the side of the ship.

He awoke the next morning red-eyed and ill-tempered and began to set out his breakfast ingredients with grim determination.

∾

The results of his early morning endeavours, which have already been described, again finished up overboard and, with no cheese left to quieten the pangs of hunger, Captain and Engineer did what they could with a loaf of bread, a pack of butter and a tin of orange marmalade.

For the next two days (as the *Vital Spark* made her passage to the forestry pier, loaded up such a quantity of cut timber that her deck was so heaped with it that the puffer's rowing-boat had to be unshipped and towed astern, and headed down the Sound of Mull to Oban to replenish food-stocks) a succession of quite appalling meals were served in the fo'c'sle and — more often than not — hurled angrily over the side a few moments later.

When the stocks of bread ran out, and the company was reduced to staving of their growing hunger pains with months-old ship's biscuit, the Mate began to fear for his safety.

At four o'clock in the afternoon, the *Vital Spark* tied up at the North Pier in Oban's capacious harbour. The Captain handed the Mate the ship's mess-money for the purchase of provisions for the return voyage to Bowling and announced that he and the Engineer were going ashore for a refreshment "to waash the tastc of your cookin' oot" as he very kindly put it: and that when they returned at six o'clock they would expect that the Mate would have spent the money on food that he *could* cook, and would have an appetising meal on the table for them.

The Mate stood disconsolate on the deck as his ship-mates made off, and stared miserably round the harbour. The *Vital Spark* had the North Pier to herself. Over on the South Pier MacBrayne steamers were loading passengers for the evening services to Tobermory to the west, Fort William to the north.

In that moment, Dougie saw a solution to all his problems.

~

Para Handy and Macphail returned from the Lorne Bar with heavy hearts, each imagining what horrors might be waiting for them on the mess-table.

To their astonishment, it was neatly laid out with plates of sliced and buttered bread and teacake, pancakes and a selection of fancies — there was even a single rose in a small vase as a centre-piece.

As they seated themselves, the Mate went to the stove and with pride took from its oven three plates of delicious, crisply-battered haddock fillets with golden chips and tastily-minted peas.

Wordlessly, the crew fell to and demolished the delicious food set before them.

"Well, Dougie," said the Captain, finishing the last morsel of currant-cake and pouring himself another cup of tea, "I don't know whether to thank the Oban proveesions, or the improvement in your cooking, but that's the best meal I've had for months!"

And even the Engineer grudgingly concurred.

The miracle continued all the way to Glasgow. Breakfast before leaving Oban was a revelation — crisp bacon, gold-en-yoked eggs and sausages of a spicey perfection. Indeed the Mate insisted on buying fresh provisions that morning, and sent his shipmates for an early constitutional towards Ganavan while he did so.

Lunch at Crinan (where they shared passage through the canal with MacBrayne's *Cygnet*), served after the Captain and Engineer, at Dougie's insistence, had stepped ashore for a refreshment to set their appetites up, comprised roast leg of lamb with mint sauce, new potatos and carrots followed by jam roly-poly with a delicious custard sauce.

They arrived to berth overnight at Tarbert just twenty minutes before MacBrayne's *Iona* left for Ardrishaig, there to berth for the night herself. Tea, when Captain and Engineer returned from the Harbour Inn, consisted of cold roast beef with a delicious salad and another fine selection of cakes and pastries.

Breakfast (again at Tarbert) and then lunch at Rothesay, where the Mate insisted on berthing to replenish his supplies, and sent his shipmates up to the Argyll Arms for a drink at his own expense, were again a revelation of their temporary cook's new-found culinary skills and there was even talk of readjusting the whole duty rota of the *Vital Spark* on Sunny Jim's return.

But late supper at Bowling, where they berthed at ten o'clock, was a repeat of the stomach-churning disasters of the outward trip. Greasy bacon, half-raw Lorne sausage, cold tinned beans.

"My Cot, Dougie," said Para Handy in disgust, pushing his plate away, the food on it virtually untouched. "What on earth went wrong tonight?"

"Simple," said the Mate, "there's no MacBrayne shups here."

"What in bleezes d'you mean?" asked the mystified Captain.

"What d'you think?" replied the Mate: "You surely didna think ony of that good cooking wass *mine*?

"Wi' our skiff handy in the watter astern, I've been rowing to the MacBrayne boats in Oban and Crinan and Tarbert and Rothesay and *buying* meals ready-made from the passenger-galley cooks.

"It cost me money oot of my ain pocket, what wi' the extra for the food, and givin' you two beer-money to get you oot the way whiles I did ma 'shopping': but at least it wass worth it no' to have your abuse aal the way from Mull to Gleska the way I had it aal the way from Gleska to Mull!"

*FACTNOTE*

I am not sure what the good folk of Kirkcudbright did to merit Sunny Jim's observations about the town's notorious abilities for celebrating a wedding in style!

Shipboard catering — at least in the context of provisions

for ocean-going passengers — must always have been fraught with problems in the days before the invention and general use of stabilisers. Early (and not so early) accounts of Transatlantic liner passages tell tales of woe in all classes, for of course sea-sickness is no respecter of persons.

Most poignant perhaps are the stories of society ladies in the first-class acommodations in the luxurious days of White Star and CGT, both expecially renowned for their cuisine, who spent the entire week of the crossing prostrate in their cabins, with the double frustration of failing to make their mark on their fellow-passengers at the elegant functions and soirees, and unable to keep down so much as a cup of bouillon, never mind the caviar and lobster and tournedos and out-of-season fruits.

And of course, for all of this irretrievably lost opportunity and gone-for-ever delights, they had paid handsomely — very handsomely. More than one purser recounts being importuned on arrival at New York for just one jar of caviar to compensate in some way for the outlay which had been lost — overboard.

Catering on the Clyde steamers rarely encountered weather problems and was surprisingly good, most particularly on MacBrayne's vessels: and even allowing for the horrendous inflation in the generations since, it seems to have offered remarkable value as well. In 1911 MacBrayne's first class fare from Glasgow to Ardrishaig and return was 6/- or just 30p: while for a mere 4/6 (22p) more, the excursionist could enjoy a package of breakfast, lunch and tea.

In *The Victorian Summer of the Clyde Steamers* Alan Paterson reprints the day's menus on one sailing of MacBrayne's *Lord of the Isles*. Breakfast offered (among other choices) Salmon, Fresh Herring, Steaks, Ham and Eggs, and a whole range of breads, rolls and trimmings. Dinner included Salmon again, plus Roast Beef, Boiled Mutton, Roast Lamb, Fowl, Tongue, Assorted Sweets, Cheeses. High Tea was a simpler repast of just Fish, Cold Meats, Boiled Eggs, Fancy Breads and Preserves.

And the costs? Breakfast was 2/- (10p) as was High Tea. Dinner was 3/- (15p).

I reckon Dougie did pretty well by his shipmates if that was the kind of fare he was putting on the table!

# 36

## *A Stranger in a Foreign Land*

Para Handy's blinkered devotion to the West Coast and its islands is legendary. "Have you never regretted that you didn't decide to go foreign yourself, Captain?" I asked him one evening as we sat on the pier at Gourock watching the Anchor liner *Columbia* pass the Tail o' the Bank at the start of her passage to New York.

"No, not really," said Para Handy without hesitation. "I would neffer have had the dignity of my own command if I had, for wan o' the qualifications for bein' Captain wi' the likes of the Anchor Line or the Blue Funnel is that you have to pass a wheen o' examinations in seamanshup and navigation and the like, and I wass neffer a man for examinations.

"Forbye, you canna learn seamanshup oot of a book, whateffer they say, it iss something you either have or you have not, and ass for navigation, weel, my idea o' navigatin' is doon to the Garrioch Heid, first right for Tighnabruaich, second right for Ardrishaig, straight on for Brodick, left for Saltcoats — that kind o' thing. Aal this business wi' sextants and chairts and compasses and the rest is way beyond me. It iss wan thing for the men who have the agility for them, like Hurricane Jeck for example — he has a heid for figures and he passed for his Master's Certificate the fastest effer in the merchant marine.

"It wass a peety he lost it chust aboot ass quick, but ass Jeck himself would say, what's for you wullna go by you, and what you're no meant to have you wullna keep.

"The wan thing I disagree wi' him aboot in sayin' that iss when it comes to the matter o' money, for I'm sure that there wass neffer anybody better suited to *have* it than

Jeck. Money could have been invented for him, he spends it wi' such dignity and style that it is a privilege simply to waatch him doin' it. But then at the same time, you see, it iss exactly because of that that he can neffer *keep* it. It chust runs through his hands like watter from a tap."

I felt it best to offer no opinion on the question of Hurricane Jack's suitability to be a member of the moneyed classes.

"But I wass abroad myself, chust the wan time" continued the Captain, "and I decided then and there that wance wass enough for me."

I stared in surprise. "I had no idea," I said. "When was this, and where to?"

"Luverpool," said the Captain. "Chust before I got the command o' the *Vital Spark*."

"But Liverpool isn't *abroad*, Captain," I protested. "Liverpool is in England."

"Weel, if England issna abroad then I would be very pleased if you wud tell me what it iss," said Para Handy scathingly and with considerable conviction. "They are a very strange sort of a people indeed doon there. They aal taalk a lenguage that you simply canna understand, they dinna drink whusky, their beer iss like watter, not wan o' them hass so mich as a single word o' the Gaelic, they canna mak' a daicent bleck pudding or bit of breid, nor cure bacon, nor catch fush, they've neffer even heard o' Hurricane Jeck, they dinna like the pipes, and instead of amusing themselves wi' something ceevilised like shinty, they play some sissy game caalled cricket."

Before an attack set on so broad a front, and one so vehemently delivered, I was for a moment speechless.

"Well, Captain," I said after a moment, "that is a different way of life to ours, perhaps, but it does not make England a foreign country. I am sure that many English people who come to Scotland would be just as entitled to describe *us* and *our* ways as foreign if they applied the same criteria as you have."

"I am sure I have neffer applied a criteria in my naitural Mr Munro," said the Captain indignantly, "and I would be grateful if you wud chust bear that in mind."

I decided that this was neither the time nor the place to embark on a short lesson in semantics.

"And in any case," Para Handy continued, "any Englishman trying to miscaall *us* as foreigners wud be in serious trouble. I am a peaceable man, myself, and wud simply try to persuade him of the error of his ways in a chentlemanly fashion, but the likes of Hurricane Jeck wud have a mair immediate and violent means of debating hiss misconceptions wi' him."

"Tell me more about your visit to Liverpool..." I prompted.

"I wass between chobs at the time, ass I said a while back. I wass waiting for the *Vital Spark* to be laaunched, and I had signed aff a gabbart I'd been crewing oot of Ardrossan, I chust couldna stand her skipper, he wassna a chentleman at aal.

"So I wass lookin' for a berth for two weeks or thereby, and when I made an enquiry at the Ardrossan Docks Office they telt me that there wass a shup o' the Burns Line on a charter cairgo run to Luverpool that wass short of a deck-hand, and I got the chob the same mornin'.

"The shup wass the *Lamprey*, she wass usually on the regular Belfast service but she had been chartered to tak' a load of steel plate from Harland and Wolff's to wan o' the shipyerds in Luverpool.

"We wass two days in Belfast takin' the cairgo on board. I have a lot of time for the Irish, they could be chust ass good ass the Scots if it wassna for those few miles of sea cuttin' them aff from us. I ken that their whusky is different, but then you dinna really notice that after the third gless or thereby, for you get kind of used wi' it.

"We had a very rough passage across the Irish Sea to Luverpool and wi' the load of steel plate the shup took a fair pounding. I wass the happy man when we cam' safe to the docks.

"Efter the steel had been unloaded the owners wass trying to find a cargo of some sort for either Belfast or Ardrossan so they could mak' somethin' oot of the home trup — I can tell you there iss nobody near ass greedy ass a man that owns a shup, he canna stand sein' it no' makin' money wi' effery turn o' the propellor.

"So for two days we wass coolin' our heels in Luverpool. There wassna mich to do, and we wass runnin' desperate low on coin, we didna have ass much ass would pay for even chust the wan wee quiet dram. I had got friendly wi' wan o' the stokers, a laad caaled Danny, frae Stornoway: Danny had wance been a piper wi' the Bleck Watch and he still had his pipes aboot him — he practiced oot on the poop deck when he wass aff duty — so I put a proposeetion to him.

"I telt him that they wudna often ha'e the chance to hear a daicent piper in Luverpool, and if we went into the toon and he played and I went roond wi' the hat, we wud surely mak' enough to put oorselves in funds for a refreshment.

"Danny chumped at the idea, dashed doon below to get his pipes and aff we went.

"We picked a spot where two o' the main streets crossed, and there wass a big public hoose at each corner.

" 'This'll do fine and dandy,' says I. 'The chentlemen comin' in and oot o' the Inns wull be pleased enough to hear a cheery tune. Wait you and you'll see. We wull do weel here!'

"Danny sterted to tune up his pipes, and wud you credit it, he hadna been blawin' for mair than a hauf a meenit when a big fella wi' a long white apron, and a bleck waist-coat on him same ass he wis a meenister, came rushin' oot o' wan o' the public hooses.

" 'Whit sort o' racket d'ye caal this,' he shouted, very red in the face. 'Are you tryin' to scare my customers away? Whit the bleezes is yon man daeing?'

" 'It iss aal right,' said I: 'stop you and you wull see something worth listening to in a meenit. For the moment he iss simply tuning his pipes.'

" 'Tuning them is it, for peety's sakes.' howls the man. '*Tuning* them indeed! And wull you tell me chust how the bleezes he's meant to know when he *has*?'

"And he disappeared into the public hoose. Twa meenits later, when Danny wass chust gettin' warmed up wi' *The Glendaruel Highlanders*, he cam' oot again, wi' a smaall cairdboard box in his haunds, and went across the street and into the ither three public hooses, wan efter another.

"When he cam' oot o' the last Inns, he walked over and tipped a wee pile of sulver oot o' the cairdboard box into the kep I was holding.

" 'Now,' he shouted, purple wi' rage by this time, 'That's frae me and my fellow publicans. Wull you please now be reasonable for we are aal trying to run a business here. Wull you and your frien' now *please go away!*'

"Well, we wassna weel content at the way we got the money, but at least we had enough for a few refreshments. 'We'd better no' go near wan o' these hooses, Danny' said I, 'we shall look for a likely-looking Inns close by.'

"We foond this wee public hoose doon an alley and in we went and I ordered up two drams. 'Drams?' says the barman, 'What in tarnation is *drams*? We dinna sell drams in here.'

"So we ordered beer, and I can tell you it wass chust like drinking coloured watter. Mr Younger would neffer get awa' wi' foisting rubbish like that on your average thirsty Gleska man. But we had paid for it, and we would drink it if it killed us. Danny had his pipes under his airm, of course, and after a meenit the barman leaned over the coonter and said, quite jocco, 'We dinna get mony bagpipers in here.'

" 'Wi' coloured watter at saxpence the pint, I'm not at aal surprised aboot that,' said Danny. And we never got to feenish the beer, they threw us oot.

"By this time the public hooses wass aal shutting for the efternoon. Danny stopped a man in the street and asked him where we could get a refreshment. 'The only place iss the cricket metch,' says the man. 'The Inns there iss open aal day.'

" 'I havna the faintest notion what a cricket metch is,' says Danny. 'But if the public hooses are open, who cares?'

"We paid oor sixpences to get in the gate, and made for the refreshment rooms. There wass a whole wheen o' chaps in white shirts and troosers standin' in the middle of a field throwing a red ball at a man haudin' some sort of club. Personally I dinna think this cricket is a game at aal, it's some kind of a magic ritual, for ass soon ass the wan that wass throwin' the ball hit the man wi' the club on the legs, aal the ithers threw their arms up in the air and shouted 'Howzat!' — and wud you credit it, at that very instant the rain came *pourin'* doon!

"The Inns kept open, but efter an hour or thereby they wudna serve ony more to Danny and me. We'd been blethering awa' in the Gaelic and they thought that we wass the worse for drink and said it wassna a lenguage at aal, it wass chust us so fu' we couldna speak. 'If Hurricane Jeck wass here,' says I quite angry, 'You wouldna get awa' wi' refusing *him*.'

'Hurricane *who*?' says the man behind the bar.

"We sailed for Ardrossan the next morning wi' a half cairgo of pit props, so it wassna a total loss for the owners.

"But the food on the way hame wass deplorable. They'd stocked up the galley in Luverpool, and aal we got wass bleck pudding filled wi' lumps of fet, rubbery breid, tasteless streaky bacon wi' nae cure to it, and fush that aromatic you wouldna put it doon to a cat.

"Don't talk to me aboot England no' being a foreign country. I wass there — I've seen it for myself!"

And I thought it best not to argue with the Captain, but to take him for a quiet glass of something with which to wash away the taste of such an unhappy — if misinterpreted — memory.

FACTNOTE

The Anchor Line was established by two brothers — Nicol and Robert Handyside — in Glasgow in 1856 and lasted for exactly a century. The name 'Anchor Line' was only adopted in 1899.

Though usually thought of as a Clyde-based transatlantic company, Anchor traded to America from a score or more of European and Mediterranean ports, and to India and the East.

The *Columbia* was a three-funnelled passenger and cargo liner of just over 8000 tons, almost 500ft in length and carrying 345 passengers in first class, 218 in second and 740 in steerage to take advantage of the booming traffic and she sailed mostly on the Glasgow to New York run, with a regular call in Ireland on the outward journey to take on emigrant familes. She served as an armed merchant cruiser (renamed the *Columbella*) in the First World War, was sold to Greek interests in 1926, and was finally broken up in 1929.

There was a complex network of shipping links between Scotland and Ireland in the early years of the century, and G & J Burns of Ardrossan held a substantial share of this. Later amalgamated to become the Burns-Laird Line, they moved the centre of their operations to Glasgow and a generation ago their handsome vessels provided a comfortable and reliable overnight service to ireland from the Broomielaw, and their cargo ships criss-crossed the Irish Sea and the North Channel.

Harand and Wolff in Belfast were — with Vickers in Barrow-in-Furness — the only serious rivals to the Clyde Yards on the western seaboard. The Belfast builders are probably best remembered nowadays for the *Olympic* and above all for the *Titanic*, the two giants which (with the later *Britannic*) were intended to set the seal on the superiority of Ismay's White Star Line. Instead they nearly destroyed it.

There is a piece of maritime folklore associated with the

naming of the *Britannic* — as there later was with the naming of the *Queen Mary*. It is said that the original plan had been that the three huge sisters, which dwarfed anything else on the high seas at the time of their launch, were to have been named *Olympic*, *Titanic* — and finally *Gigantic*.

But legend has it that the sheer horror of the *Titanic's* loss convinced the company that to call their third ship by such an arrogant and boastful name would simply be to tempt providence (particularly after the bitterly-regretted claims about the unsinkability of her sister) and the plan was shelved, with the patriotic and uncontroversial *Britannic* being chosen instead.

# 37

## Cavalcade to Camelon

It was just past two o'clock of the afternoon of a fine Saturday in early May. The *Vital Spark* lay against the stone facing of the passenger quay on the east side of Craigmarloch bridge on the Forth and Clyde Canal.

A welcome, idle weekend was in prospect for her crew. She was scheduled, first thing on Monday morning, to load a cargo of cask whisky from the Rosebank distillery at Camelon, on the western fringes of the historic Burgh of Falkirk. Until then a long and lazy meander across central Scotland was in prospect, a passage no longer plagued by the taunts of the urchins of the towns and villages which fringed the canal. The manner in which a previous generation of those youthful predators on the inland voyages of the vessel was devastatingly dealt with — thanks to the ingenuity of Sunny Jim — has already been set out in one of my earlier accounts of the travels and travails of the *Vital Spark*, and is now firmly entrenched in the folklore of today's towpath tearaways who therefore give to the puffer a wide (and respectful) berth.

Para Handy and Macphail were seated on the main hatch in a most companionable silence, replete with fried sausages and potatos and in lazy contemplation of the tranquil canal. To their right hand the silver ribbon of its waters curved out of sight along a gentle bend towards Kirkintilloch with, on the nearer bank, the towpath: and on the farther, a long phalanx of mature trees at their freshest springtime green.

The Captain stretched luxuriously and reached into the flap of his trouser pocket for his oilskin tobacco pouch and his safety matches.

"I tell you, Dan, on a day like this I think that there iss a lot to be said for a landlocked life. There iss not the lochs and the bens, to be sure, and the view iss not what it iss when you are comin' doon Loch Fyne, but then neither iss the weather either. A peaceful existence!"

The Engineer nodded.

"True enough, Peter," he said. "But wud ye no' get awfu' bored wi' it, aye jist the same places and the same faces year in and year oot, the same cairgos and the same carnaptious duvvles to deal wi' at the locks? At least we get some sort of deeversity on the ruver, and a lot o' different harbour-masters yellin' at us for no good reason, no' the identical yins a' the time."

"You are probably right," conceded Para Handy. "And for sure neither iss there the same opportunity for cheneral high-jinks or entertainment to be had. I mean to say, chust look at Dougie and Jum!"

The Mate, ever the optimist whether confronted with the lively tidal waters off the pier at Brodick or, as here, with the dark depths of a sluggish canal, could be seen a couple of hundred yards away seated on the bank with his legs dangling over its edge. In his hands was the *Vital Spark*'s acknowledgement of the tenets of Izaac Walton — a ten-foot bamboo pole: from its tip there dangled a length of tarry twine terminating in a rusting hook baited with a worm whose luck had run out when Dougie had spotted it, sunning itself on the grassy bank, at precisely the right time for him — but very much the wrong time for it.

Sunny Jim was more strenuously employed on the broad swathe of grass beside the imposing but at present unopened Craigmarloch Refreshment Rooms, widely patronised in summer by excursionists and day-trippers on the canal. He was playing kick-about with a handful of local youths with a battered football which had been spied floating, forgotten and abandoned in one of the locks at Kirkintilloch on their passage through them that morning: and commandeered enthusiastically by their young deck-hand.

The Captain viewed with mixed emotions the prowess demonstrated by his young shipmate as he showed quite remarkable skill with an impressive display of the traditional game of 'keepie-uppie' with boot and knee which had the Craigmarloch youths staring open-mouthed in amazement.

"Nimble enough wi' his feet, right enough," he said. "But for why? What good does it do the laad? It is chust the same as chumpin' through girrs, that iss aal it iss, fine enough for a penny street-show but I am sure and you could neffer be making a livin' from it.

"And as for Dougie...! Has he effer, I ask you, caught a fush in his naitural? I am telling you, Dan, if we had to depend on Dougie Campbell's skills for the proveeshuns on the vessel then we would aal surely sterve."

"Hairmless enough, Peter," replied the Engineer, on whom the peace and beauty of his surroundings had wrought an unexpected and most unusual air of goodwill. "For surely you need to enjoy some divershun in this world, as weel as work? Life iss no jist aboot the daily grind, as it says in the Scruptures, there has tae be a chance for ." But he surreptitiously and shamefacedly hid the copy of his newest penny novelette under a fold of hatch tarpaulin as he spoke.

Para Handy snorted. "That's ass may be," said he: "but the day that Dougie brings us in any sort of catch, or the day that we get ony good out of Jum's fancy tricks wi' a foot-baal, iss the day I'll take and treat you aal in the nearest Inns at my expense!"

"Weel," said Macphail darkly, "Ah heard you say that, Peter, so be sure Ah'll keep you to it."

"Chance would be a fine thing," said the Captain, undismayed and unperturbed, and set about filling his pipe.

A few minutes later the two men stretched out across the main hatch and dozed fitfully in the warm sunshine.

Time passed.

On the towpath Dougie fished — but caught nothing. On the grassy bank the football hopefuls set up goals marked by folded jackets and played five-a-side and, when an ill-judged shot sent the ball spinning into the canal, pushed its perpetrator into the water (despite his protests) to retrieve it.

Time passed.

At three o'clock the peace was shattered. A horse-drawn wagon came clattering down the narrow, winding road from Kilsyth and pulled into the forecourt of the Refreshment Rooms. Three young women in the black dresses and white pinafores of waitresses or parlour-maids jumped from the bench behind the driver's raised seat and moved towards the building: two men began to unload boxes and crates from the dray.

The driver, a smartly-dressed individual in a brass-button navy blazer and with a jaunty straw boater, took one glance at the panorama of angler, footballers and puffer and came rushing over to the quayside against which the *Vital Spark* was lying.

"Get this eyesore out of here this minute!" he yelled with such ferocity that Para Handy was wide awake in a moment. "Are you crazy? In thirty minutes the *Gipsy Queen* will be here with the first excursion party of the year from Glasgow, and I've got little enough time to get their teas ready as it is. This is a berth for the gentry and their ladies, not a dumping-ground for a filthy coal-boat. Get it shifted this very minute!

"And you lot," he added, rounding on the footballers without pausing to draw breath, "away to Hampden Park if football's all your brains can cope with. Don't waste my time with it here!"

"And you," turning to Dougie — for he was obviously determined to leave nobody out, "have you got a fishing licence?"

Para Handy got to his feet and drew himself up with dignity. "I am sure and there iss no need to take that attitude," he said, "for we have effery right to be here same ass you. But ass it happens we were chust on the point of leaving anyway so I will not put you to any further trouble..."

~

"Why wass he tellin' you to go to Hampden Perk?" the Captain enquired of Sunny Jim shortly afterwards as the *Vital Spark* negotiated one of the locks between Castlecary and Bonnybridge.

"Jist bein' clever by his way o' it," said Jim. "It's the Cup Final today. Wush I *could* have been there, Raith Rovers and the Bairns."

"Bairns?" asked Para Handy in a puzzled tone. "Whit the bleezes iss the Bairns?"

"Falkirk, of course," said Jim. "They cry them that frae the toon's slogan: 'Better meddle wi' the de'il than wi' the bairns o' Falkirk.' A spunky team."

"Falkirk!" shouted a contemptuous voice from the depths of the engine-room. "They couldna play cat's-cradle, never mind fitba'. The Rovers wull eat them alive."

Before Jim could take up the challenge, Para Handy

remembered something more important than an argument about football.

"We've nothin' for oor teas," he cried, "what wi' Dougie's usual success wi' the fushing, and the shops'll be shut by the time we get to Rosebank. Wheneffer we get to Bonnybridge Jum will have to make a wee excursion to get some bacon and eggs from the grocer's."

Nobody paid too much attention, when they moored by the towpath at the village, to an abandoned, empty chara-banc slewed across the road at the Wellstood Foundry, its front wheels splayed out like the flippers of a seal. It was obvious that the axle had broken and the vehicle was hope-lessly immovable.

"Poor duvvles," said the Captain. "And a Sunday School trup or the like by the look of it — see the bunting and the flegs on her! I chust hope that they dinna have much fur-ther to go."

~

He had the answer to both those questions a few minutes later when Jim returned (with Dougie, who had chummed him on it) from his shopping excursion — with a bizarre following.

Behind them came some 15 or so young men, smartly turned out in matching blazers and grey trousers, each car-rying brown canvas holdalls. At the van of this party were half-a-dozen older and distinguished-looking gentlemen, one carrying with exagerrated care a large silver cup, its handles pennanted with navy-blue and white ribbons.

A large crowd — half the population of Bonnybridge, by the look and sound of them — followed this group, whooping, cheering and cavorting exuberantly.

Both Jim and the Mate were grinning with delight as they came up beside the puffer. The frock-coated gentleman carrying the silver trophy held up his hand to the cheering crowds behind him. Their noise died away and he turned towards the vessel.

"Captain," he said to Para Handy. "I would deem it the most enormous favour, since I understand that you are headed for the Rosebank Distillery, if you could give my fellow-directors and our boys passage. Our charabanc, as you can see, has met with an accident, and I do not want to disappoint the crowds waiting us in the town, nor the horse-carriages awaiting our arrival at the road-end to drive our boys into their home-town in their hour of triumph."

Para Handy was non-plussed. "What boys? What hour of triumph?"

"Why," said the gentleman: "here is the Falkirk football team and here we are on our way home with the Scottish Cup. You surely will not deny the boys their glory? Nor yours, either, for I am sure that your kindness will be well rewarded..."

The puffer's passage those last four miles to Rosebank on the western outskirts of the team's home town remains among the very happiest moments of Para Handy's maritime life. On either bank, cheering crowds raced along beside them: the team stood on the main-hatch, the silver cup held aloft in pride. At masthead and from the stern jackstaff flags and bunting, recovered from the charabanc, fluttered proudly in the evening sunlight.

At the Rosebank basin the waiting crowd had to be numbered in thousands and the rapturous reception for the team and its directors split the heavens. But all good things must come to an end, and within minutes the triumphant 'Bairns' had climbed aboard the brightly-decked open coaches which awaited them, and driven off towards the town centre and a gala civic banquet.

Heroes of the moment in their own more modest way the crew were hailed ashore, taken to the Rosebank Inn, and enthusiastically 'treated' by a large party of Falkirk supporters.

"Let this show you," said Dougie to Para Handy good-naturedly, "that I can fetch home mair than fush — and that Jum's football skills are not aal in vain, for it wass he that recognised the team at the roadside at Bonnybridge."

"And don't forget," chipped in the Engineer, "that means you're due to treat us now as weel — for I telt ye I wuddna forget whit ye said on the canal! Mine's a dram!"

*FACTNOTE*

The earliest passenger traffic on the Forth and Clyde Canal was not leisure travel, but workaday journeys or, at least, travel with a purpose. And since the boat service offered was not only faster but also much more comfortable than the coach-and-horses which were the only alternatives in the canal's early years, it prospered and grew. In time, though, the convenience and comfort of the water-borne transport was overtaken in every respect by the development of firstly the rail network and then the motor-car and charabanc.

By the early 1900s the canal boat companies almost exclusively provided pleasure cruises in purpose-built vessels which ran afternoon, evening or full-day excursions from Port Dundas in the centre of Glasgow. The *Gipsy Queen* was almost the last and probably the most capacious and luxurious of them all. Although restricted in size (like the working puffers) to an overall length of under 70' by the dimensions of the locks she had to navigate, she had three decks, the lowest (fully enclosed) having a tea-room capable of seating 60: and a lounge as well.

Craigmarloch, in a sheltered and handsomely wooded valley, was the most popular destination for charter parties and scheduled excursions alike, and the Restaurant and Tea Rooms were opened in 1905 to provide a necessary service (and indeed a *purpose* to the whole outing, namely a couple of hours ashore) in what was otherwise a remote and inaccessible corner.

Though I was born and brought up in the West, both my father's and mother's forebears had connections with Falkirk and the surrounding district and from an age when indeed I knew no better I was therefore inducted as a supporter of Falkirk Football Club and I have never regretted that despite the vicissitudes of the last 40 years. The Club is something of a Cinderella in Scottish football and a glorious uncertainty as to likely performance goes as they say 'with the territory'. Not for nothing is 'Expect the Unexpected' an unofficial rallying-cry for many Falkirk fans. All teams have their ups-and-downs, but ours are often particularly dramatic: and traumatic. A team which can travel to Parkhead as hopeless underdogs and come away with the points can also host a home game against a minor Division minnow in the Cup — and lose.

But we *did* win the Cup in 1913 against Raith Rovers: and again (and I own to being old enough to have actually been there) in 1957 against Kilmarnock. A modest gap of 44 years between these landmarks seems somehow appropriate in all the circumstances. Pragmatic and superstitious Falkirk fans the world over — and there *are* Falkirk fans the world over, and great is their kind camaraderie — therefore have high hopes for 2001.

PADDLE POWER — *In a cavalcade of another category, half-a-dozen sail-powered fishing vessels get the benefit of a steam-driven tow out of Campbeltown Loch, presumably on a day of adverse wind or tide: or both. The high freeboard of the fishing boats is as striking as the astonishing beam displayed by the tug, although this may simply be exaggerated by the camera angle. However, at least the procession would mean a brief respite for the hard-driven fishing crews.*

# 38

## *Scotch and Water*

As the *Vital Spark* passed the end of Meadowhill Quay on her way down river, at that point where the river Kelvin debouched into the Clyde, Para Handy leaned from the wheelhouse to watch with particular interest the delicate manoeuvres of the craneman who was busily occupied in lowering, with a quite impressive precision, a gleaming and curiously shaped copper tank into the fore-hold of a small three-island steamer.

"A still," he said enviously to the Mate, who was seated below him, cross-legged on the main-hatch. "A *still*! I wonder where it's bound for? Campbeltown, I wouldna wonder. My chove though, it iss a real whopper! If you had wan o' them at the foot of your drying green you would be set up for life!"

"Or *daein'* life mair likely," remarked Macphail, easing himself out of the engine-room, "and wi' little chance of ony remission for guid behaviour neither."

Para Handy ignored the comment. "I am chust aawful vexed that Jeck is no' with us, for he'd be maist interested in her," he continued. "It has aalways been his ambition to go in for what you might caall serious commercial production, raither than chust pickin' awa' at the business wi' a pocket-size version that canna do much more than turn oot the odd bottle or two for frien's or family.

"He wass very disappointed that we neffer once had a contract to cairry a still whiles he wass on the vessel. I told him the hold chust wassna big enough to tak' wan, but he wass aalways hopeful that we would get the chance of wan as deck cairgo. His idea wass that we could say that we had lost it overboard in heavy weather and have the dustillery chust claim off their unsurance, for he aye had the notion to land a still on Eilean Loain, at the head of Loch Sween, and set up in business on his own account.

" 'Loain iss well-wooded and we could hide the operation withoot ony trouble," he would point out: 'forbye, there iss no a hoose within a mile of the island and anyway they are aal Highland chentlemen in that part of Argyll, they would be well pleased to have a local enterprise such ass a smaall, privately-owned whusky still on the doorstep and would neffer even think to let the Customs people know that there wass something there for them to investigate. Indeed it would be fine and handy for the Loch Sween men: maist o' them are carryin' on their own private operations in the same line o' business and when we wass buying grain in bulk for our dustillery we would look efter their needs at the same time, and shup barley in for them at cost.' "

Macphail snorted. "The man should be locked up!" he said. "He iss nothin' but a one-man crime wave, if you ask me."

"But I didna ask you," said the Captain brusquely, "so awa' back doon and play wi' your enchines and leave us in peace."

The engineer climbed back into his cubby and slammed the metal hatch angrily behind him.

"That's put his gas at a peep," said Para Handy firmly. "There iss only wan way to treat a man like Macphail and that iss to let him know who iss master on the shup!"

Sunny Jim, who had been perched up in the bows as the puffer made her way down river, came aft and sat down beside Dougie on the hatch.

"So Hurricane Jack never got his still, eh?" said he.

"Not while he wass with the *Vital Spark* he didna, no," said the Captain: "but he did when he was working one summer ass a deck hand on the *Ivanhoe*."

"How on earth did a steamer come to be cairrying cargo?" asked Sunny Jim incredulously: "and whit way could a deckie manage to steal it?"

"I didna say it was cargo, Jum," said Para Handy patiently. "It wassna like that at aal. What happened wass that Jeck *installed* a spirit still on the vessel. As he said to me when he wass makin' his plans, a moving target iss that much more difficult to hit, it iss neffer in the same place two days running and if a bottle or two of the white spirits wass to come on the market in, say, Tarbert on a Thursday mornin' and be intercepted by the chentlemen from the Excise Offices, who would effer think that the source of it might be moored at Bridge Wharf on Friday afternoon?

" 'The point is, Peter,' said Jeck, 'the powers that be aal-ways expect a stull to be a kind of a fixed asset, ass they say in financial circles, no' something that's aye on the move.'

"Putting her on a steamer wass a brulliant notion, but the real stroke of genius, which you would expect from a man of Jeck's natural agility, was to put her onto the *Ivanhoe* of aal the vessels on the Clyde. I mean, even if a whisper effer came to the ears of the Customs men that there was a shup on the river traipsing aboot wi' a portable still on board, which offeecial would effer jalouse that onybody would have the sheer effrontery to put it on the wan and only temperance steamer on the Firth? They would be ass like-ly to expect to find the Grand Master o' the Ancient Order of Rechabites calling for a round in the snug bar of the Saracen's Heid at the Gallowgate.

"Of course, it wass chust a wee machine, but it wass perfectly capable of distilling two bottles of spurits each trup that the *Ivanhoe* made, and Jeck wass neffer effer an over-ambitious man, what he couldna either sell or swallow himself he wassna interested in.

"The Golden Goose he chrustened it, and each evening he came off the vessel at the Broomielaw wi' two bottles under his shirt, wan to tak' home and the other to sell discreetly at the pier-head. He wassna greedy neither, three shullings the bottle wass aal he asked."

Sunny Jim burst in with the question he had been desperate to ask for some minutes. "Where on earth," he enquired, "did Jack put the stull on the shup, and how did he hide it?"

"One of Jeck's responsibilities," continued the Captain, "was the regular inspection and maintenance of the lifeboats. Aal their equipment — oars, water-bottles, flares, biscuit-boxes, signal lamps and the like — wass aal protected from the weather and the depredations of ony passing stevedores or light-fingered passengers by a heavy tarpaulin cover.

"There wass one boat chust abaft the paddle wheel at each side of the shup but they were far too much in sight of the Officers on the brudge: but there wass a third one at the stern, lying inboard on a cradle chust immediately above the shup's galley.

"It wass ideal. That piece of deck wass out-of-bounds to the passengers, it wass hidden from the brudge by the line of the upper deck which formed the roof of the aft saloon, and since aal the ventilation shafts and chumneys from the stoves in the galley came up aal aboot it, nobody wass going to notice one more wee vent pipe in among aal that lot, and nobody would think it at aal oot of the ordinary if there wass an occasional smell o' barley aboot the place.

"Jeck stayed aboard late one night till aal the crew was ashore and then he removed a couple of the thwarts from the boat to give him room and bolted doon a wee copper stull wi' a paraffin burner and a funnel vent that he'd bought from an acquaintance.

"It was plain sailing from then on. Each mornin' he'd sneak on board really early wi' a big jar o' home-made fermented barley wash, tip it into the still, prime and light the burner, and away to his duties. At denner-time he would dump the lees of the wash in the river and set up the second distillation. Each evening he would decant the day's production out of the jar below the condenser and into a couple of empty bottles, cork them firmly, and head off.

"From the start of the summer season in May efferything went as smooth as silk for Jeck. He had to take a couple o' the other deck hands into his confudence. There wass occasions when there wass towerists leaning on the after rail o' the promenade deck watchin' what Jeck wass up to on the stern deck below them, and someone official-lookin' wass needed to go up to the promenade deck and clear them awa' from the after end o' it till he had finished his business. But that wass no problem.

"Jeck made his fatal error of chudgement at the time of Gleska Fair. The shup wass absolutely packed wi' truppers day on day.

"Till now, Jeck had neffer been tempted to sell at retail, ass you might say: he wass quite happy to dispose of the output of the Golden Goose at wholesale price, and by the bottle. But during the Fair he suddenly realised that, what wi' the demand for a place on the boats, there was many truppers takin' the *Ivanhoe* not *because* she wass a teetotal boat (as wass aalways the case in other months), but *despite* it, and because they wass chust gled to get passage on *any* doon-the-watter steamer.

"The result wass that Jeck and his shipmates wass constantly being importuned by very thursty-looking Gleska chentlemen as to whereaboots the Bar wass and where refreshments wass being sold. Their language on being told that the shup wass teetotal would have shamed the Trongate on a Saturday night, neffer mind the driest shup on the river!

"Jeck wass sorely tempted. When he did his sums he realised that the bottles he wass selling at chust three shullings would bring in three times as much if he wass to sell the contents by the gless, and he had a stockpile of spurits at home to top up the two bottles a day that the Golden Goose wass producing. It could be a very profitable Fair Fortnight if he wass careful.

"What decided him wass that he found an old unused paint-locker let into the paddle-box casing on the starboard side of the shup, across the passageway from the viewing platform for the enchines. It had wan o' these splut-doors that let you open the upper part of it and keep the bottom half shut. And though it wass a busy spot, efferybody wass watching the big pistons on the enchines, they wass the most popular sight on the shup, and nobody was lookin' at the casing wall at aal.

"First thing the next morning Jeck shut himself into the cubby wi' half-a-dozen bottles of spurits, a stack o' paper cups, and a wee wudden box for the money. His shupmates were on commission at a penny a gless and it was their chob to identify ony chentlemen that looked in need of a refreshment. They wass told that if they went to Jeck's locker and knocked on the door once and then three times — rat: tat-tat-tat — then it would be Open Sesame, and the whisky wass sixpence a gless.

"For five solid days the money chust poured in, and Jeck wass so delighted with the way things was going that he volunteered for a Sunday shift, a thing he'd neffer done before aal his time on the vessel. He wass busier than effer that day, for what with it being the Sabbath there wass double pleasure for the chentlemen in being able to get a dram, and the news o' Jeck's shebeen spread like wildfire through the shup.

"Tragedy struck at chust past mid-day. Jeck had been pouring almost non-stop since the *Ivanhoe* had left Brudge Wharf at nine o'clock, and when there wass a sudden wee lull in the knockin' at the cubby door, he thought nothing of it and was quite glad of the chance to draw breath. Though ass a rule Jeck neffer, effer drank while he wass on duty he thought he would treat himself to chust the wan wee dram. He wass enchoying the first smack of it when there was a kind of a scratching at the door. Jeck opened the upper-half wi' one hand, the gless of spurits held tight in the other, and asked cheerily and politely (for he wass aalways the perfect chentlemen) 'How many wull it be boys, speak up and dinna be feart, we're aal Jock Tamson's bairns on the good shup *Ivanhoe*' — and found himself staring into the horror-struck faces of the shup's Captain and First Officer.

"Nobody had thought to warn Jeck that the Sabbath run wass the occasion for the Captain to make his weekly inspection of the shup, and that no corner or compartment wass effer likely to be overlooked. Indeed, Jeck found oot later that the Captain had even been in under the tarpaulin o' the stern lifeboat and the only reason the still had survived wass that the Captain had neffer seen wan in hiss life, wouldna have recognised wan if it wass comin' doon Renfield Street on a Number Three caur, and thought that Jeck's Golden Goose wass some new piece of equipment for purifying watter that the lifeboat suppliers had installed during the annual overhaul o' the boat.

"But he had no difficulty in recognising wan o' his own crew wi' a gless in his hand, and a stack of bottles at his feet, and they didna even wait till *Ivanhoe* got back to Gleska, Jeck wass thrown aff at the next stop, Kilcreggan, and since the shup refused him passage on the return leg he wass stuck till next day with only the clothes he stood up in. Mercifully, the local polis wass a kind of a second cousin, and Jeck got the use of wan o' the cells for the night."

"What did Ah tell ye," Macphail shouted from the engine-room at this point. "Justice at last! The man's nothing but a natural jailburd! He shouldna even be allowed oot loose."

"You're just jealous, Macphail," said Para Handy wearily, "and not chust of Jeck's popularity, but because you're no' on the *Ivanhoe* and nobody effer wants to look at *your* engines!"


*FACTNOTE*

Bootleg liquor didn't start with Prohibition in America: indeed it could well have been earlier Scottish immigrants who brought the traditions of illicit stills to the Land of the Free! From the 18th century onwards there was a constant running battle across Scotland between the government enforcers on the one hand and the do-it-yourself distillers on the other.

Nor (to scotch another myth, and I apologise for the verb) were illicit stills confined to rural locations. There was probably as much home-made whisky circulating in Glasgow as in the rest of the country put together at the height of the traffic.

The other side of the coin were the temperance movements which crop up elsewhere in these tales. *Ivanhoe*, the Clyde's first and only teetotal steamer, was however the product of a response to general public demand rather than the direct result of temperance campaigning. The plain fact was that by the late 1870s more and more families and excursion parties were being dissuaded from traditional Clyde cruising because of the anti-social behaviour of a small minority of travellers, and the mismanagement of a handful of steamers, which became floating shebeens of the worst sort, and whose reputation undeservedly sullied that of other operators as well and got the whole Clyde steamer industry what we would call 'a bad press'.

The *Ivanhoe* was a most handsome ship, and a resounding success in her early years: as the drink problem elsewhere was better managed, and a degree of discipline was restored across the fleets, demand for a strictly teetotal ship fell away and in 1897 she was purchased from her original owners and operators the Frith of Clyde Steam Packet Company by the Caledonian SPC for the sum of £9,000, and sailed fully licensed from then on.

Incidentally, I have taken at least one liberty with the facts in presenting this story. The *Ivanhoe* never sailed down river on Sundays during her temperance years. There was something of a moratorium on Sunday sailings from about 1880 to 1895 as a direct result of the horrific problems of the Sabbath-breaking booze-boats (there is no other word which can satisfactorily describe them) of the 1870s.

The sight, sound and smell of the magnificent engines which drove the blades was *the* great spectacle, and memory, of a day spent on the paddle-steamers. And since the real bars aboard were usually on the same deck level as the observation areas at which the public in general (and small boys in particular) could spend hours gawping at such raw power in action, the adult male's euphemism for a trip to the bar was 'let's go and look at the engines, shall we?' And, on the *Waverley*, it still is today!

COASTAL COMMERCE — *I have been unsuccessful in tracing the history or ownership of the* Planet Mercury *but she is seen here, riding very light indeed, at an unidentified pier. She is very typical of the small 'three-island' coastal steamers of the early years of the century, so called from the raised fore, main and poop decks rising like islands above the well-decks fore and aft. She was certainly large enough to carry Para Handy's copper pot-still!*

# 39

## *Many Happy Returns*

I was striding purposefully along Sauchiehall Street towards Charing Cross railway station, intent on catching the earliest possible train home to Helensburgh, but my progress was slower than I could have wished, for the pavements were thronged with shoppers — and sightseers — on this, the first Monday of the traditional Glasgow Trades Fortnight.

As I dodged round yet another family group rooted like a rock in the surging flow of pedestrian traffic, quite transfixed by one of the stunning window-displays in Messrs Treron's elegant emporium, there was a touch on my shoulder and, turning, I was surprised to see the mate of the *Vital Spark* behind me, with a large brown paper parcel tucked under one arm.

"How are you yourself, then, Mr Munro?" asked Dougie. "You seem in a terrible hurry, to be sure. Wull ye no' tak' time to come up to Spiers' Wharf and see the Captain, for we iss there chust waiting for a cairgo o' cement which shows no sign at aal of arrivin' and he would be very pleased to see you."

I explained that, much though I would have liked to take him up on the invitation, I must decline. I was in a hurry to get home early, I added, as today was my birthday and my family, I knew, had a surprise waiting for me and it would not be wise for me to delay the meal which my wife would have lovingly prepared.

"Your birthday, indeed," said Dougie. "Well, I wush you many happy returns — on behalf of us aal on the shup. I chust hope you have a mair propeeshus day than poor Para Handy had a few years back on a sumilar occasion."

And, as we proceeded together along the street, he unfolded an extraordinary tale.

~

It had happened many years previously, when the *Vital Spark* was less than a year old, and Para Handy and his crew were relative strangers who were just beginning to get to know each other.

It was long before Sunny Jim had joined the ship. His cousin Colin Turner, the Tar, fulfilled the functions of deckhand and chef de cuisine on board. It was so long ago that Macphail was still in a state of honeymooner's euphoria with his engines — a state which did not prevail for very much longer. It was long before Para Handy's marriage and Dougie himself, still a young man, had only three children (as against the current count of eleven) and — though they had crewed a sailing-gabbart together on several occasions — had yet to acquire that intimate knowledge of his Captain's character and situation which comes with familiarity.

One April afternoon the puffer was lying alongside the cargo jetty at Tarbert on Loch Fyne. Her cargo of coal had just been discharged but there was no sign of the load of pit-props from the local sawmill which she had been contracted to convey to Ayr for inland despatch to the coalmines around Darvel. Dougie and Macphail were seated in companionable silence on the main hatch: the Tar was wiping off the coaldust besmirching the wheelhouse windows. Para Handy had retired to the fo'c'sle.

It was from that confined space that there now suddenly issued a deep groan followed by a long, protracted sigh.

Alarmed, Dougie rose from the hatch and peered down the open companionway into the crew's cramped quarters.

All he could see of the Captain was the top of his head. Para Handy was standing at the foot of the ladder, holding in his right hand the ship's solitary mirror (which was badly stained and cracked, and which normally hung on a nail on the end of the engineer's bunk) and studying his face in it, his left hand scratching at his stubbly chin. Dougie stared in some surprise, for the mirror was normally used by the Captain but once a week, on the occasion of his customary Sabbath shave, and at no other time.

Again Para Handy groaned, and shook his head at its grubby reflection.

"Man, man," the Captain muttered half under his breath, so that the Mate had to strain to catch the words. "Man, man. Tomorrow iss the bleck day indeed. Bleck, bleck. Today chust a young man at the height o' his prime, but tomorrow is the watter-shed for it iss not chust anither ordinary birthday, but the big wan. The big zero. The big 'O'. And efter that old age, and nothin' to look forward to but totterin' doon the hill to the grave."

And he put the mirror down with another heartrending sigh and vanished out of Dougie's line of sight in the direction of his own bunk. Moments later, the Mate heard the creak of wood as Para Handy climbed into it and lay down.

Dougie walked back to the main-hatch, where Macphail had now been joined by the Tar.

"Boys," said Dougie. "We must do somethin' to cheer the Captain up. Tomorrow iss his birthday, and no' chust a usual one. This is what Para Handy has caaled the 'Big Zero' and it iss getting him doon. Poor duvvle, I had neffer realised it, but this means that he must be fufty tomorrow!"

"Fufty!" exclaimed the Tar. "*Fufty*! I find that very hard to believe, Dougie."

"Me too," said the Mate, "for he iss the sort of man that seems neffer to change in the very slightest way from wan year's end to the beginnin' o' the next, chust the same aal the time."

"Ah'll no' disagree wi' that," said Macphail sharply. "He's aye struck me as a cantankerous auld fool, a dangerous combination of a man, ignorant and thrawn all at the same time."

Dougie paid no attention.

"We must gi'e him a perty tomorrow," he said, "and let him see that this birthday of his is nothing special and most certainly nothing to be depressed aboot — that it iss no different to any other except that it's an even happier one for him. Otherwise he'll be in a bleck mood for weeks, and we do not want that to happen, laads, do we?"

And with the unhappy memory of some of their Captain's previous tirravees all too fresh in their minds (such as the never-to-be-forgotten occasion when he announced that he was giving up drink and indeed did — for all of three days which felt, to his crew, more like three months) his shipmates nodded in agreement.

~

For the next few hours there was feverish but guarded activity in and around the *Vital Spark*.

A whip-round of the available resources of the crew produced the princely sum of two shillings and fourpence, but the Tar then pointed out that a figure as well-known in Tarbert as Para Handy was could surely expect some interest in (and pecuniary contributions to) such a landmark birthday as what everyone, in deference perhaps to the implications of the actual figure, now referred to simply as 'The Big Zero'. Only the Tar periodically shook his head in disbelief (which Dougie found quite touching and indicative of an admiration of his Captain and his apparent youthfulness which he had simply not realised the young man so strongly felt) and muttered "Fufty! *Fufty!* It fair makes you think!"

The funds available to celebrate the auspicious landmark in the Captain's life soon mounted up. The crew, wisely restricting their collecting-round to the local Inns, found that there was an encouraging support for their cause not only from many habitues of these establishments but from their owners as well.

"Peter Macfarlane has been a staunch supporter of mine over a lot of years," observed the landlord of the Harbour Bar in the sort of response typical of his colleagues in the Tarbert and District Licensed Trades Association, "and it wud be churlish not to give him the encouraging word and the helping hand in his hour of need. Fifty! I find that very hard to believe."

By late afternoon Para Handy's 50th Birthday Fund stood at the very handsome total of two pounds twelve shillings, and there now began a debate as to how best to dispense this magnanimous sum for the better pleasing of its unsuspecting recipient, who dozed the day away fitfully in his berth on board the puffer.

It was decided, after some heated discussion, that two-thirds of the funds collected should be expended on the purchase of a smart new navy-blue pea-jacket for the Captain. His own had seen much better days and was sadly frayed at neck and cuff, but was, even in that state, worn with pride on the Sabbath and on other special days or circumstances, for Para Handy was a man who would have been a commodore if he could, and retained pride both in his command and his appearance.

This still left almost a pound in the kitty, ample to finance a modest refreshment the following morning, on board the *Vital Spark*, for those who had made some contribution to it and who could be relied upon to help to cheer the Captain up on his day of gloom. The pea-jacket would be presented to him at the same time, by Dougie, on behalf of the assembled company.

When the crew awoke the following morning no hint was given to the Captain that anyone other than himself was aware that this was a special day. When Para Handy, as usual, went ashore after breakfast to telegraph the Glasgow office of the owner of the *Vital Spark* (and on this occasion to protest the delay in the arrival at the quayside of their return cargo, and to wait for a reply) the opportunity was taken to complete the purchases necessary for the surprise party, and assemble the company on board the puffer to await the Captain's return.

The publicans brought with them the beer and spirits for which Dougie had paid the previous evening and the very last three shillings was entrusted to the Tar, who was sent ashore to make the last-minute purchase which was (the pea-jacket aside) to be the centrepiece of the party.

"Go you to MacNeill's Bakery," said the Mate, "and get the very best iced cake you can for a half-a-crown. Then go next door into the newsagents and buy one of they gold lettered cardboard favours you get for laying on top of the icing, one that says 'Congratulations and Many Happy Returns on your 50th Birthday.' And buy a wheen o' wee cake candles at the same shop to put roond the edge."

The Tar pocketed the coins, muttering again to himself, "Fufty! I still dinna believe it. Fufty! *Never*!" and went off to carry out his instructions.

On his return (Para Handy thankfully still not having finished his business at the Telegraph Office) he was sent below to the fo'c'sle where the pea-jacket lay, neatly parcelled, on one of the top bunks.

"When I gi'e you the shout," said Dougie, "and you hear us aal sterting to sing 'Happy Birthday to you', stick the pea-jaicket under your arm, light the candles on the cake and bring it up on deck."

～

Ten minutes later Para Handy appeared on the stone quayside and stared in astonishment at the company gathered on the deck of the *Vital Spark*.

"Mercy," he exclaimed. "What iss the occasion for this, boys?"

"You're the occasion, Peter," said the landlord of the Harbour Bar. "Dougie found out that it's your birthday, and a rather special one, and we decided we should mark the occasion. It's not every day you reach 'The Big Zero', eh, Peter?"

"Well, well," said Para Handy, delighted, and cheering up quite dramatically, "It iss at a time like this that a man finds oot who his friends are.

"It iss indeed 'The Big Zero' (though I cannot imachine chust how Dougie knew aboot it) and it iss a date that iss a reminder of time passing and a sobering thought indeed for any man when he reaches his fortieth birthday."

Dougie, at the back of the crowd and adjacent to the hatchway down to the fo'c'sle, blanched.

"Colin," he whispered urgently to his shipmate at the foot of the ladder, "Para Handy's 'Big Zero' is his *fortieth* birthday, no' his fuftieth. We're in big trouble when he sees thon cake!"

"We're in bigger trouble than you think," replied the Tar, "for I told you time and again I couldna believe it wis Para Handy's fuftieth birthday. He looks an auld man to me.

"I wis sure it wis his *sixtieth* — and that's the number on the favour I bought for the cake…"

*FACTNOTE*

Glasgow's highly-regarded and usually independent Department Stores are now nothing but a memory for — with the honourable exception of House of Fraser in the pedestrianised and improved Buchanan Street — they have succumbed to the changes in retail trading patterns and changes wrought (or so the retailers would have us believe) by consumer preferences.

It is passing strange though, that in London there survive such household names as Harrods, Selfridges, Army and Navy Stores, Harvey Nichols, Fortnum and Mason, Liberty — many more: while in Glasgow we have long lost the echoing galleries of Pettigrew and Stephen, Copland and Lye and, missed most of all, Treron on Sauchiehall Street, a seminal legacy of Edwardian architecture sadly gutted by a disastrous fire. The store was lost but at least the City Fathers decreed that its original fascia must be preserved and it now houses, among other residents and tenants, the respected MacLellan Art Galleries.

Spiers Wharf at Port Dundas, on the Glasgow branch of the Forth and Clyde Canal, was named for an Elderslie Tobacco baron whose influence in canal development in late 18th century Scotland was considerable. His warehouses survive, overlooking the now landlocked basin, converted into offices and town flats for the upwardly mobile.

Tarbert or Tarbet — there are at least three places in Scotland bearing the name — derives from the Gaelic for 'Isthmus' and the topography of each confirms that.

Tarbet on Loch Lomond stands just over a mile east of the Loch Long village of Arrochar while in Harris in the Outer Hebrides Tarbert on the Minch coast of the island is less than a mile from the Atlantic shoreline to the west.

Best known of the Tarberts, though, is that on Loch Fyne where once again just about a mile separates the sheltered waters of that Clyde estuary loch from the Atlantic seaboard to the west which gives access to the islands of the Hebrides and the towns and villages of western Argyll.

In every instance, tradition speaks of Norse longships hauled by brute force across the narrow isthmus between one stretch of water and the next. At Tarbert in Argyll such manoeuvres made sense — not just in the semi-mythological reports of Viking incursions, but into recent historic times. Small fishing boats could readily be moved overland from coast to coast with less difficulty than they would face in undertaking the dangerous alternative of almost 150 sea miles round the notorious Mull of Kintyre in some of the stormiest waters in the country.

# 40

## *Here be Monsters*

Para Handy was more than happy to see that the puffer would be sharing the first of the long flight of locks at Banavie, at the base of that triumph of engineering ingenuity known to all mariners on the Caledonian Canal by the sobriquet of Neptune's Staircase, with two small yachts.

"It will mean more hands, and the more hands that we have, then the lighter the work for us all," he commented to the Mate as they contemplated the daunting series of locks — eight in all — which rose in front of them, tier on tier for more than quarter of a mile, and which the *Vital Spark* must now negotiate to gain access to the tranquil waters of the canal and a lazy lock-free six mile passage to the entrance to Loch Lochy.

It was some years since Captain and crew had last negotiated the canal. Most of their work was in and around the waters of the Clyde and the west coast lochs, but just occasionally the owner managed to secure some business which took them out of those familiar surroundings.

They were bound for Drumnadrochit on Loch Ness, in ballast, to collect a cargo of railway sleepers which had been brought down to the lochside from the big Forestry Sawmill at Cannich twelve miles inland. It promised to be a contract quite fraught with difficulties, for there was no pier at Drumnadrochit and, in a tideless inland loch, no way in which the *Vital Spark* could be brought close inshore on the flood to ground on the ebb. When Para Handy pointed out these problems to the owner, he was assured that the forestry team from Corpach had been loading such cargos successfully for many years, and that they would be perfectly capable of doing so once more.

It took four hours for the little flotilla to climb the locks to the top of Neptune's Staircase and, by the time that summit was reached, all hands were exhausted with the constant effort of manoeuvring the heavy wooden sluice-gates of each lock by muscle-power alone.

Para Handy consulted the pocket watch suspended from a nail in the wheelhouse.

"Six o'clock. I think we will chust moor here for the night and make oor way up to Drumnadrochit at furst light," he announced firmly. "We have had a long day and I think that tomorrow wull be longer. And a smaall refreshment would be very welcome after aal oor exertions at the locks and I seem to recall that there is an Inns hereaboots."

The crew's frustrations on discovering that the Banavie Inn was at the foot of the lock system rather than at its summit may be imagined.

"Well, if I had known that then I am sure we could have made good use of it while we were negotiating the first lock," said a disgruntled Captain: "aye, and carried a canister or two of refreshments to keep us cheery on the way up."

"Knowin' you lot," put in Macphail, who was more nippy-tempered even than usual after the struggles of the past few hours, "If you'd been drinkin' your way up the locks then Ah'm sure you'd have forgotten, half-way up, which way she wis meant to be goin', and then for sure you'd have taken her right back doon to the bottom and had it do all over again."

"Pay no heed, Dougie," said Para Handy with dignity. "The man iss chust in a tantrum because he has had to do a day's work for wance, instead of sittin' in yon cubby of his with his nose in wan o' they novelles. Are you comin' with us, Dan, or are you chust goin' to stay up here and worry aboot what iss likely to be happening to poor Lady Fitzgerald and her man in the next episode?"

With ill grace the Engineer went to the pump and washed himself and a few minutes thereafter the three senior members of the crew headed off towards the Inn, leaving the unfortunate Sunny Jim on unwonted and (for him at least) unwanted guard duty.

"I am truly sorry, Jum," said the Captain as they left: "but this iss unfamiliar territory to us and I dare not risk leaving the shup unprotected. Who knows what the natives might steal on us if they had the chance."

"Ah suppose you think this is Red Indian country," remarked the Engineer sarcastically. "In any case, who in their right mind would want tae steal onything aff of this auld hooker? There isnae a decent piece of marine equipment on her, and the local pawn wuddna gi'e much for yon old watch of yours."

~

The trio were in much better spirits and a more amicable frame of mind when they returned just before midnight, for they had had a good run at dominoes, playing the locals for drinks, and an ungrudging conviviality prevailed. Even the discovery that their night watchman was fast asleep in his bunk, and by the look of him had been so for some hours, and did not even so much as stir when the shore-party tumbled noisily into the fo'c'sle, did not ruffle the Captain's equanimity.

"Och, you wass probably right, Dan," he conceded. "There iss not a lot to steal from the *Vital Spark* and in any case I am sure that the locals iss aal true Highland chentlemen."

Nobody was foolish enough to remind Para Handy of that cheerily expressed opinion when, at first light, Sunny Jim staggered up on deck to look at the weather, and found two individuals in the act of jumping onto the canal bank with the oars of the puffer's dinghy over their shoulders.

~

The oars, recovered from the towpath where the thieves dropped them in their flight, were firmly lashed, upright, to the mast of the *Vital Spark* as the puffer proceeded to make passage up Loch Lochy and Loch Oich, and then came to the historic little town of Fort Augustus at the foot of Loch Ness.

"You know," confessed Para Handy from the wheelhouse window as the vessel nosed out onto the dark waters of Scotland's longest loch, "if it wassna for having to work aal those dam' locks by hand there would be a lot to be said for a command on the canal for I am sure that you would neffer have to worry aboot the weather or the wund or the fog. An easy life!"

His crew, who had back-breakingly worked their way through every single one of the locks, at each of which their Captain's only contribution to the process had been shouted (and all too often contradictory) instructions emanating from that same wheelhouse window, said nothing.

The puffer arrived at Drumnadrochit later that afternoon, too late for any work to be started that day, although the forestry men had got there ahead of the *Vital Spark* and a huge stack of sleepers lay piled up on the shore beside a tiny concrete slip.

Para Handy surveyed the scene with a marked lack of enthusiasm.

"How in bleezes do they propose to get aal of that out to the shup?" he asked querulously. "We cannot get closer in than 50 yards and I for one am no' goin' swimmin' for anyone."

~

He had his answer in the morning.

By eight o'clock the loading process was in full swing, with two foremen from the sawmills — one ashore and one on board the *Vital Spark* — supervising and co-ordinating the operations.

A raft some twelve feet square lay alongside the concrete slip, attached by two ropes to the collar of a towering but placid Clydesdale horse which, having been led down the slip by its handlers, now stood in the loch to the front of the raft up to its hocks in the water.

Once the raft was loaded, the two handlers — who wore only canvas trousers cut off at the knee, and heavy boots with substantial, studded soles — took one rein of the bridle apiece and led the horse across the sandy bottom of the loch till they were in up to their waists and the the loch bed began to deepen rapidly. At this point the cargo was within twenty yards of the puffer, lying in the deeper water, and the forestry foreman on board the *Vital Spark* threw a light rope, lead-line for a heavy hawser which was itself coiled round the drum of the puffer's steam-winch. The handlers unloosed the patient horse, Macphail started up the winch at the foreman's signal, and the raft was reeled in to the side of the ship as an angler might reel in a fish. The men in the water, who had retained one line attached to the stern of the cargo-carrier. pulled it back once it had been unloaded and returned with it and the horse, once more set within its traces, to the shore.

The process continued all morning till the hold of the *Vital Spark* was full and a substantial deck cargo had been built up on the main hatch.

Para Handy watched the proceedings with some admiration.

"Now that iss chust astonishing," he said. "And that horse iss a wonder. Wass she no' awful hard to train, for I'm sure and she canna like the watter at aal."

"On the contrary," the foreman laughed. "She just loves it, for most horses are great swimmers. We sometimes have a job keeping her in the shallows. She'd be swimming out with the raft given a half a chance!"

Para Handy looked appraisingly at the sleepers stacked on the main hatch.

"I think that will do us," said he. "It iss not ass if we only have to take them doon the loch. We have to get back doon to Gleska and I will not overload the shup."

"Fair enough," said the foreman. "You know your own business best. But we would ask one wee favour of you, it will not be a problem I'm thinking, and that is to let me put just three new wooden mash-tubs for the distillery at Fort William on top of the lot. If you would just drop them off at the distillery pier, I know that the maltings manager will see that it is made worth your while."

Para Handy nodded his agreement and the foreman then bellowed instructions to the shore party. Three very large barrels were rolled down the slip roped together in line, and the first of them attached to one of the Clydesdale's towing ropes.

Just what happened was never too clear. Probably one of the handlers slipped on a rock and took his colleague with him, but next second the two men had let go of the horse's bridle and disappeared, briefly, under water.

By the time they surfaced, spluttering, the horse was gone. Pulling this much lighter burden behind her with ease, she splashed out into the deeper water, kicked out, and began to swim out past the *Vital Spark* with the three barrels bobbing in her wake. As she past the puffer she turned to the south and proceeded to swim along parallel with the shore.

" 'Dalmighty," exclaimed the foreman. "She's off! Please get your dinghy in the water, Captain, and I'll row after her and catch her. Otherwise she'll probably swim a couple of miles or more before she decides she's had enough and heads for the shore"

Launching the dinghy was the work of a moment — but of course it was then realised that her *oars* were firmly lashed to the puffer's mast. By the time these had been loosed, the horse was a hundred yards away and the prospects of catching her slim.

The foreman and the puffer's crew watched the horse with its attendant barrels move into the distance, silhouetted darkly against the mirror-brightness of the still surface of the loch.

"I'll tell you something," chipped in Sunny Jim after a moment, laughing delightedly. "See wi' jist the heid o' the horse oot o' the watter like that, and they three barrels like humps behind it, the whole shebang fair pits ye in mind o' a dragon: or better yet a sea-serpent, eh?"

Para Handy chuckled.

"Aye Jum, that'll be right. A monster in Loch Ness! Now that *would* be something to excite the towerists, eh?"

And, helping the foreman into the dinghy, he rowed him ashore to find a pony and trap with which to pursue his errant charge along the road which wound along the lochside.

"You and your monsters, Jum!" protested the Mate. "All I know iss that this wan has cost us the chance of a dram from the distillery, and that iss most certainly a monster inchustice, to be sure!"

*FACTNOTE*

Telford's Caledonian Canal was a formidable undertaking for the technology of the age. It took 18 years to complete and was opened formally in 1822. Using the natural fault of the Great Glen and the string of lochs (Lochy, Oich and Ness) which gave immediately navigable waterways over two thirds of its length from Corpach at the head of Loch Linnhe to Inverness on the Moray Firth, it is 60 miles long and vessels traversing it have to negotiate 29 locks.

The government of the day was first moved to find the funds to build it by the exigencies of the Napoleonic Wars. A sheltered passage from Scotland's East to West coasts, wide enough and deep enough to enable frigates and small merchant vessels to use it, would help the Navy to deploy ships to and from the various theatres of the maritime war more readily: and it would offer a safer passage for merchant and fishing vessels, one that would shelter them not just from the storms of the Pentland Firth but from the intrusions of the French privateers which skulked off the Scottish coasts on the lookout for unwary and defenceless prey.

The flight of eight locks at Banavie was an engineering marvel, an achievement without parallel at that early stage of canal development and still today an impressive prospect.

What can one say about the Loch Ness monster that either hasn't been said before or is palpable nonsense?

It would be very satisfying to believe in its existence and I suppose that it must be real enough in one sense, for it has spawned an immense tourist industry, and lured individuals and organisations from the patently dotty to the seriously scientific, and from all quarters of the globe, to expend years of effort and enormous sums of money in an attempt to track it down for the discomfiture of non-believers.

All this despite the fact that the first and most famous of all the Loch Ness photographs — the 'Surgeon's Picture' of 1933, the basis really for all the subsequent monster mania of the last sixty years, has now been acknowledged — by no less an authoritative voice than that of its perpetrators — as a quite deliberate hoax.

At one time there were two distilleries at Fort William though they were under the same ownership and the second one operated only for a few years at the turn of the century. Both stood on the river Nevis, and were served by a private jetty on Loch Linnhe. The water for both was drawn from a single well, high up on the slopes of Ben Nevis.

# 41

## *The Tight White Collar*

From the window of the Inns at Crarae, Para Handy watched with interest the comings and goings in and around the pier of the little Lochfyneside village — a popular destination in summer for day-trippers, and a much-loved oasis of peace for those who were fortunate enough to manage to secure rooms in one of its handful of boarding-houses for the Fair Fortnight.

The steamer from Glasgow had just berthed, and was disgorging the usual motley selection of human kind. The *Vital Spark*, with Sunny Jim just visible — perched on her stern-quarter with a fishing-line — was sharing the inner wing of the wooden pier with two local fishing boats.

At that moment, the three man crew of one of these vessels came in sight, having just left the Inns by the front door and now striding across the lochside road to the pierhead. As they did so they were confronted by a group of Ministers, unmistakable in the dark frock-coats and contrasting white collars which were their badge of office, making their way up to the village from the excursion steamer. Suddenly aware of the presence of the approaching gentlemen of the cloth the fishermen hesitated momentarily and then side-stepped to the right, thus giving the clergy as wide a berth as the narrow pierhead allowed, before proceeding onwards and down towards their skiff.

Para Handy turned to his Engineer and Mate and remarked: "Well now, there iss a sign of the times and no mustake! It iss not aal that many years ago that a fisherman meetin' a Meenister on his way to his vessel would chust have turned for home again and neffer sailed that day. It wass thought to be duvvelish bad luck, and a sure sign of disaster or poor, poor fushin's at the very least, to meet with the clergy like that. Yet here is Col MacIlvain and his laads cairryin' on aboot their business quite jocco, and them efter meeting not chust the wan Meenister but a good half-a-dozen o' the species! Changed days indeed!"

Macphail nodded.

"Right enough," he said: "Ah've seen jist one English munister on his holidays turn back the hauf o' the Tarbert herring fleet at the very height o' the fushin's in the good days, by takin' a daunder alang the quay at the wrang time o' day!"

Dougie snorted.

"Chust nonsense," he protested, "superstitious nonsense. There iss no more ill-luck aboot a Meenister than there iss aboot ony o' God's creatures. The man that tells you different doesna ken ony better and that's the truth of it! It would tak' mair nor a Meenister to keep me from my shup any hour of the day, I can assure you of that."

"Mind you," Para Handy observed, "I think it must be admutted that there have been many times when it hass been the fushermen or the sailormen — Brutain's hardy sons! — that have made life difficult for the Meenisters.

"Hurricane Jeck hisself wass aalways gettin' into trouble wi' the Church for wan reason or the ither..."

"Ah'm no' surprised in the very least aboot that," interrupted Macphail caustically: "that man has the happy knack o' gettin' into trouble wi' onything that lives or breathes. Dear God, he wud pick a fight wi' a dry-stane dyke if ye were tae gi'e him the opportunity!"

The Captain paid no attention.

"There wass one time," he continued. "that Jeck was asked by wan o' his kizzins, whose wife had chust had a new bairn, if he'd be the Godfather to it" — there was an explosive spluttering as the Engineer nearly choked himself on a mouthful of beer — "and of course Jeck said yes, he'd be delighted. You know yourselves that he iss the kind of a man that would neffer willingly refuse onything to onybody, for he has aalways been the perfect chentleman.

"The chrustening wass to be at St John's in Dunoon, a fine kirk and congregation and a most handsome building. The trouble came from the fact that the wean wass to be laaunched, as you might say, ass a pert o' the evening service and no' the morning wan ass usual, because Jeck's kizzin and his wife couldna get doon to the town wi' the bairn till the afternoon, what wi' them aal livin' away oot in the muddle o' nowhere on a wee ferm that they tenanted from wan o' the MacArthurs up at the head o' Loch Striven.

" 'Don't you worry about a thing, Jamie,' said Jeck to his kizzin. 'Rely upon it that I will be there for you, and in the very best of trum! For to be sure, us Maclachlans must stick together in the hour of need! We aalways have and we aalways wull! I wull come over to Dunoon on wan o' the efternoon boats and meet you outside the Kirk at six o'clock.' He wass lodging in Gourock chust then, and had a kind of a chob loading coals onto Mr MacBrayne's shups at the Cardwell Bay bunkering pier, for he wass doon on his luck at the time.

"Well, Jeck wass early to his bed on the Saturday, and without even a single dram in him, for he wass taking the duties of the next day seriously to heart: so much so that when he woke on the Sabbath he decided that he would come over to Dunoon early to be sure of being there on time, for he wass that determined not to let his kizzin doon.

"At eleven of the clock next morning he presented himself on the pier to tak' the first shup he could get with the idea of a meat dinner at the Argyll Hotel and then a quiet stroll on the sea-front till time for the service, and what shup wass it but the *Dunoon Castle* herself, the most notorious of aal the 'Sunday Boats', on an excursion from Broomielaw to Rothesay?

"Jeck neffer paid heed, it wass chust a twenty meenit crossing and it was neither eechie nor ochie to him whit shup it was, so he boarded her without realising it.

"The bar had been open since the moment the shup had cast off from the Broomielaw but even that wouldna have mattered as Jeck wassna thinkin' aboot drink at aal that morning" — once again the Engineer seemed to encounter problems getting breath, and once again the Captain paid no attention — "but the very first person he clapped eyes on when he got aboard her wass his old shupmate Donald Baird, who'd been his Furst Mate on the clupper *Port Jackson*. The two of them hadna seen each other for near on five years.

"Donald had been two hours on the vessel, and the most of them spent in the Refreshment Saloon, so he wass feelin' no pain at aal. And he wouldna tak' *no* for an answer, neither.

" 'To bleezes, Jeck,' said he with some conviction, when

Jeck told him where he wass bound for and why, and chust why he wouldna tak' a dram in the by-going either: 'you have aal the day to get through before tonight's chrustening, and I am sure that nobody wull force you to tak' a refreshment if you are set against it. Stay on board chust for the baur! We have a lot of catchin' up to do, and since the shup wull get back to Dunoon from Rothesay at five o'clock that gives you plenty of time for you to present yourself at the Kirk.'

"Jeck aalways finds it very difficult to refuse that kind of an invitation, ass bein' a true chentleman iss aal a part of his upbringing and his cheneral agreeableness. He would neffer wullingly hurt a fly, neffer mind the feelings of his fellow human beings! So while the shup crossed over to Dunoon he stood at the rail with Donald and exchanged the news of the last five years. But then ass soon ass the vessel was away from Dunoon and past the Gantocks on course for Innellan and Rothesay, did he not allow himself to be inveigled doon to the Refreshment Saloon 'for chust the wan wee gless of ale for the sake of the heat that's in the day' ass Donald put it: and though Jeck had little enough coin with him, for he wass doon on hiss luck yet again poor duvvle, ass I have told you already, Donald had chust been paid off efter a seven month trup to the Far East wi' mair money than he knew what do do with, and he simply wouldna let Jeck refuse his hospitality for aal his protests.

"The outcome wass inevitable. By the time the *Dunoon Castle* got back to Dunoon at five o'clock Jeck wass in chust ass good trum as Donald. The dufference, of course, wass that Jeck — being a perfect chentleman in efferything he did — could carry his dram and it wass only when you were really up close that you became aware that the man was not totally in control of himself but was operating by unstinct raither than logic, and that ass a result onything might happen — and probably would.

"There wass aalways a most stumulating atmosphere of complete uncertainty aboot, wheneffer Jeck was in good trum!

"Jeck and Donald had a tearful farewell, and Jeck headed off to St John's Kirk. He had a half hour to wait before the kizzin arrived, so he sat on the wall in Hanover Street and took a few good deep breaths of the Cowal air, and sooked on a wheen of candy-striped baalls he'd had the sense to buy from a sweetie barrow on the esplanade.

"By the time the chrustening perty arrived, and they wass aal ushered into the vestry o' the Kirk, Jeck *looked* the pert right enough: but there wass still enough drams coursin' through hiss veins to float a toy yat, and his view of the proceedings wass hazy to say the least. But, ass you know, wi' aal the cheneral agility he had, only Jeck himself would have known it.

"The only wan o' the perty that jaloused that maybe efferything wass no' chust what it seemed wass the Meenister himself. But he said nothin', until they wass in the Kirk and when, half way through the chrustening, Jeck was handed the wean by the mither and telt to tak' it up to the Meenister so that it could get the watter splashed over it.

"At that point the Meenister got his furst real whuff o' Jeck's breath — and in spite o' the candy-striped baalls he'd been sookin' ye wouldna have needed to be a bloodhound to realise that there wass that much spurits to it that you could have set it alight if you'd had a match — and asked him in a piercing whisper that could be heard aal roond the Kirk: 'Are you sure you're fit enough to hold that child?'

" 'Fit enough to haud it?' cried Jeck loudly, and he grupped the bairn in both airms and held it ass high over his head ass he could stretch and waved it aboot from side to side, 'fit enough to *haud* it? Man, I'm fit enough that if you chust gi'e me the chance I'll tak' it ootside right noo and throw it over the roof of the Kirk, steeple and aal!'

"Jeck's Glenstriven kizzin has neffer spoken to him since, and the St John's Meenister iss now aawful wary of ony chrustenings which involve sailors or their femilies: so mebbe the men of the cloth should be ass superstitious noo aboot the fushermen o' Crarae as the fushermen used to be aboot the Church!"

The pierhead now being clear of crowds, and the steamer having departed for her ultimate outward destination — Inveraray, by way of Furnace — the three shipmates left the Inns and headed back towards the *Vital Spark*.

"If we get away within the half-hour," said Para Handy, pulling his watch out of his trouser pocket, "we can be in Rothesay by eight o'clock and ready to load the Marquess of Bute's potatos first thing tomorrow."

There was a sudden, protesting croak from the Mate.

"Peter," said he, agonised: "look who's talkin' to Jum at the shup! It's the Reverend McNeil, our Parish Meenister."

Both Dougie and his Captain (with their wives) were members of the same congregation in Glasgow. The difference between their membership of it, however, was that though the Minister did not approve of the Captain's predilection for a dram, he was aware of it — and prepared to tolerate it. The Mate, on the other hand, had for many years now successfully pretended to both his wife and his Minister that he was of a Rechabitic and therefore strictly teetotal persuasion.

"He must have been wi' the excursion perty and recognised the vessel when they came ashore," Dougie continued. "I canna let him find me like this, he'll smell the drink on me and it's no chust that he'll put a bleck mark on me for it wi' the Kirk Session, he'll tell the mussis and my life wull not be worth living, I can assure you.

"I'm awa' to hide. Tell him I'm not on the shup this trup, tell him onything you like."

"Shame on you Dougie," said the Captain, "I thought you told us back there in the Inns that no Meenister would effer keep you from boarding *your* shup? You cannot surely have forgotten that aalready?

"Forbye, he hass seen us!"

And with a cheery wave, he strolled down the quayside to shake the Minister by the hand.

*FACTNOTE*

In earlier generations superstition was rife in every fishing community from Cornwall to Shetland and took some quite bizarre forms. For some, it was unlucky to mention pigs (or pork, which must have somewhat restricted the choice of victuals on offer at mealtimes) and other animals which must never be talked of at sea included ferrets and rabbits.

Whistling on the quayside when the wind was from the east was another taboo in some ports, while refusal to sail on a Friday was more widespread. Sticking a knife into the mast (for wind) was a good-luck omen for some, a bad-luck certainty for others.

Almost universal were the superstitions associated with the clergy of all denominations. To meet a minister or priest on the road to the harbour was bad enough, to have one come aboard the boat for any reason was a portent of certain disaster.

'Sunday Boats' became a notorious feature on the Firth during the last decades of the 19th century. The Licensing Acts then in force forbade the sale of alcohol on the Sabbath save only to so-called 'Bona Fide Travellers' or to Hotel residents. But a number of enterprising (or to put it rather more accurately, avaricious) Glasgow publicans spotted that the restrictions of these Acts did not apply to ships: and realised that there were enough thirsty Glaswegians to make an investment in a battered old paddle-steamer a most rewarding speculation.

Their resulting Sunday fleets consisted of boats which had no pretensions to be family cruising vessels — or indeed cruising vessels in *any* sense. They were floating shebeens but (and here was the ace card) they were *legal* shebeens, and earned huge profits for their owners. Andrew McQueen summed up the whole sorry state-of-affairs very accurately in his *Clyde Steamers of the Last Fifty Years*, published in 1924:

'Travellers by these boats were almost entirely drouths out to secure the alcoholic refreshment denied to them ashore. The boats were simply floating pubs, and their routes and destinations were matters of little moment. It is probable that, when they arrived home, a large proportion of the passengers had no very definite idea as to where they had been.'

From the excesses of the 'Sunday Boats' (and the *Dunoon Castle* was the most ill-reputed of them all) came the development of the temperance steamers: and the amendments to the Licensing Acts in the late 1880s which banned sales of alcohol on Sundays aboard any vessel returning to her port of departure on the same day, and effectively closed down the Sabbath breakers.

# 42

## *That Sinking Feeling*

Para Handy laid down the previous day's edition of the *Glasgow Evening News* (the most up-to-date account of the world and its ways presently available in the Harbour Inn at Ardrossan) with a snort of disdain.

"I chust cannot think what the Navy iss coming to, I said it to Dan a meenit ago" he confided to Dougie. Macphail was standing up at the bar talking to one of the engineers off the *Glen Sannox*, which had just completed her last run from Brodick. "What sort o' men are they employin' ass captains or helmsmen nooadays? Here iss another Naval shup agroond on the Lady Rock in the Firth of Lorne.

"Where the bleezes iss the Admirulity recruitin' these days? At the weans' boating pond at Kelvingrove? That makes three of His Majesty's Shups grounded on the Lady Rock skerry this year alone, and we're no' into October yet. It's not even ass if the rock wassna well enough lit, you ken that it is fine enough yourself, Dougie: you've seen it often: mony's the seck of winter coals we've humphed ashore there.

"At this rate poor King Edward'll be runnin' oot o' shups to send up there — or onywhere else."

"It's probably the same shup aal the time, Peter," observed the Mate. "or mebbe the same skipper. For there iss some shups, and some men, that chust seem to have a jinx on them.

"Did I neffer tell you aboot the mustress's Uncle Wulliam? He's retired noo, but he wass a deckhand, then a mate, and finally a skipper on wan or ither o' the Hays' boats aal his working life and given what befcll him it's a miracle the owners kept him on for mair than a month. It wass wan disaster efter anither!

"At least when he didna have the command, he couldna really do aal that mich damage and it tended to be sma' beer.

"When he wass deckhand, mony times when he would be throwin' a line ashore for the longshoremen or the pier-hands to catch hold of, he'd throw it short and then discover it wassna even the right line: it would be chust a spare length of rope he'd flemished-doon *beside* the right line — for tidiness by his way of it — that wassna attached to onything on the shup, and they lost coont o' the fathoms and fathoms o' good rope he cost them, lyin' at the bottom of the river.

"More than wance, when he wass ashore himself to put a bight of a mooring-line over a bollard, he would pit it on wan that wass already cairrying the hawser of a steamer and you know yourself what the steamer crews can be like. They chust threw the top rope over the side of the pier, and Uncle Wulliam's vessel went driftin' off — if they were lucky.

"If they were *unlucky*, the bight of their line got aal fankled wi' the hawser of the steamer, so that wherever she went, they went too. The steamer crews never bothered to unfankle it, for them it wass chust a fine amusement, takin' poor Uncle Wullie's shup in tow ass if it they wass takin' a dug for a waalk on a leash. Wan time the *Inveraray Castle* towed them aal the way from Port Bannatyne to Colintraive before the Officers on the brudge of the paddle-steamer realised that they wassna alone in the Kyles!

"Ass Uncle Wulliam moved up the ladder o' command wi' Hays, and only the good Lord knows how he ever did, his capacity to make a mess of things increased dramatically. The mair he wass given to do, then the mair there wass that could go wrong, and maist usually it did."

"I canna understand how John Hay put up wi' it at all," put in the Engineer, who had rejoined his shipmates. "He wisna a man famous for his tolerance, wis he?"

"Right enough," said Dougie. "The faimily aalways used to say that Uncle Wulliam must have had some kind of a haud over John Hay, that he'd caught him wi' a drink in him on a Fast Day, or tellin' fibs to the Board o' Tred.

"But it wassna that at aal, of course: it wass chust that John Hay liked to have a man aboot the place that wass like a clown at a circus, good for a laugh so long as the herm he did wassna too serious, and it made John Hay feel important, like wan o' they auld medevial kings wi' his own Court Jester.

"But, ass I say, when Uncle Wulliam wass made Mate, there wass more scope for disaster.

"He showed that in fine style. His very first assignment ass a Mate went wrang — I canna chust mind the way of it — and for the next few years he wass shufted from wan shup o' the Hays' fleet to anither, none o' the skippers wanted him for long because something wass aye goin' to pieces when he wass aroond. Finally he was berthed on a puffer that was sent to the wee pier at Sannox, at the north end of Arran, for a cargo o' barytes ore from the mine up the glen.

"It iss a horrid cairgo to load and unload: mercifully we've neffer had a contract for't on the *Vital Spark*. What you may not know, then, iss that it iss a most terrible *heavy* cairgo. A bucketful o' barytes weighs an awful lot mair then a bucketful of onything else you care to name. So ony shup hass to be very careful how mich of it she takes on board, and her captain hass to work oot the load very carefully.

"Onyway, in came Uncle Wulliam's boat on the high tide, and they put her alangside the jetty and ass the tide went oot she beached herself, for there wassna mich watter at the inner end o' the pier.

"The boat wass chust a three-hander and wance she wass berthed, and still no sign of the quarry men comin' wi' the cairts of barytes, the skipper told Uncle Wulliam that he would leave him in cherge while he went to the Inn at Sannox vullage for a wee refreshment, and off he went and took the enchineer with him.

" 'If onybody frae the mine arrives,' said the skipper, 'tell him I'm at the Inns and whenever he wants to get the loading sterted, he can send for me, it's jist hauf-a-mile away. In the meantime, jist you keep an eye on the boat — and dinna you daur touch a thing,' he added emphatically, for Uncle Wulliam's reputation for makin' trouble had come before him.

"Chust ten minutes efter they'd left, the furst o' the Sannox Mine cairts appeared wi' two big Clydesdales in the shafts, and a squad o' men to help load the shup.

"There wass a kind of a chute wi' a funnel on tap of it fixed to a trolley on the quay, and the whole shebang could be swung roond and pointed doon into the hold of any vessel lying alangside. Then the ore wass chust shovelled from the cairts into the funnel and went whooshing doon the chute like snaw off a dyke and into the hold.

"Aal the crew of any shup had to do wass point the mooth o' the chute in the right direction and get the trolley it wass moored to moved effery now and then so that the ore wass evenly spread in the hold.

"So when the first o' the cairts arrived, the foreman leaned over and shouted 'Puffer ahoy! Hoo mich o this dam' stuff can ye take?'

"Uncle Wulliam wass chust aboot to give the man the captain's message, when he thought to himself that it would be a grand surprise for his skipper to come back and find the chob aal done for him: mebbe it would be good for Uncle Wulliam's career too if he showed the unitiative.

"So, instead o' doin' what he wass told like a sensible chap would have done, he shouted back 'Chust you go ahead and fill her up wheneffer you're ready!'

" 'Fill her *up*?' said the foreman, quite flummoxed. 'Are ye sure ye ken whit ye're daeing?'

"Uncle Wulliam drew himself up to his full height and adjusted his peaked kep (he'd bought a white-topped wan ass soon ass the news of his promotion cam' through) and replied sherply: 'You concentrate on looking efter your horses, and allow me to know what iss best for the shup!'

"The foreman shrugged: it wassna his affair. For the next two hoors the Clyesdales and their cairts kept the barytes comin' doon to the shup, and by that time the hold wass full quite to the brim.

"The foreman got Uncle Wulliam to sign a sort of a paper givin' the tonnage she'd taken aboard, and off he and his men went.

"Chust as the loading sterted, the tide had turned and aal this time since then the flood had been coming in. The first inkling Uncle Wulliam had that something wassna right wass when he realised that the water wass creeping up the side o' the shup and the shup wassna moving at aal, she was stuck fast on the bottom as she had been at the foot o' the ebb. She wass that overweighted doon there wass no way at aal that she wass going to float!

"By the time the skipper and enchineer came back from the Inns the only parts of the shup that wass above watter was the mast, the wheelhoose, the ventilators and the funnel.

"It took them three days wi' buckets and shovels at low tide to empty enough barytes oot o' the hold for the shup to be able to refloat herself."

"And Hay's didna seck the man, not even efter that?" asked Para Handy in astonishment.

"Not them," said the Mate. "I can only think they believed that secking him would bring ill-luck on the firm — or that greater responsubility would mebbe improve the man, for it wassna aal that long efter the Sannox uncident that they gave him a shup of his ain.

"He wass to tak' her into Auchentarra on Loch Linnhe for a cairgo of granite from the wee quarry there.

"They cam' in at the peak o' high tide: the jetty was near awash wi' it and they had to lie off for an hour for the ebb to tak' some watter away and give them a chance to berth and make fast.

"Next morning they began to load up, but the quarry wass a good mile from the pier, and they had chust the wan cairt, wi' chust wan horse, and it took a couple of days to get the chob done.

"They took the granite doon to Oban, unloaded it at a private wharf at the sooth end of the bay, then back again for anither load from Auchentarra aboot three days efterwards.

"Wance the shup wass full to the line again, Uncle Wulliam made his farewells wi' the quarrymen, and cast off.

"This time they only got two hundred yerds oot towards the mooth of the bay when she grounded! What Uncle Wulliam had not realised wass that when they'd put in the previous week they'd come in on the spring tides, and the soundings he'd taken then on the way in, and back oot again, wassna the normal ones.

"There wass a sand-bar across the mooth of the bay which neffer had more than 10ft of soundings at normal high watter. But at the springs, there wass well over 16ft of watter on it at high tide.

"When Uncle Wulliam lifted his first cairgo, he'd come in and gone oot on the springs, drawing 11ft aft when she wass loaded, but wi' plenty mair than that under the keel he'd done so withoot any bother.

"This time, though, he wass well and truly stuck. It would be two weeks before the tides wass near enough the springs to give the shup enough watter to refloat herself. Meantime they had the choice of either throwing the cairgo overboard to free the shup, or sitting it oot.

"Uncle Wulliam telegraphed to the Hays' office in Kirkintilloch for instructions. Raither to his surprise, their reply was to tell him no' to dump the cairgo, chust to bide where he was and wait for the springs.

"He wass surprised: I neffer wass," the Mate concluded. "I think that Mr Hay realised it would be less dangerous for the company and its shups, no' to mention the world at large, chust to leave Uncle Wulliam stuck on a sandbar somewhere in Lorne for a fortnight, raither than have him goin' aboot loose."

"Well, Peter," observed the Engineer: "now ye'll mebbe stop fretting aboot the Admirulity. At least they havna got Dougie's Uncle Wulliam on their books. Jist as weel, or we'd be doon to wir last torpedo-boat-destroyer if his record in the merchant fleet wis onything to go by!

"Mebbe that wis why Hay never sacked him: perhaps the guvernment paid a subsidy to keep him oot of the Navy!"

*FACTNOTE*

There were three steamers named *Inveraray Castle* on the Clyde during the 19th century, and it is even thought that one of them was built as early as 1814, just two years after Bell's pioneering *Comet*.

The third ship of the name is the best-known. She was built in 1839 and was in service for almost 60 years, during which period she was twice taken into dry-dock and lengthened — a not unusual practice at that time.

She is believed to have spent her entire career on the Glasgow to Inveraray run — out one day and back the next — and provided the sort of passenger (and light cargo) service to the smaller piers and remoter communities which was beneath the dignity (or beyond the capabilities, due to their sheer size) of the giants of the steamer fleets.

Most of the Clyde puffer fleet belonged to John Hay and Company of Kirkintilloch. That business was in operation for almost 100 years and over that period the firm owned more than 90 of the little boats. They built most of what they owned, too, at their Kirkintilloch yard. Ross and Marshall of Greenock were another significant owner, starting as shipowners later than Hay but remaining in the business longer. They too nearly celebrated their centenary.

UNLUCKY FOR SOME — *Here is Naval Patrol Boat 13 well and truly aground somewhere around Kintyre in the first decade of this century. Built in 1907, powered by Parson turbines, these little craft — 185ft in length but with a beam of only 18ft — were capable of 26 knots. Number 13's luck did not improve: she was lost in 1914 although not through enemy action, but collision with another naval vessel in the North Sea.*

There was indeed a barytes mine in Glen Sannox and the ore was notoriously heavy for its bulk. Extraction of the mineral began in 1840 but at some point later in the Victorian era the whole operation was closed down by the then landowner (the Duke of Hamilton) on what seems to have been purely aesthetic or ecological grounds. A surprisingly late 20th century knee-jerk reaction to find a century earlier!

After the First World War the mine was opened once again. It had its own private jetty just outside Sannox village and, by then, a light railway to haul the ponderous raw material down to the waiting puffers. The mine closed for good shortly before the outbreak of the Second World War but it was during this period of its history that the ore really *did* 'sink' an unfortunate puffer and its unsuspecting or inexperienced skipper. Indeed, I am indebted to a reader of my first collection of Para Handy tales for relating to me his own recollections of just such an unexpected incident at the little Sannox pier!

Strangely, I cannot find the bay of Auchentarra, with its dangerous sandbar lurking to trap the unwary, in any maps that I have of the Loch Linnhe area.

# 43

## *A Boatman's Holiday*

I was standing on the pier at Rothesay passing the time of day with Para Handy, whose beloved vessel lay in the outer harbour waiting the arrival of the local contractor's carts so that a cargo of road-chips could be unloaded.

It was early on a scorching August afternoon: the capital of Bute was already overwhelmed with visitors but their number was in process of being substantially augmented by the crowds who could be seen streaming ashore from the *Iona*, calling on her way to Tarbert and Ardrishaig, having left the Broomielaw at noon on the afternoon run which supplemented the *Columba*'s morning service on the route during the peak season.

"You would wonder where they are aal going to stay," remarked the Captain, watching as fathers struggled down the gangplank with the family's tin trunks and hat boxes while elsewhere on the pier anxious mothers desperately waved a rolled-up umbrella (only the very foolish ever came to Bute without one) to try to catch the attention of an unengaged shore porter with an empty handcart who could wheel the luggage along the esplanade to their chosen hotel.

"There iss times when I think that the island will chust up and sink under the sheer weight o' the numbers. If there iss ony hooseholds in the toon that iss not sleepin' in their beck yerds whiles the hoose is earning coin from towerists packed in hauf-a-dozen to the room, then they must be gey few and far between."

"What do you and Mrs Macfarlane do yourselves when it comes to holidays, Captain?" I enquired, curious: "presumably you have seen enough of the West Coast resorts all the other 50 weeks of the year, and choose something very different?"

"Mery and I very rarely go awa' at aal," Para Handy said. "I am no' mich of a traiveller, other than at my work. And if I can get the twa weeks o' the Fair off, then we ha'e Gleska almost to oorselves. Half the city hass gone doon the watter somewhere and the toon iss deserted.

"You have no idea how peaceful it iss in the Botanic Gairdens, or Gleska Green, or Kelvingrove, when there iss no crowds. And it iss the same wi' the shops, and the tea-rooms, and the picture palaces and aal the rest. There iss no crowds to fight your way through, and the shopkeepers and the rest is most obleeging, they're dam' gled to see ony customers at aal when the maist of their regular tred iss spending their money on sticks o' rock and Eyetalian ices somewhere aboot Innellan or Saltcoats.

"Certainly Gleska's no' a place you'd think to tak' your holidays in ony ither time o' the year but I assure you, in the second hauf of July, you could go a lot further and do a lot worse."

"An interesting concept, Captain," I said: "I confess I have never thought of it that way. In any case, I admit that I enjoy a change of scenery and surroundings, myself."

"Oh, we are not total stay-at-homes," said Para Handy. "We have been doon to England, we stayed at Bleckpool for a week wan year. It iss a strange toon, full o' the English, and the maist of their hooses is built oot o' brick wi' nae harling, it looks like a hauf-feenished building-site.

"We went doon by train frae Gleska, and when we got there we took a horse-cab to the hoose we wass booked into, for it wass a fair step oot of the toon centre.

"Aal the way through the toon Mery kept pointin' oot the number o' temperance hooses to be seen, they wass clustered at every street corner. I'd noticed it myself, and I wass getting a bit anxious aboot it, I can tell you.

"But Mery wass delighted, and she remarked to the cab-driver that Bleckpool must be wan o' the most abstentious holiday-resorts in the country, and the chentlemen that owned the temperance hotels deserved to be congratulated for their convictions.

" 'It's not chust exactly what you're thinking, Ma'am,' said the cabbie: 'though in one sense *convictions* is the right word to be using.

" 'You see, of aal the dry hooses you see, aboot hauf of

them *wants* a licence but cannae get it frae the magustrates because o' the reputation they have: and the other hauf *used* to have a licence — but lost it for the way they wass running the hooses, chust drinking shebeens they wass, wi' constant fighting and noise and broken glesses and the polis aye being called by the neighbours, and clamjamfreys and shenanigans every night.'

"That raither changed Mery's opeenion aboot Bleckpool and she wass gled to get oot of it efter the week — though I managed to find some cheery company roond aboot the pier. But wild horses woudna drag Mery beck!"

∼

The Captain shrugged. "I must admut that I am not chust exectly comfortable staying in a hotel myself.

"Mony of the big wans are so highly-polished and stiff-necked that you are feart to sit on the chairs or waalk on the flairs in case there iss an extra cherge on the account, and the staff are aal so high-falutin' that you are feart to ask them for onything and, when you do, their accents is that posh you could cut them wi' a knife and you canna under-stand wan single word they are saying.

"And the smaal wans that I have been unlucky enough to stay in have usually been run by a man wi' a problem wi' drink and a wife that canna cook, so you get short-measure at the bar and short-shrift in the dining-room.

"The staff is either ower 80 and that wandered and trauch-led that the guests think *they* should be serving *them* raither than the ither way roond: or else they're laddies of aboot 12 years wi' weel-scrubbed faces and a habit o' picking their teeth wi' a matchstick when they think nobody's looking.

"I mind fine wan time a few years back, before the *Vital Spark* wass built, I wass working for a man that owned two or three boats that sailed oot o' Girvan. And did wan o' them no strand herself — or more accurately, did the man that wass supposed to be in cherge of her no' strand her, and him doon below in the fo'c'sle with aal the rest o' the shup's company and enchoying a refreshment when she ran agroond — on a sand bar in the Soond o' Raasay, on her way to Portree from Kyle.

"McTavish, him that owned the boat, secked the entire crew the meenit he got the report of it. I wass on my leave break at the time myself. This wass long afore I got married, of course, and I wass chust perambulating aboot Gleska and having a gless noo and then in wan o' the Hieland public hooses aboot the toon.

"McTavish caaled me back from my leave and sent me up wi' an engineer and a hand to bring the shup back doon to Girvan. I can tell you, I was not at aal happy aboot the chob. We had to get her refloated first, she wass still on the sand: and then we had to hope the propellor wassna damaged: and aal the time we would be aware of the owner waatching efferything that wass going on, through his agent in Portree.

"If things didna work oot then heaven help us, for he wass a short-fused man withoot an ounce of Chrustian charity in him, and he'd secked mair men for less reason than a Tarbert trawlerman's had sair heids on a Sabbath morning.

"We went up by train to Mallaig, and got there late afternoon. There wass only two boats a week to Portree, wan sailing the morn's morning — which iss why he'd sent us up that day — wi' the next no' due till fower days later.

"Lord help us if we missed that boat! And she sailed at half-past five in the morning! There wass a kind of a night-clerk in the Hotel, a man of 75 if he wass a day, very shaky on his feet and as deaf as a post.

"We made sure we wass early to bed, I can tell you. We had a room on the furst floor o' the Hotel wi' three beds in it, at the head of the stairs from the main haall.

"While the other two went up to make their ablutions, I went in search of this night-clerk.

"I found him cleaning the boots o' the commaircial chentlemen who wass the Hotel's only ither patrons, in a basement room wi' no light but wan solitary candle.

" 'We've to get the Skye steamer at half-past-five', I bellowed in his ear, 'and we daurna miss it! Ye'll need to mind to gi'e us a caall at half-past-four. Room three at the heid of the stair.'

" 'Aal right,' says he, 'that's no bother. Room three, heid of the stair, half-past-four for the half-past-five steamer — and ye dinna need to shout, I'm no deaf!'

"We found out later that, come the morning, he had forgotten which room wass to be knocked for the steamer, and he chust went to the tap o' the hoose — room 33 — and worked his way doon. You can imachine the abuse he got alang the way!

"But it took him a long time to work his way doon for the

ither chentlemen wass ill to rouse, them no' expecting the caall in the furst place, and verra displeased indeed when they were given it.

"When he finally knocked on the door of room three it wass too late.

"I woke up wi' this voice shouting through the keyhole: 'Are you the chentlemen that wants the caall for the early boat?'

" 'Yes,' I yelled back. 'Thanks! we'll be down for our breakfast in a jiffy.'

" 'Och, ye needna fash yersel's', he shouts: 'tak' your time, you've plenty of it. It's six o'clock and she's well on her way to Kyle by noo. She left hauf an hoor ago. There wass no need to waken you at aal, I chust did it because you asked me to.'

"So," concluded Para Handy, "that wass wan 'holiday' that cost me my chob, for MacTavish brought in a crew from Inverness and we were secked. I should chust have stayed in Gleska and taken my leave."

~

With an imperious blast on her powerful steam whistle the *Iona* announced her intention of departing and the admiring flotilla of small yachts and rowing boats which had been gathered around her gleaming black hull like pilot fish round a whale scattered hastily as the steamer's bow and stern ropes were cast loose from the pier bollards and the paddle-blades began to turn.

At that moment came an anguished feminine cry of "Wait, wait for us, please: please wait!"

Turning, the Captain and I saw a strange little cavalcade come hurrying from the esplanade, along the connecting roadway to the pierhead.

In the van was a woman of perhaps 40 years, gesticulating quite frantically with an umbrella. Hers were the shouts.

Behind her, making the best speed he could, was one of the town's shore-porters with his barrow. On it lay the lady's luggage — and one other accoutrement: the lady's husband. Fast asleep and with a contented smile on his face, his rosy cheeks suggested how that contentment had been achieved, and why the couple were in grave danger of missing the steamer.

The *Iona*'s Captain, on the wing of the bridge, took the

scene in at a glance — and gently nudged his vessel back towards the quay for the minute necessary for the lady and her luggage to be gallantly assisted aboard across the paddle-box by two of the ship's crew: and for the husband to be less ceremoniously taken in a fireman's lift and dropped onto a convenient bench.

Para Handy sighed.

"There is no justice, is there? We went sober to our beds and lost our chobs. That chentleman probably neffer went to his at aal last night and not only did he catch his ship, it wass his wife that he has to thank for that.

"If that had been Mery and me, I doot the mustress would have gone aboard and left me at Ro'say pier wi' a label roond my neck printed, 'Not wanted on Voyage'.

"And you know, she would have been quite right!"

*FACTNOTE*

Blackpool has been a favourite holiday destination for generations of lowland Scots and its 'Golden Mile' with its end-of-the-pier-shows, the tower, the ballroom, the funfair, have entertained millions and still attract the summer hordes at the end of this century. I wish the Clyde resorts had been as fortunate in fine-tuning and marketing their appeal for them we might still have had steamer fleets!

Of all the famous Clyde names, only that of the veteran *Iona* comes close to eclipsing the legendary *Columba*.

She was the third steamer of that name to be built for the Hutcheson fleet at the Govan yard of J & G Thomson in a space of just nine years!

The first *Iona*, launched in 1855, put in just seven seasons on the Clyde when her speed and manoeuvrability were noticed and she was bought by the American Confederate States for service as a blockade-runner in the Civil War. Ignominiously, however, she never got past the Tail o' the Bank, being run down by the steamship *Chanticleer* off Greenock when she was running without lights. As soon as she had been sold to the Americans a second *Iona* had been ordered from Thomsons yard, but this one never even entered service before she was snapped up by agents of the Confederacy. She got a little further on her voyage to America than her predecessor, though not much: she foundered off the island of Lundy in a Bristol Channel storm.

I suppose we only had a third *Iona* actually on the Clyde

because the American Civil War was coming to its end as she was being completed!

She was the largest vessel on the river at the time of her launch and for style and opulence she was not to be surpassed till 1878 when David MacBrayne, now controlling director of the Hutcheson fleet, ordered (again from Thomson's Govan yard) the incomparable *Columba*, a full one-fifth again bigger than *Iona* but very much based on her proven, successful design.

*Columba* had a long career as MacBrayne's adored flagship before going to the breakers in 1936 at the venerable age of 58, but here she had to give best to *Iona* which had seen an astonishing 72 years service when she, too, went for scrap that same year.

Who could have foreseen a hundred years ago that industrial, commercial Glasgow would indeed become a serious holiday destination — though Para Handy and his wife did not have the lure of such delights as the Burrell Collection or the restored Merchant City or the Mackintosh legend to tempt them!

THE ELEGANCE OF HORSEPOWER — *The suspicion is that this photograph was commissioned from the MacGrory brothers on the day that its Campbeltown owner-driver took delivery (probably by a steamer and possibly even by a puffer) of this handsome Hansom-cab, a fashionable conveyance designed in the mid-19th century by its eponymous inventor Joseph, but in fashion till well into the early years of the 20th century.*

# 44

## *Santa's Little Helpers*

I encountered Para Handy and Hurricane Jack quite unexpectedly as they emerged from the Buchanan Street doorway of the Argyll Arcade late on Christmas Eve, the Captain's oldest friend clutching a large rectangular parcel wrapped in shiny brown paper printed overall with the name of the shop on which every schoolboy's hopes would that night be concentrated — the Clyde Model Dockyard.

"Last minute shopping indeed, Captain," I exclaimed : "and from the Clyde Model Dockyard itself! Who is the lucky lad?"

Para Handy, looking rather embarrassed, just mumbled something unintelligible and made to move off but Hurricane Jack, laying his burden carefully on the pavement, straightened up with a sigh and remarked pointedly, "It iss real thirsty work, this shopping business : and a rare expense ass weel : I'll tell you that for nothing."

Sensing a story, I persuaded the two mariners to join me for a seasonal dram in a convenient hostelry in neighbouring St Enoch's Square. But it took a second glass to start the flow of the narrative, and then a third before the whole sorry tale was unfolded for me.

It had all begun three days previously...

~

A freezing fog had enveloped the lochside village all day, and darkness was rapidly closing in on the short December afternoon when the indistinct silhouette of a steam-lighter loomed out of the gloaming and the fully-laden little vessel eased its way into the basin at the Ardrishaig end of the Crinan Canal.

In the wheelhouse of the *Vital Spark* Para Handy breathed a sigh of relief as he bent down to call into the engine-room at his feet. "Whenever you're ready, Dan," he said, and with a rattle and a clank the propeller-shaft stopped turning and the puffer drifted the last few feet onto the stone face of the quay.

"My Cot," said the skipper, as Sunny Jim leapt ashore with the bow mooring rope and slipped its bight over the nearest stone bollard, "I wass neffer so relieved to see the shup safe into port. Ever since we came round Ardlamont I have been frightened that every moment wud be our next."

Indeed it had been an uncomfortable passage up Loch Fyne, for it was there that the weather had closed in on the puffer and Para Handy had steered his course towards Ardrishaig more by instinct than anything else in fog which restricted visibility to less than fifty yards.

"It's chust ass well that Dougie iss not here," said Hurricane Jack, materialising out of the gloom on the cargo-hatch just forward of the wheelhouse. "A fine sailor when we are safe in port but tumid, tumid when we are at sea."

It was four days before Christmas and Dougie the family man had bargained with the bachelor Jack to stand in for him on this unexpected last-minute charter to Inveraray with a cargo of coals. Not that the Mate himself was particularly keen to spend the festive season cooped up with ten screaming children in a tenement flat in Plantation, but the Mate's wife was determined that he should do so, and she was certainly not a lady to be argued with lightly by anyone, and least of all by her husband.

Once the puffer was safely berthed, Para Handy went ashore and up to the Post Office to send a wire to McCallum, the Inveraray coal merchant, explaining why his cargo had been delayed.

McCallum's response, delivered to the *Vital Spark* half-an-hour later by a diminutive telegraph boy, proved that the spirit of the season of peace and good will to all men had not reached certain quarters of Upper Loch Fyne.

"You wud think that we was responsible for the fog," complained the Captain as the crew made their way up the quayside towards the Harbour Bar. "Well, all I can say iss that he will get his coals tomorrow if it lifts, but I am not prepared to risk the boat chust to keep Sandy McCallum's Campbell customers happy."

~

Next morning the fog had indeed dispersed and the puffer made an early start for Inveraray. Since one and all were anxious to get home in time for Christmas, the unloading of the coals was achieved in record time. As soon as the cargo was safely ashore in the early afternoon, and carted to McCallum's ree, the crew prepared to set sail at once without even a cursory visit to the bar of the George Hotel.

However, just as Sunny Jim was loosing the last mooring rope, the owner of the Hotel himself appeared on the quay-side, quite out of breath, and carrying a large cardboard box.

"I heard you were at the harbour, Peter : I wonder if you would do me a kindness," he asked, "and deliver this for me? It's my nephew's Christmas present — my sister's laddie — and it should have gone up to Glasgow yesterday on the steamer, but with the fog the *Lord of the Isles* turned back at the Kyles and I've no way of getting it to town in time other than with yourself.

"My sister's house is just off Byres Road, and I'll give you the money for a cab..."

~

"Would you take a look at this!" cried Hurricane Jack fifteen minutes later, emerging from the fo'c'sle with the box — minus its lid — cradled in his arms, and an excited grin on his face.

Para Handy was about to protest at the cavalier way in which Jack had satisfied his curiosity, but when he saw the contents of the box for himself, he peremptorily summoned Sunny Jim to take the wheel and hurried for'ard to join his shipmate.

The box contained a magnificent train-set — a gleaming green and gold locomotive, three pullman coaches, and a bundle of silver and black rails.

"My chove," said the Captain enthusiastically. "Iss that not chust sublime, Jeck! There wass neffer toys like that when I wass a bairn and needin' them, or if there wass, then I neffer saw them.

"I'm sure it wouldna' do ony herm if we chust had a closer look at it aal..."

In no time at all, the rails — which formed a generous oval track — had been laid out on the mainhatch, the carriages set on one of the straight sections : the two mariners were peering curiously at the engine itself.

" 'Marklin, Made in Chermany',," said Para Handy, reading the trademark stamped on the underside of the chassis. "Clever duvvles, but I canna see the key and I canna imachine chust how on earth we're meant to wind the damn' thing up."

Hurricane Jack took the engine out of the skipper's hands and looked closely at it. "This isn't a clockwork injin at all, Peter," he said at length, reaching to the box and taking out of it a small tin which he opened to reveal a number of round white objects like miniature nightlights. "It's wan o' they real steam ones. You put some watter in the wee biler, and then you light wan o' these meths capsules in the firebox, and off she goes.

"I'm sure it wouldna' do ony herm if we chust tried her oot chust the wan wee time..."

However, despite their best efforts, neither Para Handy nor Jack had any success in getting the model engine fired up.

"Can I not have a shot at it please, Captain?" called Sunny Jim plaintively from the wheelhouse, whence his view of proceedings down on deck was frustratingly limited.

"Haud your wheesht and mind the wheel, Jum," replied Para Handy brusquely, "and leave this business to men who are old enough to ken what they're doin'. But you could maybe give Dan a call and ask him to come up here for a minute."

It was of course the puffer's engineer who finally cracked the problem of propulsion and in a few minutes the little train was chuffing importantly around and around the oval track, the three seamen on their hands and knees, spellbound, beside it.

Jim's repeated pleadings to be allowed to join in the fun were totally ignored.

"Is that aal there is to it?" Jack asked after a while. "I'm sure she wud run faster withoot all they carriages..." An experiment which was soon put to the test, and as soon shown to be true. Even that improvement, however, palled after a few minutes more.

"I'm sure and she wud be able to go faster if we took her aff the rails," suggested Para Handy : "and she'd certainly be able to go further..."

Moments later, with Para Handy on his knees at the after-end of the mainhatch and Jack at the fore-end, Macphail having retired to his lair with a snort of derision, the rails had been packed away and the little locomotive was racing to and fro the full length of the hatch, set on its way by one of the mariners, and then caught at the far end by the other, turned about, and sent on the return trip.

"Careful, Jeck," cried Para Handy : "dinna drop it, whatever you do!"

"Can I no' come doon and have a wee shot wi' it?" pleaded Sunny Jim again from the wheelhouse, and in that one fatal moment the damage was done.

Para Handy turned irritably to remonstrate with his persistent deckhand and as he did so the little engine, racing back from Hurricane Jack's end of the hatch, hurtled off it as it reached the momentarily unattended after-end, bounced once on the deck and, in a gleam of green and gold, soared over the low bulwarks of the puffer and sank, with one briefly echoing plop, into the salty depths of Loch Fyne.

"Jum!" yelled Para Handy accusingly. "Wull you chust look and see whit ye've been and gone and done noo..."

~

"An expensive high-jink, Captain" I said as we parted company on the corner of Argyll Street and Union Street. "But so long as you deliver the new set safely, and so long as neither giver nor receiver ever find out that you had to buy it, or why..."

"Chust so", said the Captain somewhat shame-facedly, and he and Hurricane Jack went off in search of a cab while I made my way back to the newspaper office.

~

It was several weeks before the *Vital Spark* was in Inveraray again but one February morning she lay at the outer end of the pier loading a cargo of pit-props.

Just after mid-day the owner of the George Hotel came down the quayside and called to Para Handy, who was supervising the work of the derrick from the deck. Dan Macphail was at the winch and Hurricane Jack and Sunny Jim were up on the pierhead roping bundles of the timber together.

"I just wanted to thank you for delivering that Christmas gift in Glasgow for me, Peter," the hotelier shouted. "Very much appreciated, and the laddie just loved his train.

"Funny thing, though : I must be losing my memory I think, for he wrote me such a nice letter about the train set and its fine *red* engine when I would have sworn blind that I had bought him a *green* one."

"Aye," Sunny Jim began : "But the toy shop wis sold richt oot o' the greeeeeaaaAAAAAH...!"

"Sorry, Jim" said Hurricane Jack loudly and pointedly, lifting the metal-shod heel of his heavy boot from where it had crashed down onto the toe and instep of the deck-hand's left foot. "Ah didna see you there..."

*FACTNOTE*

The Clyde Model Dockyard in the Argyll Arcade, the L-shaped indoor shopping mall which links Buchanan Street and Argyll Street, was so much part of the myth and folk-lore of West of Scotland schoolboys of my own and previous generations that it almost comes as a surprise to find that it *doesn't* have an entry in the Collins Encyclopedia of Scotland.

Argyll Arcade today is inhabited by nothing but wall-to-wall jewellers, but go back a generation and it housed a wide range of shops of which the Model Dockyard was the undisputed mecca.

Its window displays were legendary, the stuff of magic, dreams of the unattainable. Before plastic came to destroy the quality and character of toys the magic names of Hornby, Meccano, Trix, Mammod, Dinky, Basset-Lowke, Marklin, Frog and other legends of railways, roadways, air-ways and seaways in miniature dominated that plate-glass paradise and its groaning shelves.

At Christmas, even in the decades of continuing short-ages which stretched well into the fifties, the Dockyard somehow managed to acquire stock which eluded lesser contenders, and scrums of anxious youths fought for places at the windows to see what was available before rushing home to pen anxious lists for their own personal present providers — before the limited, but quite priceless, stocks ran out.

I was living many miles from Glasgow when the Dockyard finally closed: victim presumably of the mass-produced, mass-marketed toys which for all their greater availability in shopping malls everywhere — and their relatively greater affordability — seem inconsequential and insubstantial trivia in comparison to those earlier delights.

Those who remember the solid chunkiness of a post-war Dinky Toy taxi-cab (any colour you wanted so long as it was black and green or black and wine) with its uniformed driver seated in his cab, open to the elements: or the challenge of getting the best from Meccano sets with which everyone else seemed to be so much more adept than you were: struggling with balsa-wood ship or aeroplane kits: the acrid smell of modelling paint and varnish: the surprisingly versatile rubber Minibrix, precursor of Lego and a valuable adjunct to Hornby Gauge 0 train layouts.

Those who remember such delights will never forget them, and will only regret that the toys which thrill their own children seem at once made so slipshod and slapdash (though technically out-of-sight), and so ephemeral (though imperative possessions for their one brief hour of fashionable fame) by comparison.

# 45

## *The Black Sheep*

T he disdain with which the Deck Officers of many of the crack paddle-steamers, and the officials at the more fashionable Clyde resorts, treat the puffers which cross their paths and frequent their harbours is as nothing compared with the calculated and insulting pretensions to superiority which are often directed at the little boats and those who work on them by the private yachts which they encounter — and the larger the yacht, then usually the larger the degree of derision with which they are treated.

Such opprobrium, however, comes not from the *owners* of the yachts but from their *crews*. This is particularly cruel, for as often as not these crewmen are of the same stock and background as the crews of the puffers, and the gabbarts and steam-lighters, which are the butt of their jibes and sneers.

I suppose it is merely symptomatic of the inadequacies of human nature that many who succeed in 'bettering' themselves, whether financially or socially, should then desire to kick away from beneath them the ladder by which they climbed to such new and giddy heights — and to pretend that they never had anything in common with those less fortunate occupants of the lower rungs of that same ladder (namely their former colleagues and equals) at the same time.

And no individual can be more cutting in these circumstances than one who only *pretends* that he has improved himself, but knows full well that, despite superficial outward appearances, he has in fact signally failed so to do.

Para Handy, fortunately, was a man of a kindly and

forgiving nature, and though he could be hurt by the unfeeling comments of former acquaintances who had moved on from the rigours and frustration of the coastal cargo trade, he was not prone to harbour grudges and was more likely to forgive and forget than to remember and plot revenge.

There are, however, exceptions to almost every rule and in this instance Para Handy's exception was Donald Anderson.

Anderson was a small, dark-haired and dark-featured individual with twitchy movements and a shifty look. He rarely if ever smiled and when he did (usually at the discomfiture or distress of another) it was, to trot out the old cliche, with his mouth only and not with his eyes.

Yet it had not always been so. Para Handy's very first posting afloat, as deckboy on a sailing gabbart trading out of Bowling, had been shared with Donald Anderson and the two lads, who were both of the same age, had struck up an immediate friendship.

In part they were drawn together by the unfamiliarity of their new surroundings, the uncertainty as to what the future held for them, and the sometimes unreasonable treatment meted out by the senior members of the gabbart's crew. In part, though, they had much in common despite the startling difference in their backgrounds — Para Handy brought up in a remote corner of Argyllshire, Anderson the unmistakable product of inner-city Glasgow. For the two years they spent on the gabbart, the two were inseparable.

Their paths diverged when they reached the age of 18.

Para Handy, determined to chart a career in the mercantile arm of shipping, signed on as deckhand on a larger gabbart carrying a wider range of cargos over longer distances.

Donald Anderson, when he learned of this, gave the very first indications of the sort of man he would one day become.

"Ye dinna catch me dirtyin' ma haun's ever again if I can help it," he said cuttingly. "Ah'm fairly dumbfoonered at ye, Peter Macfarlane. Ye can keep yer gabbarts frae noo on for me, for Ah've got took on by MacBrayne as a steward in the third-class saloon on the *Grenadier*, regular hoors, a fancy uniform jaicket and three meals a day, and that's only a start. So you can be thinkin' o' me, and the dufference between wis, each time you is shuvveling coals or roadstone or some other filthy cairgo in some god-forsaken Hielan' hell-hole on a cauld January day.

"Ah actually thocht ye'd some sense, but ye're naethin' but a Hielan' stot efter a', and that's whit ye'll stay."

"I dinna care much aboot clothes and ootward show, but you may as weel may get yoursel' into a uniform jecket if that is what you want, but it's for sure that you will neffer get your own command as a kutchen-porter if you live to be a centurion," was all that the young Para Handy replied, and Anderson gave him a foul look and they went their separate ways.

∼

Over the years, Para Handy heard snippets of gossip about his former friend, and they occasionally encountered each other in some corner of the west.

Anderson did not keep his job with MacBrayne for long, for once into his steward's uniform his attitude to the patrons of the third-class accommodation to whose needs he was supposed to attend became quite insufferably patronising — only ministering to the whims of the gentry in the first class lounges and saloons could merit *his* attentions and match *his* pretensions — and after just three months he was looking for another post.

He then spent twenty years going foreign — on the Greenock to Nova Scotia service of the Allan Line as a senior steward, by his own account. The truth was more mundane. Once again found wanting in his care of the paying passengers, he was demoted to acting as mess 'boy' for the ship's engineers. He passed many fruitless and frustrated years trying to 'improve' his position by obtaining a cabin post with one of the other transatlantic shipping companies but his record, resentment and reputation always preceded him, however, and he stayed where he was.

"At least his uniform fits him, even if his estimation of his own importance doesna," remarked Para Handy to the Mate one day after they had encountered him in a dockside public house in Govan. "I am chust sorry for the Allan enchineers, it must be like bein' danced attendance on by a yahoo wi' a superiority complex. How they keep their hands off him I chust cannot think."

By the time Para Handy had his own command,

Anderson was back on the Clyde, having tried the patience of the Allan Line and its engineers just once too often. He drifted from one unhappy job to another — a washroom attendant at the St Enoch Hotel, a doorman at the Mitchell Library, a porter at Central Station, a boating-pond steward at Hogganfield Loch, a park-keeper at the Botanic Gardens. Anderson would take *anything* — as long as it gave him a clean-hands and non-labouring occupation, a uniform, and the opportunity to fawn ingratiatingly upon his superiors and treat contemptuously those he saw as his inferiors.

And through the passing years and the ups and downs he lost no opportunity, when their paths crossed, to sneer at the chosen career of the skipper of the *Vital Spark*, belittle his status, and contrast their circumstances to his own imagined advantage.

~

Late one Friday evening Para Handy guided his command gently through the narrow dock entrance at Rothesay and into the outer of the two harbours which lay sheltered by the great length of the town's main steamer pier.

Apart from a few small fishing smacks lying against its inner face for the weekend and a couple of skiffs bobbing to moorings in the centre of the basin, the only other occupant of the harbour was a handsome, yellow-funnelled steam yacht of similar length to the Vital Spark, but with a much narrower beam and a graceful look about her which the unfortunate puffer could never hope to emulate.

"Ready when you are, Dan," the Captain called down the speaking tube to the engine-room, and Macphail cut the power to the propellor and the *Vital Spark* drifted the last few feet onto the quay wall.

The accident was the merest trifle, the result perhaps of a sudden, slight flaw of wind catching the port quarter of the puffer — for she was in ballast, and riding high enough in the water to present a sail-like profile to a surface breeze: but whatever the reason, as the way came off her she gently — ever so gently — nudged her bows against the stern of the yacht and tipped that vessel just fractionally to starboard so that her fenders squeaked against the stone quay, and her main halyards slapped softly against her mast.

There were two immediate and contemporaneous results of this quiet coming-together.

From beneath the awning stretched across the fore-deck, where the owner and his party sat contemplating the peaceful charm of Rothesay over the rims of their cocktail-glasses, a tall figure rose to his feet and, glancing towards the wheelhouse of the *Vital Spark*, enquired in concerned tones: "Is everything all right with you Captain — no problems, I hope?"

At the same time a small, white-jacketed figure came hurtling out of the stern galley shaking his fist in the direction of the *Vital Spark* and mouthing a torrent of abuse. It was Donald Anderson.

Para Handy, ignoring him completely, doffed his cap with a nod of the head to the owner, and apologised for the mishap. "I am chust anxious aboot the yat," he concluded.

"Please don't concern yourself, Captain. The *Carola* is a sturdy little ship. I should know — I built her myself! And she has taken much more punishment many, many times when I've misjudged my approach to a jetty!"

And with a smile he turned away — and to Para Handy's relief and satisfaction sent Anderson (who had recognised the Captain and now stood glaring malevolently at him) back down below with a curt word and an angry gesture.

∽

The following afternoon the *Vital Spark* came bucketing round the north end of Arran into Kilbrannan Sound in a strong south wind. The barley she had loaded at Rothesay was destined for one of the Campbeltown whisky distilleries.

Dougie caught Para Handy's arm and pointed towards the Kintyre coast. "Is that no' that yat we saw in Rothesay?" he suggested anxiously. "And does it no' look as if she's in trouble of some sort?"

Indeed the *Carola* it was, and — plainly drifting uncontrolled and without power — she was rolling alarmingly in the rising waves that came marching up from the stormy Mull to the south.

Fifteen minutes later the *Vital Spark* had passed a line to the yacht and begun to tow her back across the Sound to the shelter and safety of the bay at Lochranza.

∽'

At the yachtsman's insistence the crew of the *Vital Spark* (after a toilet supervised by her Captain, a toilet as thorough and as demanding as any they had ever inflicted upon themselves) dined on board the yacht that evening.

Para Handy had at first been most reluctant to accept the invitation and excused himself on the grounds that he and the steward of the *Carola* were acquaintances of long-standing but that they "didna get on".

"Don't concern yourself about that," said the yachtsman. "The man was only taken on temporarily for this one week, my regular steward being sick. And in any case, he's not on board any longer. I'd had more than enough of his insufferable behaviour before we reached Rothesay, and when I heard and saw how he treated you after that little incident last night, I sent him packing. I am used to having nothing but gentlemen on the *Carola* whether as guests or as crew, whatever their background may be. *Gentlemen!*" he repeated with emphasis.

"In fact," he observed at dinner, "I am absolutely certain that Anderson was responsible for the engine failure this afternoon and my engineer agrees. Somebody loosened one of the connecting rods so that after an hour or two it was bound to shear. It did not do that by itself."

"I think I might know where the polis could get a haud of him..." Para Handy began.

"No, not at all," said the yachtsman firmly. "There are some people not worth bothering about even to see them getting their due deserts. Some people are beneath contempt. And that man is one of them."

Para Handy could only nod in agreement.

*FACTNOTE*

The career of MacBrayne's *Grenadier* was a perfect illustration of just how far-ranging that company's operations were.

She spent several years on long-haul services out of Oban to the far North West Highlands, and latterly she was employed on the day-trip business of the bread-and-butter Oban money-maker, the excursion to Iona, for the Abbey and a touch of the mystery of the Celtic Church: and on to Staffa, for Fingal's Cave.

In winter she was often brought down to the Clyde to take over the daily Ardrishaig service from the *Columba* and she was the only MacBrayne paddle-steamer to be requisitioned for service in the First World War. Returned to the Oban station in the 1920s she came to a tragic end, burned out at the South Pier in 1927.

Donald Anderson's grudging service at the Mitchell Library would probably have been deployed in the second building which that institution occupied, in Miller Street, from 1889 to 1911.

The Library moved in that year to the purpose-built premises which it has occupied ever since. The Mitchell was originally endowed by a Glasgow tobacco merchant and has become one of the largest Libraries in Britain — despite not having the right of the British Library or Trinity College Dublin to a free copy of every book published in the U.K. Its Glasgow Room is a goldmine of information, from the trivial to the earth-shattering, about the West of Scotland: and the staff the most knowledgeable and user-friendly in the business.

The steam-yacht *Carola* was built (possibly as an 'apprentice piece') in the yard of Scott of Bowling for the family of Scott of Bowling in 1898. 70ft long, and powered by a two-cylinder compound engine, she was used by the family for day excursions on the Clyde. Despite the fact that she had no cabin accommodation she was also used for longer excursions, sometimes as far as Oban by way of the Crinan Canal. She would undertake those journeys in a series of day-long stages, the family and their guests going ashore each night to sleep in a local hotel while the crew bunked down on board.

Derelict and abandoned in the River Leven, she was about to be broken up when she was rescued and taken down to Southampton to be restored by an English enthusiast.

Subsequently purchased by the Scottish Maritime Museum and brought back to the Clyde, she offers the opportunity for quiet contemplation of the river, in summer, from the decks of what is perhaps the oldest remaining sea-going steam yacht afloat.

# 46

## *On His Majesty's Service*

I
t was a pleasantly sunny May morning, but Para Handy
watched the Postman coming along the quayside at
Bowling Harbour with some distaste, for he could see,
clutched in that worthy's right hand, a buff-coloured
envelope obviously intended for delivery to the *Vital Spark*
and, in all probability, addressed to her Captain. Para Handy's
experience with buff-coloured envelopes was that they were
usually the harbingers not of good or welcome news but of
unwanted ill-tidings, most usually of a monetary nature.

"What iss it this time," he demanded petulantly, "another bill from Campbell's Coal Ree? Ah've only jist paid for
the last lot of assorted stanes he delivered in April."

The postman, handing over the envelope, shrugged apa-
thetically and made off without a word.

Para Handy watched his wiry figure step briskly out along
the quayside and back towards the village.

"You would think," he observed to the Mate, "that Lex
Cameron would treat me wi' chust a little more respect,
given what I know aboot him that his bosses at Post Office
headquarters up in George Square dinna: and what they
might want to do aboot it if they did!"

"What's that, Peter," queried Macphail, joining the other
two on the main-hatch.

"Last Chrustmas Eve it wass," said the Captain, "right
here in Bowling. You two — and Jum — had gone ashore for
a refreshment while we wass waiting to go up the canal to
Port Dundas, but I had stayed on board in the fo'c'sle wi' a
mutchkin of spurits to make up a hot toddy for myself, for
you'll mind that I had a terrible dose of the flu at the time,
and wass feeling pretty sorry for myself.

"Onyway, Lex Cameron came alongside up on the quay wi' the mail, and gave a bit of a whoop to see if there wass anyone on the shup, so I shouted on him and doon he came. Since it wass Chrustmas the least I could do wass to offer him a dram, ass any Chrustian chentleman would do, and he perched on the end of Dougie's bunk and drank it, and then made such a production oot of banging his empty gless doon on the table that I had to gi'e him anither.

"That wass when I realised that the man wass fairly in the horrors wi' the drink, and he had aboot ass much spurits aboard him aalready ass would have filled a bucket, but he didna have Hurricane Jeck's agility when it cam' to carryin' them.

" 'Are you aal right, Lex?' says I, 'I think maybe you should get yourself hame before you do yourself a mischief.'

" 'Ah canna dae that,' says he: 'the wife'd kill me if she saw me in this condeetion, Ah'll be a' right, jist help me up the ladder, Peter, and Ah'll get on wi' the roond. It's aye the same at Chrustmas, my regulars a' have drams waiting for me for the sake o' the season, and if Ah dinna drink them they would think Ah've taken offence at them.

" 'Jist see me ontae the quayside and point me at the vullage and Ah'll no' tak' anither drap o' spurits, Ah'll jist get the roond feenished and go and sleep it aff at ma brither's hoose.'

"I neffer saw Lex for a month or more after that," the Captain continued, "and when next I did I asked him how he'd got on that Chrustmas Eve, had he got the mails aal safely delivered and made peace with his mustress.

" 'Ah made peace wi' the mustress a' right, Peter,' says he: 'but there wis no way I could huv feenished the round, Ah wisna fit for't by then.'

" 'So what did you do,' I asked: 'did you get wan of your mates to feenish it for you?'

" 'Dod, no,' says Lex: 'Ah could hae got the sack straight off for bein' fu' and in cherge o' a load of mails. No, there wis only wan thing tae dae, and Ah done it. Ye ken there's a mail box at the harbour entrance up yonder? Weel, I jist emptied my bag of a' the letters and packets in it, and posted the whole lot back again, and went hame.'

"And that's the man who canna be bothered to give me the time of day," concluded Para Handy with disgust, and he examined the small brown envelope suspiciously. "Whit does *OHMS* mean?" he enquired, studying the imprint on its top left corner.

"*On His Majesty's Service* of course," said the Engineer.

"And for why would King Edward be writing to me," asked Para Handy incredulously, "for I'm sure I'm no' in his obleegement in any way."

"Dinna be so daft," said Macphail. "It's no a letter frae the King, that jist means it's an offeecial letter o' some sort. It wull be frae the Tax Office, or the Customs and Excise men, or something like that."

Para Handy shivered apprehensively. "I am sure I am beholden to nobody for nothing," and he ripped the envelope open and pulled out the flimsy sheet which it contained.

It was merely notification of a minor amendment, with regard to the lighting of Pilot Vessels, to the Merchant Shipping Acts of 1892, 1897 and 1904.

"Well, that iss a great relief," said the Captain. "I neffer see these brown unvelopes but my hert sinks. I mind the trouble my mither's cousin Cherlie got into wance wi' the Tax people when he had that big ferm at Dunure, it wass the ruination of the man, and him the only member o' the femily that wass effer likely to mak' serious money.

"The trouble wass he hadna paid a penny piece of Income Tax for years, but eventually they caught up wi' him and he got a whole series of abusive letters demandin' to know whit way he hadna been keeping in touch and letting them know how he wass getting on, and threatening the poor soul wi' aal sorts of hellfire and brumstone if he didna pay up fast.

"I wull say this for Cherlie, he could aalways tell when he wass in real trouble, and he recognised that this wass the time for drastic action, so he pulled his tin trunk oot from under the bed, counted oot two hundred pounds, put them into a paper poke, and took the train from Ayr up to Gleska an went to the Tax Office.

" 'Cherlie Mackinnon from Dunure Ferm,' says he to the man at the desk by way of introduction, 'and I've been getting a wheen o' letters from ye, so I thocht I'd best come and see you to straighten it aal oot.' And he tipped the money oot o' the poke onto the desk counter.

" 'Two hundred pound,' he says: 'and I think that should see us straight. So, if you're happy wi' that, I'll be on my way back to the ferm': and he headed for the street door.

"The clerk wass aal taken aback but he recovered himself enough to shout to Cherlie, 'Wait a meenit Mr Mackinnon, I'll have to give you a receipt for this money.'

"Cherlie wass almost in the street by this time but he

stuck his head back round the door and said, 'No, no, my mannie. You mustn't do that! That's *cash* — for peety's sake, you're neffer goin' to pit that through the *books*, are ye?'

Para Handy shook his head sadly. "Poor Cherlie, the Income Tax people went into his affairs wi' a most duvvel-ish ill-wull till he wass left with nothin' but the breeks he stood up in, they took the ferm off him to pay what they said he owed, and that wass the end of the only chance of a puckle money that either the Mackinnons or the Macfarlanes effer had aboot them!

"It iss chust a pity that Cherlie didna have the natural sagiocity and deviousness of Hurricane Jeck, for likely he would have had the ferm yet!

"While Jeck had the happy knack of spendin' money as if it grew on trees and aal he effer had to do wass chust wander oot and pick some more, he wass also pretty skilfull at keep-ing it oot of the hands of the Revenue and the Excise Officers.

"Wan time, when he wass wi' the Allan Line, he had bought himself a smaall barrel of white spurit from a private enterprise still run by an acquaintance o' his in Plantation, and installed it in the fore-cabin of the vessel he wass on. He wass a popular man wi' his shupmates that trup, and his price for the gill wass very fair.

"When they put in at Halifax in Nova Scotia Jeck still had a mair than half-full barrel o' illicit spurits in the fo'c'sle, and no intention at aal of surrendering it to the Canadian Excisemen, though he knew that they would be coming on board to search the shup. What he did wass, he got an empty whusky bottle from the Officer's Mess and filled it wi' watter that he coloured wi' a wheen o' burnt sugar so it looked like the real stuff.

"When the Excisemen came aboard and doon to the fo'c'sle — with the barrel of spurits lying on a trestle in the corner, quite openly, and wi' a spigot at the fore-end of her — Jeck admutted straight away that he had some unde-clared whisky that wass due for a surcharge.

" 'But chust the wan bottle, chentlemen,' he said, pro-ducing the bottle o' coloured watter from his locker, 'and I wull gi'e ye a wee taste so ye can assess it yourselves for strength and cheneral cheerfulness, but ye'd better watter it doon a bit for it iss strong stuff!' And did he no' get two glesses, and pour a gill or thereby of the coloured watter into them, and then chust as cool ass you like wander over to the barrel o' white spurits and fill the glesses up from the spigot! And the two Excisemen smacked their lips and said that yes, it wass a fine bottle of spurits, but there would be two dollars duty to pay, and when Jeck paid it they went off quite jocco, neffer for wan moment jalousing that there had been a barrel in the corner of the fore-cabin wi' aboot 12 *gallons* of whusky in it!

"The only time that I effer heard of Jeck getting the worst of an encounter wi' the Customs or the Excisemen wass when he came back to Liverpool on that same trup.

"The barrel of spurits wass near enough finished but Jeck wass dem'd if he was going to leave ony of it behind. So the morning they docked he got ootside as much of it as he possibly could."

"And knowing Jack," interposed the Mate, "I would imagine that was a pretty impressive intake."

"Chust so," agreed the Captain: "in fact that wass his undoing. When he'd taken what he could carry internally, ass you might say, there wass still about two bottles-worth of spurits left in the barrel so he got two empty bottles, filled them, wrapped them in two dirty shirts, rammed them into the legs of his rubber boots, and stuffed the boots into the very bottom of his dunnage-bag under a pile of jerseys and oilskins and the like.

"Then he hoisted the bag onto his shouthers, and off like a full-rigged ship to the Customs Shed. By the time he got there, what wi' the fresh air and the amount of good spurits he had on board, for the first time in his life Jeck didna really know whether it was the Old New Year or a wet Thursday in Crarae.

" 'Have you onything to declare?' asked the Customs man, poking the dunnage-bag Jeck had laid on the coonter.

"Jeck beamed on him with immense kindliness. 'Have I onything to declare?' says he, glowing with the greatest of good-wull to aal men, 'yes indeed I have, but I am a sporting chentlemen and I will give you a chance to make some money on it.

" 'I'll bet you a pound you canna find it!'

"Poor Jeck spent the rest o' the day in some sort of a cells in the Customs-shed sobering up while they decided what to do with him, and he missed his train to Gleska.

" 'I tell you, Peter,' he said to me later: 'if the Government go on at the rate they're goin' now they wull run oot of things to tax! A chentleman iss not a free man in this country any more, he iss hounded for his money from wan day to the next.

" 'Where will it aal end? Aboot the only things they havna taxed yet are horses or bicycles to pay for the roads, or pianos or harmoniums in the hoose to pay for their entertainment value, or the watter in the teps. That would be the final insult — it's bad enough paying tax on whusky, chust imagine if you had to pay tax on the watter to pit in it!' "

Para Handy got to his feet and stretched. "Anyway, the owner wull be taxing us for idling awa' the day if we don't make a start. And I dinna want to stert gettin' broon unvelopes from him, apart from the wans wi' the pey in them!"

*FACTNOTE*

The original idea for this story came not just from the firm conviction (held, I am sure, by many) that with only a very few exceptions buff-coloured envelopes are not worth the bother of opening them, but also from the very vivid memory of a postman who served an office in which I once worked — but wild horses will not make me reveal which town that was in!

He did indeed arrive with our mail one Christmas Eve, rather the worse for wear, and he did indeed partake of a dram or two at the party which was in full swing that day in what was otherwise a rather conformist place of work, and after leaving the office, he did indeed post the contents of his satchel in a handily-placed letter-box — and go home: via the pub.

The first Allan Line ship to cross the Atlantic from Greenock sailed from that port in 1819. She was a small brig, the *Jean*, but she was forerunner of the huge fleets of vessels which flew the Allan Line flag independently across the Atlantic for almost 100 years. Though Glasgow remained their head-office Allan Line ships also provided services across to North America from Liverpool and Le Havre. The business was bought over and amalgamated with Canadian Pacific in 1915.

Typical of the larger Allan ships to be seen on the Clyde in the first decade of this century was the *Grampian*, a 10,000 ton liner built by Stephens of Linthouse for the Canadian service. While undergoing a postwar refit at Antwerp she was virtually gutted by fire, handed over to the insurers, and finally broken up four years later in 1925.

I don't know what it is about Customs at airports or seaports but it seems that even the most innocent person will suffer a harrowing guilt on the way through the Green Channel.

I always imagine that there is a large hand suspended in space above my head pointing unmistakeably in my direction, and I shiver yet at the recollection of coming through the Green Gate at Glasgow Airport when our family were kids, and the two of them looked up at me and shouted in piercing voices that seemed to echo round the hall for an eternity 'Is this where they're going to stop you and search you, Daddy?'

Para Handy would find it hard to believe that almost everything in sight is indeed taxed nowadays. They maybe haven't taxed horses for using the roads — but they've hammered cars. And though pianos are, I think, still exempt, TVs have taken a bit of a beating.

God forbid that they should ever tax books!

A COMPANY AT CARRADALE — *Just disembarked from the* Kinloch *are Campbeltown's Boy's Brigade unit, en route to their summer camp. Not 'On His Majesty's Service' but seeing themselves as very much a serving and serviceable organisation, the movement was near its peak at this period and was a valued asset in the local community and a formative influence on youngsters from country and city alike.*

# 47

## *All the Fun of the Fair*

Tarbert Fair was in full swing and a great press of people was constantly moving hither and thither: along the shore road from the steamer pier to the inner harbour, where excitement at the finishing line of a rowing race was reaching fever pitch: from the inner harbour back to the steamer pier, to meet arrivals off the incoming *Lord of the Isles*: and from every direction to the centre of the town and out along the West Loch Tarbert road towards the showground and amusement park.

Finely turned-out open carriages accoutred in highly-polished brass and gleaming leather, their immaculate horses driven by a smartly-dressed coachman and occupied by young ladies in their brightest finery and twirling parasols, contrasted strongly (and strangely) with the carts in from the country — crammed with four generations of the same family, work-begrimed, drawn by a single patient Clydesdale. Poles apart in every regard but sharing the same excitement and sense of occasion on Tarbert's annual big day.

Aboard the steam-lighter tucked into the innermost recess of the coal harbour, ablutions were in progress as her crew made ready to join in the excitement. She had berthed just an hour earlier, after a helter-skelter dash (or the nearest thing to a helter-skelter dash of which she was capable) from Carradale, where she had been discharging cement.

Macphail, still querulous and ill-tempered after the exertions he had been called upon to make in piling on the coal in a vain pursuit of the extra knots demanded by the Captain, was in the *Vital Spark*'s bows with a blunt safety razor and the ship's mirror, scraping at his face with an expression of considerable concentration and periodic protests as he nicked his skin.

Captain and Mate shared the puffer's ablutions bucket at the fore-end of the main hatch. Dougie, despite Para Handy's caustic comments as to the superfluity of the gesture (given the almost total absence of hair upon his head) was shampooing vigorously, while his commander was using copious applications of soft-soap to rid his hands of a layer of caked-on cement.

Sunny Jim alone was ready for the fray. His melodeon lay at his feet as he stood on the after-end of the same hatch and amused himself (and several passers-by on the quayside) with a brisk display of step-dancing for which his whistling provided the only music.

"Will you lot get a move on," he cried in exasperation a few minutes later, when he stopped to draw breath. "It's a fair that's on for wan day, no' a fortnight, and besides for all the good you three auld fogeys are likely to get oot of it, ye're a' jist wastin' yer time."

Para Handy was on the point of retaliating caustically to these unkind remarks when there came the tuneless toot of a rather feeble ship's whistle and another puffer appeared round the head of the jetty and drifted down towards the *Vital Spark*.

"Oh no," said the Captain, swivelling round to inspect the new arrival, "oh no, for peety's sake. It's the *Cherokee*! I had raither hoped they had emigrated wi' the Klondike men, but then I should have kent better. We'll neffer be rid o' Rab Gunn, the man's like the proverbial bad penny."

Gunn's *Cherokee* was one of the few skipper-owned puffers to be encountered on the river, though in fact she spent most of her time on the Forth and Clyde and Monklands Canals, ferrying coals from the mines to the furnaces of the Lanarkshire steel mills, and finished iron and steel from there to the shipyards on the upper Clyde. That meant that, thankfully, her path only rarely crossed that of the *Vital Spark*.

The origins of the strained relations between the two skippers were lost in history, though Para Handy's constant references to Gunn as a 'lowland loon' and that worthy's dismissal of his rival as a 'Hielan' haddie' did little to smooth the way to peace and harmony.

This antipathy extended to the two crews as well. Gunn's Mate, Big Fergie, was an ox of a man with an arm like a side of beef and a temper on a short fuse, of whom gentle Dougie kept well clear. Morrison, the Engineer, was a mean-spirited man with a weakness for gambling and a reputation for cheating at cards while the Deckhand, known simply as Towser, was a swarthy young man with gold ear-rings and long, straggly hair.

"Ah'm amazed yon rust-bucket o' yours is still afloat," roared Gunn from his wheelhouse as the *Cherokee* eased her way into the berth immediately astern of the *Vital Spark*. "Ah heard she'd been hit and sunk by an oaring-boat aff Skelmorlie!"

"Iss that so," said Para Handy huffily, hastily completing the last of his own toilet and hurrying to join his crew, who now stood waiting him on the quayside: "well, that chust shows you that you shouldna believe a word you hear in those disgraceful low-country shebeens you spend your days in!

"I am more than a little surprised to see you in Loch Fyne at aal, there's no caall for coal-gabbarts up here. And besides wi' your navigation abulities I didna think they let you loose outside the canals for even you canna get lost in there, aal you have to do is follow your nose. It's different oot here on the real river. Are you sure you havna taken the wrong turn at the Garrioch Heid, are you no' meant to be in Ayr right noo for a load of nutty slack from the mines aboot Cumnock?"

"Very cluvver," riposted Gunn. "You are much too smart for your ain good, Macfarlane. I wuddna normally gi'e you the time o' day aboot it, but jist to pit you in your place Ah'll tell ye for nothin' that the *Cherokee* is on her way tae Inveraray for a cairgo o' baled wool frae the Argyll estates. Ah'm sure an' you wush you could get a classy job like that but you've nae chance wi' yon tarry old hooker o' yours."

Para Handy drew himself up with dignity. "Classy chob? You mean you caall shuftin' a few bales of greasy wool a *classy* chob? We are off later tonight to the heid of the Loch to load a *real* classy cargo furst thing tomorrow at Cairndow! The cases and baggage of the biggest shooting perty of English chentlemen effer seen in Upper Loch Fyne. Tarry old hooker, indeed!"

And, turning away, he picked his way across the quayside — an operation which had to be undertaken with some care, as it was in the course of being resurfaced in places and stacks of cobblestones and low pyramids of roadstone had been deposited where repairs were being carried out.

~

The crew returned to the puffer at dusk, foot-weary but more than content with life after a splendid day at the Fair.

The Engineer's years of shovelling coal had stood him in good stead at the Test-Your-Strength Stall and his mighty hammer blow had sent the wooden shuttle flying up the vertical post to ring the bell at the top with a reverberating, satisfying clang: and won him a bottle of whisky which, in the euphoria of his success, he had generously agreed would be shared with his colleagues.

Sunny Jim, relying on his nimble-footedness to see him through, had put himself forward at the Boxing Booth (to the horror of the pacifist Mate) and successfully survived three rounds against the promoter's protégé, largely by virtue of running rapidly backwards round the ring, but had nonetheless qualified to win the half-crown on offer for the achievement, and used it to treat his shipmates at the Harbour Inn on their way back to the boat.

Even the lugubrious Dougie, cautiously investing his sixpence to enter the incense-filled tent of The Mystic Maharajah of Mysore, had emerged happily when that necromancer (actually an out-of-work riveter from Yorkhill) prognosticated nothing for him but future success and early promotion. For the next month or so he was on the look-out, whenever the *Vital Spark* was in port, for the arrival of the telegraph boy bringing news of his posting to his own command — till he gradually forgot the whole affair.

Para Handy had enjoyed a particularly satisfactory day, for he had early on made the happy discovery that two of his cousins were on the Fair 'Committee' and had spent a pleasant hour or so in that crowded and convivial tent enjoying the hospitality of the Fair's organisers.

That happy atmosphere of universal goodwill was destroyed in an instant when the crew reached the edge of the quayside where the puffer had been moored.

There was no sign of her.

Para Handy blanched: "My Cot," he said, 'Issn't this the bonnie calamity! The shup's been stole on us! Whateffer wull the owner say!"

Sunny Jim caught hold of the Captain's sleeve and tugged

at it, pointing towards the stern of the *Cherokee*, where Rab Gunn sat on a coil of rope puffing contentedly at his pipe and looking on innocently.

"If ye're looking for that rust-bucket of yours," he said, "Ah think ye'll find her over at the steamer pier. We jist left her there wance we'd finished wi' her.

"You see, my boys decided to earn a penny or two from the towerists and we wisnae going to use wir ain boat, and spoil wir ain reputation. Wance the last steamer had left we set your tarry old hooker up as a sort of a floating funfair and gave them free trups roond the bay. But we made a fortune aff the entertainment! Big Fergie carried on a Boxing Prize Match doon in the hold and though wan fella caught him wi' a lucky poke in the eye for the rest o' the time he jist plain murdered them, it wis like takin' toffee aff af a bairn. Morrison ran a school o' Find-the-Lady on the foredeck and Towser wrapped himself in a couple o' blankets and did the genuine Gypsy Rose Lee in the fo'c'sle. We took in near on four pund, and the lads are aff to spend their share.

"Ah'm just staying on board to keep an eye on the shup, for Ah ken whit you Hielan' stots can be like when your temper's up!"

And with a sarcastic, satisfied laugh he stood up, stretched luxuriously, and made his way along the deck and down the hatch of the fo'c'sle.

Para Handy, dejected and at a loss for words, shook his head sadly and, motioning the crew to follow him, set off on the half-mile walk round to the steamer pier.

Once again, Sunny Jim caught him by the sleeve and pointed, but this time towards the assorted building materials which had been left on the quayside overnight by the construction gang.

"Captain," he whispered urgently, "is that no' a tar-biler over there? And iss that no a length of hose connected tae it, wi' a handpump on the side of the biler?"

"Aye," said the Captain, "what of it?"

"Well," said Jim "D'ye no' think, if someone were to tiptoe aboard the *Cherokee* wi' the end of yon hose while Gunn's asleep and before his crew get back from the Inns, and slide aside jist wan plank on the hatch, that we'd have a fine chance to get back at them...?"

∾

Sharing the contents of Macphail's bottle of spirits in their thick tea-mugs was a welcome bonus, but the crew were in high spirits (for very different reasons) as the *Vital Spark* chugged out into Loch Fyne half-an-hour later and set her course for a moonlight run north to Cairndow.

"I chust wush," said the Captain, "that I could be in Inveraray tomorrow morning to see Gunn's face when they open the hatches to take that cargo of wool on board.

"Some chance! Not with three inches or more of liquid tar lying on the floor of the hold. That was a sublime notion of yours, Jum, chust sublime. There iss no getting away from it. I could wish though that there had been more tar in the biler than that but at least it will give them something to think aboot.

"There's no doot at aal now as to which shup is the tarry old hooker now, eh, boys? Gunn'll no' shout that at the *Vital Spark* again in a hurry!"

*FACTNOTE*

The second *Lord of the Isles* featured in my first collection of Para Handy stories. Launched from D & W Henderson's Meadowside Yard in 1891, she was an acclaimed and handsome ship which in no way could eclipse the Columbia, but which ran her close in terms of public loyalty and affection, and could almost — but not quite — match her for speed.

The Captain's reference to the Klondike has, of course, nothing to do with the operations and practices of the rusting and battered fish-processing factory ships which have followed the herring fleets round Scotland in recent decades, but everything to do with the great Canadian Gold Rush of 1897.

Only the Californian bonanza of the late 1840s exceeded the Klondike for madness and mayhem, but of course that was located in a (slightly) more accessible and (certainly) more amenable environment. And lasted just a little longer: the Klondike was over and done with in less than four years.

The Klondike River in the Arctic North-West of Canada, on that country's border with Alaska, came to public notice when gold was discovered in its creeks and those of its tributaries. Both the climate and the terrain were implacably hostile. Wintertime temperatures fell to 50 degrees below centigrade and the area of the strike could only be reached with the very greatest of difficulty, either up the Yukon river or by way of treacherous mountain passes from Alaska.

Yet despite those almost insurmountable hazards nearly 30,000 prospectors and camp-followers streamed into the area. Shanty towns sprang up overnight. In all probability the owners of the saloons and brothels did rather better out of the 'strike' than did any of the miners. Dawson City, the self-created 'capital' of the gold fever country, reached a peak population of about 20,000. Only about 300 households remain there today.

The country fairs which criss-crossed Scotland on their travels were the eagerly awaited event of the year in many of the most isolated communities and their 'attractions' did indeed include the notorious boxing-booths to which any local aspirants of the 'noble art' were lured (to provide entertainment for a paying audience) by the promise of a shilling or two if they could last a round — or three rounds, depending on the generosity of the proprietor — against the veteran thugs who were the stock-in-trade of the whole enterprise.

Cairndow Church, at the northern arm of Loch Fyne, has a unique octagonal parish kirk, built in 1820, which attracts visitors year round. The loch itself at this point is now heavy with the cages of salmon-farms.

*ROLL UP, ROLL UP!* — *The annual Fair or Show was the highlight of the summer for many isolated Argyllshire towns and villages, and here the McGrory brothers have captured some of the atmosphere of those occasions. To the left, the tall post of the 'Ring-the-Bell' test of strength towers above the twin booths of conjurers, and to their right, catching the attention of the passers-by, is a boxing booth, the gloves for unwary challengers hanging from poles across its frontage.*

# 48

## Cafe Society

M rs Macfarlane looked appraisingly at her husband over the rim of her breakfast tea-cup and came to a decision about something which she had been mulling over in her mind for some days.

"Peter," she said firmly, "I think it is high time that I invited Mrs Macphail and Mrs Campbell to tea. You spend most of your life with their husbands yet I've only met them once, very briefly, at our wedding. And," she added with a smile, "since I had a lot of more important things on my mind that day, I don't think I gave them the attention they deserved. It would be nice to get to know them a little better."

Para Handy grimaced.

"I am not sure that that iss such a good idea, Mery," he said hesitantly, picking his words as carefully as he could. "Effer since we got married I have made a point of keeping my home life quite separate from the shup. Besides, the three of you mightna get on, and that could strain relations between the menfolk, and it's herd enough ass it is bein' cuvil to Dan when the moods iss on him, or copin' wi' wan of Dougie's tirravees if he's had a bad weekend at hame."

Mrs Macfarlane bridled.

"Are you suggesting that I am difficult to get on with?"

"Not at aal, Mery," he said hastily. "You are sublime, chust sublime, and the wumman that couldna get on with you would be a sorry case indeed."

And so the necessary arrangements were made and, the following Thursday, when their men were buffeting through a March gale in the Sound of Mull, the three ladies took a lavish tea together at Mrs Macfarlane's neat flat on the second floor of a trim red sandstone tenement, just off

Byres Road, which boasted a quite astonishing wally close showing an unmistakable influence of the Orient in its design and colours.

The Captain's menage was accounted by the two visitors to be a most desirable and beautifully furbished apartment and was much admired, although in the course of conversation Mrs Campbell remarked that she understood, from what she had read in the papers, that electric lighting was about to be made generally available in that part of the city: and perhaps Mrs Macfarlane could persuade the Captain to make the necessary investment to add its advantages to the many the house already possessed. And Mrs Macfarlane agreed that this would indeed be a subject worth broaching with her husband.

The three ladies got on famously, and their cosy tete-a-tete in the Macfarlane menage was soon followed by a return invitation to Annie Macphail's Plantation home, where over an even more lavish tea a quite exhaustive discussion took place on the merits or otherwise of being domiciled so close to the river with its riveters and hooters and fog: above all, fog: with the balance of opinion finally coming to the conclusion that King's Park and its environs (to take just one example) was, really, quite close enough: and that Mrs Macphail would have to have a word with Dan on that very subject at some suitable occasion in the near future.

The ladies met two weeks later at Lisa Campbell's many-bedded pied-a-terre in Ibrox. The day was carefully planned by their hostess who succeeded in emptying the house of its 12 noisy siblings for the two hours duration of the tea-party by giving them each a jelly-piece and a penny for their fares and sending them on the long, slow tram-trip from Paisley Road West out to Airdrie, and back.

It was a ruse that had saved her sanity before this, and it did not let her down that afternoon. Nor did her catering, for she served a tea even more sumptuous than those proferred at Byres Road and Plantation, conscious that she was entertaining the widow of a baker who would have high standards in that department.

Once more the conversation ranged widely. Mrs Macphail, who was herself one of a large family of five brothers and four sisters and came originally from Bowling, stressed the great value of a house (be it ever so humble a house) somewhere in the country and with a garden of its own, when it came to allowing parents the luxury of a little peace and privacy from the noisy demands of their numerous offspring. Impressed, Mrs Campbell concurred with the Captain's wife's proposal that she really should speak to Dougie about the problem and canvass *his* opinion as to the feasibility of a move when he returned that night from Bowling.

So pleasant had these meetings been for the ladies that nobody thought to call a halt now that the wheel had come full circle, as it were. Indeed Mrs Macfarlane, who was now planning to be hostess a second time, hit upon a novel and really quite exciting idea in relation to their next get-together, and began to make preparations for it.

~

The Captain was home for the whole of the following weekend and there was a subject which he must — reluctantly — broach with his wife.

Reluctantly because he genuinely hated to do or say anything to upset her in any way at all: but reluctantly also because for all her aura of gentle kindness and unstinting affection, Mrs Macfarlane could, when roused, be found to have considerable backbone when it came to defending her position and her rights as a woman.

"Mery," he said, tentatively, when the dishes had been cleared away from the tea-table and the two sat quietly at their ease on either side of the parlour fire, "are you planning to have ony more o' these tea-pairties wi' Dan's and Dougie's wives?"

"Why, certainly," his wife replied, brightly: "such charming ladies, and we do seem to have so much in common — apart from our husbands being shipmates. We really look forward to meeting and I am planning something rather special for next time."

Para Handy scuffled his slippers on the rug. "Weel, Mery, it iss like this. The laads are upset aboot some o' the things you have aal been talking aboot, and the way they are now being nagged at aboot it aal."

Mrs Macfarlane bridled. "I am sure I do not know what you mean, Peter."

"It iss this business of hooses, the three of you agreein' that I should be puttin' in the electric for a stert: I am not made of money, you know that fine.

"And that Dan should mak' a move to get awa' from the ruver chust because it's foggier there than up at Hyndland or Gilmorehill. I neffer heard such umpident nonsense. Dan *likes* the ruver, he wis born and brought up on the ruver and he's no more intention of leavin' it than of emigrating to Canada. If Dougie wass here he would tell you himself. Forbye, Annie Macphail was perfectly content wi' their wee hoose there till you and Lisa Campbell got sterted on her.

"And then you are tryin' to get poor Dougie to move awa' frae Ibrox! Dougie canna *staun'* the country! The laad was brought up in Cowal, for peety's sake, and he saw mair rain in the first ten years of his life than maist men see in their three-score and ten. As he says, at least in the city there's aye somewhere fine and handy to tak' shelter if the heavens open, and usually somewhere that you can find some company to pass the day wi' and get a gless in your haund at the same time."

Mrs Macfarlane gave her husband a steely look.

"If we wasn't meant to try and better ourselves," she said with conviction, "the good Lord would not have given us ambition! If you had not had any ambition you would still have been a deckie on a gabbart."

"That iss not the same at aal," countered her husband. "It iss in the nature of a man to mak' the best he can of his *career* for the sake of his faimily but it iss neffer the place of the faimily to try to change his *character*, and that iss what the three of you are daein'. Dan would be lost away from the ruver and Dougie would be right oot of place oot o' the toon and if the three of you cairry on like this there wull be no *Vital Spark* and no crew for we'll be at opposite ends o' the country. Forbye, you wouldna like to be put to live somewhere you wassna comfortable wi' yourself, Mery. You wouldna want change chust for the sake of it."

"Nonsense," said Mrs Macfarlane sharply, "for a start I moved here from Campbeltown without making a fuss about it when we got married. It is a matter of adjusting and making the best of the circumstances wherever you find yourself, not complaining when there is nothing to complain about. Annie and Lisa have my full support."

And she retired, frostily, to iron the Captain's shirts in the kitchen ready for his departure the following morning.

When Para Handy returned from an eight day trip to Islay and Jura, he found his wife in subdued mood.

"What ails you, Mery?" he asked anxiously as she greeted him at the door absent-mindedly, and turned away without proferring her cheek for a kiss.

She shook her head.

"Now, now," said the Captain. "Something's wrong. What have I done — or not done?"

"Oh, it's not you, Peter," she said at length, sitting on the arm of her chair in the parlour, "it's me. You were right about our tea-parties. We went about them all wrong, trying to outdo each other with the baking and the accessories and then trying to improve the poor woman's house that we were in. Well, we have all learned our lessons.

"This week was my turn to have Lisa and Annie round, but I had the notion to take them up town for a fancy afternoon spree and we went to Miss Cranston's Room de Luxe in Sauchiehall Street."

She shuddered at the memory.

"I have never been so embarrassed in my life! I knew I had made a mistake from the moment we went through the door!

"The place was full of nothing but society ladies from places like Bearsden or Whitecraigs or Eastwood or Milngavie. There were more fur-coats hanging on the racks at the door than you would find running about in a zoo, and as for the hats!" — she shook her head in disbelief — "the hats! Lisa and Annie and I felt quite out of place among all that finery, for all that we were dressed in what we thought was our *own*."

Para Handy nodded sympathetically. "It iss chust what I have been trying to tell you, Mery: let us be happy with what we have and with where we were meant to be."

"But it got worse," said his wife, "the waitress that came to serve at our table was a Campbeltown woman I had been at school with and she recognised me, I could see that: but she pretended she did not, and ignored us as much as she could, and spilled the tea on the tablecloth when she put the pot down, and never brought us fresh hot water, or offered us extra cakes, the way she did at all the other tables.

"And when the bill came, I did not have enough money to pay it it was so huge, and had to ask Lisa and Annie to help out.

"I have never been so ashamed and angry all at the same time."

"And I am sure you neffer looked bonnier either," said Para Handy with some fervour, and comforted her, "for when the colour comes to your cheeks when you are upset or cross, there is not a prettier gyurl in aal Scotland. And besides, you were never out of place in there, you are a finer lady than aal the toffs o' Gleska pit together, and I am proud to be your man."

At which Mrs Macfarlane blushed most becomingly, and clapped her husband gently on the shoulder.

"Keep your teas wi' the other wives by aal means, Mery, for it iss good that you are all frien's. But neffer try to change the way the world is, and certainly leave well alane wi' the way we are, and Dougie iss, and Dan.

"We're aal Jock Tamson's bairns on the shup, and on shore, and that's the way we want it to be — and nobody is goin' to alter that — not even our wives!"

*FACTNOTE*

Of the ladies of the three senior members of the crew only Para Handy's wife Mary makes more than a fleeting appearance. There is just one brief veiled reference to Dan Macphail's domestic circumstances, though Dougie's wife makes her mark (in *The Mate's Wife*, one of the earliest of the original stories) when she turns up at Innellan pier on pay-day to collect the Mate's wages, 'with her door-key in her hand, the same ass if it wass a pistol to put at his heid'.

Para Handy tells us that she is down on the first steamer from Glasgow any Saturday that the puffer is inside Ardlamont (the outer margin of the Kyles of Bute) so she is not a lady to be taken lightly and certainly not one to whom one would willingly take home an opened pay-packet.

To introduce the three ladies to each other was a temptation impossible to resist.

Glasgow had certain catering institutions, including among their number the venue chosen by Mrs Macfarlane for the ladies' afternoon tea, which were unique to the city, or so at least it seemed, and which though they had their origins at the turn of the century, lived on into the second half.

For serious eating, whether of lunches or high teas, a Scottish speciality rarely encountered nowadays, there were the three restaurant businesses founded and operated by three redoubtable ladies, whose names were almost always given in full when their establishments were being referred to. These were the respected restaurants run by Miss Cranston, Miss Buick and Miss Rombach and though targeted at the middle to upper class family market they were also very popular lunchtime venues for Glaswegian businessmen.

A second, distinctive, Glasgow institution was the basement coffee-house, very much the preserve of the male, and the haunt of the lawyers, accountants and merchants who made up so much of the middle-class commercial backbone of the city centre. The chain of tobacco-shops owned by Mr George Murray Frame had in their depths a dark, wood-panelled, dimly-lit subterranean room redolent of coffee and tobacco smoke and crammed full in mid-morning (and most other times of the day) of men in dark suits, whose dark topcoats and bowler hats festooned the wooden hallstands at the foot of the stairs which led down from the shop above.

The formidable Miss Cranston was one of the early patrons of Charles Rennie Mackintosh and her (and his) Willow Tea Room, in which every detail of interior design bears his stamp and seal, is a major attraction still in Sauchiehall Street.

*For Richer, for Poorer — No two photographs from the MacGrory Archive better illustrate the yawning gap between Edwardian rich and Edwardian poor than these dramatically contrasting depictions of the crofter or smallholder in his donkey-cart and landowner with shiny top-hat in his pony and trap. The Trabant and Ferrari of 90 years ago!*

# 49

## The Sound of Silence

**P**ara Handy studied the telegram which had just arrived from the owner of the *Vital Spark* with details of her next assignment. "Lighthooses!" he exclaimed petulantly. "More of him and his dam' lighthooses: I dinna care if I never see wan again ass long ass I live."

The puffer was lying at Rothesay where I was changing steamers for a long-promised visit to old friends in Lamlash, and the Captain had seen me on the quayside when I disembarked from the *Lord of the Isles* and invited me on board for a mug of tea. Our exchange of the gossip of the river as we sat side-by-side in friendly and relaxed familiarity on the vessel's main-hatch had been passing the time very pleasantly until we were interrupted by the arrival of a Telegraph Boy complete with scarlet bicycle and low, black, chin-strapped pillbox hat.

"So what's the call of duty this time, Captain?" I enquired, as that mariner angrily tore the flimsy telegram into shreds and consigned the fragments to the winds.

"Well," he said: "at least it's no' coals this time, for that is the worst cairgo of them aal, ass I have told you before now. But this wull run it close for we're to tak' in the oil in barrels for the generators at the lights on the Ailsa Craig and roond the Mull o' Kintyre, and I sometimes think, from the way the crew behave and the sheer tumidity of them aal, that we iss an explosion waiting for somewhere convenient to happen when that is oor cairgo.

"We daurna smoke on deck by Dan's way of it — and him wi' a fire going in the stokehold that wouldna have disgraced Emperor Nero: and Dougie iss that nervous that he iss not at aal happy if Jum hass the galley stove goin' in the fo'c'sle to boil a kettle for oor teas or potatos for oor denner so we feenish up livin' on mulk and rabbit-food.

"I neffer, effer eat ass much in the way o' lettuces and raw carrots and that sort of rubbish in a whole twelve-month ass I do on a single week's fuellin' run to the lighthooses — and aal chust because my crew are feart o' havin' an open flame on the shup. They are chust feart for their lifes! If Dougie wass here he would tell you himself.

"I aalways tell them that a load of whusky, though it might be a much more welcome cairgo for aal sorts of reasons, iss chust ass likely to blow them to Kingdom Come ass a load of kerosene or paraffin — but wull they lusten? Wull they bleezes. You are talking to a brick wall wi' them."

$\sim$

It was therefore with some anxiety that I first came across the accounts, a week later, of an accident which had befallen a steam-lighter in the course of her duties in servicing the lighthouse which guides mariners safely past Davaar Island at the mouth of Campbeltown Loch and into the welcoming shelter of that capacious harbour.

It appeared that the vessel involved — un-named in those first reports of the mishap carried in the earliest editions of the *Glasgow Herald* — was carrying kerosene to the light-station. She was struck by an errant starting-flare fired from the trim motor-launch acting as floating club-house and starter's office for the Campbeltown Yacht Club's annual regatta, which was in process of setting the yawl class off on a triangular course from the island to Peninver on the Kintyre peninsula, across to Blackwaterfoot on Arran, and back to the finishing-line at Davaar.

The rocket had landed on, and set fire to, a small heap of waste rags on the puffer's foredeck. Onlookers reported that within seconds a middle-aged man, thought to be the Mate of the vessel concerned, had dived overboard followed immediately by a young deck-hand and, just a fraction later, by an older man who had been seen scrambling out of the engine-room hatchway at the stern of the boat.

This left on board just one man, presumed to be the skipper of the vessel, who had been alone in the wheelhouse when the flare struck.

By the time this man — described by at least one paper

as the 'hero of the day' had run to the foredeck to extinguish the flames with a bucket of water hauled from the sea, dashed below to the engine-room to set the machinery to the off position, and returned on deck and made for the wheelhouse, it was too late. The puffer ran firmly aground on the sandy tidal-flats below the lighthouse, and stayed there till the next high-tide floated her off that same evening.

"I wass bleck burning ashamed for them aal," said Para Handy bitterly the next time I met him, and questioned him about the incident — for of course, as later editions of the paper had confirmed, the steam-lighter involved in the incident was indeed, as I had suspected from the first, the unfortunate *Vital Spark*.

"Not wan scrap of courage or initiative between the three of them," he continued, "but they did weel enough for themselves right enough! Aal three of them was picked up by the Yat Club's safety-launch and taken into Campbeltoon and treated like royalty, ass if they had been real shupwrecked sailors and no' chust three faint-hearts that had shamelessly neglected their duties to save their necks! And there wass I marooned on the shup, nothing could get alongside her till the tide turned, and there wassna so mich as a drop of wholesome Brutish spurits aboard, nor the makin's of a hot meal neither.

"Meanwhile that crew of mine wass safe ashore bein' wrapped up in warm blankets at the Mussion to Seaman's Hostel, and coaxed to tak' chust the wan more wee hot whusky drink, and spoon-fed wi' soup and chicken, and generally made heroes of."

I agreed with the Captain that it must really have been an infuriating experience.

"Aye, and outfuriating ass weel," he protested, "for when they wass interviewed by the chentlemen of the press when we got back to Gleska two days later (and no disrespect intended to yourself, Mr Munro, you'll understand) here and did the reporters no' sort of agree wi' them that the only reason I had stayed on board wass that I couldna sweem and that the three o' them had had to dive off to get a boat to rescue me, because our own skiff had a hole in her from where *I* had hit her onto a rock skerry aff the mooth of the Sliddery Water when *I* wass oot poaching in Arran the previous night.

"Dam' leears — we wass *aal* oot poaching in Arran the previous night!

"Onyway, I have made it clear to the owner: I am not cairrying kerosene effer again wi' that lot and I am gled to say that in aal the circumstances, he has agreed to that."

"Well, that should reduce the visits you have to make to the lighthouses, Captain," I said: "and given that you don't like them, that should suit you fine."

"Aye," said Para Handy, scratching his ear. "They chust do not agree wi' the Macfarlanes and I am not surprised. Look at my brither Keep Dark, noo — he wass six months in wan o' they rock lights aff the Pacific coast of America. Keep Dark went foreign for mony years, and wan time in the nineties he hit rock-bottom in San Francisco, poor duvvle, he wass ashore from wan o' they nitrate cluppers, they wass on passage from Valparaiso wi' a load of guano. That iss the most desperate cairgo you could effer imagine! Loadin' it iss unspeakable and the smell of it is in effery cranny o' the shup, you cannot escape it at aal.

"And that very first night Keep Dark got kind of separated from his shupmates and found himself alone and up a back-alley in the derk which is no' the kind of thing you'd wush on your worst enemy in San Francisco. He got shanghaied poor duvvle, by a gang that wass crewin' up wan o' the Yankee Cape Horners — naebody would shup on wan o' them of his own free wull — and though he managed to sneak ashore three nights later afore she wass ready to put to sea, by that time his own shup had sailed without him and he wass stuck in America with only the clothes he stood up in.

"His luck changed, he met up wi' a man that wass in cherge of the lighthooses on the coast roond aboot, and him orichinally a Macfarlane from some wee vullage sooth of Oban. He offered Keep Dark a posting to wan o' the rock lights, ten dollars a month aal found, and of course my brither chumped at it.

"The lighthoose wass on tap of a rock chust off a long kind of a headland, and man but it wass a desolate place. There wassna a hoose within miles, and the landing on the rock in a wee bit skiff from the lighthooses relief shup wass a nightmare.

"The worst of it though wass the fog. Keep Dark said it wass fog even on from wan day to the next, it chust neffer lifted at aal week in and week oot, and effery 45 seconds your ears was split wi' the blatter o' the huge foghorn on the cliff edge not 20 feet from the keepers' living room at the foot o' the tower.

"There wass only two of them on the rock and they worked six hours on, six hours off round the clock: it wass a funny kind of a shuft, said Keep Derk, but you got used to it. You even got used to climbing up to the tap o' the tower wance effery half hour to trum the light, and mak' sure aal was hunkey-dorey up there — no' that it would really have mattered whether the light wass on or off, because wi' the constant fog the light wass aboot as much use as a teeto-taller at a Tiree funeral.

"What you chust *couldna* get used to, though, said Keep Dark, wass the foghorn. It near deeved him to utter distrac-tion, five seconds of sheer hell every 45 seconds night and day. It wass bad enough when you wass on waatch, but it wass when you wass trying to get some sleep that you felt like goin' up to the tap of the tower and throwin' yourself aff it.

"The other keeper wass an American caalled Purdie, a smert enough man, and he'd been on the station for years. 'Ye'll soon get used tae the foghorn,' he says to Keep Dark wheneffer he'd be complainin' aboot the din, 'and then you'll be like me — I neffer, effer hear it nooadays. It chust forms a pert o' the naitural background ass far ass I am con-cerned and I am totally unaware of it goin' aff at aal. Wait you and you wull see.'

"Keep Dark didna believe him, he wass at his wut's end wi' the din and he wass even thinkin' aboot tamperin' wi' the foghorn's automatic mechanism to shut the dam' thing up, even if it wass only for a half-an-hour.

"In the end, he didna need to. It did it for him! Wan night he wass on duty and Purdie, who slept like a log from the moment his heid touched the pillow, despite the fact that that dam' foghorn wass shakin' the very foondations o' the tower wi' the racket it wass making, wass snoring chently in his bunk ass peaceful ass if he wass in a boat drufting on some silent and deserted loch.

"Keep Dark wass sitting at the table reading an old news-paper and trying to pretend he couldna hear a thing when — withoot him knowing onything aboot it at first — there must have been some kind of a mechanical failure on the clockwork motor that ran the foghorn and set it aff auto-matically (it wass aal worked wi' some kind of a fantoosh self-winding hydraulic enchine) and it broke doon.

"So there wass Keep Dark, coonting in his head till the time the next blast was due — you got that you did that withoot even noticin' it, he said, it wass some kind of a defence system the body put up — and when he got to '41,42,43,44,45' and braced himsel' for the roar o' the horn, nothin' happened.

"Total, blissful silence for the furst time in the three weeks he'd been on the tower.

"What *did* happen, though, wass that Purdie wakened in a flash and leaped oot o' his bunk in a panic shouting '*Whit in the name of Cot wass* **that**?'

"Lighthooses!" said Para Handy firmly. "Dinna talk to me aboot lighthooses. They are nothin' but a trial and tribulation. If Keep Dark wass here, he would tell you himself."

*FACTNOTE*

Para Handy's family are only hinted at in Neil Munro's original stories, but at least we know that he was one of ten sons, 'all men except one, and he was a valet'. We are told the by-name of four of the others. They were (and it would be a fascinating if unproductive exercise to speculate how they got such unlikely nicknames) the Beekan, Kail, the Nipper — and Keep Dark.

Did Keep Dark get his sobriquet by virtue of the fact that he had worked on a lighthouse? Probably not, but that is my excuse for featuring him in this tale!

Davaar Island lies like a cork in the neck of a bottle at the entrance to Campbeltown Loch, its cliffs pierced with caves in one of which a local artist, Alexander Mackinnon, secretly painted — in 1887 — a representation of the Crucifixion which still forms a place of pilgrimage today. A shingle spit almost one mile in length connects Davaar to the mainland and although it appears to offer a safe and dry crossing, many walkers have been caught out by the flooding tides and it needs to be approached with caution.

The island gave its name to the Campbeltown Shipping Company's eponymous screw-steamer, launched in 1885. She was a beautiful little ship with a clipper bow, figurehead — and twin funnels set close together aft of the bridge. In 1903 she underwent a series of alterations which included replacing the twin funnels with a single smokestack. She gave four decades more of service before going to the breakers in 1943.

The first British maritime incursions to the Pacific were the 18th century naval or privateering expeditions in search of the fabled treasure galleons of the Spanish colonies in Peru and the Philippines.

Over the next century the clipper trade to and from the Pacific coast of South America was founded on three cargos — copper ore from the mines of Central Peru, nitrates from the arid deserts of Chile, and guano from the bird-islands offshore. Poor Keep Dark was sailing before-the-mast at the peak of these detested contracts.

All were loathed by the crews as foul cargos to be avoided when possible — nitrate was particularly susceptible to fire, for example — but the guano cargos were unquestionably the worst.

Guano was formed, quite simply, by the droppings of a thousand generations of seabirds as it accumulated on their isolated, uninhabited and uninhabitable breeding rocks and islands lying offshore. On some islets the guano deposits of millenia were more than 200ft deep.

LEAD KINDLY LIGHT — *This is Davaar Lighthouse, on the eastern tip of Davaar Island at the entrance to Campbeltown Loch, and plainly there is some sort of regatta in progress. The two-funnelled steamer heading towards Campbeltown is the* Davaar *of 1885 and we can date the photograph as prior to 1903 for in that year she was reboilered and as a consequence of that alteration, her twin funnels were replaced by a single, broader smokestack. Her passenger lounges were enlarged and extended at the same time.*

# 50

## *Twixt Heaven and Hell*

The *Vital Spark* came lolloping into Loch Broom, and Dougie heaved a sigh of relief as they were drawn into its sheltering arms and the white-capped waves of the open sea dwindled into the distance astern. In ballast (she had come to the northerly port of Ullapool to load a consignment of cured herring in barrels for Glasgow) the puffer had been accorded a lively reception by the notorious waters of the Minch from the moment she had passed out of the protection of the Sound of Sleat.

"Man, but your tumid, Dougie, tumid!" said Para Handy from the wheel, "neffer happier than when you're safe inside the Garroch Heid. But the shup wass built to tak' this and more."

"Maybe the shup wass," replied the Mate, "but I am sure and I wass not. It iss at times like this that I think it would be no bad idea to look for a shore chob. At least the grund stays in the wan place and you are not aalways lookin' for something to hold on to, to stop you bein' thrown across the room!"

"Ah'm no' so sure aboot that," said Macphail, poking his head from the engine-room hatch. "Depends whaur ye are. Take Sooth America for unstance, when Ah wis there wance wi' the Donaldson Line there wis that many earth-quakes goin' on, the streets wis heavin' like wan o' the penny-rides at Henglers's, and if ye went ashore for a refreshment, ye daurna pit yer gless on the table for fear it wis cowped."

Para Handy snorted. He had a very low threshold of disbe-lief in the matter of the Engineer's tales of his world travels and on more than one occasion had poured total scorn not just on the particular experience being recounted, but on the whole notion of Macphail having ever been further from the tenements of his native Plantation than the Irish Sea.

"Well, there's nothin' earth-shattering aboot Ullapool," said the Captain. "For they are aal aawful Hielan' up here, the only excitement o' the day iss when the mail comes in from Inverness and it iss usually a week late even so. If it wassna for the herring-boats in season to help keep the place cheery, it might ass weel close doon for aal that ever happens."

Indeed the town itself, a couple of streets of neatly presented white buildings on a promontory which terminated in the harbour itself, seemed asleep. The few remaining East Coast boats which came to the port for the brief herring season were at sea, and the only signs of commercial activity were the darkly-smoking chimneys of the two curing stations, all that were left of the once huge numbers of processing factories which had crowded Ullapool before the virtual collapse of the fishings thirty years previously.

"My brither Alec, the wan that wass in service and we didna talk aboot, Napkin Heid we cried him, he wass a year butling at wan o' the big Estates a few miles north o' the toon," Para Handy continued. "He didna have a high opeenion o' the place at aal, and the man he wass working for wass the worst of it. The Laird had a quite dreadful reputation: he wass a most terrible man for the drink: he wass a gambler at the cairds and a maist unsuccessful wan at that: and the parlour-maids — not chust in his ain hoose but in aal of the big hooses, and even the Manse too — learned soon enough to run for their lives if the Laird wass aboot and wi' a dram on board.

"He wass the despair o' his poor wife. She was more than twenty years younger than him, a kindly soul Alec said, but no match for the Laird, and efter Alec had been in the man's service for six months or thereby, the poor wumman chust upped and left him and went hame to her own people in Dingwall and took the weans wi' her.

"That wass when things started to go really doon hill at the Big Hoose, Alec said. There wass nobody to even try to keep the man in check, the drinking perties went on aal night, and the cairds wass played seven days a week, for there wull always be disreputable cronies to gather roond a man like the Laird ass long ass he has his money.

"Within a couple of weeks of the wife leaving, Alec wass the only servant left at the hoose, aal the wummen had fled, and Alec himsel' had had mair than enough of it and was lookin' oot for anither place.

"The Meenister took to comin' oot to see the Laird, he thought it his Chrustian duty to save sich a dreadful backslider, and tried to persuade him to get back on the straight and narrow.

" 'To bleezes wi' your straight and narrow,' said the Laird. 'Is it no' enough that I come to the Kirk releegiously every Lord's Day?'

" 'You may come to the Kirk,' said the Minister, 'but you always sleep through the service, and the congregation iss beginning to complain aboot it.'

" 'Nae doot,' replied the Laird, 'but that'll only be because of my snoring keeping *them* awake. What else can you expect when you preach nothing but hellfire and brumstone? Lustenin' to wan o' your sermons would turn milk sour.'

"From that you can imagine that relationships between the Laird and the Manse wass very strained."

The *Vital Spark* was now less than a hundred yards from the harbour and Para Handy, calling down for the engines to be stopped, let her drift slowly towards the stone quay. Sunny Jim moved forward and made ready to leap ashore with the bow rope.

The reception committee waiting on the quayside to welcome them to Ullapool consisted in its entirety of two very small, dirty and ragged urchins of about eight years of age, one engaged in throwing stones at the wheeling seagulls, and the other picking his nose.

"What wass also clear to Alec by now," the Captain continued once the mooring process was complete and the crew retired to the fo'c'sle to brew up a pot of tea, "wass that the Laird wass chust destroyin' himself wi' drink.

"But it wass a fever that took him before the drink had had the chance to feenish the chob. For three days he lay at death's door, but if you thought that would have concentrated his mind on higher things, you can think again. He kept a bottle hidden under the bed and made sure Alec had it topped up: he wass aalways tryin' to grab hold of the nurse that the local doctor sent in to look efter him: and whenever the Meenister, good Chrustian soul that he wass, came to see him, he cursed him and his whole Kirk Session to bleezes.

"Then came the morning when Alec answered a knock on the door to find the Minister on the step.

" 'A fine day, Alec,' said he as my brither took his coat. 'And how is the Laird this morning? I do hope his temperature is no higher than it was last night?'

" 'I wass speculating aboot that very thing myself, Meenister, and hoping chust the same ass you: though I wouldna be counting on it,' said Alec. 'for I think it could well be a great deal higher by now. You see, the Laird passed awa' at three o'clock this morning.'

"So there wass Alec withoot a billet, though a relieved man to have got oot of his last one. But the Meenister put in a word for him wi' the owner o' the Bay Hotel, here in the toon, and he took Alec on as Head Porter. The Hotel's still here, but it iss changed oot of aal recognition for it has a drinks licence noo but when Alec worked there it wass a Temperance Hoose.

"Alec could tak' that or leave it, he wassna *for* drink the way Hurricane Jeck iss, for instance: and in spite of aal the months of misery wi' the Laird, he wassna *against* it neither.

"What he *wass* against, though, wass the miserable kind of a clientele the Hotel attracted for the maist o' them wass the sort of folk that looked ass if they'd neffer had so mich ass wan single day's enchoyment out of life. Good Templar families on holiday: or commercial travellers of the Rechabite persuasion (and little enough business they could expect to do in Ullapool, what with the shopkeepers no' wantin' to offend the sensubilities of the fushermen that made up the maist of their regular custom by havin' ony truck wi' teetotallers): or Meenisters — Meenisters maist of aal.

" 'It wass that miserable in that Hotel, Peter' he said to me after he'd got oot of it, 'that in comparison wi' it, a day in an undertaker's office would have been mair like a night at the Music Halls for cheneral hilarity and entertainment.'

"Mercifully he didna have to thole it for long, for he got the seck wan November morning chust a couple of months after he'd started.

"There was some kind of a Presbytery Convention in the toon and Ullapool wass chust hotching wi' gentlemen of the cloth, there wass dog-collars on effery street corner and needless to say the Bay Hotel was chammed to the rafters wi' them. If it had been a gloomy place afore, it wass like a wet day in Rothesay noo, prayer-meetings in effery room and faces efferywhere ass lang ass the Parliamentary Road.

"That morning was the third day of the Convention and Alec wass at his wut's end, but he wass up at the crack o' dawn ass usual and laid a fine log fire in the big open fireplace in the main lounge, then took up his post at the Porter's Desk in the front hall.

"Pretty soon the Meenisters began to come doon stairs in ones and twos and foregaither, ass they did the first thing effery morning, for a wheen o' prayers and a lugubrious unaccompanied psalm or two in the lounge. That wass usually feenished by quarter to eight or thereby, and at eight o'clock it wass Alec's duty to go through the various public rooms wi' a gong, to summon the residents to their breakfasts in the dining-room.

"When he went into the lounge to do chust that, there wass mair than a dozen Meenisters in their bleck frockcoats and white collars clustered aboot the fire, some o' them toasting their backs at it, others warmin' their hands, for it wass a frosty cauld morning outside and the Hotel wass far from warm.

" 'Yes,' one of the older Meenisters wass saying ass Alec came into the room, 'I enchoyed a positively apocalyptic dream last night — I dreamed that I wass in Heaven!'

" 'And what wass Heaven like,' asked one of the younger ones.

" 'It wass very much like our Convention,' replied the older man solemnly, 'a meeting-place and a gathering-place for the faithful and the penitent.'

"Alec told me later that he chust could not have resisted the temptation that now overwhelmed him. He coughed, and the group round the fire turned towards him.

" 'That is aal most interesting, chentlemen,' said he, 'for I too had a most prophetic dream last night. But where you, Sir, dreamed of Heaven I dreamed that I was in Hell.'

"There was a pause till one of the chentleman asked: 'And what was *that* like?'

" 'It wass chust exactly like the fire in this hotel lounge,' said Alec brightly, 'you could hardly see the flames for Meenisters!'

"He wass oot on the street wi' his tin trunk within 20 minutes but it was the very best thing that effer happened to him. Not only did he get oot of the Bay Hotel and oot of Ullapool, but he took a tumble to himself and gave up working in service and got a proper chob.

"He's a potman at the Horseshoe Inn in Gleska now, happy ass larry, and quite reconciled wi' the rest o' the faimily, for the maist o' my cheneration o' the Macfarlanes wouldna talk to him whiles he wass in service.

" 'It iss like a new lease of life, Peter,' he told me the last time I saw him, and the latest word iss that he iss getting married next month to wan o' the barmaids."

"Well, there you are Peter," said the Engineer, laughing: "you were wrong in what you said a while back — it seems they do get earth-shattering events happening in Ullapool! Jist ask your brother — Ah'm sure he'd agree!"

*FACTNOTE*

Para Handy's (unnamed) brother is referred to (working as a valet and disowned by the his nine siblings) on the very first page of the first of Neil Munro's original tales — *Para Handy, Master Mariner*. I felt that following the tale of Keep Dark in the previous chapter such an unlikely relative had to be worth investigating!

Ullapool was founded on fishing, has had two hundred years of feast and famine as the herring shoals have come and gone and come back again, but now earns its keep almost entirely from tourism. Though Loch Broom in recent years has been crammed with catchers and mother-ships from almost every country of Northern Europe and some from even further afield, only a tiny handful of small wooden vessels are locally owned and crewed (almost exclusively for shellfish) and no shore-based curing stations remain. The processing of the catch is now carried out on the fleet of klondykers anchored out in the Loch.

Just as Neil Munro's home town of Inveraray was designed and built from scratch as a planned entity by the Duke of Argyll in the 1740s when his new Castle was also constructed and the old Castle and Village demolished, so Ullapool too is an artificial creation.

Here, though, the builder was not a local landowner and the motive was not for the sake of elegance and prestige. Ullapool was identified as the perfect location for a fully integrated fishing town ideally placed to exploit the huge herring shoals of the Minches.

Thus the town came into being in 1788, the brain-child of the British Fisheries Society, with the necessary constituent parts for catching the fish, processing the fish, and servicing the fleet. Thus there were, in addition to the curing stations, a variety of other shore-based operations including boat-yards and ship-chandlers, cooperages and net-works. In season not just the boats but the majority of the shore-workers moved into Ullapool in those days when an army of workers spent each year following the herring shoals on their mysterious migrations around the coasts.

In 1974 Ullapool replaced Mallaig and Kyle of Lochalsh as the terminus for the direct sea-crossing to Stornoway. One perhaps unforeseen side-effect of that decision was that it placed the Inverness to Kyle Railway Line, world-famous for the stunning beauty of its meanderings across some of the most evocative and remote landscapes in the United Kingdom, but economically very fragile, under almost constant threat of closure. So far the conservationists have managed to fend off the pragmatists but its long-term future is still far from assured.

# 51

## A Matter of Men and Machinery

Dougie, who was seated atop the wheelhouse with paint-pot and brush, touching up the black boot-topping on the puffer's funnel, pointed over the puffer's bows and observed: "This must be him comin' noo."

Para Handy turned round from the sternpost, where he had been making some minor adjustments to the rope fenders, and peered along the empty cobbled vista of Yorkhill quayside towards the distant dock gates.

A small figure, hunching forward slightly as he walked and clutching a shabby canvas holdall, was rapidly drawing near the *Vital Spark* with quick, purposeful paces.

"He looks hermless enough," observed the Captain, "and there iss not much of him, to be sure!"

The Mate slid down from the wheelhouse roof and joined him against the rail on the puffer's port quarter. The approaching figure took the last few paces which brought him abreast of the two shipmates and leaned down towards the vessel, whose deck was a few feet below the level of the quay.

"I am sure I must have mistaken my instructions," he observed to the pair quietly in a soft voice with the clipped tones of the east coast discernible in it. "and taken a wrong turning somewhere in the docks. You are not by any chance Captain Peter Macfarlane? I think, surely, that you can't possibly be."

"Oh but I am," said Para Handy cheerfully. "And you'll be Angus Napier? The Docks Office told me to expect you some time this afternoon. Welcome to the smartest boat in the tred. This iss Dougie Campbell, my Mate. Throw us

354

your portmanteau and come aboard. I can assure you we are mair than pleased that you are here, for we have been marooned in this wulderness for the last two days."

With a strangely twisted expression on his face Napier complied with these instructions slowly and uncertainly, and clambered down the iron ladder set into the face of the quay and onto the deck.

He looked about him almost apprehensively.

"And this is really the *Vital Spark*?" he enquired in a doubtful voice, "and you're expecting an engineer...?"

~

Forty-eight hours previously misfortune had struck the puffer or, more accurately, her engineer when Dan Macphail, at home in Plantation for the weekend, had been suddenly taken ill with severe stomach pains which were quickly diagnosed by the doctor summoned by his anxious wife as appendicitis.

Now Dan languished in the Western Infirmary awaiting a decision about an operation and the owner of the *Vital Spark* had been forced to look for a relief engineer. The ship, meanwhile, lay idle at Yorkhill fully-laden with the annual cargo of winter coals ordered by their Laird for the islanders of Canna, unable to fulfill her obligations under that contract till a temporary replacement for Macphail could be found.

"Could you and your Mate not manage the conning and the running of the vessel?" had been the owner's first question when Para Handy reported the situation at his office on Monday morning. "I am sure that between the pair of you you're as familiar with the engines as Macphail himself, and there is little enough to do except keep the furnace fired."

"Not I!" exclaimed Para Handy in some horror. "I leave aal that side of the business to Macphail. My place iss on the brudge o' the shup, no deevin' aboot amang aal the coals and grease and bilers like wan o' the bleck geng on the *Lusitania*. It iss the naavigation and cheneral management of the vessel that iss my responsibility, and a heavy one it iss.

"Besides, you wouldna want the *Vital Spark* to end up the same way as Wullie Jardine's *Saxon* did a year or two back?"

"What happened to her?" enquired the owner, curious.

"She was dam' lucky no' to be sunk." said Para Handy. "Wullie had a furious argument wi' his engineer, old Erchie Begg, one November night when they wass berthed in Dunoon and had gone ashore for a smaal refreshment, and they fell oot aboot their relative importance to the shup.

" 'Caal yourself an enchineer do you,' howled Wullie when Erchie suchested that because of his qualifications he was the key man on board. 'Ah've seen better-qualified men than you drivin' a dustcairt for the Gleska Corporation. *You* run a shup indeed! My Lordie, you couldna even run a tap!'

" 'Iss that so,' retorted Erchie, 'well then I would like to see you tryin' your hand at the controls o' the engine-room. Ony fool can *steer* a boat, Lord knows, Ah did it in my bath when I was a bairn, but it tak's brains to *drive* wan, and you couldna drive a nail intae a plank.'

"There wass more, much more, in the same comradely vein for the two wass in their best insultin' trum what wi' the refreshments they had taken and the upshot of it aal wass that they agreed that, next mornin', the Engineer would tak' the wheel ass they left the Coal Pier at Dunoon, whiles Wullie would be doon below makin' sure the engines didna break.

"What had seemed a good idea at midnight wass very much less attractive at seven o'clock on a dark winter mornin' but the two o' them wass that thrawn neither would admit it, and Wullie went doon to the engine-room while Erchie sauntered into the deckhoose and grabbed the wheel and pretended to himself he'd been doin' it aal his naitural.

"The Mate, who'd been told to keep well clear and leave the two eejits to their ain devices, cast off the bow and stern ropes and she began to druft off the pier-head. Erchie rang doon for full-speed ahead and Wullie tried to mak' some sense of aal the levers and gauges in front of him.

"For a few minutes there wass no sound apart from a series of muffled curses from doon below, then there wass a grindin' and a crunchin' and the propellor began to turn. For a while both men thought efferything wass hunky-dory, till there wass a loud screech on the whustle to the engine-room and Erchie roared doon the voice-pipe 'You auld goat! You've got her goin' astern instead of aheid!'

"Next thing came the crunchin' and the grindin' sounds aal over again, followed by silence and then mair cursin', lots mair cursin', wi' chust occasional bursts of the shaft turnin' for a meenit and then stoppin', and then turnin' again, till finally in a last flurry of un-Chrustian language Wullie admitted defeat and yelled up the voice-pipe for Erchie to get back doon below and sort things oot for he chust wassna able to cope wi' it at aal.

"There was a short silence, then Erchie called quietly doon the pipe 'Weel, Ah dinna think there's mich point in me comin' back doon right noo, Wullie, for Ah'm pretty sure Ah've chust run her onto the Gantocks onyway.'

"And indeed he had, right at the top of the tide, and it wass a full twelve hoors before they wass able to float her off again!

"Naw," concluded Para Handy firmly. "We're no sturrin' till we get an engineer." And, in view of the evidence which he had just had put so graphically before him, the owner agreed with some alacrity that Para Handy should register the temporary vacancy with the employment exchange at the Clyde Docks Office as a matter of urgency.

∽

The bemused Napier set foot on the puffer's deck with an air of reluctance and stared about him in disbelief, pulling off his jauntily-tilted blue peaked cap to scratch at his head with all the signs of an inner turmoil.

Para Handy led him to Macphail's dark subterranean domain. The East Coast man looked even more distraught as he cast his eyes over the cramped engine-room with its single bunker, its single furnace, single boiler, single-pistoned power unit and single propellor shaft: its ramshackle tangle of dank pipes stained here and there with rust and marked by dark streaks of oil: its basic controls and almost total absence of instrumentation of any description.

"There she is, then," said Para Handy with some pride. "Iss she not the beauty?"

There was an awkward silence.

"Is this *it*, then?" Napier asked finally. "I mean, where's the rest of your crew for a start..."

"Oh," said the Captain, "Jum wull be back at any meenit, he has chust gone ashore for some provisions ass I was determined to mak' a start ass soon ass you got here. We have lost two days already and our customer is becoming impatient at the delay, he has been sending telegraphs to the owner's office to say so."

Napier looked no more at his ease. "So — er — this 'Jum': is he my stoker, or my greaser, or my machine-man? And whichever he is, where are the other two? And how the blazes does your regular man find enough space for them all to carry out their duties in a cupboard like this?"

Para Handy stared at the relief engineer uncomprehendingly.

"Jum iss our deckhand and cook," he said: "and a good cook he has become over the years, you will be well fed aboard the shup I can assure you! But Jum has no business effer to be in the enchine-room at aal: it iss your own responsibulity entirely and neither Jum nor nobody else wull interfere with that, I can promise you ."

Napier gaped on the Captain. "D'you mean to tell me you are sailing with jist one man in the engine-room? What happens when he's asleep in his bunk?"

"What do you mean 'what happens'?" retorted the Captain. "What do you think happens? Nothing happens! When he's off-watch then efferybody's off-watch."

Napier blanched. "When I saw the vessel, I had to admire your courage in undertaking the voyage and I was prepared at least to consider sailing with you for I've never been known to shrink from my duty. But with no proper crew — man, you're all mad! You will never, never make it to Canada in this tub!"

"*Canada*," exclaimed Para Handy. "For peety's sake, who the duvvle said onythin' aboot Canada? What do you think this is — the Allan line? We're chust takin' some coals in to *Canna*. Does Dougie look the sort of a man who would risk the North Atlantic in anything smaaller than the *Olympic*? As for me, a Macfarlane neffer shurked, but there are lumits!"

The other looked mightily relieved. "Well," he said, "I have been sent here under false pretences, for I'm a deep-sea man myself, waiting to take up the Chief's post on the new Ben Line ship that's fitting out at Fairfields right now, and when I asked at the Docks Office yesterday about the chance of a berth to fill in the time, they told me that you were looking for an engineer for a round-trip — to Canada!"

"That clerk must have cloth ears! And I must say you gave me the devil of a fright! What's more, I take my hat off to your own engineer: I'm too spoiled by having a huge squad at my beck and call. I could no more run this engine-room on my own than I could navigate to

Australia — your man's worth his weight in gold and I hope you realise it."

~

Para Handy and Dougie were delighted, on their return to the boat thirty minutes later after they had treated Napier to a dram to compensate for the waste of his time, to discover that not only was Sunny Jim back — as expected — and frying sausages in the fo'c'sle, but Macphail himself was esconced among his engines and examining them anxiously to see if they had come to any harm during his absence.

"Dan!" cried the Captain, beaming with enthusiasm, "we are fair delighted to see you back! What happened to the appendix?"

"Appendix my eye," replied the Engineer. "It wis naethin' but a bad spell o' indigestion and the Hospital wisnae weel pleased wi' ma ain Doctor for gettin' it wrang.

"Huv I missed much?"

"Nothing at aal, Dan," said Para Handy. "Nothing at aal. There wass some talk of takin' her to Canada" — the Engineer paled — "but, och, it came to nothing, it wass chust a baur. Let us chust get some steam up, and we will tell you aal aboot it some other time."

*FACTNOTE*

The Gantock Rocks lie about half-a-mile south-east of Dunoon Pier and must have claimed many maritime victims large and small over the centuries, particularly in poor visibility and rough seas. Although they are now well-lit, and in spite of all the modern aids to navigation, they still do — as was demonstrated by our last and much-loved paddler *Waverley*, which was stranded on the reef but fortunately with no casualties and no serious damage to her hull.

The largest ship ever to have been sunk by the Gantocks was the Swedish ore carrier *Akka* which went down in April 1956. Six of her crew were lost in the tragedy, which was apparently caused by steering-failure when she slowed down in order to pick up the river-pilot for her voyage upstream to Glasgow. The 5,500 ton ship, with an overall length of 440ft, struck the reef on her port side, ripping a huge hole in the hull, and remained afloat for only a matter of a few minutes.

The White Star liner *Olympic* was built in the Belfast yard of Harland and Wolff and handed over to her owners on May 31st 1911, the same day on which her sister *Titanic* was launched. An overall length of nearly 900ft ensured that these new ships far exceeded their German and Cunard rivals in size as well as in the opulence of their accommodations. They were designed to deliver profits as well as prestige, though, being powered by newly-developed engine systems which combined efficiency with economy, and capable of carrying 2,500 fare-paying passengers in three classes.

Hidden from these passengers were the echoing caverns of the engine room and, worst horror of all, the stokehold where (till the use of oil-fuel rendered their thankless, repetitive tasks redundant) armies of men laboured on the back-breaking work of coaling the furnaces for the 29 boilers which powered the ship.

Known in the shipboard slang of the period as the 'Black Gang', most of the stokers employed on the British Transatlantic fleet were Liverpool Irish. Harsh conditions bred harsh men and stories of quarrels and sometimes lethal fights — usually among themselves, though occasionally with other members of the crew and even more rarely with particularly brutal Officers — are a part of the legend and lore of the age. However they invariably maintained good relations with the galley, which they provided with fuel and whose fires they helped maintain. In return, the cooks passed to the stokehold men what became known as the 'Black Pan' — uneaten food left over from the sumptuous menus provided to First Class Passengers.

The 'Black Pan' was at its bounteous best during spells of bad weather — the more prolonged, the better!

# 52

## *May the Best Man Win*

Para Handy and Dougie were seated in Castle Gardens in Dunoon watching the world go by on the esplanade below them. It was the middle of July, the weather was set fine, and the town was packed with holidaymakers and day visitors. A quarter of a mile away at the Coal Pier a thin drizzle of smoke rose skywards from the black-topped red funnel of the *Vital Spark*, awaiting a consignment of logs to be carted down from Glen Masson.

There was a sudden buzz of interest on the thronged pavement and a scatter of applause, and a wedding-party came into sight and headed for the Argyll Hotel. Bride and groom occupied the first carriage-and-pair and in a second one, following closely behind, were bridesmaids, the best man, and the ushers.

"A wedding," sighed Para Handy sentimentally. "I can neffer see wan but I think aboot my own."

"And I neffer see wan but I try to forget aboot my own," said the Mate gloomily.

"Neffer!" said Para Handy, "Lisa iss a fine, managing wumman if a bit headstrong chust now and then, and you have a family to be proud of. Brutain's hardy sons!"

"Aye," replied the Mate, yet more gloomily still. "All twelve of them."

Para Handy felt it was time to focus his companion's attention elsewhere.

"Hurricane Jeck wass best man at a weddin' in Oban a few years back," he observed. "Man, they still taalk aboot it in the toon to this day!

"I wass ashore myself on leave at the time, and met Jeck hurryin' up Buchanan Street towards the railway station.

" 'The very man,' says Jeck. 'I have time for chust the wan wee gless before my train leaves, and I need your advice, Peter.'

"Jeck had been asked earlier in the week by an old frien' of his from Barra if he wud be his best man, he wass being merrit next day in Oban on a Kilmore gyurl, and this wass Jeck heading for the train for the two of them wass to meet up in Oban that night, and stay over at the Crown Hotel before the wedding the following morning.

" 'What it is, Peter,' says Jeck, quite flustered, 'iss that I havna a notion whit's expected of me. You know me, Peter, I've made dam' sure never to be tied doon, and the result iss that I have neffer effer been at *any* wedding in my naitural, neffer mind my own!

" 'So tell me, what's a best man, and what's he to do?'

"Weel, I gave Jeck a quick run through on the duties and the responsubilities o' best men: he didna like the bit aboot answering the toast to the bridesmaids, said he wassna much for public speaking, but I told him not to worry, by that time in the proceedings efferybody would have had a gless or two and the place would be fine and cheery.

" 'The most important thing you have to do, Jeck, is to get the bridegroom to the kirk on time, smertly turned oot, and above aal else — sober. Every bride's mither aye thinks that nobody is good enough for her lass, and if the gyurl's intended turns up late, and looking ass if he had been dragged through a hedge backwards, and reekin' o' spurits, then I promise you that that merriage iss off to the worst of aal possible sterts.'

" 'Thanks Peter,' says Jeck, looking at the clock in the public hoose we wass in, 'I wull remember. On time, smert, sober. You can rely on me!'

"And with a quick shake o' the haund, he was off like a whippet to catch his train.

"It wass some months before I heard what way things had gone for Jeck and his frien' in Oban. The news wassna good and the cheneral feeling wass that neither was the prognostications for the merriage.

"The groom wass a MacNeil from Castlebay, a fine, cheery chap wi' shouthers on him like an ox, by name o' Wullie. He wass in the Navy at the time, and he'd met the bride the previous summer when the fleet wass in Oban, and she wass workin' ass a waitress at a wee temperance hotel at the back o' the toon. The two of them met at the

Argyllshire Gaithering in August and by the time Wullie's ship sailed at the end of September, he wass an engaged man. The gyurl — Constance, her name wass, but she answered to Connie — wass a MacRobb from Kilmore.

"Her faimily didna take too kindly to the news that she wass engaged to a sailor — though they'd neffer met him and didna really know mich aboot him — but Connie assured them he wass a true and considerate chentleman, and then she spent the winter saving money and gaithering together aal the bits and pieces for her bottom drawer.

"Wullie couldna get ony leave till the wedding itself, so aal the arrangements had to be left to the MacRobb faimily. They booked the kirk — St Andrews, on the esplanade: and promised a fine reception efter, wi' places for 40 o' Wullie's faimily and frien's from Castlebay.

"On the evening Jeck arrived in Oban Wullie wass all on his own for the Barra fowk wass comin' to Oban overnight on the steamer and wudna get there till the morning. So they had agreed that efferybody would mak' their ain way to the Kirk, and chust meet up there for the service at eleven o'clock.

"Jeck met Wullie at the Crown Hotel, ass arranged, and the two of them exchanged news, aal very quiet and restrained, and had a fish tea in the hotel dining-room.

" 'I am seeing you're early to your bed tonight, Wullie," said Jeck firmly, 'for it iss my responsubility to deliver you to the Kirk on time and in appropriate trum for the occasion.'

"And the two of them agreed they would have chust a ten minute stroll on the esplanade, and then go to their rooms.

"This wass the point at which things sterted to go seriously wrong for, while they wass at their teas, they hadna noticed that a naval cruiser had come into Oban Bay and when they got to the esplanade, the toon wass chust hotching wi' seamen, and worst of aal, it wass the shup Wullie had been on till chust three months earlier, so aalmost efferyone o' the navy that the two of them encountered on the pavements wass a friend of the groom's — and when they heard that he wass getting married the next day, they chust wouldna tak' no for an answer in relation to the matter of a gless of somethin' to celebrate.

"I would like to think that Jeck did his best to protect Wullie from himself, but I am chust not sure. It would have been hard enough to protect Wullie from *Jeck* in normal circumstances. And I do not know exactly what happened, for the two main players in the game have no recollection of it, for reasons that wull become obvious, and I canna very well ask the Navy to hold an unquisition into it aal.

"The pair foond themselves press-ganged by aal Wullie's former shupmates, and soon they wass in among a lerge perty of sailors visiting aal the public hooses of Oban wan by wan, and bringing an unfectious air of goodwull and happiness wi' them whereffer they went.

"The following ten hours or so iss a mystery and Jeck's next connection wi' reality cam' at aboot nine o'clock the followin' morning when he woke up, fully clothed, underneath wan o' the airches o' McCaig's Folly above the toon. Efter less than a meenit — he wass aalways very quick makin' a recovery from this sort of situation, he'd had lots o' practice — Jeck remembered where he wass, and why. And realised that there wass no sign of Wullie!

"But chust then, he heard somebody snoring, very loud, and a wee investigation resulted in the discovery of Wullie asleep under the next airchway, and in a terrible state! Jeck realised that *he* probably looked jist as bad, but he hadna a mirror aboot his person. Wullie's clothes was aal damp and stained green wi' the gress he'd slept on, he'd lost his collar and tie, his hair wass a mess and he wass in sair need of a shave. Possibly worst of aal wass that for some reason that Jeck could not fathom or remember, Wullie had a whupper o' a bleck eye.

"Jeck woke him urchently and reminded him whit day it wass.

" 'My Cot,' says Wullie, 'we must get back to the Hotel and get bathed and shaved and changed. It's less than two hours to the wedding!'

"If Jeck had thought things couldna get ony worse, he wass very wrang. When they got to the Hotel, the proprietor wouldna let them in. Apparently they'd rolled up to the hotel aboot two in the mornin', wi' a whole perty o' sailors, demanded drinks aal roond, and threatened his person when he refused. They had only left when the owner sent for the polis.

" 'Well at least let us get oor clothes,' Jeck pleaded. 'The man iss getting married at eleven o'clock.'

"'Heaven help the bride,' said the hotelier, 'but I'll gi'e ye back yer stuff — wance ye settle the bill.' Jeck and Wullie went through their pockets — but they didna have a penny piece between them.

" 'In that case,' said the hotelier, 'I'm holding onto your luggage till ye pay what's owin'. That's the law, that's what I'm entitled to do, and that's what I'm doing.'

"Jeck pleaded and better pleaded, but the man wouldna budge an inch. The two of them made the best attempt to tidy up they could in the waash-room at the station, then hurried out along the esplanade to the Kirk.

"I dinna ken what the Meenister thought, but he said nothing though he had bad news for Wullie. 'I didna realise you wass coming over in advance' (Wullie hadna a clue what he meant by that) 'but the rest of your folk are coming on the overnight boat, aren't they?' he asked and Wullie nodded. 'Weel, I'm afraid to tell you she had a biler failure and she'll no' be in Oban till two this efternoon. I presume you wull want to put the weddin' off till then?' And when Wullie said no, just to go ahead, the Minister looked puzzled, and said he would have to send word to the bride and her party, but they could be there in under half-an-hour. Wullie didna understand that, neither.

"So it wass twenty minutes past eleven when Wullie and Jeck took their places at the fore-end of the altar, wi' naebody in their side of the Kirk at aal, and naethin' but strangers — the bride's pairty — on the ither.

"The organ struck up *Here comes the Bride* and Jeck and Wullie wass aware of the gyurl and her attendants comin' up the aisle and when they reached alangside and Wullie turned to smile at her he foond himsel' lookin' at a total stranger. 'Who on earth are *you*?' screamed the bride, and Wullie said he could ask her the same thing. The Meenister near threw a fit and said angrily to Wullie, 'What sort o' shame are you bringin' to St Antonys wi' a stupid prank like that!' 'St Antonys' yelped Jeck, 'I thought this wass St Andrews?'

" 'Naw, said the Meenister, furious, 'St Andrews is a hunner yerds further along the front. *Our* groom is a fine young man from Colonsay and his faimily, but the boat has broke doon, which iss why I couldna think how *this* groom got here at aal.'

"So Jeck and Wullie were an hour late for the real weddin', and by that time the bride wass chust gettin' ready to go hame for she thought she'd been left at the altar. She wass ready enough to tear Wullie to bits, whateffer his condition or excuses, but when she saw the state of him and the best man, and gaithered what had been going on, she near enough *did* go hame.

"Eventually the wedding went ahead. Things didna get ony better efterwards, neither, though by noo Jeck wass past caring and in any case the trouble wass being caused by Wullie's faimily.

"What neither Wullie nor Jeck, nor the faimily, had known wass that the MacRobbs and their kin wass strict teetotallers, very staunch Rechabites to a man, and the reception wass in the Oban Temperance Halls without a refreshment in sight.

"The MacNeils spent their time ignoring the bride's pairty and complaining loudly about the lack of Highland hospitality and how they'd been brought aal the way from Barra under false pretences and I am ashamed to say that some of them went out to the toon for a gless, and brought several bottles back wi' them for the rest o' the company.

"By the time it cam' time for Jeck's speech there wasna mich point makin' it for the maist of the MacRobbs had gone hame and the few that hadna — the younger, bigger men — wass having a donnybrook wi' the MacNeils: and the bride was in hysterics in the ladies' cloakroom.

"So if you effer get depressed thinking aboot your ain wedding, Dougie, then think aboot *that* one. That'll cheer you up!"

*FACTNOTE*

Castle Gardens remains a very pleasant spot from which to watch the passing show, though sadly there are few movements of shipping on the river and Dunoon Pier, onto which the Gardens look directly down, once a crossroads of steamer services both complementary and competing, now offers no spectacle other than that of the arrival and departure of the regular CalMac boat from Gourock.

The Glasgow to Oban Railway, in the days when Hurricane Jack made the journey, would have taken him to the west coast port by way of Stirling, Callander and Killin Junction on one of the most scenic railway journeys in Europe.

By 1965, despite some half-hearted attempts by BR to attract additional patronage by putting observation cars — some with a conductor/guide — on the peak summer services, it was obvious that the Beeching Axe would include

THE WEDDING PARTY — *In my factual companion to Para Handy's world* In the Wake of the Vital Spark *I used as one of the illustrations a photograph of a different Campbeltown wedding and was thrilled and quite fascinated to receive a letter from a lady who could identify most of the 'sitters' as her own forebears. Can anyone help out in the same way with* this *splendid period piece?*

this beautiful but tortuous route. The Dunblane to Crianlarich section was closed, the track uprooted, and trains for Oban henceforth left from Glasgow Queen Street and travelled up Loch Long and Loch Lomond on the much shorter former LNER line to Crianlarich and on to Oban.

McCaig's Tower, to give it its proper name, is an incongruous but very distinctive feature of the town's sky-line overlooking the bay and the Sound of Mull, and offering from its elevated position fine views of what are perhaps the most dramatic sunsets in the West.

A replica, albeit on a reduced scale, of the Colosseum in Rome, work started on it in 1897, and the stated intention of the excercise was that of providing work for the unemployed labourers of the district. This was the first but it certainly has not been the last of purported 'job creation schemes' which have been a feature of the Highland economy on many occasions since.

The big difference here, however, was that the funds for this project came, not from the public purse, but from a retired Oban businessman, one John McCaig, who was himself a shareholder in the Oban and Callander Railway Company — and the owner of the town's North Pier. The project was never carried through, work ceasing in 1898, and since rumour has it that had it been finished it was intended as some sort of monument and mausoleum for the McCaig family, it is probably just as well.

The Argyllshire Gathering, held every August, hosts some of the top Solo Piping competitions and is very much a key date in the social calendar for the great and good of that part of Argyll, whose Duke is its hereditary Chieftain.

# 53

## The Appliance of Science

W ith almost every year bringing some further, dramatic advance in the range of navigational and mechanical instrumentation and infrastructure (and domestic comfort) available to mariners the world over I have always been forcefully struck by the apparent failure of even the most basic improvements to the sailors' lot to come (or be brought) to the attention of Captain and crew of the *Vital Spark*.

Year on year that most kenspeckle component of the entire Clyde puffer fleet remains firmly anchored to the anachronistic maritime technology of the year in which she was launched, even in terms of her domestic arrangements.

Thus (to take just a few examples) the revolution of wireless communication has passed her by, as has the more widespread installation of the repeating engine-room telegraph: the now normal provision in the wheelhouse of a handsome, brass-cased instrument combining compass, chronometer and barometer: the switch to electrical incandescent lighting: the provision of running water from a central tank: and the use of bottled gas for the purpose of cooking.

Aboard the *Vital Spark*, therefore, Para Handy still puts in to the nearest village blessed with a Post Office to communicate by telegram with his Head Office, and gives his instructions to the engine-room either verbally, or with a tap of the boot on Macphail's flat cap. A small pocket compass of very dubious accuracy is the sole aid to navigation, and the battered tin alarm-clock hanging by a string from a nail in the fo'c'sle the only rough guide to the real time.

Weather prediction is always accomplished first thing each morning by sending Sunny Jim up on deck to see if it is raining or not. Dougie still trims and curses dimly-flickering, temperamental oil-lamps for the ship's navigation and safety after dark. On deck, Sunny Jim rinses out dirty pots and dishes in a bucket of sea-water, and down below in the fo'c'sle he cooks on a smoking coal stove.

Thus the facilities enjoyed aboard the speeding *Columba* are as far removed from those deployed on the wretched puffer which she regularly leaves in her wake, as the accoutrements to hand in the douce terrace houses of Kelvinside are an advance upon the amenities of a Hottentot hut.

Given Para Handy's blind devotion to his command this was not an easy topic to broach, but encountering the mariner on Dunoon pier recently I took the opportunity to draw to his attention the favourable reception accorded to the recently-electrified tram service on Bute, and asked whether he foresaw, in the near future, any likely major improvements to the maritime services on the Firth — and particularly to the lot of the puffer-men who provided so many of them.

"None that I can really think of," he replied, catching hold of my elbow as he did so and steering me gently, unobtrusively and almost absent-mindedly (though with unerring accuracy) in the very precise direction of the Licensed Refreshment Room located at the eastern end of the pier.

~

"But surely there are many things which would help make life easier for you," I continued a minute or so later as the barman wiped our corner table with a damp cloth before setting our glasses on it. "What about weather prediction, for instance. A barometer would allow you to make some sensible judgement about likely conditions over the next twenty-four hours…"

"Barometer!" exclaimed the Captain, almost choking on his drink. "Don't talk to me aboot barometers. They are nothin' but a snare and a delusion, as it says in the Scruptures.

"The owner sent one doon to the vessel a year or two back wi' a wee note ass to how to work it, and said it would help us plan our week better if we had some idea of the likely condeeshuns when we wass at sea. I am not a thrawn man, so though I didna like it I hung the dam' thing up in the fo'c'sle and effery morning and effery evening I would be lookin' at it to see what it said.

"It aalways pointed to the same thing. *Set Fair*. It didna matter if we wass marooned in Tobermory wi' a howlin' gale, or stranded in the fog in Ardrossan Harbour, or gettin' snowed on like we wass in the Arctic, but us chust in Colintraive. *Set Fair*. That was the message even on, month efter month.

"I stuck it oot, for it wassna my property and anyway I had learnt chust to ignore it, but we had Jeck wi' us for a couple of trups and I tell you he took ass ill to that dam' barometer ass if it had been a temperance campaigner in the Yoker Vaults at the Gleska Fair Weekend.

"He finally snapped one mornin' when we wass comin' doon from Arrochar. It had been rainin' on like a second Flood for three solid days and we wass aal on a short fuse ass a result. Mebbe I should have seen the warnin' signs the previous night, for Jeck had spent maist o' the evenin' swearin' at the barometer ass if it wass personally responsible for the doonpour.

"Chust before mid-day I wass in the wheelhouse, wi' Jeck and Dougie off watch in the fo'c'sle, when suddenly the fore-hatch crashed open and Jeck came clatterin' on deck wi' the barometer clutched in baith hands.

"He jumped onto the main hatch and held the barometer high over his head wi' its face to the sky, and the rain wass harder than ever and the clouds wass that low you could have touched them wi' an oar.

" '*Set Fair*!' bellowed Jeck. ' *Set Fair*, is it, ye eejit! Weel maybe ye'll believe the evidence o' yer ain eyes noo, ye leein' blackguard!' — and he fair shook the implement in his hands and thrust it up and into the worst o' the rain — 'Tak' a good look at that. *Set Fair* my auntie!'

"And wi' a final roond o' curses I wouldna give myself a red face by repeating, he swung the barometer round above his head several times for luck and sent it hurtling up and oot and over and into the loch and oot of oor lives forever.

"Naw, I am not a great man for any o' these new-fangled gadgets at aal, for you almost neffer find them to be aal they is cracked up to be. I am chust perfectly content so long as I am provided wi' the staples that have made us Brutain's hardy sons," the Captain concluded, mournfully staring into his now empty glass with a pointed purposefulness to which I felt it best to respond.

∾

Para Handy's frustrations with the recalcitrant barometer, however, were as nothing compared with the encounter with the new technologies which he experienced a couple of weeks after our conversation in Dunoon.

The incident is best related as it was reported in the columns of the *Greenock Telegraph* in the following terms, which I here reproduce by kind permission of the Editor of that respected journal:

### A NEAR MISS AT ARDNADAM
(National Press please copy)

After exhaustive enquiries by the piermaster concerned, the steam gabbart *Vital Spark* has been held solely responsible for the regrettable incident at Ardnadam Pier at 10 p.m. last Saturday night which resulted in minor damage to the structure of the pier and to the upperworks of the paddle-steamer *Dandie Dinmont*, which was berthing at the time. Of more immediate concern was the mental and physical distress occasioned to a large number of excursionists, of both sexes and all ages, who were waiting on the pierhead to board the steamer for their scheduled 'moonlight-cruise' return journey to Craigendorran.

It transpired that, as part of a planned refurbishment of the puffer, her owner had contracted with the Ardnadam Foundry for the supply of a new remote-control signalling apparatus between wheelhouse and engine-room: and a steam-whistle of improved design and performance.

These had been fitted under the supervision of the Captain and Engineer of the steam lighter, though we understand from the foreman of the Foundry that there had been constant bickering and altercation between the two as to the most effective way of achieving satisfactory installation of the new equipment.

With benefit of hindsight it is now apparent that certain grave errors and miscalculations occurred and that neither piece of equipment was correctly instated.

The results were unfortunate to say the least.

As the *Dandie Dinmont* approached, the Captain of the steam lighter, which had been tied up alongside the head of the pier, loosed his moorings and signalled for dead slow astern in order to move slightly inshore to leave a clear berth for the steamer. Unhappily it is now apparent that the signalling device had been installed back-to-front and the instructions which were displayed in the engine-room in fact called for emergency full-speed ahead.

The puffer collided bow-first with the paddle-box of the approaching steamer but, mercifully, the damage was slight as even at maximum revolutions the acceleration of this type of vessel is notoriously ponderous.

On realising what had happened (though not, unfortunately, why it had happened) the engineer of the puffer engaged full speed astern, at which the vessel proceeded to bear down on the pierhead, now crowded with the steamer's intending passengers.

In the wheelhouse the vessel's Captain, powerless — in the time available — to prevent the imminent collision with the pier, pulled sharply on the lanyard of the new steam-whistle to sound a warning.

Unfortunately the valve-pipe from the boiler which was intended to power the whistle had been erroneously connected not to the tubing at the base of the whistle shaft, but to an old, narrow and disused ventilation pipe which led directly into the base of the vessel's smoke-stack.

As a result, instead of producing the intended warning whistle, deployment of the lever which should have controlled that instrument sent a great blast of scalding steam straight up the shaft of the funnel and resulted in the immediate and widespread emission of an enormous cloud of smoke and soot of quite volcanic proportions which, in the prevailing wind, was deposited thickly onto the pier and onto the persons and clothing of all those standing upon it.

It is understood that several parties are consulting their lawyers as a result of this contre-temps, and that when last seen the Captain and Engineer of the steam-lighter were on the point of exchanging blows on the mainhatch as the vessel, still under power but not apparently under control, drifted out from the pier and vanished into the darkness.

~

I was glad that some weeks passed before I again encountered the Captain.

In the meantime, although I cut out the newspaper's report and pasted it carefully into my commonplace book, I have made a mental note never again to broach with Para Handy the subject of the new technologies.

I would hate to see him blow his top again.

*FACTNOTE*

Till the very end of their era, the puffers were the most basic of vessels, embellished with few refinements and even less evidence of modern technology.

They relied on the seamanship, experience and total familiarity with the waters they sailed which were the hallmark of their skippers and their crews. Indeed as more one than former puffer man has told me, that instinct was often more to be relied on than the best efforts of modern science. Those most gifted were able to 'feel' a storm coming in from the west, or 'sense' the imminence of fog before it closed in — and take the appropriate avoiding action in good time.

Ardnadam Pier, some 70 yards from shoreline to pierhead, was the longest of the Clyde piers. Indeed it still *is* because it has survived as a result of having been the pier which served the US Navy throughout their 30 year lease of the anchorage of Holy Loch as the North Atlantic base for their quite unholy nuclear submarines. Improved and refurbished, scrupulously maintained as a result of its totally unforeseen strategic importance, the venerable pier is today in immaculate condition, set fair to celebrate its 150th anniversary in 2008.

The communities centred around Holy Loch and its immediate environs, were — at the zenith of communication by water on the Clyde — the very heart of commuterland both in terms of travel to work (in Glasgow), and travel to shop (either in Greenock or closer at hand in Dunoon.) As a result, within a space of just a few miles on the Cowal shore of the Firth, there were steamer piers at Blairmore, Strone, Kilmun, Ardnadam, Hunter's Quay and Kirn. All had regular communications with the principal Cowal pier at Dunoon, and with the railheads of Gourock, Greenock and Craigendorran, as well as the Broomielaw or Bridge Wharf in the heart of Glasgow itself.

The *Dandie Dinmont*, launched from the Partick yard of Messrs A and J Inglis of Pointhouse in 1895, was the regular Holy Loch steamer for most of her working life. Named, like all steamers in the North British Company's fleet, after a character from one of Sir Walter Scott's novels, she was 195' overall with handsome saloons fore and aft. Her contemporaries in the North British fleet included the remarkable *Lucy Ashton*, a product of the *real* 'Upper Clyde', built by Seath's of Rutherglen in 1888. Only MacBrayne's *Iona* — broken up in 1936 after no less than 72 years in service — could be regarded as a more potent link to the Victorian era. 'Lucy' survived two World Wars and was only withdrawn from service in 1949, still within the living memory and, above all, the practical experience of countless Clyde enthusiasts.

# 54

## *The Gunpowder Plot*

Many residents of the West Highlands are angry at the way in which successive governments have used the area as a convenient dumping ground for industrial activity of a risky nature — such as the manufacture of explosives: or for testing the efficiency and effectiveness of a wide variety of experimental maritime or martial hardware — from submarines to land mines.

Many *more* residents would be equally angry if they were aware of such activity in the first instance, but it is in the nature of government to admit little and divulge less, and as a result obfuscation of the truth is nowadays an art form in political and military circles.

Thus one of the better-kept secrets of the Ardlamont peninsula is the presence, in the tiny clachan of Millhouse on the narrow winding road from Tighnabruaich to the Otter Ferry, of a not insubstantial manufactory of black gunpowder — established two generations ago in 1839. It is indeed from this very enterprise that the little village derives its name, though the majority of visitors passing through it (and there are, sadly, very few of these despite the general growth of tourism on the fringes of the Firth of Clyde) are unaware of its presence. They assume that the group of buildings enclosed within a high dry-stone wall and just visible from the road, through a barred iron gate bearing a nameboard reading simply 'Mill', are intended for the more acceptable and less controversial activity of grinding corn or barley.

Even Para Handy himself, regular habitue of the Kyleside piers though he is, never ventured inland of Kames and thus remained in total ignorance of the existence of that

Gunpowder Mill until the bizarre chain of events, which are here related for the first time, were set in motion by a peremptory summons to the offices of the owner of the *Vital Spark*.

The Captain made his way along the Broomielaw in the direction of those rarely-visited premises with considerable trepidation, mentally reviewing the events of recent weeks with the aim of identifying in advance the (hopefully minor) peccadillo for which he was about to be called to book.

He need not have worried. The owner himself greeted him in the lobby and, throwing a comradely arm over Para Handy's shoulder, ushered him into his inner sanctum, sat him down, and offered a cigar from the humidor atop his leather-inlaid desk.

"We have been commissioned to undertake a rather unusual and challenging contract, Peter," said the owner: "and it was at once clear to me that only the *Vital Spark* could be trusted to fulfil it satisfactorily."

Para Handy positively glowed with pride.

"There is a vessel wrecked on the Burnt Islands to the west of Colintraive," the owner continued. "Just a small schooner, but her cargo must be recovered urgently. The salvage team have reported to her owners that the only type of ship able to come near her is a puffer, which can get alongside and then ground on the shoals when the tide goes out."

He spread out a sea-chart — one of the very few that Para Handy had ever seen — on the desk between them.

"A larger steamship would have far too much draft to come into this channel even at high tide, and of course no sailing vessel with any sort of keel would be able to ground on the ebb tides without heeling over to such a degree that she wouldn't be able to work her derrick.

"It's either a steam-lighter, or nothing."

"Well you need have no fear at aal on that score," said Para Handy confidently, "for the *Vital Spark* iss more than capable of doing the chob."

"Good!" The owner smiled expansively. "I was sure that would be your reaction, Peter: and I am sure too that there could well be a modest bonus for her Captain once the job is complete."

There was a pause as the implications of that last, and unrehearsed, statement sank in to both parties.

"So what iss her cairgo, then?" asked Para Handy — more out of a desire to fill that embarrassing silence than from any real concern about the matter.

"Butter," said the owner after a moment. "Salted butter: from Islay, in barrels for export."

At which juncture the owner shuffled his feet noisily under the polished mahogany desk, and twisted uncomfortably in his swivel chair before ringing the bell at his right hand and, when his clerk put his head round the frosted-glass door from the outer room with an enquiring glance, instructing that worthy to fetch the bottle of whisky from the safe and pour two generous drams.

～

"Are we no' puttin' in to Colintraive for the night?" queried Dougie with some surprise as the smartest boat in the coasting trade hiccuped past that attractive settlement at eight o'clock the following evening.

It was a pleasantly mild late September gloaming and the lights of the little Kyleside village twinkled invitingly in the gathering dusk, those of the Inns on the low ridge above the pier particularly conspicuous and especially promising of a warm welcome and good company.

"Owner's orders," said Para Handy. "He iss frightened that there could be something stole from the wreck — from her accoutrements or her cairgo. Remember what Hurricane Jeck got up to in the Kyles wi' yon steam yat the *Eagle* that her owner abandoned at Tighnabruaich! He strupped her of efferything that wassna nailed doon — and maist o' the things that wass as weel! So the owner wants us to moor chust off of Burnt Island ass a deterchent to ony o' the light-fingered chentry, and then to go alongside her and ground on the ebb at furst light tomorrow to transfer the cairgo."

Once they had dropped anchor 50 yards from the sorry-looking remains of the two-masted schooner *Caroline Anne*, her foremast broken off at deck level and lying athwartships with rigging and sails trailing overboard in a tangle of sodden rope and canvas, Para Handy — to the crew's disgust — produced a piece of paper from his trousers pocket and recited a watch roster for the hours of darkness.

～

Sunny Jim, on the dawn shift, was astonished to see — as

the light grew brighter — that there were crowds assembled on the water's edge to either hand. Those on the Bute shore had had an arduous walk over rough country to reach their viewpoint, for this northern tip of the island was barren and normally without any human presence. Today however a goodly number of men, women and children were to be seen on the rocky beach, many of them (just like their counterparts on the opposite shore) studying the *Vital Spark* closely through binoculars or telescopes.

When the puffer was successfully beached alongside the stranded schooner the unloading process began, as a cargo consisting of small wooden barrels was transferred from the hold of one ship to the hold of the other in netting slings. From the shore came great whooping cries of "Oooooh!" each time the laden sling was swung between the vessels, and a hearty cheer once its load had been safely lowered into the main-hatch of the *Vital Spark*.

"Ah cannae think whit's so interestin' aboot a cairgo o' butter firkins," protested Macphail for the umpteenth time, as another whoop marked the progression of a fully-laden net from schooner to puffer: "and it's no' as if they havnae seen plenty o' shups stranded on the Burnt Islands afore noo. There must be precious little doin' in Rothesay or along the Kyles if this is seen as entertainment for a family day oot!"

"They iss a funny kind o' firkin, forbye," said Dougie, "for I have neffer before seen Islay butter packed in barrels wi' a bleck Jolly Roger flag pentit' on the lids — usually it iss the picture of a coo."

"Naw," said Macphail with a snort, "that disnae surprise me at all, that's their trade-mark. Maist o' the fairmers in Islay are naethin' but a crew o' pirates: they'd rook ye blind sooner than look ye in the e'e. If ye'd mind whit we wis payin' for tatties in Port Askaig last month then ye'd hiv tae wonder that they dinna mak' ony visitin' seaman walk the plank aff the toon pier-heid as a deevershun for the lieges on a Setturday nicht.

"Onyway, if it's flags ye're on aboot, did you ever see wan as trauchled as thon auld rag hingin' on the *Caroline Ann*?"

And he pointed aloft to the schooner's mast-head, where a plain red burgee, tattered at the edges and stained by a continuing exposure to the weather of many years, flapped idly in a light southerly breeze.

At which moment, the last load having been swung

aboard the *Vital Spark*, Sunny Jim (acting on instructions given earlier by his Captain) launched the puffer's punt and rowed off towards Colintraive and its well-stocked Inn with a pocketful of change and two large tin canisters.

At the same time Para Handy himself, overhearing his Engineer's caustic remark about the schooner's burgee, glanced up at it in curiosity — and saw something which made him draw his breath in sharply, and scurry off into the wheelhouse.

～

"No, no, put your money away, there is no charge at all," said the landlord of the Colintraive Inn as he filled the second of the *Vital Spark*'s canisters and Sunny Jim, who had been rummaging clumsily in his pocket for the money, looked up in astonishment.

"Just tell Para Handy that he has given us more entertainment this morning than we've had for many a month," continued the landlord: "and besides, I had a wee bet that you *would* unload the cargo safely — so I have won a few shullings for myself, as the maist o' the folk thought that Peter would blow the shup to smithereens."

Jim croaked wordlessly as the landlord concluded:

"Aye, it takes a strong hand and a sherp eye to trans-ship near on fufty tons o' gunpooder just as calmly as if it had been barrels of herring — or butter, come to that."

～

On board the puffer Para Handy, ashen-faced, appeared at the door of the wheelhouse with a copy of Brown's Manual of Signals in his hand.

"Dougie, pit oot thon pipe this meenit. Dan, away you and dowse the fire in the enchine-room and the stove in the fo'c'sle and if either of you have matches aboot your persons then throw them over the side o' the shup.

"We are standing on a floating bomb! A red burgee flies ower a ship that's cairryin' explosives. Butter firkins my eye — we've chust loaded up wi' kegs o' gunpooder. We canna unload them again and I wull not abandon shup: neffer let it be said that a Macfarlane flunched at the hoor o' danger. But there iss only wan way this shup iss going up-river — and that iss under wind-power. Break oot the mainsail for there will be no fires aboard the vessel from noo on. I do not care how long it takes."

~

It took three days — for puffers, while notoriously slow under power, are positively plodding under sail.

The passage of the *Vital Spark* up river started out in convoy fashion as Sunny Jim, refusing point-blank to set foot aboard the vessel till her lethal cargo was safely unloaded, followed her in the punt, maintaining station a hundred yards astern. He finally bargained with his ship-mates for a tow-line in exchange for the two canisters of Colintraive ale, and slept through most of the subsequent voyage upstream.

News of the puffer's condition and cargo spread like wild-fire before her and, sporting her red burgee (a warning as potent as the hand-bell of a medieval leper) she was given a wide berth by all the traffic on the river. But she was cheered to the echo by the curious crowds on the bank — crowds which became denser as she neared the centre of the city, lured to this most unusual spectacle of a floating bomb by the reports carried in the *Glasgow Evening News*.

Her owner, uncertain whether to be outraged or flattered by the attention focussed on his wayward craft, met Para Handy on his eventual arrival at Finnieston with cautious cheerfulness.

This was only slighty diminished when it was made clear to him that the promised bonus, now that the entire crew of the puffer were privy to his deceptions should — far from being split four ways — now be multiplied four times. He cheered himself up with the thought that the original Gunpowder plotters had paid a far higher price for *their* deception.

FACTNOTE

The Cowal peninsula and the shores of Upper Loch Fyne seem to have been singled out as highly convenient dump-ing grounds for undesirable military activity for more than a century.

The US Navy has only recently withdrawn its Polaris Submarine Base from the Holy Loch just a couple of miles from Dunoon — a presence which made not just the adjacent, innocent villages of Kilmun or Sandbank but the entire Central Belt of Scotland one of the most obvious potential targets for a primary pre-emptive strike by the former Soviet Union throughout the uneasy decades of the cold war.

Our immediate forebears maybe did not have the misfortune to live with that particular threat hanging over their heads, but they were certainly no strangers to an unwanted military or armament facility deployed into their midst without so much as a 'by your leave'.

Thus at otherwise idyllic locations such as Furnace on Loch Fyne, Clachaig in Glen Lean west of Dunoon, and Millhouse, just inland from Kames on the Kyles, gunpowder and other explosives were manufactured over a period of close on a hundred years.

Operations at Furnace (where the established presence of a huge granite quarry had produced generations of locals inured to the thump and the threat of daily detonations) closed in the 1880s after a horrendous explosion left more than 20 dead.

The black powder manufactory at Clachaig lasted a decade or two longer and some of the original worker's cottages, renovated and restored, are happy homes today.

The Millhouse works were shut down only in the 1920s, despite a series of catastrophic accidents over the previous century which resulted in heavy loss of life and (if the contemporary newspaper reports are to be believed) were sometimes to be heard — and even felt — as far away as Rothesay and Inveraray.

The finished products from Millhouse ware indeed shipped out on schooners from a private jetty at Kames, to which the kegs were transported on horse-drawn carts — their wheel rims at first cushioned by leather and, later, by rubber.

Anyone who has seen that classic edge-of-the-seat 1950s French film *Les Salaires de Peur* (The Wages of Fear) about truckers offered premium payment to drive potentially lethal loads of nitro-glycerine several hundred miles across unsurfaced roads in mountainous terrain will have some idea of how the drivers of those carts may have felt as they went about their duties!

# 55

## *Nor any Drop to Drink*

In the balmy, early evening of midsummer's day, the *Vital Spark* lay against the inner face of Inveraray pier. In the afternoon the thermometer had touched 80 degrees fahrenheit, without so much as a whisper of wind, and even now, at six o'clock, there was not the slightest promise of any freshness in the air and the heat remained overwhelming.

The puffer's crew were spreadeagled on the main-hatch: Para Handy, vainly seeking some shade in the wheelhouse, leaned his elbows on the sill of its opened fore-window and surveyed the crowds thronging the pier and its approaches with a somewhat jaundiced eye.

Preparing to board the steamer *Ivanhoe* were the several hundred members of a special charter party. Special in more ways than one, for this was a strangely silent crowd. Though it included scores of children of an age-group which would normally be expected to be of a boisterous and undisciplined disposition, these particular youngsters were marshalled into subdued groups under the watchful eye of straight-backed ladies of an angular build, a frosty mien and a certain age — and all apparently sharing a taste for unseasonably drab and voluminous garments.

The balance of the company was comprised of perhaps one hundred couples, presumably the parents and grandparents of the silent children, conversing in small groups in a whisper, their heads down: occasionally, just occasionally, a few of the men-folk glanced wistfully towards the frontage of the town, dominated by the prominent white facade of the Argyll Arms Hotel. The last components of the party were about one hundred younger men and women who were also gathered in supervised clusters, all men in this one or that, all girls in these others.

Gliding through the crowd with beady eyes which seemed to peer everywhere and take in everything were a dozen or more stiffly erect figures in black frock coats, high-buttoned waistcoats, and tall, shiny-black stovepipe hats, and carrying tight-rolled umbrellas, the glint of white dog-collars (largely hidden behind full sets of Dundreary whiskers) the only departure from unrelieved black in their whole attire.

"A Good Templar's summer ooting," said Para Handy with a degree of acerbity, to nobody in particular: and he shivered in spite of the heat. "Now there iss a sight to mak' the blood run cold! There is chust aboot as much spurit of happiness, good-wull and harmony in that gaitherin' ass would fill an empty vestas box!

"They'll have been at the Cherry Park for a tent-meeting and a picnic, and then a march back doon the toon to the pier. Cheery days! Look you at aal they bible-thumpers wi' the chuldren, and aal they spunster wummen chaperonin' the lasses, crampin' their style and makin' sure they keep them awa' from the lads and dinna let ony couples go wan-derin' off into the woods or up wan o' the closes. Then there's a wheen o' bleck-coated meenisters to stop the men-folk from sluppin' off to the bar of the Argyll Arms or the George Hotel for chust the wan wee Chrustian dram and a necessary refreshment on a thirsty day like this!

"I am thinking they would be better to hire in a whole pack of collie dugs and drive the puir duvvles through the town ass if they wass a flock of sheeps, for if you ask me that iss what they aal are, and that iss surely how they are treated by their weemen and their meenisters: if Dougie wass here he would tell you that himself."

Indeed the thronged pier dispersed an aura of gloom totally at odds with the brightness of the day, and in dismal contrast to the cheery joie-de-vivre and bonhommie which were dispensed in large measure to all and sundry by the typical excursion party.

Certainly the crew of the *Vital Spark*, and perhaps the whole of Inveraray as well, breathed a sigh of quiet relief when, at half past six and with the boarding process com-pleted, there was a toot (even *that* a subdued one) on the *Ivanhoe*'s whistle and the paddler moved out into open water and headed off back towards Ardrossan.

"In a sense," observed Para Handy half-an-hour later, as the crew settled onto a bench in front of the Argyll Arms Hotel and contemplated the play of light on the trees of Duniquaich over the top of a pint pot, "in a sense they only have themselves to blame, puir craiturs, but at the same time there iss many of the menfolk chust bludgeoned into the Templars, or maybe the Rechabites forbye, by their wummenfolk, wi' no chance at aal to mak' an escape. I mean, would *you* want to argue the rights and wrongs wi' maist o' the wummen we saw on that pier today? They certainly pit the fear o' the Lord in me. I am thinkin' that maist men would simply do what they wass told ass long ass the wummen wass around, and do what they wanted to do themselves ass soon ass they were on their own.

"And when you get them on their own, the maist o' the Templars men are chust ordinary mortals like the rest o' us."

"I'm sure an they didna bring mich business to the Inveraray Inns today, though," observed Macphail. "The Licensees' herts must sink to their boots when they see the *Ivanhoe* offshore. If she had been the *Lord of the Isles* wi' a works' ootin' frae Fairfield's yerd that wud hae been different, Ah'm thinkin'."

"You would be surprised, Dan," said Para Handy, "at chust how profitable a temperance excursion can be for the licensed trade if aal the arrangements are in the right hands."

Sunny Jim sensed a story.

"Go on, Captain," he prompted. "What d'ye mean?"

"It wass many years back," said Para Handy. "Hurricane Jeck and me wass crewin' a sailin' gabbart that turned a penny for a man in Saltcoats.

"We were to load a cargo o' bales o' wool from Lochranza, and we arrived there late one Friday evenin' and went ashore for a gless of something at Peter Murdo Cameron's Inn, chust along the road from the head of the pier.

"Cameron was in a bleck mood, that wass plain to see, and Jeck asked him what wass the matter.

" 'Chust my luck,' says Cameron, 'you can imachine how very few excursion perties we get comin' to Lochranza, the maist o' the steamer passengers we see iss those aboard the *Kintyre* goin' to or from Campbeltown. Precious few effer comes ashore *here* for a dram. If it wassna for the likes of you, Jeck, and the herring boats in season, and the workers on the big estate, there would be little point openin' a bar in Lochranza and little chance o' makin' a livin' from it.

" 'So when we heard yestreen that there wass an excursion comin' to Lochranza tomorrow — aal adults, too — on a special charter on the *Glen Sannox*, you can imachine that I got quite excited and ordered in extra supplies from the distillery up the road, and brought in more beer on the dray from Brodick this mornin'. It wass going to be like Chrustmas and Hogmanay rolled into one, I told myself. Then this afternoon we foond out what this excursion perty consists of. Chust Rechabites from Fairlie. *Rechabites!* And me with effery penny I could raise invested in drink for them. It'll be months before I clear the stock I've bought in, and the most of the beer will have turned sour, wait you and you will see.

" '*Rechabites*! They'll be the ruin o' me.'

" 'Tush, Peter Murdo,' says Jeck reproachfully — and he wass quite jocco — 'for a Lochranza man you are givin' up aawful easily. The average chentleman of the Rechabite persuasion has exactly the same proportions of a thirst as you or me, it is chust that he hass rather less of an opportunity to indulge it, especially when his wummenfolk are aboot him. Tomorrow you will have to see to it that the men get a run at the refreshments and you will do very well.'

" 'But that's just it,' cried Cameron. 'The wummenfolk wull be aal aboot them aal the time, and forbye Lochranza iss chust a wee place. They canna lose each other ass if this wass a lerge metropiliss like Campbeltown. They daurna come in to an Inns.'

" 'Well then,' says Jeck, 'you will chust have to cater for the wummen at the same time, and whiles they are busy at their teas and scones who iss to know what their menfolk might be up to? Get yourself up early the morn's morn, wi' a wheen o' your frien's (and wan or two wives ass well) and I will show you.' "

Para Handy paused to drain his glass, and look pointedly at the Engineer as he set it on the table in front of him. Macphail took the hint and signalled to a passing barman.

"I must admut," the Captain continued, "that I thought Jeck had taken leave of his senses. But I had reckoned without the man's cheneral agility. He wass sublime, chust sublime!

"On Saturday morning we were up to the Inns at first light. You will mind, Dougie, that there iss a big white board

along the front o' the hoose with PETER M CAMERON'S
spelt oot on it in big bleck-painted wudden letters, and then
inside there iss a corridor, and off it, two big rooms — the
bar to the right, and a room on the left wi' tables and chairs
where ye can take your refreshments in peace and ring a
wee bell when you are wantin' anither gless.

"What Jeck did wass to tak' aal the letters off the board
along the front o' the hoose, mak' another 'O' oot o' the lid
of a herring firkin, and hammer the letters back up on the
board but this time so that they spelt oot TEMPERANCE
ROOMS.

"Then he sent for a can o' white paint and a wee brush,
and on the door in the corridor that led into the bar he
wrote 'Coffee Room and Smoking Parlour — Gentlemen
Only': and on the door to the sitting room he wrote 'Tea
Room — Ladies Only'.

"And he got Cameron's wife, and three of her friends, to
go and bake up a stock o' buns and scones and fancies that
wouldna have disgraced a Baker's shop, and to fetch over
aal their cups and saucers and plates and teapots and the
like.

"He had Cameron put on his best Fast Day suit, and his
wife a bleck dress and white peenie, and the two o' them wi'
silver trays under their airms, and had them meet the
excursionists at the heid o' the pier as they came off the
shup at wan o'clock.

"Jeck himself stood at the Inns door and greeted the
ladies wi' a most gracious bow that it wass a preevilege to
behold, and ushered them aal into the big Tea Room.

"The chentlemen were asked to wait in the roadway till
aal the ladies wass seated, and then Jeck invited them to
come into the hoose.

"It chust needed the wan quick question at the entrance
to find oot exactly what sort of refreshment the chentlemen
were most anxious for, and ony that wass true teetotal-
isators (and there wassna but a handful o' them) wass quietly taken into the hoose next door where Jeck had
arranged wi' Cameron's neebour that she would provide
teas for any o' the chentlemen that wass soft enough in the
heid to want chust that and nothin' else.

"It wass a roarin' success! Cameron took more money in
that day than he had effer seen before in a week, and his
wife and her friends did such a great tred wi' the ladies in
the Tea Room that she wass able to pit new curtains right

through the hoose wi' the profits on it. A total waste o' money, Cameron thought that, but he couldna complain.

"Jeck had thought of efferything. When it wass time for the steamer to sail, and the chentlemen wass leaving the Inns by the back door, Jeck even had a boy there passin' oot pan drops and soor plooms to the chentlemen so their wives wouldna jalouse chust what kind o' coffee and tea *they* had been drinking!

"Cameron had even struck a bargain wi' the Lodge Secretary that they would come back again the next month. 'The best ooting we have ever had,' said that worthy, 'for you have opened up a new world to us, Mr Cameron'. And Cameron had the grace to admit that if it hadna been for Jeck there wouldna have been any sort of new world for the Rechabites to open up at aal.

"Jeck got a half-a-case of whusky for his troubles, and Cameron gave me a crate of Bass beer, and that evening we loaded the wool and set off for Gleska.

"Next time we called at Lochranza we found that the planned return trup had been caaled off. There wass some things that even Jeck chust couldna legislate for.

"The chentlemen had aal gone back on board smelling as sweet as a nut, thenks to the lozengers and the boilings that Jeck had dispensed. What he could neffer have foreseen or prevented wass that some of them wass that cheery they began to sing on the trup home — loudly. And it wassna Moodey and Sankey neither. When the wummenfolk heard a roaring chorus of *The Foggy Foggy Dew* come echoing throughout the shup from the fore-saloon where the chentlemen had gathered, they realised something wass going on and a few enquiries wass put urchently in hand wi' some bemused and befuddled husbands, and the game wass up.

"But it was a rare high-jink while it lasted!"

*FACTNOTE*

Victorian and Edwardian society had an ambivalent attitude to drink and its problems and an ambivalent way of coping with the situation as well.

These were the generations which saw the peak of the Temperance Movements (although they were in serious decline by the end of the 19th century) but at the same time they were also the years of almost unlimited and

THE SUMMER 'TRIP' — *Not, on this occasion, anything as depressing as a Templar's Outing but, probably, either a School or most likely a Sunday School picnic. These were common enough in the west of Scotland until well into the 1950s but are nowadays, I'm sure, a thing of the past. Higher standards of living and above all the wider availability of the ubiquitous motorcar mean that there is no novelty or excitement in an annual day-out by coach or steamer.*

unchecked consumption of alcohol.

Temperance movements were usually led by the 'middle' classes, the objects of whose campaigning were — inevitably, but all too frequently unjustifiably — the 'working' classes.

Drink was perceived as a social problem with well-defined class boundaries and the heavy consumption of those more fortunate in their circumstances was accepted with good-natured tolerance while over-indulgence by the 'lower orders' was railed against and vilified.

The two most influential Movements were the splendidly-titled Independent Order of Rechabites (British in origin and dating from the 1830s) and the Good Templars, imported from America in the 1870s. It is a fact that in both cases women were often leading protagonists. Where else, in the stifling chauvinistic atmosphere of the mid-Victorian era, could a woman hope to make her mark in the world? It was true also that there were as many backsliders and time-servers as there were genuine converts and followers among the male membership. Neil Munro makes several references to the standing of the Temperance Movements in the Para Handy, Erchie and Jimmy Swan stories. The Movements were accepted by then as legitimate targets for gentle humour — not cruel mockery: for mild parody — not merciless pillory.

There was even a brief nod in the direction of the teetotal lobby from the shipping companies. The *Ivanhoe* was a brave experiment, an alcohol-free vessel commissioned for and managed by a group of Clyde owners and operators — not for the benefit of the Temperance Movements, but for the sake of families whose enjoyment of the amenity of the Clyde was on occasion not just threatened but destroyed by the excesses of a raucous minority.

By the 1890s the problem of drink on the ships (which in any case history has probably, in retrospect, exaggerated) was more or less under control. The worst excesses had been snuffed out as operators improved supervision and control, and common sense and acceptable behaviour prevailed. The *Ivanhoe* reverted to the role of a typical Clyde steamer of her day.

Tea was no longer compulsory aboard her: but neither was strong drink.

# 56

## *Para Handy's Ark*

Sunny Jim sighed hopefully. "Ah sometimes wush we could have some sort of an animal on the shup," he said. "A dug, for instance. It's aye cheerier when there's a dug aboot the place. I think it's thon constant tail-wagging: it's infectious."

"The only things infectious aboot dugs is fleas," said Para Handy sharply, "And we are not having a dug on the vessel, so you needna even think aboot it. I have not forgotten the sorry business wi' yon Pomeranian that you borrowed a few years back, Jum, and I have no intention of repeating the experiment."

"Aye," put in the Engineer innocently, "you're kind of unlucky wi' animals when I come to think o' it. There wis the dug: and of course there wis yon cockatoo..."

"I wull not be reminded of that incident!" said the Captain indignantly. "Mony's the sleepless night it cost me."

"...and there wis that coo at Lochgoilhead," continued the Engineer remorselessly: "and your so-called singin' canary, and the tortoise, and of course Jeck's Fenian goat, and..."

Para Handy, who had been perched on the edge of the main-hatch smoking a peaceful pipe while Dougie took a trick at the wheel, leaped to his feet with an angry snort and marched off towards the bows, where he made a great show of studying the pier at Carradale — their destination with a cargo of slates, and which was now in plain sight — with such concentration and interest as to suggest that he had never seen a similar construction in his life before.

"Aye," said Macphail to Sunny Jim, "he disnae like any

reminder aboot those episodes at all. The man's no' canny when it comes to animals. He's no' very canny when it comes to human beings either, come to that.

"But Ah doot he means it, Jum: aboot the only animal you'd be allowed to put on board this vessel wud be a goldfish in a bowl and even then he'd find some way of stoppin' you. Para Handy and animals jist disnae mix."

Late the following afternoon, with the Carradale slates safely ashore, the Captain received a telegram from the owner advising that their next cargo was a farm-flitting from Millport on the island of Cumbrae — its ultimate destination unstated.

The news did not greatly please the Captain, for farm-flittings were not his favourite consignment.

They required that the hold had to be carefully packed with any number of teachests crammed with clothes and linen and crockery and saucepans and all the minutiae of life, followed by the flotsam and jetsam of the farmhouse furniture, then — almost always — an awkward deck-cargo of a plough and a harrow and the carts which had brought most of the plenishings to the pierhead in the first place, and finally (just to top off the whole improbable mixture) the farmer and his family.

Para Handy therefore supervised the berthing of the puffer at Millport Old Pier the next day with ill-disguised displeasure, and looked around him for his cargo. There was no sign of it.

"That chust aboot puts the lid on it," he complained to nobody in particular. "Not content wi' contracting a vessel as smert ass the *Vital Spark* to luft a mixter-maxter cairgo mair suited to a common coal-gabbart, they cannot even arrange for the goods to be here ready for us when we arrive.

"How much longer are we going to be kept hangin' aboot Millport chust like we wass on holiday?"

The rhetorical question was soon answered.

A stockily-built, red-faced man in a suit of good tweeds walked onto the pier and up to where the puffer lay.

"Captain Macfarlane?" he enquired.

"Chust so," said Para Handy: "and you wull be Muster MacMillan. But where is oor cairgo?"

"Here they come now," said MacMillan, pointing to the pier gate and (before the startled Captain could respond by asking what on earth the man meant by referring to his cargo as 'they') a strange procession came into view, coaxed along by six or seven farmhands with sticks.

Para Handy stared in total disbelief.

There were half-a-dozen cows, at least 20 blackface sheep, a sturdy Clydesdale, a couple of sows (one with a litter of tiny piglets) and a surly-looking boar, a few geese, rather more hens and ducks, and a couple of border collies.

"There must be some mustake," the Captain spluttered, "we wass contracted for a ferm-flitting."

"And what do you think this is, Captain?" MacMillan asked. "It is certainly not a menagerie."

"But a ferm-flitting iss the furniture and the chattels," Para Handy protested. "Naebody flits the *animals*. They stays on the ferm."

"Not in this case, Captain," replied MacMillan. "I am moving my livestock to a new farm. It is perfectly straightforward."

"Not from where I am standing," Para Handy countered. "Forbye we havna the facilities on board the shup for lookin' efter live animals, even if we had the knowledge for it."

"But Captain," said MacMillan, "they will only be on board for half-an-hour. Our destination is Fairlie, that is all, and my own men will be travelling with the beasts. All of the loading and unloading will be their responsibility. You are being asked simply to steer the ship two miles across the bay to Fairlie Pier and you are being paid handsomely for it."

"The owner iss mebbe being paid handsomely" was Para Handy's somewhat caustic response. "There iss nothing in this for the poor crew. But, if it iss only for a couple of miles, and if your men wull handle the beasts, then I suppose we must chust grin and bear it.

"But I don't suppose your men are going to be responsible for cleaning up the mess on the decks of the smertest vessel in the coasting trade, though — eh?"

MacMillan ignored the suggestion, and at his signal the loading began.

An hour later Para Handy stared in pained disbelief from the wheelhouse window at the state of his beloved ship. The cattle were in the hold, lowered there by slings, and the

Clydesdale stood patiently beside the mast. The pigs had been confined to the bows with a hastily-improvised pen knocked together by the farmer's men from a few wicket gates, but the sheep roamed everywhere and the poultry disputed with them for the limited deck space available.

"This iss chust a nightmare," the Captain imparted to Dougie almost tearfully, "and I only wush that I could wake up and find oot that it wass!"

At that juncture MacMillan came along the quayside and Para Handy stepped out on deck to speak with him. "I am most grateful, Captain," the farmer said. "There will be two cattle-trucks waiting at Fairlie and my men will have the animals ashore in no time. There is just one small thing, though: please don't say that the cargo is from Millport. I — er — don't want some of my rivals over in Ayrshire to know that I am moving my stock out of the island.

"Nobody will be interested, but — just in case they do ask — I would take it as a personal kindness if you would simply say that the beasts are from Arran." And leaning forward, as if to shake the Captain by the hand, he pressed a piece of folded paper into his fingers — a piece of folded paper which, when Para Handy examined it in the wheelhouse a moment later, proved to be a five-pound-note.

"There iss something chust not right aboot aal this Dougie, and I am sure and I do not know what to make of it at aal. And what on earth am I going to say in Fairlie if they ask me where we are from? A Macfarlane doesna tell a lie for any man!"

"Well," said the Mate, pragmatically, "let's chust hope that nobody asks."

~

Nobody did — because nobody needed to.

The *Vital Spark* was met, as she approached Fairlie, by a figure in dark blue uniform wielding a large magaphone and with a small crowd at his back.

"Puffer ahoy!" shouted the policeman. "Stand clear! You are not allowed to land those animals here, nor to tie up alongside. No other pier on the river will take you, either."

Para Handy paled, and turned to the farmer's foreman, who was crouched down, hiding, at the starboard side of the wheelhouse.

"What in bleezes iss goin' on here," he demanded. "Iss

this stolen property we are carrying?"

"Naw, it's worse than that," said the foreman wretchedly. "Wan o' the small ferms on the west side of Cumbrae has a suspected ootbreak o' foot-and-mouth disease, MacMillan foond oot aboot it yesterday, but since he'd already booked your boat to move his stock to a ferm he's bought at Hunterston, he wis jist hoping that he could get the beasts safely awa' and landed at Fairlie afore the news got oot. It seems he wis too late."

Para Handy's reappearance at Millport was met with an even angrier rebuff than he had received at Fairlie.

"The only reason that the polis iss no here to greet you in person, Peter Macfarlane," howled the irate pier-master, "iss that he has that scoundrel MacMillan under arrest for trying to move cattle oot of a controlled zone, and he is undergoing some prutty severe questioning doon at the polis office right now.

"If I wass you, I would chust get oot of here fast afore you're booked yoursel' ass an accessible after the fact, or whateffer the expression iss."

~

The next three days — the worst three days of his life, Para Handy maintains, and he will expound upon them at great length to anybody prepared to listen — have passed into the legend and lore of longshore gossip on the Clyde.

No port or harbour on the river would allow the puffer to enter or moor, far less unload a cargo which was becoming more and more restive and (it has to be said) foetid as well. Para Handy even made a bold effort to attract the attention of the press and through them, perhaps, the sympathy of the public by trying to take his floating zoo right up-river to the Broomielaw, but he was frustrated by two of the Clyde Port Authority's launches which forced him to turn back at Renfrew Ferry.

The one concession that was made by Authority was made not to the crew of the *Vital Spark* or the farmer's men but to her live cargo: feedstuff and water for the animals was delivered daily by another puffer especially chartered for the occasion by one of the animal charities. The human beings on board were reduced to a diet of salt herring and potatos.

Relief came on the fourth day when the results of all the

tests undertaken at the suspect farm on Cumbrae were completed — with negative results. A collective sigh of relief went up along the river and not just from the Clyde coast's farmers: there were some mightily relieved sailors as well, when the good news was finally communicated to the *Vital Spark* by one of the Greenock Pilot Cutters.

"You are more than welcome to land your cargo anywhere you like now, Captain," said her skipper: "and I would imagine that somewhere with a public house close at hand would be your first choice, after all that's happened?" And with a laugh he turned back to his own bridge and gave the order which sent the cutter swiftly on her way, throwing up an impressive foaming wake as she did so.

It was with great deliberation, but great satisfaction as well, that Para Handy, ignoring the protests of MacMillan's men and insisting on his right as master of the vessel to make all the decisions appertaining to her safety and convenience, reached that decision — and landed the animals back at Millport.

"Well, now MacMillan can stert aal over again," he observed to Dougie, "if onybody'll deal wi' him. Which I doot. He's pit *his* foot in his mooth chust the wan time too many, I'm thinking."

*FACTNOTE*

Dan Macphail's unkind references to his Captain's earlier misfortunes need no explanation for those who are familiar with Neil Munro's original tales. The watery fate of the unfortunate cockatoo is a classic.

The two Cumbraes lie just off the Ayrshire coast between Largs and Hunterston. Little Cumbrae has been uninhabited in historic times except by the keepers of its lighthouse, but Great Cumbrae was a popular holiday destination for many years and still attracts a loyal following. Millport, the capital, was served by two steamer piers but this did not save the resort from the so-called 'Siege of Millport' in July 1906 when the steamer companies refused to pay increased pier dues to the Town Council and withdrew all services.

Everything from puffers and motor launches to rowing boats and yachts was dragooned into service to convey holidaymakers (and business travellers) in and out of the island, for the effects of a protracted shut-out would be an economic disaster for the island. In July the resident population was swelled five-fold with the arrival of the Trades Fair visitors.

After some behind-the-scenes wheeling and dealing a compromise was reached and normal service resumed within the week. One has the feeling that the shipping companies themselves could not have afforded a protracted strike since not only would their steamers be losing revenue, thanks to the loss of all passenger traffic, so also would the railways which owned the steamers and which themselves normally carried the crowds from Glasgow down to the Ayrshire piers — at a considerable profit.

In the years before the Erskine Bridge and the Clyde Tunnel and the Motorway across the Clyde there were many ferry services for vehicles and passengers from the upper reaches of the river down as far as Erskine. Here and at Renfrew there were two chain-ferries, which pulled themselves undramatically but quite efficiently to and fro across the river by steam-powered pawls clanking their way along a fixed chain.

Both these vessels came in on concrete slips at either bank so the state of the tide was of no concern to them. Further up the river, where ferries operated to stone quays, significant tidal implications stimulated the development of the ingenious 'elevating ferries' of Finnieston, Whiteinch and Govan. Their carrying-decks were not attached to the hull which provided the flotation — they were in fact platforms suspended from three perpendicular girders to each side, port and starboard, raised or lowered by steam-winches according to the state of the tide, and so could always be docked at the same level as the quays.

# 57

## *Follow My Leader*

The *Vital Spark* had just threaded her way through the narrows of the Kyles, en route to Tarbert with a load of salt for the curing stations, when the staccato beat of paddle-wheels echoed across the water astern of the puffer. Para Handy, at the wheel, turned to identify the approaching vessel.

A few minutes later, as the Captain feigned indifference under the pretence of studying the shoreline of the island of Bute to port, a smart two-funnelled paddler in the livery of Mr David MacBrayne swept past perilously close on the puffer's starboard beam at full stretch, with an imperious and quite unnecessarily prolonged blast on her whistle, and then sped off towards Tighnabruaich pier, laying out as she did so a phosphorescent twin-track, turbulent wake in which gleaming ribbon the hapless *Vital Spark* lurched and dipped with the awkward ungainliness of a floating bathtub.

Sunny Jim, who had been down in the fo'c'sle frying up sausages for the crew's dinner, came scrambling up on deck to find out what was responsible for sending half the contents of the pan skittering across the stove.

"Ye clown," he shouted after the vanishing paddler: "that's the maist o' wir denner on the deck! So mich for conseederation and the rule o' the road!"

"Neffer heed him Jum," said the Captain, "it iss not worth your while getting aal hot and bothered. Yon's Sandy McIver and his precious *Grenadier*, behavin' ass if he owns the river, but I can assure you there wass a time when he wass chust ass angry wi' the *Vital Spark* ass you are wi' him noo. And he's neffer forgotten nor forgiven either, in spite of what it says in the Good Book, which iss why he dam' near runs us doon every time he sees the shup.

"Dan or Dougie will tell you aal aboot it."

But Macphail was busy in the engines and Dougie, off watch, was catnapping in the fo'c'sle so with a little persuasion, once he had his pipe going to his satisfaction, Para Handy told the tale.

~

"It aal happened twelve years ago chust a matter of a few weeks after the shup had been launched, and we were on the very first trup wi' her ootside Ardlamont Point. We'd had a few teething problems. The cargo hatch wass letting in watter at the fore end and we'd had to have some of the deck planks caulked, the steam-winch wass the very duvvle to get sterted, the shaft wass leakin' oil and the biler wass apt to prime. But over the piece we got aal this set to rights.

"Worst of aal, though, wass that after less than a week the steam whustle broke doon and the same day that happened, while we wass laid up wan night in Bowling Harbour, somebody stole the stern lamp on us while we wass ashore takin' a refreshment.

"Well, I wassna goin' to risk the vessel in the river without the lamp. We do chust occasionally meet up wi' a shup wi' a better turn o' speed than the *Vital Spark*, Jum, and because of that it iss chust a sensible precaution to be showing a light astern at night. And it would have been madness to sail without a steam whustle, for how would we let a slower shup know we wass preparin' to pass her" — here Para Handy totally ignored the exaggerated snort of derision emanating from the engine-room at his feet — "or cope wi' fog on the Firth?

"Ass luck would have it, there wass an old steamer in the basin at Bowling, waiting' her turn to go into McCulloch's bone-yerd to be broken up for scrap. Sorley McCulloch owed me a few favours for aal the bags of coal he had from me over the years for what the owner doesna see willna hurt him, and I am a great believer in havin' frien's in effery port in the river, for you never ken when you might need them: so Sorley didna tak' mich persuasion to let me have the stern lamp and the steam whustle off the old shup.

"The lamp wass fine, a wheen bigger than we really needed, and set on a higher sternpost than wir ain, but she gave oot a most spendid illumination and there wass no chance of us bein' run doon in the derk if any shup comin' up astern of us should happen to have the pace to overtake the vessel.

"It was the steam whustle that wass the real cracker! Aal solid brass you could see your face in wance the boy had her polished to rights. It wass designed for a shup many times bigger than the *Vital Spark* and when you gi'ed her a blaw, for a stert you dam' near drained oot aal the steam from Macphail's biler tubes and you sure as bleezes put the fear o' daith in whateffer shup you wass passin', or the harbour-master and the longshoremen at whateffer pier it wass that you wass comin' into. We soonded like the *Campania*.

"I tell you we had some high-jinks the next week or two! When Dougie was at the helm, he chust couldna resist blawin' the whustle at any excuse at aal and Dan got real vexed wi' him. It wassna chust playin' havoc wi' his steam pressure, it wass fair dingin' his hearin' wi' the noise o' the blasts. Worse, since he neffer knew from wan moment tae the next chust when Dougie would take it into his heid to let her go, and since he was aye hunkered doon wi' his nose buried in wan o' his penny novelles, he lost coont o' the number o' times that he got sich a fleg when the whustle went aff that he jumped up and banged his heid on the deck beams in the enchine-room.

"If Dougie was here he would tell you himself...

"It wass two weeks efter the new lamp and whustle wass put on the vessel that they really proved their value, but that wass also the occasion when we fell foul o' McIver in the *Grenadier*.

"We wass on the same trup we are today — from the Broomielaw to Tarbert wi' a load o' salt. The dufference wass that, wance we had discharged the cargo, we wass to go up to Lochgilphead for a ferm flittin' that wass to be took over to Otter Ferry on the other side o' Loch Fyne.

"You ken yoursel' what Loch Gilp is like, chust a great spread o' mudflats at onythin' less than half-tide, the toon itself standin' at the heid o' the shallowest stretch o' watter on the river, worse even than the Holy Loch. Of course, that's why Mr MacBrayne's terminal is at Ardrishaig three miles sooth, for there's no right pier at Lochgilphead. A steamer couldna come near it even at high watter. There iss chust a jetty for the likes o' the local fishin' smacks and even the *Vital Spark* couldna get alongside it. We would have to beach offshore at half-tide and the flittin' would be brought alongside on cairts.

"Well, we lay overnight at Tarbert after we'd unloaded the salt, and went ashore to peruse the neebourhood, ass you might say. But we were back on board early. Hurricane Jeck was no' wi' us, ye'll understand. There wass chust me and Dan and Dougie and a young laddie caaled Campbell, the sowl, and him from Fort Wulliam tae. He couldna help that either, the puir duvvle, but they're awful Hielan' roon' aboot Fort Wulliam.

"The thing wass we had to be up sherp in the mornin' to take on some coal for oor ain bunkers — the owner had some sort of an arranchement wi' wan o' the Tarbert merchants. What herm the owner had ever done him I dinna ken, but it really didna bear thinkin' aboot when you saw the quality and quantity o' stanes we wass takin' on. We wanted to be away by eleven at the latest if we were to get to Loch Gilp at the right time o' the tide ready to pick up the flittin'.

"Ass it wass it wass half past eleven afore we nosed oot o' the harbour. The Inveraray Company's *Lord of the Isles* wis chust on the point o' pullin' awa' from the main steamer pier, efter loadin' up an excursion party for Ardrishaig and Inveraray, and it wouldna be long before the MacBrayne steamer frae Gleska was due to arrive on passage to Ardrishaig. Indeed ass we headed north we saw the *Grenadier* comin' thunderin' up the Loch frae the sooth, wi' McIver standin' oot on the wing o' the brudge and tryin' to look important. The man neffer had the presence for it, but then when you had wance seen Hurricane Jeck tak' a shup into a pier, onythin' else wass chust a let-doon.

"Though it wass a bright sunny day when we set off, within chust ten minutes we had run into a dark fog-bank that wass that thick, you could have cut it up intae blocks wi' a knife and sold it as briquettes.

"I tell you it wass me wass relieved we had the new sternlight for I knew fine the *Lord of the Isles* wass in our wake, and I didna fancy suddenly findin' her chust a few feet aff oor rudder and lookin' for a right-o'-passage. Dougie lit the lamp and raised it ass high ass he could up the stern-post, I put the laddie up into the bows wi' a bell tae ring to let us ken if he saw or heard onythin' ahead, and we picked oor way up the loch.

"Sure enough, in due course we heard the whoop o' a steamer's whustle dead astern and efter a few meenits we could chust mak' oot the foremast lights and the navigation lights of a shup. It wass the *Lord of the Isles* sure enough. I gave a quick blast on oor ain whustle effery noo and then to mak' sure she knew we wass there, but wi' the illumination o' the new stern lamp there wass no doubt she had seen us. She held her position for a half-an-hour and then we saw her lights swing off to port, and she picked her way in to Ardrishaig pier a mile or so away.

"Ten minutes later, and there came a whustle blast immediately astern again, a kind o' a signal maybe — two shorts, a long and two shorts again.

" 'I canna think who this is,' said I to Dougie, 'but we'd best let him ken we're here.' And I blasted oot the same tattoo on our own new whustle.

"The unseen shup gave the signal back, so we replied again. He whustled. We whustled. I tell you there wass some din on the Loch that mornin', Macphail put his heid oot o' his cubby and said a few un-Chrustian things, but if this unknown shup wass that close astern o' us — despite the bright lamp that he could surely see — then I certainly wass not goin' to risk the vessel by keepin' quiet.

"Occasionally we could mak' oot the masthead light of whatever shup it was that wass followin' us, and at times even the loom o' her bows when the fog lifted for a moment.

" 'I dinna like this at aal, Dougie,' I said. 'She's too close for my likin'.

" 'Neffer mind Peter,' says he. 'We are certainly well into Loch Gilp by now and if we chust swing to starboard and anchor, then she can go where she wants, and we can bide our time till the fog lifts.'

"I put the wheel hard to starboard with a final, long blast on the big whustle, shouted on Dan to stop the enchines, and sent Dougie for'ard to let go the anchor.

"And three things happened aal at wance.

"First, we ran oot of the fog-bank ass suddenly ass we had run into it, and there were the white hooses of Lochgilphead chust a mile ahead.

"Next, from our port quarter came a desperate, furious clang on an enchine-room telegraph ringin' and ringin' ass if somebody's life depended on it.

"Last, from the same direction there wass a most awful grinding sound like steel on stone, and the ear-spluttin' crash of falling objects, breaking glass, and smashing crockery, splintering wud and so on, that seemed to go on and on for effer. When it did stop, their wass such a racket of cries and shouts and screams — and curses too — that you would swear that the day of chudgement had come to Loch Fyneside.

"When I turned to see what the commotion wass, here wass the bow half — no more — of a big shup pokin' oot o' the fog. She had run herself fast aground on the Loch Gilp shallows and I could mak' oot her name quite plain. It wass the *Grenadier*.

"Dougie and me unshipped the punt, and rowed over to see if we could help. But the paddler wass fast aground on an ebbing tide and she'd be where she was for seven or eight hoors till the sea came back.

"McIver was leaning over the brudge-wing chust beside himself and bleck in the face wi' rage.

" 'Macfarlane,' he bellowed wance he recognised us. 'Where the bleezes did you get thon lamp, and thon dam' whustle? Are ye oot o' yer mind completely pittin' gear like that in a steam gabbart?

" 'Ah wis followin' ye because Ah thocht ye wis the *Lord of the Isles* and I thocht ye wis pickin' intae Ardrishaig. No' intae this — this — this *sump*,' he howled as he saw the Loch Gilp mud-flats, which were quickly dryin' oot as the tide went doon.

"The owner heard aal aboot it and made me get rid o' the bonny new lamp and the braw big whustle. But I'd had good value oot o' them. There's no' another skipper on the Clyde can boast o' havin' personally grounded wan o' Mr MacBrayne's most treasured possessions — when he wassna even on board of her!

"In aal fairness Jum, I dinna grudge poor McIver a few sausages cowped on our deck. I cowped mair than that on his!"

*FACTNOTE*

Lochgilphead indeed never did have a steamer pier, for the head of the shallow loch was quite inaccessible to vessels of any size. The town was served by Ardrishaig, whose commodious pier also marked the staging post for passengers proceeding on to Oban and the Western Highlands by way of the Crinan Canal, this being the eastern point of entry to that waterway.

MacBrayne's *Grenadier* was a handsome, clipper-bowed

ROTHESAY HARBOUR — *The view across the town's outer harbour, as seen from the pier, looks towards a seafront silhouette which has been much altered in relatively recent years. Many of the buildings to the right of the picture have now been demolished, and the landscaped and pedestrianised spaces of Guildford Square have been created in their place.*

paddler launched in 1885. For most of the year she was based at Oban but she became a regular replacement for the *Columba* on the Glasgow to Ardrishaig service during the off-peak months. Her end was dramatic and tragic — destroyed by fire at Oban pier in 1927 in one of the very few incidents involving Clyde or West Highland steamers which resulted in loss of life, in this case her Captain and two of her crew. As far as I know *Grenadier* was never aground, but her predecessor *Mountaineer* stranded in fog on rocks lying off Lismore near the entrance to the Sound of Mull and, though passengers and crew were taken off without any problems, she became a total loss.

The Cunarder *Campania* was built at the Fairfield Yard on the Upper Clyde in 1893. The largest (620' overall) and fastest (23 knots) of her brief generation of Transatlantic liners, she held the Blue Riband for four years from 1893 till 1897, losing it in that year to the Norddeutscher Lloyd liner *Kaiser Wilhelm der Grosse*, fore-runner of the next generation and, again, the world's largest ship. From that date mastery of the lucrative North Atlantic passenger trade rested with the Germans till Cunard in 1906 put into service those two incomparable sisters, *Mauretania* and the doomed *Lusitania*.

In retrospect, in a quite unexpected way, *Campania* exemplified the breathtaking pace of maritime development by breaking new ground both at the beginning and at the very end of her career.

When launched she was the first Cunarder to be fitted with twin screws and the first of that company's ships, therefore, not to have been provided with some form of auxiliary sail-power (an extraordinary anachronism from our standpoint, but the norm in the Victorian era) and thus the first designed to be wholly reliant on her engines.

But just 25 years later, when she was lost at sea following a collision in the Firth of Forth with the Battleship *Renown*, she had passed her last four years of life (after conversion in 1914) *as an aircraft-carrier*, the maritime base and mobile platform for a form of transport so undreamed-of at the time of her launch that even to have put it forward as a possibility would have been to invite the ridicule reserved for dabblers in science fantasy.

# 58

## *The Rickshaw and the Pram*

The papers had for days been full of nothing but increasing speculation about the impending confrontation between the Russian and Japanese Imperial Fleets in the Far East, and loud and long had been the argument and debate, involving our politicians as readily as our naval strategists, as to the relative strengths (and weaknesses) of the two participants.

Encountering Para Handy seated on a bollard on Princes Pier on a fine evening in late May, I determined to canvass the opinion of a mariner of so many years experience as to the merits or otherwise of the opposing forces.

"What is your opinion of Admiral Rojdestvensky's strength in terms of capital ships, Captain," I enquired. "Do you think he is capable of outgunning Togo's forces sufficiently to overcome their superiority in range?"

"Eh?" asked Para Handy.

"Well, let me put it another way. The humiliation the Russians suffered at Port Arthur last year must weigh heavily upon their commanders at this juncture. Do you see that as a 'plus' — an incentive to greatness: or a 'minus' — a collective millstone round their necks?"

"Pardon?" said Para Handy: "I really do not have the furst idea what you are talking aboot, Mr Munro."

"Good Lord, Captain," I exclaimed, astonished. "Have you not been following the news? Is it possible that you do not realise that — even as we speak — the naval forces of Japan and Russia could well be locked in battle in the greatest confrontation in the history of war at sea: a battle which could well determine future sovereignty and autarchy across the whole Far Eastern political and social theatre, with devastating consequences for the rest of the world? That right now, the first shots could well be bracketing the ships in the van of the two fleets and determining the course of history for decades to come?"

Para Handy twisted on his bollard and squinted up at the blue sky and the golden glow of the evening sun.

"Well," he said, "they're certainly getting a grand day for it!"

～

As we made our way into the railway station and headed towards its convenient Refreshment Rooms I endeavoured, but with scant success, to explain to the Captain just why the eyes of the world were anxiously turned towards the Sea of Japan.

"I have neffer had much time for the Chapanese," he confessed as we carried our glasses to a table set in the fresh air and affording fine views across the Firth to the Gareloch, "running aboot in rickshaws ass if that wass a fit occupation for a chentleman. Or iss that the Chinese? No matter: and ass for the Rooshians, well Macphail wass in among them several times when he was goin' foreign, and he hassna a good word to say for them. Durty duvvles, by aal his accoont of them, livin' on raw fush and potatos, and nothin' to drink but some kind o' fulthy firewater that would rot your boots.

"What iss the hairm in lettin' the pair o' them knock aal seven bells oot of each other, and then step in and pick up the bits and pieces that we want for oorselves?"

Reflecting that British Foreign Policy over several generations had often followed that particular stratagem, I felt it best to change the subject.

"What have you been up to of late," I asked. "And what is the news on the river?"

"Little enough," said he, "though there wass that wee bit of excitement we got involved in at Crinan basin last week, you maybe heard aboot it, when Callum MacAndrew the lock-keeper's wife had the truplets."

I confessed that this was all news to me, and asked for some more details. "Triplets are certainly real cause for celebration," I said. "A rare event indeed!"

"Chust so," said Para Handy: "and the celebrations wass nearly an even rarer event. If it hadna been for Dougie's agility and a bit o' quick thinking from Sunny Jim then there chust wouldna have been ony celebrations at aal. This was the way of it.

"Callum MacAndrew's wife iss a second cousin of my ain, from Strathshira, and of course the news o' her truplets had been trumpeted the length and breadth of the west. We was on oor way to Colonsay wi' coals, and ass soon ass we put into the first of the locks at Ardrishaig, Fergus McKay the lock-keeper wass down to the shup to give me the good news and ask us a favour.

"Callum's brither works as a cooper at Glendarroch Distillery at Ardrishaig, and wheneffer he got word aboot the truplets he had a confabulation wi' wan o the men in the still-room and he promised to divert a wee firkin' o' spurit to help wet the heids of aal the weans. 'Wi' three o' them to be toasted it's a terrible expense for Callum if we dinna make a wee contribution and onyway it's no' really costing the dustillery,' said he firmly, 'but chust the Excisemen. And who cares aboot them at a time like this.'

"The question wass, wance the spurits had been liberated oot o' the warehoose, how wass they to be taken to Callum's hoose at the Crinan Basin up at the ither end o' the canal? This wass what Fergus hoped that the *Vital Spark* could do for the faimily — and of course I said no bother, no bother at aal."

At that point I felt I simply had to make some comment. "Really Captain," I observed, "I am disappointed in you: I thought that you had foresworn this sort of high-jinks. You have had all too many close calls with the law in the last year or two."

"Blood iss thicker than watter," said Para Handy firmly. "Would you have had me desert my cousin and her man in their hour of need? Forbye, I am firmly of the opeenion that effery Hielan' chentleman is entitled to a dram o' his native spurit withoot the unwanted intervention of Excisemen, for I am sure that the spurits have been around a lot longer than they have.

"So we waited in the basin for Callum's brither to appear wi' the wee firkin.

"Weel, he finally did appear — but empty-handed.

" 'Issn't this the calamity!' he cried. 'You will have to tell Callum that there will be no whusky, the Excisemen spotted us takin' the firkin oot o' the Warehoose and we had to throw it into the Darroch Burn and mak' a run for it! It wass either that or the jyle for us, but I am aawful vexed, for there wull be no spurits to toast the bairns up at the Crinan Basin!'

"It wass Dougie who saved the day. He minded that the Darroch Burn, efter it had passed by the side waall of the dustillery where it provided the power for the watter-wheels that drove the enchines for the paddles in the mash-tubs, ran on doon the glebe and *under* the Crinan Canal by way of a kind of a tunnel before it spult oot into the Loch.

" 'There iss a a sort of an iron grill in the tunnel under the canal,' said he, 'which stops aal the broken bits of bar-rels or whateffer from blockin' the watter channel. If the firkin wass thrown into the Darroch, then that iss where she wull be.'

"And you know, Dougie wass quite right! We went up the canal as far as the Darroch Burn and he chumped oot onto the towpath and doon the side to the culvert o' the stream and sure enough half way through it, and stuck at the metal grill, wass the firkin o' whusky, chust ass good ass new!

"I can tell you that Callum's brither gave Dougie a real hero's welcome when he got back aboard the vessel wi' the firkin under his oxter!

"We took it on board and hid it well under a loose plate in the hold, chust in case of ony maraudin' Excisemen chumpin' the shup on passage, and off we went.

"It wass when we reached the Crinan Basin that we realised that oor troubles wass chust beginning.

"The Excisemen wass not goin' to give up aal that easy! Pert of the problem of course wass that the Glendarroch wass the only dustillery in that pert o' the country and so they had nothin' else to do wi' their time but poke their long noses into her business. And the rest of it wass that they were dam' sure they knew why the whusky had been taken, and chust exactly where it wass bound for — for they knew fine aboot Callum's truplets by noo, and indeed so did the hauf o' Argyllshire — and they were determined not to lose the firkin withoot a fight.

"When we tied up at the Crinan basin we could see Callum's hoose chust a few hundred yerds along the tow-path and hear the sounds of celebration coming from inside — though they wass aal a bit muted, withoot the whusky necessary to get them properly under way. And between the *Vital Spark* and the hoose there were four or five Excisemen from Glendarroch, aal trying to pretend they wassna there, but keepin' a very close cyc on the fowk that went in and oot o' the hoose.

" 'My Chove,' I said to Callum's brither. 'they chust dinna give up, do they? But I cannot see how we can get the firkin past them and up to the hoose for the perty.'

"Then Sunny Jim appeared at the wheelhoose door.

" 'Captain,' says he: 'Am Ah no right in thinkin' that Callum and your kizzin have a wean already?'

" 'Right enough, Jum' I said: 'a laddie of 16 months. But what has that to do wi' it?'

" 'Weel,' said Jim: 'I wis jist thinkin', if wan o' the Aunties or Wives in the hoose wis to tak' that wean oot in its pram for a hurl. And if they wis to come doon here to the shup. And if the pram wis taken on board and — when the Excisemen wisnae lookin' — if the wean wis taken oot for jist a meenit and the wee firkin shoved underneath the mattress on the pram...

" 'Weel,' he concluded. 'I think it wud be a brave Excisemen who wud try to inspect a wean's pram for a wee barrel o' whusky if ye chose the right sort of Auntie or Wife. For if they are onything like some o' the wans Ah've seen in this pert o' the world then I maybe dinna ken what they wud do to the enemy but by the Lord, they frichten me!'

" 'Jum', I said, 'again you are chust sublime. There iss nobody can touch you for cheneral umpidence and sagiocity, unless it iss Hurricane Jeck himself, and he has mony years of advantage over you!'

"And that is chust exactly what we did. Dougie strolled along to the hoose and had a word wi' Callum, and he got his Great Aunt Agnes (her that looks ass if she had fell oot o' the tap of the Ugly Tree and hit aal the brenches on the way doon) to tak' the elder bairn oot for a hurl in his pram, and we put the wee firkin in under him chust like Jum suggested.

"It would have taken the Brigade of Guards to have the courage to interfere with Great Aunt Agnes and the whusky got to the hoose wi' no problem at aal. We waited about 30 meenits chust for the look of the thing afore we made our move, then we got Macphail to dampen doon the furnace, locked up the wheelhoose, sent Sunny Jum to collect hiss melodeon from the fo'c'sle, and set oot along the towpath to the lock-house.

"The Excisemen hung aboot for anither hour or thereby and then admutted defeat and went aff to sulk somewhere else, for wance they heard the soond of singin' comin' from inside the hoose they realised they'd been duped again: but there wassna wan thing they could do aboot it by then because wance whusky is in the gless it disnae have a name tattooed on it and the drams we wis drinkin' could have come from anywhere — even though we aal knew fine what the true facts o' the matter might have been.

"Now admuttedly, Mr Munro, that is aal maybe no' chust as earth shattering as the events in Chapan that you were goin' on aboot earlier, but at least they are closer to home.

"And since it wass us comin' from the East that took the rise oot o' the Excisemen in the West, then maybe that wull give you some thoughts ass to how things wull turn oot for the Emperor and the Tsar at the end o' the day!"

*FACTNOTE*

There had not been any really significant large-scale naval encounters since the Battle of Trafalgar of 1805 until the 20th century was ushered in with the short-lived Russo-Japanese War of 1904-05. The development of capital ships and their armament had been, largely, a matter of theory and the naval architect's drawing-board rather than close encounters by substantial naval forces in a war zone.

Though there were land battles in the war, notably in Manchuria and North Korea, it is remembered principally for the two naval encounters between the protagonists. In July 1904 the Russian Pacific Fleet put out from Vladivostok and was annihilated by the Japanese. Then in one of the most flambuoyantly tragi-comic episodes in the whole history of war, the Tsar dispatched the Russian *Baltic* fleet to the Pacific to avenge the destruction of their compatriots.

This voyage of more than half-way round the world by way of the Cape of Good Hope took many months but by May 1905 the Russians were in Japanese waters. The two fleets met on May 28th 1905 at Tsushima and the result was another catastrophe for the Russian navy. They deployed 37 ships against the Japanese: Togo's fleet sank 22 of them including six of the eight battleships, largely thanks to the superior speed and fire-power of his own capital ships. That was only surpassed when the first of the British *Dreadnought* class, then on the stocks at Portsmouth, started to enter service the following year.

There was only ever one distillery at Ardrishaig.

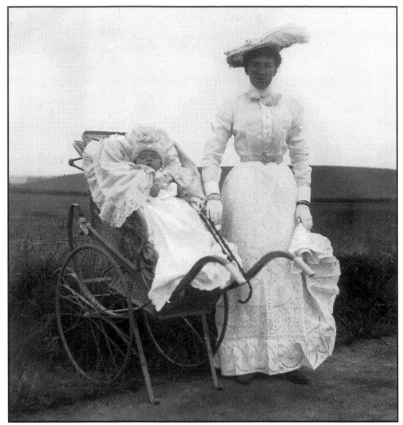

PROUD PARENT — *The moment I came across this wonderful photograph of proud mother and (presumably) pampered offspring in the MacGrory collection I knew I simply had to write a story involving a pram to give me an excuse to include the picture in the book! And now you are reading it. It is probably not the case that the child is just about to slide out of the base of the pram, but it certainly looks like it!*

Glendarroch was one of the first of the 'modern' generation of distilleries created after the new Excise Act of 1823 set the industry on its organised, commercial, large-scale (and legal) journey.

Glendarroch opened in 1831 and passed through several hands in the course of its long history. At its peak, the distillery had an output of 80,000 gallons a year but its last owners, the Glenfyne Distillery Co Ltd, finally shut it down in 1937 after more than a century of continuous production. Its buildings were put to a variety of uses in the decades thereafter, though they have now been completely demolished.

And yes, there was a stream: there were in fact *two* streams to serve the plant. One, the Ard Burn, provided the water for the distilling process: the other powered the water wheels.

This second stream, the Darroch, flowed down the glen from the distillery and passed under the Crinan Canal by way of a narrow culvert before finally debouching into Loch Gilp and so to Loch Fyne.

# 59

## *Sublime Tobacco*

Once breakfast was finished, the Captain felt in his pocket for his pipe, then reached into his overhead locker and pulled out a yellow oilskin tobacco pouch. Opening it, Para Handy stared disbelievingly into its interior, sighed, and shook his head in resignation.

"My chove," he said: "I chust do not know where the tobacco goes and that iss a fact. I could have sworn there wass a good two or three oonces left when I put her away last night, but now here she iss quite ass empty ass Old Mother Hubbard's Cupboard..." And he paused at this point to glance suspiciously across the table at the *Vital Spark's* Engineer, who was the only other smoker on the vessel.

"You needna look at me like that," said that worthy, quite indignantly, pushing his empty breakfast plate away and picking up his mug of tea. "Ah widna use the rubbish that *you* smoke tae smoke a finnan haddie. Ah've mair respect for ma throat. You call that tobacco? Ye'd be as weel to stick your heid doon the lum o' the shup and tak' a few deep breaths. Ah'm sure that wid be better for ye."

Para Handy ignored him.

"It's you that iss lucky you are not a smoker, Dougie," he said to the Mate somewhat enviously. "You chust wudna believe the expense of it!"

"Oh yes I would," said the Mate gloomily, with thoughts of the large family his wages had to support uppermost in his mind. "I most certainly would: it's only the cost that stops me, otherwise I'd be puffin' awa' wi' the rest of you. It wass only getting married that went and put a stop to my smoking. When I wass younger I had a different kind of a pipe for every day of the week."

"Smokin' wass cheaper then, though," continued the Captain, as he salvaged the last few shreds of tobacco from his pouch, laid them carefully into the bowl of his pipe, and reached for a match. "Folk were more wulling to trate you, or to share if you were oot of the makin's yourself" — and here he paused to stare meaningfully at Macphail, who was re-filling his own pipe from a well-stocked pouch, but the Engineer paid no heed — "whereas nooadays it's such a price!

"If you're smokin' your own tobacco, aal you're thinkin' aboot iss the expense of it, and you put scarcely enough in your pipe to get it going. Whiles if you're in company where a baccy tin or a pooch iss passing roond, on the ither hand, and so you're smokin' someone else's, then your pipe iss rammed that tight it wullna draw!"

Sunny Jim, who preferred to spend what surplus he could glean from his wages on more rewarding indulgences such as favours or ice-cream sundaes for his girl-of-the-moment, chuckled quietly and observed: "Weel, you could save a lot o' money by buying your vestas from thon jenny-a'-thing shop at Blairmore where you got them at last week!"

~

The puffer had been bound for Ardentinny for oak-bark from the forestry plantations in Glenfinnart when, just as they were abreast of the pier at Blairmore, the Captain had realised that he was out of matches — and remembered also that there was no shop of any decription at Ardentinny.

It was the work of just a few minutes to put in to the pier and from there Sunny Jim had been dispatched to the general store to purchase a carton containing two dozen large boxes of matches. The transaction completed, the puffer continued on her way and three miles further on put inshore and beached as close to the road as she could, close beside Ardentinny's little church, and waited for the arrival of the first forestry dray with its load of oak-bark.

Captain and Engineer, in a rare moment of camaraderie, had sat themselves side-by-side on the main-hatch in the warm afternoon sun and filled their pipes.

Para Handy passed the newly-bought carton of vestas to Macphail, who took out one of the boxes, carefully extracted a match, and struck it on the side of the box. There was a slight crackle, a momentary spark, but nothing more. He tried again. And again. Exasparated, Macphail threw the dud match away and selected another. The same scenario was repeated. He tried a third. The same again. Cursing, he tried another box, and then another and another, but always with the same negative result.

Para Handy, who had been impatiently waiting to get his own pipe lit, could finally wait no longer and snatched the carton of boxes from the Engineer's hands. "You couldna light a fire wi' a can o' kerosene, Dan," he complained testily: "see the metches here, you chust havna the knack for them at aal."

But the Captain fared no better than the Engineer had done, and in disgust Macphail finally went aft to the engine-room and put a taper into the red-hot coals in the furnace, and from that the two men lit their pipes.

Para Handy studied the carton and its worthless boxes of vestas contemptuously.

"Jum!" he shouted.

Sunny Jim, who was down below peeling potatos, came scrambling up on deck a moment later.

"Jum," said the Captain, "I want you to tak' this dam' carton o' vestas back to Cherlie Paterson's shop at Blairmore. Tell him they wullna strike at aal, I want either my money back or else a new carton wi' boxes in it that work."

Jim's protests at being forced into a six-mile round trip over such a relative triviality were disregarded and the puffer's young hand soon found himself stepping out along the coast road with the worthless carton under his arm. His annoyance at being sent on such a trifling errand soon vanished, for it was a most beautiful afternoon, Loch Long was at its spectacular best, the birds were in full song and the wild flowers bordering the roadside were at their colourful zenith — and he was *not* having to trim oak-bark in a dusty, sweltering hold.

When Sunny Jim presented himself at the store in Blairmore and disclosed the nature of his errand, the proprietor was totally unimpressed.

"There's naething wrang wi' my vestas," he said angrily, "You tell Peter Macfarlane that."

"But they wullna *light*!" protested Jim.

"Willna light?" exploded Paterson. "See me wan o' they

boxes and I'll show you whether they light or not," and he grabbed the carton, took out a box, extracted a match and then, leaning forward slightly as he did so, struck it vigorously on the seat of his trousers.

The match immediately burst into flame.

"See whit I mean?" roared the proprietor.

"Ah see whit you mean," replied Sunny Jim quietly, "but I dinna think either Para Handy or Dan Macphail ha'e ony intention of walking six miles from Ardentinny and back jist to strike a match on the seat of *your* breeks every time they want a smoke."

He got his new carton.

~

The Captain laughed at the memory of that. "Aye, you did weel there, Jum: I wush I'd been wi' you for the sake of seeing the expression on Cherlie Paterson's face!

"And *you'd* have enjoyed seein' the expression on Dan's face yon time we bumped intae thon yat the *Blue Dragon* up at Eisdale. We bumped into her in more ways than wan, in fact, for we came into the wee harbour just efter derk, no' expecting ony ither boats to be there, and towing our own dinghy, for we had a deck cairgo of a flittin'. Here and did we no' clatter the yat wi' the dinghy ass we came in.

"The owner wass on deck in a flash, but when he saw there wass no damage done he couldna have been nicer aboot it, and invited us aal on board for a refreshment."

The Engineer, who had been twisting uncomfortably in his seat, said firmly "Dinna you say anither word, Peter, that wis a lot o' years ago, and it's not a very interestin' baur onyway."

"Oh, I'm no so sure aboot that," replied the Captain. "We will let Jum be the judge!

"Onyway, Jum, after he'd given us a gless wi' something warmin' in it, the yat skipper passed roond a box o' big Havana cigars for us to try. I said no, thanks, if he didna mind I would stick wi' the pipe — but Dan here, who'd neffer smoked a cigar in his naitural, picked oot the biggest wan in the box and lit it up quite jocco.

"Two meenits and he wass chust ass green in the face ass the gress on midsummer day, and two meenits more and he wass up and oot the cabin like a lamplighter and aal we could hear wass him bein' no weel ower the side o' the yat!

It wass a while before Dougie and me let him forget aboot that, I can tell you: and I had to feenish his dram for him that night, too!"

"Och, he's so smairt," said the Engineer, both embarrassed and petulant at once. "Jist ask him aboot the time we wis cairrying the shows for the Tarbert Fair from Brodick, where they'd been for the week afore that, over to Loch Fyne.

"Wan o' the sideshows for the Fair wis a man that had a kind of a trained monkey, that could sit on a perch and stand on its haun's, and jump through girrs, and put on a wee bit of a cloak and tak' it off again, and go in among the folk on the end of a leash wi' a kind of a silver cup in its haun's tae collect the pennies."

It was now the Captain's turn to look uncomfortable. "What on earth is the point of draggin' up old stories this way," he asked Macphail with some fervour, but the Engineer continued as if there had been no interruption.

"Para Handy wis fairly taken wi' the monkey," he said: "and wis aye gettin' the man that owned it too pit it through its paces as we crossed the tap o' Kilbrannan Soond and headed up Loch Fyne.

"When the monkey wis given a wee tin drum and a stick tae bang it with, Para Handy wis that tickled he stuck his pipe in his mooth so he'd baith haun's free to slap his thighs, for he wis laughin' till he wis sair.

"At that the monkey leapt onto his shouthers, pulled the pipe frae his mooth, and went and sat on the side of the vessel and tried tae smoke it itself! Para Handy very near fell aff of the main-hatch he wis laughing that mich, watching the beast tryin' tae imitate whit he'd been dae'ing.

"He didna laugh long! The monkey near choked on the baccy smoke and it pulled the pipe oot of its mooth quicker than it had put it in, looked at it a moment with whit ye'd hae sworn wis an expression of disgust — and then hurled Para Handy's best and only genuine and original meerschaum ower the side o' the shup and into the Loch. So it wis an expensive joke for the Captain that day!"

"Well," said Jim with conviction, "If I wis ever tempted to stert smokin' I'd jist have to remind masel' aboot the mess you two cloons manage tae get yoursel's intae. It's my considered opinion ye're naethin' but a pair of eejits tae cairry on wi' the pipes at aal. They seem to involve ye in an awful lot of aggravation and expense, and I canna see that it's worth it for the sake of a whiff of tobacco."

"Ah," said Paa Handy dreamily, "but that iss where you are aal wrong, Jum. Tobacco is sublime — chust sublime. If Dougie wass here he would tell you that himself..."

*FACTNOTE*

A 'jenny-a'-thing' was, of course, a general store which sold just about everything (as the cliché has it) from a needle to an anchor. They were the hub around which very many of the more remote rural communities revolved, and in isolated parts of the Highlands and the rural west they still are today.

The pier at Blairmore, on the Cowal coast at the entrance to Loch Long, is one of the few remaining piers on the firth and sea-lochs of the Clyde which are still serviceable and, more importantly, licensed to serve. Our last surviving paddler, the *Waverley*, calls occasionally at Blairmore to pick up passengers for an evening cruise to Lochgoilhead or Arrochar. Ardentinny never had a pier: Passengers were embarked or disembarked from the steamers (by prior arrangement, or by hailing them as they passed) by flitboat.

The *Blue Dragon* (from 1892 till 1904) and her successor *Blue Dragon II* (1905 till 1913) were owned by a quite remarkable English schoolmaster and yachtsman, C C Lynam.

*Blue Dragon* was a tiny craft, just 25ft overall, yet from the modest beginnings of day-excursions along the south coast of England Lynam sailed her further and further north and became a regular visitor not just in summer, but during winter holidays as well, to the Hebrides and West Highlands.

In the larger *Blue Dragon II* Lynam undertook voyages not just to Orkney and Shetland, but over to Bergen and then north to the North Cape and the midnight sun. She was a two-masted yawl of 43ft overall with roomy cabin-space and six berths. In 1905 she cost him just £300!

Three volumes describing his voyages (all well-illustrated and comprehensive but highly idiosyncratic, not to say eccentric) were published between 1908 and 1913. Now very scarce they are much prized by bibliophiles as remarkable accounts of Edwardian maritime adventure, and the attitudes and amenities of the age.

An encounter with a puffer, her engineer and one of the yacht's cigars is indeed related in Lynam's chronicles!

Meerschaum pipes, made from a fine white clay (the word itself derives from the German for sea-foam) were then among the most highly regarded of smoking implements and the bowls were almost always carved or moulded into intricate and decorative shapes such as character or caricature heads of men or women, whether historical or imaginary: or of beasts of myth, legend or fact.

Good early meerschaums are sought-after by collectors: and the Captain would certainly not have been happy to lose his!

# 60

## *Hurricane Jack, Entrepreneur*

Hurricane Jack clattered up the ladder from the fo'c'sle and disappeared out onto the deck of the *Vital Spark*. "Weel," said Macphail sardonically, "that's the last ye'll see of *that* five shullings."

The puffer was lying overnight at the Broomielaw where she had been spotted by the doughty Jack, who was on the last night of a brief but eventful shore leave before taking passage as able seaman on an Australia-bound wool packet: the mariner had a problem, and he had come aboard to share it with Para Handy.

Jack's problem, not unusually, was to do with money, or rather the lack of it: quite simply, his leave had outlasted his funds and his final night of freedom before a 90-day passage promised to be one to forget, rather than one to remember. Para Handy had not hesitated for one second before agreeing to fund that final spree and sent Jack ashore clutching two half-crowns. He had refused, with reluctance, Jack's pressing invitation that he should join him on the grounds that the *Vital Spark* was due to leave on the six a.m. tide. A further, overwhelming reason for refusal was that Jack now had in his pocket the Captain's entire current assets with the exception only of a handful of coppers — something which Para Handy was absolutely determined that his oldest friend should never suspect, and very unwilling that his cynical crew should ever know.

"Five shullings!" he said contemptuously, "ass if that mattered at aal. Five shullings iss nothing to Jeck!"

"It's certainly naethin' to you, noo," continued the engineer implacably, "for that's it gone for good. Yon fella has jist nae idea whatsoever o' the value o' money, nor the prunciples of ownership. It's nae wonder he's never got twa pennies tae rub thegither."

"Jeck iss the sort of man that could quite easily have been a mullionaire, if he had pit his mind to it," said Para Handy with dignity and conviction: "but what you will neffer understand, Macphail, iss that there iss some chentlemen to whom money is only a minor conseederation compared wi' the sheer enchoyment of life. And it iss his life, and ensuring the happiness of his fellow human beings, that matters to Jeck. He doesna give a docken aboot money, but I can assure you that if he ever *had* cared aboot it and put his mind to it then he could have made it hand over fist.

"That wass neffer better shown than wan time when he and I wass workin' the Brodick puffer *Mingulay*. We had come doon to Loch Ryan, wi' a cargo of early Arran Pilots for Stranraer, and when we had unloaded the cairgo late on Friday efternoon, the owner sent a telegram to tell us to stay where we were till Monday as he wass negotiating a return load o' whunstane for us.

"That suited us chust fine, and we spruced up and went ashore, for neither Jeck nor I had ever been in Stranraer before, and Jeck wass always in extra good trum in a new surroundings.

"The engineer we had wi' us wass a soor-faced man — sometimes I think it's wan o' the qualifications for the chob, no offence meant Dan, and he wassna at aal interested in seeing what sort of a toon Stranraer wass, so he stayed aboard.

"The place wass hotching! There wass weekend truppers frae Gleska, folk from the country roond aboot, visiting frien's and relations in the toon, a wheen of towerists over from Ireland, and a few from England ass weel.

"The first thing Jeck noticed wass, there wassna mich provided for them in the way of entertainment. Stranraer iss no' at aal like the Clyde holiday resorts, there iss very little diversion for ony visitors — or the toon's own folk, come to that . There wass hundreds o' ladies and chentlemen and faimilies millin' aboot wi' absolutely nothing to do.

" 'That iss a sight to behold, to be sure' says Jeck: 'chust look you, Peter, at aal these folk wi' money burning a hole in their pockets and not a thing to spend it on. This toon iss no canny at aal. A man of ony sagiocity or mental agility wouldna have a problem makin' a good livin' here for he'd have nothing by way o' competition.

"Where iss the oaring-boats for hire, or the bathing-huts, or the motor-boat trups to the lighthoose, or the donkey-rides, or the day excursions up the Firth — or doon it, mebbe — or the aquariums or menageries or circuses or fairs? This toon needs a shake to itself!'

"The second thing that Jeck noticed wass a smert two-funnelled paddle-steamer tied up at the outer wall o' the harbour, quite deserted. She hadna steam up and there wassna a man to be seen moving aboot her.

" 'Now there iss someone that issna opening his eyes to a golden opportunity,' says Jeck: 'the owner o' that shup needs to tak' a tumble to himself. Here's hundreds of tow-erists and visitors chust desperate to spend their money on *something*, and here's a man wi' chust the very thing they're looking for — but instead o' preparing for an excur-sion programme, he has her lying here like a stranded whale.

" 'Let us see if there iss onybody at hame, and we'll can mebbe put some business his way to our own advantage, for he is badly in need of some advice and encouragement.'

"When we got to the shup we saw that her port of regis-tration wass Belfast, and her name wass *Pride of Rathlin*. And it wass right enough, there wassna a soul on board. There wass one gangway laid from the top of the paddle-box to the quayside but it had a kind of steel gate across the bot-tom end of it so you couldna get on board.

" 'Strange and stranger still,' says Jeck, and we walked up past the brudge till we wass at the bow of the shup.

"And there, when we looked back, we saw a kind of a bill stuck up on the foremast, very official looking.

" 'My chove,' said Jeck, 'I've seen a few of those in my time at sea. She's been impounded!'

"I hadna a notion what he wass taalking aboot. Jeck chumped on board the shup, and beckoned on me to follow him.

"The notice wass headed WARRANT: BY ORDER OF THE SHERIFF OF DUMFRIES AND GALLOWAY in big, bleck capitals. Jeck studied the small print underneath. I couldna make heid nor tail of it.

" 'Nae wonder she's chust lying here,' said Jeck, straight-ening up. 'She's no' paid her Harbour Dues for months, and the port authorities hass had her poinded by the Shuriff's Officers, the owner daurna move her till he pays the dues and the fines. Man, Peter, whatna opportunity!'

" 'Opportunity for what,' I asked him.

" 'Why, to *unpound* her — unoffeecially, of course.'

" 'You canna get awa' wi' that, Jeck,' said I, 'it's against the law!'

" 'Aye we can,' said Jeck, cheerfully, 'it iss the weekend! The law's no here, apart from maybe wan toon polisman — but he iss sittin' wi' his feet up right now, and no' wantin' his Seturday disturbed or his Sabbath interrupted. The Shuriff and his men is awa' hame to their teas and they'll no' be back till Monday.

"Look at the crowds in the toon, Peter, and not a thing for them to do. Now how many tickets d'you think we could sell for a day cruise to the Isle of Man tomorrow? *Hundreds!* Bet your life on it! Now it iss going to tak' some organising, but we can do it if we set oor minds to it.'

"I sterted to protest, but you know what Jeck iss like when he gets cairried awa' wi' wan o' his schemes. He wudna listen to reason at aal. And you couldna but admire the sheer agility of the man when it cam' to gettin' the scheme moving.

"First thing he did, he went back to the *Mingulay* and woke up our Engineer, a man by the name o' MacFadyen, and telt him to go and find a blecksmith to burn aff the iron gate fixed to the gangway of the *Pride of Rathlin* and then go on board to tak' a look at her enchines and work oot how mony men he'd need wi' him to work her.

"His next caall wass at the toon printers. He had them run off a hundred posters advertising a *Grand Excursion to the Isle of Man* leaving at 9 o'clock sherp on Saturday mornin', fares of six shullings for adults, three shullings for weans, ony bairns in prams no cherge. Then he gave two young lads a half-a-crown apiece to go aal roond the toon sticking up the posters, with a special emphasis on hotels and public hooses where the visitors was maist likely to be.

"Then he foond oot which wass the biggest of the toon's bakers and which the biggest butcher, and he went and spoke to them and offered them the chance to run the dining saloons on the shup the next day, wi' chust a smaal percentage for himself as a pert of the bargain. They chumped at the chance, and long into the derkness there was a coming and going of handcarts to the shup ass the provisions wass loaded aboard her.

"Meantime Jeck had got a hold of the Stranraer Cooncil's Toon Crier and togged him up in his gear and sent him aal roond the toon wi' his handbell, bellowing the news aboot the next day's trup to the lieges.

"He even foond a wee brass band that wass playin' to the chentry in wan o' the biggest hotels in the toon, and offered them free meals and passage, and aal they could tak' when they passed the hat roond, if they would come on the trup and provide some musical entertainment for the passengers next day.

"Then he went and had a confabulation wi' the landlord o' the Harbour Inn, and efter some discussion and a frank exchange of views, they cam' to an agreement by which the man would run the refreshment rooms on the shup wi' the help of some of the ither Stranraer publicans that he knew well enough to trust, and for the pruvilege they would pay Jeck so much for effery bottle of spurits or barrel of beer they sold.

"Last thing, he and MacFadyen the Engineer went into the public bar at the Harbour Inn and recruited the men they needed for the enchine-room and for the deck.

"Jeck and MacFadyen slept on board the steamer that night, but Jeck made me stay on board the puffer.

" 'And I'm sorry, Peter, but I am not going to allow you on the trup tomorrow neither,' he said. 'Pertly this iss for your own good, chust in case onything goes wrang, for you are a skipper and it would a real blot on your sheet if you wass to be taken to court for piracy on the high seas, or whateffer the sheriff and his gang might cry it.

" 'And pertly,' he continued, 'it iss for my own protection ass weel. What I want you to do, ass soon ass we have sailed, is to get a couple o' the longshoremen to gi'e you a hand to shuft the puffer into the berth the steamer wass in, and nail this to the mast of the *Mingulay*' — and he handed me the Warrant that he'd tore doon from the paddler's mast — 'so that if onybody offeecial jalouses that there's something no' quite right and comes to mak' an investigation, then you simply tell them that a frien' o' yours hass borrowed the steamer for the day — and that he wull be bringing her back that night in wan piece, with no questions asked — and in the meantime the puffer iss being left ass a sort of a pledge, like in a pawnshop, for the safe return of the paddler.'

"I didna like ony of it, but you know what Jeck's like, wance he has the bit between his teeth there iss no stopping him, so I chust held my tongue.

"Next morning there wass a crowd ten deep on the quay-side by half-past-eight, when Jeck opened up the gangway. He stood at the tap of it himsel', wi' a leather satchel that he'd managed to borrow frae a conductor with wan o' the toon's charabancs round his shouthers, and twa rolls of cloakroom tickets in his hand, blue for adults and yellow for weans, and took the money.

"Wance the shup wass full — and she wass that full they couldna have squeezed the matchstick man from Hengler's on board — Jeck headed for the brudge, cast of fore and aft, and conned her out into Loch Ryan and awa'.

"The trup wass the talk of Stranraer for weeks. The refreshment rooms did a roarin' tred, for Jeck had had a word in the ear o' the landlord o' the Harbour Bar, and the prices wass set very reasonable indeed. 'Better sell 1,000 pints at saxpence than 500 at sevenpence' as Jeck put it, and the result wass there wass a great air of jollity aal the way to the Isle of Man and back.

"Jeck didna daur land her there, of course, for there would be too many questions asked, but she made three or four close passes o' the main pier at Douglas, Jeck oot on the brudge wing wi' his kep on three hairs, a cheery wave for aal the world and the whustle lanyard in his hand, keep-ing time wi' the baund, which he had playin' *Liberty Bell* in the forepeak.

"On the way back the refreshment rooms and the dining saloons wass busier than ever, and there was dancing on the promenade deck and a great sing-song going in the fore-saloon.

"She docked back at Stranraer at seven o'clock that Saturday evening, but I wassna there to see it. By that time someone had gone to the polis aboot it — Jeck was aalways convinced it wass wan o' the publicans who hadna been invited into the act by the landlord o' the Harbour Inn, and him jealous because noo Jeck had taken aal his Saturday trade awa' to the high seas.

"The local polis came roond and looked at the state of things at the pierhead, and took a good long look at the puffer and me sitting smoking on her main-hatch. He said nothin', chust shook his heid and walked away. But soon afterwards he came back wi' fower big men in dark coats and snap-brim hats, and they read something I couldna understand from a long document that wan of them held up in front of him.

"Then they came aboard the puffer and it wass made clear that if I didna go to the polis station of my own free wull then I would very quickly go the hard way.

"They arrested Jeck the moment the shup docked and the case came up furst thing Monday morning — they dinna haud back doon in Wigtonshire. In the cell Jeck had told me not to worry, he'd tell them I had chust been his dupe — I didna think that wass very flattering of him but I knew fine he meant it for the best so I didna tak' offence. And he'd have no trouble paying the fine, said he. It couldna be more than £50, and he'd taken near on £200.

"The shuriff wass the meanest-lookin chiel I'd ever come across and though I wass discherged ass 'nothing mair nor less than a fool in a rogue's clutches' ass he put it (and thenks for the kind words, I thought at the time) he threw the book at poor Jeck. He gi'ed him hiss ancestry and telt his fortune for the best pert of 30 minutes and then said: 'sentence of the court is a fine of £200 or three months imprisonment.'

"Jeck paid the fine, of course.

"As he said, money iss only money, but to give up your freedom iss to give up your heart, and to give up your heart is to cut yourself off from the happiness and friendship of the world.

"So that's wan o' the mony reasons, Dan, that I neffer begrudge Jeck anything. The man is wan o' life's leprechauns, dispensing nothing but kindness and mirth and wi'oot wan drap o' malice in him. He should be preserved ass a national monument, for he iss a credit to the human race."

*FACTNOTE*

Stranraer would probably vie with Campbeltown for the title of most isolated Scottish town were it not for its importance as the sea-link to Northern Ireland. Most of the goods coming from or going to that country, which used to trundle in and out of Stranraer by rail, are now transported by juggernauts for which the roads and (more basically still) the rolling landscapes of Wigtonshire and its environs were never designed.

The town stands at the head of Loch Ryan and it was from here, in Para Handy's time, that ships of the Larne and Stranraer Steamboat Company ran their services. Today

*THE IRISH DIMENSION — There was, around the turn of the century, an established and comprehensive steamer service around the towns and villages of the Belfast Lough, and the MacGrory brothers visited Northern Ireland on more than one occasion. Here is the paddler* Slieve Bearnagh (Mount Bearnagh) *leaving Belfast Docks. She was built on the Clyde at J and G Thomson's yard in 1894.*

there are two major roll-on, roll-off shipping terminals located on the Loch, one at Stranraer, the other at Cairnryan on its eastern shore.

More than 50 years ago the Loch was a vitally important wartime base. Its sheltered waters were home to huge squadrons of flying boats, notably the Catalinas and the larger Sunderlands which patrolled hundreds of miles out into the Atlantic to guard and protect the vast convoys of merchant ships, Britain's lifeline of hope, from the waiting U-boats whose wolf-packs lay in stealthy ambush in the Western Approaches.

Later in the war it was at Cairnryan that component sections of the 'Mulberry' floating harbour, itself crucial to the ultimate success of the D-Day landings, were constructed.

One especially poignant memory of the Stranraer to Larne service was the foundering in heavy weather off the Irish coast of the *Princess Victoria* on January 31st 1953. There was heavy loss of life in this, one of the worst-ever maritime disasters in British waters in peacetime. The ship was the fourth vessel of that name on the service: but she was also, to the time of writing at least, the last.

On the outskirts of Stranraer stands the imposing North West Castle Hotel, a popular destination for golfers and curlers (it has its own ice-rink) but once the home of the

Arctic explorer Sir John Ross. Like Parry before him and Franklin after him he was obsessed with the idea of discovering the fabled North West passage across the top of Canada to the Pacific. So was the Royal Navy, which explains why so many unsuccessful expeditions were funded out of the public purse. Ross's published account of his second voyage recounts in detail how he and his ships put in to Loch Ryan en route to the Arctic, and how he came ashore to visit home before they left.

That particular expedition sailed from Loch Ryan on June 13th 1829: it did not return to this country for more than four years coming into Stromness harbour in Orkney on October 12th 1833.

AND FINALLY — *Perhaps the greatest evocation of how the sea around the coasts of Argyll was the life of our Victorian and Edwardian forebears would not be the handsome steamers, which were the investments of the wealthy: nor the more humble steam-lighters and gabbarts which were the bread-and-butter of the employed seamen: but the simple fishing skiffs, numbered in their hundreds, which were owned and crewed by families, their skills and their knowledge (like the boats themselves) handed down from generation to generation. This picture of just one tiny corner of Campbeltown harbour says that more eloquently than words could ever do.*

*Stern views of paddlers are rare, which makes this fine plate from the MacGrory archive specially interesting. It illustrates perfectly the spaciousness afforded by the wide paddle-boxes in contrast to the fine lines of the hull itself, and the dramatic wake left by the twin blades. The steamer is the Duchess of Hamilton, and she has just turned away from Campbeltown pier and is heading out to sea towards the Ayrshire coast. When this picture was taken she was at the beginning of her career — in contrast to the unidentified square-rigged naval vessel anchored out in the bay, very much at the end of hers.*